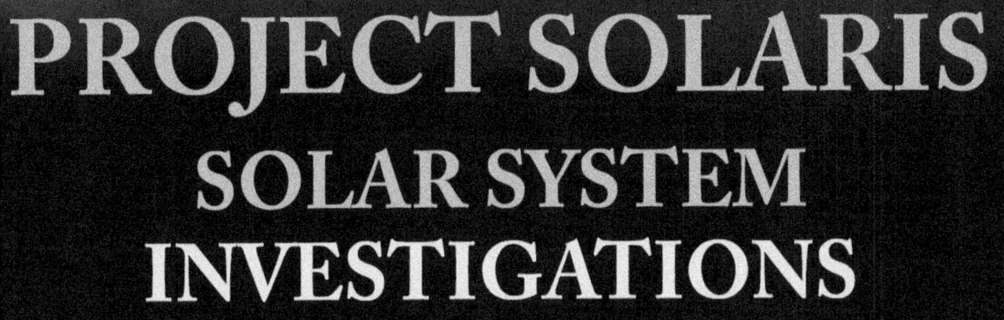

PROJECT SOLARIS

SOLAR SYSTEM INVESTIGATIONS

Paul D Escudero

WORKBOOK PRESS LLC

187 E Warm Springs Rd,

Suite B285 Las Vegas NV 89119 USA

Website: https://workbookpress.com/

Hotline: 1-888-818-4856

Email: admin@workbookpress.com

Ordering Information:

Quantity sales. Special discounts are available on quantity purchases by corporations, associations, and others. For details, contact the publisher at the address above.

ISBN-13:   978-1-963718-49-2 Paperback Version
              978-1-963718-50-8 Digital Version

REV. DATE: 04/26/2024

PROJECT SOLARIS

SOLAR SYSTEM INVESTIGATIONS

by

Paul D. Escudero

Table of Contents

Preface

As the reader explores this novel, at first glance it might seem this science fiction stands little chance of developing in real life. But when the Wright Brothers first flew their airplane at Kittyhawk, North Carolina, December 17, 1903, anyone saying America spaceflight would land humans on the moon 66 years later, would be considered crazy.

What if we build a submarine on Saturn to explore some of the great bodies of liquid helium and liquid hydrogen 66 years from now? Does that idea seem crazy to you as well?

Commander Neil Armstrong and lunar module pilot Buzz Aldrin landed the Apollo Lunar Module Eagle on July 20, 1969, at 20:17 UTC, and Armstrong became the first person to step onto the Moon's surface. Hence it wasn't so far-fetched after all.

Perhaps Earth Space Forces building a fusion nuclear-powered submarine on Saturn to explore the depths and mysteries of that gas-giant might not be out of the question if you think about it.

How would you build a submarine on Saturn in such a hostile environment where a human would always have to have on a space suit if outside a habitat or quickly perish from asphyxiation?

What are we observing now in the development of the human condition? Robotics and Artificial Intelligence grows in spiral development at a pace we never imagined. It's through the technological revolution that such a venture would be made possible.

Not only ventures to Saturn are probably likely, but elsewhere, including outside this solar system as the secret space program is forced to the surface and the public becomes aware we can travel to the stars right now just like

Ben Rich former director of Lockheed's Skunk Works stated in the 1990's during a death bed confession, which you can find easily on the internet.

What would create interest of Saturn of all places?

Our scientists think they know everything there is about our solar system and if there were alien races living on other planets, we would know by now because we would think their behavior would be like us, telegraphing our presence to the universe through vast radio and signal emissions.

Dr. Brandenberg, a nuclear physicist who helped design our

hydrogen bombs working at Lawrence Livermore Labs has written several books and has several videos on YouTube where he describes the nuclear devastation of Mars. His contention is Mars was nuked and destroyed approximately 250 million years ago.

We are discovering artifacts on Mars all the time NASA has gone to extremes to cover up. With the ongoing congressional hearings some NASA executives fearing prison time for perjury to congress are now being more forthcoming. NASA just announced they received communications from four (4) alien sources. China claims they are communicating with aliens.

If advanced intelligent life exists in places like Saturn, why would they not telegraph their presence? My theory is they know what Doctor Brandenberg knows, Mars and Atlantis on planet Earth were wiped out in a nuclear war.

NASA asked Doctor Brandenberg to investigate the high concentrations of Xeon 129 isotopes on Mars. Xeon 129 does not exist on Earth except at locations where hydrogen bomb explosions occurred at the test sites.

In case you do not know it, not only is the atmosphere of Mars full of Xeon 129 isotopes, but there are also two hot spots on Mars, including the famed area of Cydonia where the face that looks up into space exists.

Researchers have claimed to discover structures built on Mars indicating an ancient civilization. Some of those structures can be viewed on YouTube and in books that have been published.

If other civilizations on planets in our solar system are silent, and it's probably for good reason. They do not want to receive the treatment Mars and Atlantis received eons ago. In the rest of the galaxy, it's probably modus of operendus, if a civilization telegraphs their presence, it could usher in visits from unknown entities who do not have your best interest in mind.

If that's the case, why did they suddenly start communicating to us from Saturn?

Chapter One

Saturn Realization and Reactions

The sudden intercepts of radio signals NSA discovered and after a twenty- year study concluded they were not of terrestrial origin and stopped looking towards Russia, China, India, and Iran. Suddenly a new source of information created a firestorm of interest when out of the blue, unsolicited material from relatively unknown scientist Paul Morgan, approached his friend in the INTEL business in Norway who provided recordings and sophisticated measurements that tracked Saturn's position over a couple decades.

Along with the positional data matching the exact position in space where Saturn was presently showing in the night sky, he took it to a different level when he painstakingly located on Saturn the latitude and longitude where the communication signals originated. It did not make sense to anyone, as that positional data source indicated the radiators came from a large body of liquid on the planet surface.

The Arecibo Observatory in Puerto Rico used a radio telescope with its huge antenna to map the surface of Saturn over a several decade study. Scientists from Cornell University, augmented with Government scientists and a few infiltrators from the CIA, painstakingly created a map of Saturn's surface using four high frequency transmitters in frequency skipping to increase the duty cycle and refine the resolution of the measurement.

At the same time, when the Cash in Advance (CIA) boys thought nobody was paying attention, they utilized that system for nefarious activity and bounced signals off the moon to their operatives staged deep inside Russia with an unobstructed view to some of the most sensitive Soviet Weapon's developments. Using highly directional antenna's that looked totally innocuous, attached to an AM/FM radio sent reports to their sponsors and was recorded at Arecibo. Cornell scientists knew about some of that nefarious activity, and when they confronted the Cash in Advance personnel, they quickly disclosed what their price was to remain silent which was a combination of being permitted to keep living as well as some "Cash in Advance" to make them want to cooperate.

In the end, when the National Science Foundation determined they had enough Saturn planetary imagery, there was no longer any point in continuing the funding of the radio observatory, and Cornell University understood, don't rock the boat, and went away gracefully as the site has since fell into decay and is no longer a viable scientific instrument to gain further knowledge. Cash in Advance shifted communication modes thanks to a plethora of satellites that now orbited planet Earth.

***

Wilber O'Toole, CIA case officer for Project Solaris, the program to discover all there is to know about the civilization transmitting signals from Saturn and why, pulled into the multi-level parking garage in an innocuous looking office building in McClean Virginia.

The flight back from Oslo Norway didn't please Wilber O'Toole in the least bit. He knew he would probably get an ass chewing by his unfriendly superior, Pat Barton for creating a hostile environment with the Norwegian Intelligence Service locally referred to as Etterretningstjenesten (E-tjenesten). Wilber's Norwegian Intelligence Service counterpart Jørgen Eriksen was obviously under influence by his superiors to deny Wilber O'Toole access to Paul Morgan.

In the weeks leading up to the encounter and rough episodes, CIA had a few breadcrumbs in exactly what Paul Morgan possessed. If it were not for the fact Paul Morgan, who had a contact at Cornell University and was discussing some of his insights to the Saturn radio intercepts, CIA and NSA would not know he possessed such startling data. Sitting in the same room a cubicle down from the Columbia professor was one of the CIA plants that had spent time in Arecibo and subsequently reported to his superiors and case officer, the juicy tidbits he overheard Professor Proctor discussing with Paul Morgan.

Besides the briefing, Wilber knew that shortly thereafter, his boss Pat Barton would call him into his office and have a private discussion about Wilber's conduct which included threatening to kick Norwegian Intelligence Service agent Jørgen Eriksen's ass if he didn't allow access to Paul Morgan.

What a dumb son of a bitch, Wilber was thinking. Pat Barton didn't think anything such as turf battles existed. And sometimes they and the FBI rubbed each other the wrong way. The fact of the matter is terrible turf battles do exist and how could such a dumbass make up in a high position in the agency?

Even though Wilber was flying very high in the CIA's new Gulfstream 750 jet, the weather sucked and no matter where the pilot tried to fly, they were boxed in and had to fly through the remnants of a Hurricane which didn't help the upset stomach one bit.

Facial recognition and fingerprints were no longer viable. Three-dimensional biological printing allowed spies to change identity almost as fast as the mask makers when it became necessary to squeeze an agent into some location that was heavily defended.

The building Wilber entered didn't rely on facial recognition or palm prints because those methods had been compromised when hackers simply put fake palm prints into the system allowing the spy to enter a compartmentalized area.

The CIA now utilized a new system comparing DNA samples stored offline so no hacker could get to them and as the access list shifted as they normally do because of visitors or personnel changes, a new DNA matrix was brought down via two-man rule and plugged into the access system each and every day with no exceptions.

In this unmarked commercial building, that looked like an innocuous commercial office building, had an access chamber that only one person and the inspectors were allowed in at any given time. Nobody from the outside could see inside and know what was going on.

As soon as Wilber was in the access chamber and doors shut and locked via pneumatic controls, the technician had the swab and Wilber knew to open his mouth where two samples were taken on each side of his tongue. It was a timely ordeal and access was slow but not many people were ever invited into this area of the building. In five minutes, the machine gave the results. Identity confirmed, Wilber O'Toole, is cleared to enter.

Wilber went to the elevator and selected floor number fourteen when he stepped into the elevator and went up to the Deputy Director's office of Solar System Investigations (aka Project Solaris).

As Wilber walked through the area on his way to the conference room, he got a lot of stares. Scuttlebutt was that Pat Barton was either going to chew his ass or do some sort of disciplinary action for his confrontation with a Norwegian Intelligence Service agent.

Wilber didn't care because he knew in a few more weeks Pat Barton will be under immense pressure as the President would be demanding the DCI explain all this Saturn business to him in laymen's terms. An added bonus was the Norwegian Intelligence Service management could give a rat's ass what Majestic 12 and their coverup boys wanted to do. Disclosure was around the corner.

Pat Barton was just about to learn that turf wars existed, despite Pat Barton's whimsical beliefs the world was perfect, and professionals didn't step on each other's dicks all the time. This is what happens when you fill a management position with a neophyte who has no experience in cosmic intelligence gathering.

The room was evenly split between military and civilians attending. The reason why the military members were present is they operated the secret space program that even NASA was not cleared to know about. If there was a mission to Saturn, the military who were the principal operators in the secret space program would most likely do the mission with possibly one or two civilian CIA oversight people coming along for affirmative backup and vet the conclusions during post mission debriefs.

This meeting was not going to go over well because the big guy was on temporary duty (TDY) to Hawaii, doing a yeoman's job of protecting their assets.

Truth of the matter John Burkette, the Deputy Director/Planning for Project Solaris had checked into a Waikiki Hotel on the beach to have a secret rendezvous with his beautiful blonde lover Karena who was in direct control of his little head all the time.

Wilber did not know how he was going to be received at this meeting. It was just a matter of time before he and Pat Barton had their big conflict rise to the surface. Old age and treachery overcoming youth and skill wasn't going to work this time. Wilber was ready to tell Pat Barton to shove it where the sun didn't shine.

"Thanks for getting back as quickly as you did," Pat Barton said with a poker face.

"Yea that was a nice plane I flew on, but the weather sucked, and the pilot said there was nowhere to fly to avoid the severe weather." Wilber responded wondering what was in store for him later.

"Alright, let's see the eye candy," Pat Barton said.

Wilber pulled out his CIA certified cell phone that had special features. On the table was a cradle to shove the cell phone in and suddenly it was a computer terminal interfacing to the large screen briefing display that easily could be mistaken for a very large screen TV.

"I worked on this briefing while flying here. Paul Morgan showed me these images on his computer and of course my cell phone copied the sources directly off his hard drive via wireless."

"Norwegian Intelligence Service will be pissed if they discovered you stole all their eye candy," one of the other CIA members responded.

"They are not going to find out," Wilber responded. "Alright, let's see what you got," Pat Barton said.

"This is a time lapsed video Paul Morgan developed over several years. What you are seeing is his interactions as he ran the pointer over the various images and the popup boxes that show the intercepted text," Wilber stated knowing people in the meeting were already starting to disclose with their body language some astonishment.

"When you look at the colorized peaks on the images that's where he runs his computer mouse over to read what is originating in the communications hot spot," Wilber explained.

"Is that text like anything we have on Earth?"

"No. The text images could easily be Russian Cyrillic writing but it's not. It just looks similar."

"Have the Norwegians managed to decipher any of it? One of the CIA men present asked.

"No. Paul Morgan only provided this to the Norwegian Intelligence Service within the past month. The Alien language is rather sophisticated, and I think our linguists would take years to crack any of it, since we have no idea what their civilization is like," Wilber responded.

Next, Wilber showed high resolution photographs of the areas where the transmissions originated. "As you can see there are no buildings or structures."

"Then where the hell are the signals originating from?"

"There is only one possibility."

"And what is that?"

"Under the liquid surface of Saturn." "What is the liquid? Water?

"No, liquid hydrogen and liquid helium."

"How would we be able to find the transmitters?" "There is only one method possible."

"And what is that?"

"Either a probe or a submarine."

"The chances of shipping a submarine to Saturn is unlikely. A probe would be our only option.

"A probe might be insufficient for this purpose. I think," Wilber stated.

"Then how do we find the transmitters?"

"Send a person in a submersible below the surface and discover what exactly is down there."

***

Chapter Two

The Showdown

The meeting went on as people looked at Paul Morgan's eye candy, and nobody in the room took Wilber O'Toole's comment about sending a submarine to Saturn very seriously. Some of the military people present snickered under their breath wondering: is this dumbass making this suggestion some kind of crackpot?

In due time the consensus of the room was to send a probe to Saturn.

"How long will it take to design such a probe?" One of the officers from the secret space program asked knowing NASA would take several years as they milked most projects.

"It's kind of hard to estimate. We need a rocket to get it up in space."

"That's easy, I think we have a spare rocket," The general stated.

"Why do you have a spare rocket?" Pat Barton asked.

"The design work on the KH-15 ran into a few snags, we are set back maybe a year. We can have another rocket and four boosters built in time to launch the KH-15 when we think it will be ready for prime time."

"What's the snag in the KH-15 if you don't mind me asking?" Pat Barton asked.

"The KH-15 has a fusion rocket engine to move it around to avoid space junk and to get it away from the Russian satellite killers."

"You mean like the COSMOS 2547 satellite killer that was following one of our KH-12's for a while?"

"Precisely."

"Whatever happened to COSMOS 2547?"

"It was destroyed."

"What happened?"

"We didn't kill it and the Russians know we didn't kill it with our kinetic satellite killer."

"Any idea how it happened?"

"We do not know but one of our moles over there reported, the Russians have evidence, Aliens took it out."

"Anything to do with the signals from Saturn?"

"Not that we can tell. In fact, we have an invitation to meet with our FSB counterparts to discuss the matter sometime in the near future in Moscow. They have some major concerns."

"We certainly can't go there with this situation in Ukraine."

"The destruction of that Satellite rattled them. They have drastically changed their tune."

"Perhaps they can demonstrate their sincerity by pulling out of Ukraine?"

"That's not going to happen any time soon."

"Which means we will not be sending anyone to Moscow any time soon."

The meeting slowly decayed to a point where adjournment was imminent and Pat Barton suddenly said, "This meeting is now over. Please everyone, remember this is compartmentalized information and is not to be discussed outside Project Solaris offices. The Pentagon has no jurisdiction over this information, so you military members are also advised not to discuss this in the Pentagon. If your superiors press you for information, direct them to our offices and we'll brief them if we feel they have the need to know."

Everyone started to stand up and Pat Barton suddenly said, "Wilber please remain, we need to have a discussion."

Here it comes, Wilber O'Toole thought.

When everyone was out of the room and the door shut behind them, Pat Barton started the fireworks.

"Wilber, you are a valuable asset, but we cannot tolerate Cowboys like you in this agency. You managed to piss off the head of the Norwegian Intelligence Service by your conduct over there."

"Pat, I hope you understand, that had I not put the pressure on that Norwegian Intelligence Service agent Jørgen Eriksen's, I would never have gained access to Paul Morgan."

Wilber had you gone through normal protocols and conducted affairs in alignment of Project Solaris policies, all these negative communications floating back and forth via the State Department wouldn't be necessary."

"Well Pat, had I not stepped on Jørgen Eriksen's dick really hard, you wouldn't have a fraction of information I provided today."

"Wilber, you have forced me to take administrative action. I'm putting you on a day's administrative leave without pay with a warning going into your service file that indicates you Cowboy it up too often and give our agency a black eye too often."

"Pat the reason why you do not get a lot of information without paying a lot of Cash in Advance often buying tainted crap from third parties is because you have too many Girl Scouts and not enough Cowboys who know how to deal with unsavory characters."

"Wilber this is your final warning. If you step on another dick like you did that Norwegian Intelligence Service agent Jørgen Eriksen's, I'll get you moved out of here to some place where you are not capable of doing any more damage."

"Alright Pat, you do what you think you have to do, but something tells me that real soon when the President starts putting pressure on the DCI, you will wish the hell you had a few Cowboys around to handle the dirty work, because all your Girl Scouts with pristine hands, don't get much accomplished but handing out a lot of that Cash in

Advance which makes this agency look incompetent. The FSB laughs at you and your superiors.

"You really believe that crap?"

Pat you are a checkers player, and they are master chess players. The Chinese MSS has an even lower assessment of this goat fawk operation."

Wilber stood up and marched to the door and as he was leaving Pat Barton yelled, "Come back here, I'm not done with you mister."

Wilber ignored Pat's statement and continued his way out of the SKIF and soon out the building heading home, where he would change into gym clothes and head down to the waterfront park and put in a few miles and feed a few ducks and geese after he worked up a good sweat running eight miles. As a spy he had to keep in shape as death was lurking around the corner.

In his mind he recalled the snide remarks about his statement concerning using a submarine. But one thing Wilber knew, they needed to get below the surface into a helium or hydrogen lake or ocean to find out what is down there.

The technological challenges of building a submarine that could survive the rigors of liquid hydrogen or helium would be monumental. It would be the biggest engineering challenge ever attempted on planet earth.

It was obvious to Wilber they could not build the submarine here and send it to Saturn. Such a technological challenge would ultimately require building the submarine on Saturn as a kit, bolted together there. It was a foregone conclusion; they could not ship a large number of people to Saturn to build a submarine. Just how could such a device get built?

Thoughts of robots and artificial intelligence suddenly flooded Wilber's head as he was later running with all the vigor in the world along the Potamic majestic parkland.

In the meantime, Wilber would have to sit on his hands and watch the foolishness play out. Knowing how NASA operates, he knew it would be a year before that probe was mounted on a rocket ready to launch to Saturn, then it would take another six months for it to reach the planet. Another failed attempt by idiots who are constrained by mental midgets like Pat Barton who believes in the tooth fairy and didn't have a clue that ninety percent of the CIA's INTEL was collected by Cowboys not girl scouts with soft hands.

***

Chapter Three

Saturn Probe Commences

Days and weeks passed by with Wilber O'Toole's resentment for Pat Barton simmering right below boiling temperature. How can such a dumb ass get promoted to such a high level? Wilber wondered.

Unfortunately, that's how it was in government. Fair and impartial my ass, patronage and nepotism flourished in the Cash in Advance rank and file. Back in the late 1950's when Frank Wisner was Deputy Director for planning (DD/P) working directly for Allen Dulles, it was Cowboys in Action (CIA). Tracey Barnes, Richard Bissell, and illustrious members of that once proud group of Cowboys got the job done facing off with formidable enemies in Europe, Southeast Asia, Latin America, South America, and in Africa.

With the cold war running hot and critical, the Soviet Union was vast and strong. Those great Cowboys who dealt with the Soviet Union were long gone, but as a kid, Wilber O'Toole had the pleasure of meeting a couple of them since his own Papa was a Cowboy as well. Things were looking up as our Polaris Submarines now created the scenario of Mutually Assured Destruction (MAD).

Khruschev discovered the hard way during the Cuban Missile Crisis Kennedy knew where every one of their submarines were located with a great degree of accuracy thanks to Operation BORESIGHT and SOSUS. Those two programs were declassified in the 1990's by two female admirals at the detriment to the country. Boresight was no longer quite as important since the Soviets were shifting from Burst transmissions to satellite communications.

Declassification of SOSUS gave away the location of all the SOSUS arrays laid across every major body of water in the world and seems to many sheer lunacies. The admiral who ordered SOSUS declassification deserves criticism.

During the Cuban Missile Crisis when Khruschev threatened to nuke the United States with his submarines, President Kennedy informed Khruschev, we knew where every single Russian submarine was located and offered to read off the latitude and longitude locations for each one of them to prove that to be exactly the case.

When Admiral Gorshkov confirmed to Khruschev America had the locations of every one of approximately 400 Soviet Submarines and we could quickly destroy every one of those submarines, then wreck all their cities if they launched any nukes at us from Cuba. That's when the Cuban Missile Crisis abruptly ended. Within two years Kennedy as well as Khrushchev had been removed from power.

The new woke nature of the American government in general had now permeated all Federal Agencies. The Cash in Advance boys were no exception to the political overhaul done by misguided administrations making it rougher for the Cowboys to continue doing their incredible efforts to keep us safe. The attacks on the twin towers on 9/11 that took them down goes to show why you need Cowboys, Wilber thought.

Wilber O'Toole felt New York got hit because of complacency and too many Pat Barton's in high places that were diabolically counter to a successful security

operation. Wilber was grateful he was tasked with Solar Intelligence and not mired in the Ukraine quicksand. But something in the back of his head told him that if China crosses the Taiwan Straits, or North Korea attacks Japan and South Korea, he would no doubt get reassigned.

As a Russian linguist Wilber O'Toole was working on borrowed time as it was and dreaded the scenario a snake like Pat Barton could do to him such as transferred to the Russian or Ukraine desks. Even with the fear of adversarial action such as a transfer to those nebulous case officer desks, Wilber O'Toole still wasn't going to buckle under to a neophyte like Pat Barton who knew zip point chit of what Project Solaris charter required.

Every day, Project Solaris received more and more pressure from the White House via the DCI. And soon, Project Solaris personnel were all back in a highly classified meeting in their SKIF. This time the meeting included a couple contractor representatives escorted in that worked Lockheed and Boeing.

These two engineers on the staff of United Launch Alliance (ULA) a consortium led by Boeing and Lockheed often launched CIA spy satellites like the KH-13 and KH14. The KH-15 should have been launched by now but due to the technical difficulties in the nuclear fusion rocket engines thrust vectoring there were significant delays. Adding to the delays was the Vulcan rocket engine exploded during testing.

Because of Wilber O'Toole's running gun battle with Pat Barton, he was not invited to sit at the table and was next to the military brass in the chairs against the wall a few feet away from the conference room table. Wilber didn't have a lot of interest in this probe because he felt the Alien sources were submerged in a Helium Ocean and thus the probe wasn't going to accomplish much other than delay what really needed to get done.

But that's how the government operated often taking baby steps. And since no spacecraft the government would admit had been to the Moon since the Apollo missions. They had to do that all over again. They needed to listen to Elon Musk and forget the Moon and go right to Mars.

Now suddenly thrust into the forefront was the priority launch mission to get the Saturn Space Probe with full Intelligence, Surveillance, and Reconnaissance (ISR) capabilities to discover alien communications sources. The probe pie in the sky plan now led to the acquisition of a Saturn probe needed to find out exactly what infrastructure exists where those radio emanations originated.

John Burkette, Deputy Director/Planning for Project Solaris was at the head of the table showing signs of stress. He should feel stressed because DCI ripped him a new one a few times in just the past few days to get this probe launch moving in high gear. Up until now they were able to keep things covered up and with ample Cash in Advance, Norwegian Intelligence Service and Paul Morgan were keeping their mouths shut.

The scientist at Cornell University who had conversations with Paul Morgan was given his Cash in Advance to keep his mouth shut as well as a long free trip out to Southern California to work with CAL Tech at the Palomar observatory doing real science on per diem living in nice cottages in the area a short drive away via his rental car to Mount Palomar Observatory.

Working side by side with several Nobel Laureates the scientist worked at testing new optical processing systems utilizing stochastics resonance and wavelet filtering to obtain images better than the Hubble Space Telescope.

Between Hubble Space Telescope, Mount Palamar Observatory, and the massive parallel processed imagery down in Argentina, vast strides were being made in science and the exploration of the Universe. New Science was being made every day and that made people extremely excited as they viewed ongoing research and anticipated vast discoveries.

"Alright ladies and gentlemen let's get the meeting started. A friendly reminder, make sure your phones are in airplane mode. I want everyone to check it now because if you phone rings during this meeting security will be crushing it in a few minutes with our phone declassify machine."

It was kind of comical to watch the entire crowd suddenly check their cell phones. The fact they were inside a SKIF with their cell phones was unprecedented, but since it was RF shielded not much could be leaked out and God forbid anyone who did.

Most of us know we launch most of our KH-13 and KH-14 NRO satellites via United Launch Alliance. They will also soon be launching the KH- 15 satellite as soon as we resolve a couple technical issues with its fusion rocket engines."

"I'm going to introduce our two distinguished guests who are involved in the Vulcan rocket we are going to use and the Saturn Probe. Sitting right beside me is Doctor James Barnes from Lockheed. He's a missile designer and did a lot of work on the Vulcan Rocket Engines that will accelerate the capsule carrying the Saturn Probe out into space."

James Barns dipped his head in an abbreviated bow to the meeting members.

"Sitting next to James Barnes is Doctor Ronald Mattern from Boeing. There are a couple things about him I'm going to tell you but it's not to leave this room. Ronald is a great singer; I've seen him in action."

The people at the meeting gave a quick chuckle as Deputy Director/ Planning for Project Solaris, John Burke, had displayed his humor in the office several times before especially when he knew the hometown football team was going to get slaughtered in several games in recent years where it seemed changing the teams name really put a jinx on them.

"The second thing I'm going to disclose about Doctor Mattern is he is one of the finest electronics designers I have ever worked with in my past experiences.

Doctor Mattern smiled and looked fondly at John Burkette.

"As a technology user Doctor Mattern provided me with tools and equipment. Doctor Mattern is also the chief integrator of the electronics in the Saturn Probe." John Burkette added.

"Before we engage Doctors Barnes and Mattern about the Saturn probe, I want to convey to all of you, the President is getting quite animated and wants this mission to get underway as soon as possible because he fears it's only a matter of time before public awareness becomes significantly more intense," John Burkette said then looked around the room for responses.

"I know some of you are slightly bewildered we must cut time out of the schedule but believe me the pressure on the DCI is now enormous."

One of the Air Force Generals interrupted and asked, "Just exactly how are we going to shave time off. Quality isn't fast."

"We have a few people directly involved with these distinguished researchers and designer and in discussions leading up to this meeting we came up with a few questions for them. We'll start out with Guy Burgess. What questions do you have?"

"Thank you, Doctor Barnes. My first question is: Doctor Barnes, have you solved the problem with the Vulcan rocket engines?"

"Mr. Burgess, we believe we discovered the flaws in the Vulcan Rocket Engines and have been doing tests on several of them out at Area 51 and ran them up to 100% reactor power as long as we perceive they would operate during the space flight and launch of the capsule that would have sufficient velocity to arrive at Saturn in approximately four months."

"Why would it take so long?"

"At the velocity we need to achieve to reach Saturn in 4 months, we also need a two-week period to slow down in order to safely launch the probe."

"How do you slow down?"

"The capsule has a fusion reactor rocket engine just like the main rocket engines for the lift off the planet as well as retro rockets to spin the aircraft.

We simply swing the Capsule around 180 degrees and fire the rocket engine to provide the breaking."

"And all that's going to take two weeks?"

"Yes, we have done all the calculations and to get the probe precisely where you want it to land requires such precision application of flight controls."

The discussion lingered for another thirty minutes as Doctor Barnes answered a myriad of questions about the fusion reactor propulsion rockets. Then it was time to move on to the actual Saturn probe.

"Doctor Mattern, you helped to design the probe, can you please tell us a little about it?"

Wilber O'Toole was now animated and focused on every word Doctor Mattern stated. He knew they were heading down the wrong path because idiots like Pat Barton bought into this utter nonsense. But unfortunately, management spoke, and the neophyte was selected for reasons Wilber would never learn. Nepotism and patronage sure seemed like a logical conclusion.

"First of all, ladies and gentlemen," Doctor Mattern stated as he was well aware there were several smoking hot women in the SKIFF with them, "The probe has a fusion power plant that will provide sufficient power to maintain operations while the probe is in orbit for well over a year."

"What are some of the data collection capabilities of the probe?" an Air Force general asked.

"Thanks for asking the question, General. The probe has essentially all the ISR capabilities of our X-37B craft. As you know the X-37B has been flying for quite some time thus we had the opportunity to miniaturize the electronics more and the probe instrument package only takes up twenty five percent of the volume and weight of the X-37B payload."

"Any plans to do engineering changes to upgrade the X-37B with this new version of the electronics?" The Air Force General quickly asked.

"General, I know the X-37B is not a matter associated with the Saturn probe, but since there are people in the room who have a vested interest in the X-37B especially with what's happening in Ukraine, so I'm going to take a brief moment to let you know what is going on. I would also advise people in this room this is privileged information and one of our guarded national assets so please do not discuss it outside this meeting."

"Thanks," The General responded.

Doctor Mattern knew this would probably piss off Deputy Director John Burkette, for wasting valuable time on items not associated with the Saturn Probe, but this gave Boeing a cheap shot at their competitor Lockheed, that was friend and foe only because of ULA.

"Normally, as we do engineering changes thanks to our spiral development concepts we use in the X-37B program that utilizes commercial off the shelf (COTS) technology. Nevertheless, we would not have considered such a huge reconfiguration for the X-37B and saved most of that innovation for the X-37E that is now in development."

Those words struck a chord with the Air Force General who seemed to stiffen up in response.

"However, due the exigency created by Ukraine and Vladimir Putin throwing out the nuclear option terms, we decided to do a massive engineering change to the X-37B that will include the miniaturization that significantly reduces power consumption allowing us to add an additional sensor suite providing some of the same capability as the KH-14 operates in additional wavelengths and nuclear material detectors and missile prelaunch communications and transients.

"Does the orbital ISR craft remain an X-37B?" The Airforce General quickly responded.

"When an X-37B is reconfigured as I described we change the designation to

X-37BE."

"How soon will the X-37BE be ready to operate?" The Air Force general asked.

"This is very sensitive information. I can't give exact dates, but ULA will no doubt be moving a rocket to the launch pad real soon that will have an X-37BF in the disposable capsule. I would estimate the X-37BF will be over Ukraine before the end of the month."

"How long will it operate there?"

"As long as necessary. As you know we had an X-37B operating over two years for the National Reconnaissance Office (NRO)."

"What's the advantage of the X-37BF over our KH-14?" The General said as he was starting to get on John Burkette's nerves.

"This will be my last comment about the X-37BF because I have a lot of information, we might want to discuss about the Saturn Probe," Doctor Mattern said which immediately put a smile on John Burkette who wanted the General to shut the hell up.

"We must fly KH-14's at 25,000 to 30,000 miles above the planet to hide them from Russian Cosmos 2547 class satellite killers. The X-37BF which have propulsion to evade a Cosmos 2547 sister ship, remains in low Earth orbit where the telemetry we receive provides much better granularity in photonics and ESM focusing for localization of communications and sensor radiators."

John Burkette decided to ask a question to get them back on track,

"Doctor Mattern, have we done anything with the firmware of the Saturn Probe to make it more versatile in surveillance of signals we've intercepted from Saturn?"

"Director Burkette, we have a rack of equipment installed in an NRO secure laboratory where people from Johns Hopkins university who control those intercepts, process the information and monitor the telemetry with a special test set to validate the encrypted transmissions coming back to Earth send certified transmissions to ensure we receive very accurate signal measurements that can be processed and analyzed in their laboratory."

"Has there been any breakthroughs in deciphering Alien Communications?"

"Director Burkette, you would not like to hear this and I must state the signals intelligence of what we have obtained is TOP SECRET SCI with S, Y, and X special designators. Very few people in the room are cleared for that information. But what I will state is something many already know from other alien signals we processed via a secret space program, the Aliens use Tangramization in their communications, making it extremely difficult to decipher."

"What's Tangramization?" A Navy Admiral asked.

"When you get a chance after the meeting, visit the Wikipedia web site and lookup Chinese Tangram."

"Why would the Tangramize their communications?"

"Precisely for the reason why we find it almost impossible to decipher, but our communications experts also believe the Aliens have a Tangram lexicon that results in massively increased communications speed."

To say everyone in the room wasn't somehow moved by Doctor Mattern's last statement, clearly showed it by their body language.

Now they knew why the President had really put the squeeze to the DCI. The aliens suddenly broadcasting Tangramized signals we intercepted in numerous sudden bursts really spooked the Pentagon as well as the top leadership in the intelligence agencies. It could possibly mean Earth might soon have to deal with these Aliens in ways we never expected and FEARED.

"What's the overall plan for the Saturn Probe?" one of the agency members in the meeting asked.

"The probe will orbit Saturn avoiding its rings and attempt to localize the source of the transmissions. Once we feel we have a high-resolution location that matches areas Doctor Paul Morgan in Norway plotted, we'll send the probe down to the planet surface and when it gets into the thick atmosphere, control surfaces will deploy like we do with some of our missiles allowing it to glide down close to the target area and perform all the ISR measurements possible. Eventually the probe will crash land on Saturn, most likely landing in one of the oceans of hydrogen or helium."

All during the discussion Wilber O'Toole was betting against the probe. He already concluded they would not see anything because the aliens were submerged and hiding in the vast pools of liquid helium and hydrogen. But since Wilber didn't desire to get reassigned to the Russian or Ukraine desks, he kept his mouth shut and simply kept his thoughts to himself. He wondered, "How many probes would they waste before they finally realized there was only one method of discovering much about these aliens and that was with a submarine?

Wilber O'Toole was very sophisticated and intelligent and knew that to be able to build a submarine that could operate in liquid Helium or Hydrogen would require technology that would have to be invented and they needed to start developing the materials science now or it would not be feasible any time in the future.

Even though his suggestion of building a submarine went over like a lead balloon, at some point in time out of desperation they would have to take the idea seriously. And the best way to make sure it was achievable was to get Pat Barton out of the chain of command so someone with some smarts could figure it out and make it happen.

In due time the probe was fully discussed, and the meeting ended. Everyone slowly exited the SKIF conference room, and the two visitors were escorted to the front entrance. Doctor Mattern and Doctor Barnes left the building with smiles on their faces because they loved getting blank checks from the Cash in Advance boys that would eventually make their investors happy as company earnings would be impacted by all the black money they would receive for this project.

This new Saturn Probe boondoggle also meant the delay in the KH-15 launch was not going to be detrimental to their ULA profit margins since that Vulcan Rocket would now be put to immediate use. The icing on the cake was ULA would be funded to build an unexpected rocket plus boosters for the KH-15 they hoped to launch by the end of the year.

The Saturn Probe was a win-win for everyone, even though the purpose of the Saturn Probe was slightly alarming. Doctor Mattern knew far more than he could state in the meeting. Researchers at Johns Hopkins university who were joined at the hip with intelligence agencies, were quite alarmed these alien communications outclassed anything manmade by a huge margin.

Another thing Doctor Mattern could not divulge because it was shrouded in one of the greatest secrets, the Tangramization data feed coming from Saturn appeared to be part of an elaborate holographic communication system. Fractal researchers had reconstructed a few partial holographic images and with the use of artificial intelligence, it appeared they were finding a way to speed up the process. One fractal researcher estimated that within 6 months they might be able to determine how to create a constant feed of images required for real time holographic presentation.

The haunting question remained: "Who were these beings on Saturn communicating with?" Were they communicating to Saturn people on Earth? That proposal was a frightening one.

Upon arrival at his desk, Wilber O'Toole found an email from Pat Barton in his in basket. The content of the email stated, "I'm sending you to Vandenberg to look at the work in the assembly building for the Saturn Probe. A helicopter will be landing on top of the building in 30 minutes to fly you to Andrews where one of our new GS750 aircraft will be waiting for you in the hanger to fly you out there. If you must spend the night and a few days, get a rental car, and check into a hotel nearby and send me back report via secure communication. Do not discuss your findings with anyone there, only inform me what you find out."

Sounds like Pat Barton is getting nervous if he must send out a Cowboy to get a good status report, Wilber thought.

This would not be the first time, nor the last time Wilber would hop on a plane with just the clothes he was wearing. Arriving in Moscow in the winter like that in the past caused a lot of uncomfortable moments. But emergencies are emergencies. Once he got inside the warm embassy, a staffer was sent out to get him a winter coat and one of those Russian Ushanka that covered his ears for the brutal winter cold.

Wilber O'Toole had interesting memories of some of his trips to Russia, especially Petropavlovsk-Kamchatsky where he played the role of the co- pilot for an air freight company. His purpose was to obtain a microchip from one of their deep plant moles that had a profoundly large amount of Russian military secrets on it stolen off a Russian Submarine parked at the nearby Rybachiy Nuclear Submarine Base in Vilyuchinsk.

Petropavlovsk-Kamchatsky is located 4,204 miles from Moscow and 1,380 mi from Vladivostok where a large portion of the Russian Pacific fleet is home ported.

Wilber, operating under the alias Roger Keeney, was the co-pilot for the flight. The pilot, Kevin Landry was a real air freighter pilot and was a little nervous when he received his Cash in Advance pay to go along with the ruse.

The plan quickly unfolded as Wilber (aka Roger Keeney) asked the waiter where the restroom was located and quickly gave directions.

Wilber met the mole in the bathroom that he had reviewed his picture on the plane taken merely hours before, so Wilber easily recognized the Russian Spy in the clothes he was wearing and his overall image.

Wilber quickly swallowed the microchip, and it was expected he would not poop it out for a couple days. CIA experts would go through his poop carefully and extract the microchip with 16 Gigabytes of storage loaded with TOP SECRET Russian information including information and crypto codes required to decode a lot of Russian message traffic.

The San Marino Restaurant was an upscale restaurant and bar located on Karla Marksa Avenue was within walking distance of the Dolce Vita hotel where Wilber O'Toole was spending the night and would fly back the next day.

The food at the San Marino Restaurant was fabulous. Besides having great wines, the ambience was phenomenal. The white chairs were Russian style that might give one the

impression they were built during the Napoleon era. The fine linen and tablecloths and real silverware exposed some of the reasons why the food was relatively expensive. But with per diem of an Airline pilot flying between Russia and Memphis, was more than sufficient for esthetics of the alias.

The airfreight company spent vast amounts to provide Russian language skills to select pilots chosen to fly this route. Company policy was to have at least one Russian Speaker as pilot or copilot. Due to Wilber's relatively youthful appearance, looking remarkably like Tracey Barnes, one of the top operatives in the DD/P covert operations fifty years before, he would have to play the role of the copilot.

The regular scheduled copilot for this flight was sent to the bathroom on the plane before it departed Memphis, and changed clothes provided by Wilber and a mask and a hardhat to make him appear like a grounds support person who immediately walked off the airplane and was taken to a hotel where he was sequestered with room service and hookers if he wanted one until the plane returned. Wilber would simply walk off the plane and the regular copilot would have his uniform on and simply appear to drive home as if it was another day at the office.

Wilber had changed into street clothes back in his hotel on a lovely summer day and before that he went to the restaurant. He knew that no doubt he was going to be followed and all his movements watched. He assumed his hotel room was bugged and everywhere he went there would be FSB (KGB) watchers.

Sometimes there are perks in the Spy business. Today was no exception. The Russian FSB like the Chinese MSS love to initiate honey pot schemes. These intelligence agencies film you in bed with a lovely Russian Blonde or in some cases a homosexual lover and threaten to reveal that to your wife or employer especially if you are a defense contractor doing inexplicable acts with a term often used in the far east: LBFM's.

Just like out of the playbook, when Wilber returned from the bathroom a moment later with the microchip swallowed, there was the beautiful blonde arriving. This gorgeous creature was escorted to a table close to Wilber's by the equally exemplary and beautiful, lovely blonde maître d' named Irina.

This blonde now sitting near Wilber was all business. Either a hooker or an FSB (KGB) operative. The beautiful blonde's mink coat and diamonds gave the appearance of an elegant lady who had money which a high-class Russian call girl could easily afford if her Russian customers were filthy rich such as some that lived in this area thanks to mining and lumber operations. Nearby Sakhalin Island had one of the largest oil reserves in the world.

The FSB spares no expense for clandestine operations, especially in Russia. Back in the Soviet Union days when the country was poor and almost bankrupt trying to keep up militarily with Europe and the

United States, the KGB didn't spend a lot of

money. But now with various nefarious activities involving the Russian mafia and rouge FSB/KGB people enriching themselves just like Putin, the black money flowed into their coffers, and they had just as much funds as the Cash in Advance Americans.

Aida Abramova the extremely beautiful FSB operative now making eye contact with Wilber O'Toole could pass for the twin sister of the famous Russian singer Polina Sergeyevna Gagarina. Aida was a well-trained spy who knew how to use all her tools including her body. Having sex with the enemy to gain control, was no different than taking a bullet for an Army Infantryman who wanted to win the war.

Aida Abramova well indoctrinated in KGB and NKVD history, knew the impact spies have especially Richard Sorge during WW2 who informed Stalin the Japanese would not attack Russian forces in Manchuria and Siberia because they were just about to start a war with America. Hence Stalin was able to reposition 18 divisions by train from the far east for the counterattack at Moscow, and with the help of IL-2 Shturmovík Aircraft and T34 tanks that had never been revealed to the Germans were a tank busting duality that quickly decimated German forces and bagged over 350,000 POWs, saving Moscow.

As a field operative, Aida Abramova intended to work her way up in the FSB (KGB) even if she had to spend time working on her back, letting her enemies take their pleasure before she gained permanent control of them. Aida would waste no time in slicing Wilber's throat if ordered to kill him. It would not be the first time she poked a spy's eyes out if required. In the spy business it's kill or be killed.

Wilber O'Toole had no doubt this woman he would soon meet by the name of Aida could only be a call girl or FSB operator. Either way there would be flirtation and attempted seduction or recruitment.

After receiving his glass of wine, Wilber ordered the seafood plate that cost 3785 ₽ (Rubles).

The beautiful blonde also ordered food and soon received what appeared to be crab cakes and mashed potatoes.

One thing, no matter what her game was, her smile appeared infectious and there was no doubt she was flirting.

The restaurant was more than half empty as it was a little early for most Russian diners. They would start arriving in about an hour. The professional at work wasted no time on her quarry.

"Привет, меня зовут Аида."

{ "Privet, menya zovut Aida."}

["Hello, my name is Aida (pronounced I-E-DA.")]

"Приятно познакомиться, меня зовут Роджер Кини."

{ "Priyatno poznakomit'sya, menya zovut Rodzher Kini."}

["Nice to meet you, my name is Roger Keeney"]

"Вы живете здесь, в Петропавловске-Камчатском?" спросила Аида.

{"Vy zhivete zdes', v Petropavlovske-Kamchatskom?"} sprosila Aida. ["Do you live here in Petropavlovsk-Kamchatsky?" Aida asked.] «Нет, я живу в Мемфисе, штат Теннесси, в Соединенных Штатах».

{«Net, ya zhivu v Memfise, shtat Tennessi, v Soyedinennykh Shtatakh».}

["No, I live in Memphis, Tennessee, in the United States."]

« Вы американец? » спросила Аида.

{« Vy amerikanets? » sprosila Aida.}

["You are an American?" Aida asked.]

"Да"

{"Da"}

["Yes"]

«Твой русский язык так хорош. Как ты можешь так хорошо говорить по-русски?» — спросила Аида.

{«Tvoy russkiy yazyk tak khorosh. Kak ty mozhesh' tak khorosho govorit' porusski?» — sprosila Aida.}

["Your Russian language is so good. How can you speak such good?

Russian?" Aida asked.]

«Я изучал русский язык в старшей школе и колледже, затем моя компания по авиаперевозкам решила, что хочет, чтобы больше русскоговорящих летало в Россию и из России, и выплатила мне премию, чтобы я вернулся в школу в рабочее время и прошел ряд курсов в нашем местном университете. улучшить свои навыки русского языка, чтобы я мог более эффективно общаться с российскими авиадиспетчерами».

{«YA izuchal russkiy yazyk v starshey shkole i kolledzhe, zatem moya kompaniya po aviaperevozkam reshila, chto khochet, chtoby bol'she russkogovoryashchikh letalo v Rossiyu i iz Rossii, i vyplatila mne premiyu, chtoby ya vernulsya v shkolu v rabocheye vremya i proshel ryad kursov v nashem mestnom universitete. uluchshit' svoi navyki russkogo yazyka, chtoby ya mog boleye effektivno obshchat'sya s rossiyskimi aviadispetcherami».}

"I took Russian in high school and college, then my air freight company decided it wanted more Russian speakers flying in and out of Russia and paid me a bonus to go back to school on company time and take a sequence of courses at our local university to enhance my Russian speaking skills to allow me to speak with Russian Air Traffic Controllers more effectively."

«Ваше знание русского языка весьма впечатляет. Я бы не узнала, что ты американец, если бы ты не раскрыла это,» ответила Аида.

{«Vashe znaniye russkogo yazyka ves'ma vpechatlyayet. YA by ne uznala, chto ty amerikanets, yesli by ty ne raskryla eto,» otvetila Aida.}

["Your Russian skills are quite impressive. I would not know you were American had you not disclosed it," Aida replied.]

«Я чувствую себя более комфортно, летая в Россию, когда понимаю инструкции, которые нам дают авиадиспетчеры, когда мы подходим к аэропорту.

Я также слышу указания по воздушному движению других самолетов в этом районе и в результате чувствую себя более комфортно и безопасно». — ответил Роджер.

{ «YA chuvstvuyu sebya boleye komfortno, letaya v Rossiyu, kogda ponimayu instruktsii, kotoryye nam dayut aviadispetchery, kogda my podkhodim k aeroportu. YA takzhe slyshu ukazaniya po vozdushnomu dvizheniyu drugikh samoletov v etom rayone i v rezul'tate chuvstvuyu sebya boleye komfortno i bezopasno». otvetil Rodzher.}

["I feel more comfortable flying to Russia when I can understand instructions the air traffic controllers give us when we approach the airport. I can also hear the air traffic instructions to other aircraft in the area and feel more comfortable and safer as a result." Roger replied.]

Роджер и Аида отказались от десерта, их еды было столько, сколько они могли выдержать. Как только Роджер заплатил за еду и встал, Аида вдруг сказала: «Роджер, не хочешь ли ты пойти со мной прогуляться?»

{Rodzher i Aida otkazalis' ot deserta, ikh yedy bylo stol'ko, skol'ko oni mogli vyderzhat'. Kak tol'ko Rodzher zaplatil za yedu i vstal, Aida vdrug skazala: «Rodzher, ne khochesh' li ty poyti so mnoy progulyat'sya?»}

[Roger and Aida turned down desert, their meals were as much as they could handle. As soon as Roger paid for his meal and stood up, Aida suddenly said, "Roger, would you like to go for a walk with me?"]

«Да, я думаю, что хотел бы, я люблю гулять при каждом удобном случае, люблю гулять по городам и молча восхищаться людьми и их культурами».

«Da, ya dumayu, chto khotel by, ya lyublyu gulyat' pri kazhdom udobnom sluchaye, lyublyu gulyat' po gorodam i molcha voskhishchat'sya lyud'mi i ikh kul'turami».

["Yes, I think I would, I like walking every chance I get and like to walk around in cities and silently admire the people and their cultures."]

***

Chapter Four

Trip To A Dacha

The two walked at a leisurely pace, neither one of them had any other place to go. Staying cooped up in the hotel room just did not seem to satisfy Roger. They had walked about half a block from the San Marino restaurant.

Aida turned towards Roger and said, "I had to talk to you in Russian while we were in the restaurant, but I can also speak English. Since we are alone, I wish to speak to you in English and practice speaking English, if you do not mind."

Aida had that definite Russian accent she could not hide. She knew she had to get rid of that accent and speak more like an American if she ever wanted to be detailed to the west, especially into the hot den of spies around Dupont Circle in Washington DC where some of the greatest espionage adventures over one-hundred-year period occurred. Spies watching spies watching spies was not uncommon during the height of the cold war.

Aida knew walking back towards Roger's (aka Wilber) hotel would not afford them privacy and there was no way she was going to have sex with Roger while the FSB boys would be monitoring the room if they went there.

Aida had an FSB friend who flew out from Moscow quite often. He was a highranking FSB official and came out to meet with her superiors on assignments mostly to tweak their operations because they were not catching enough American spies they knew were around somewhere.

The FSB agent's name is Dmitri Vasilyevich Bortnikov, but the alias he used while in town was Boris. Only Aida knew his real name because Dmitri had banged the rims off Aida's tires a few times on a theme from Paganini.

To reward her for her excellent love making and friendship, he allowed Aida exclusive use of his dacha when he wasn't in town. Boris (aka Dmitri) had just traveled back to Moscow about a week earlier and would not be coming back for three or four weeks.

Boris would encourage Aida if he knew her assignment to get Roger to the dacha and seduce this Russian speaking American so they could determine his real activity and purpose of being in Petropavlovsk Kamchatsky. If they discovered Roger worked for the CIA, Aida would get some promotions and increased visibility allowing her a higher probability of being reassigned to Moscow or St. Petersburg where and FSB agent wanted to be for any hopes of promotions to a much higher level without taking a bullet for the team.

"Roger, there are not a lot of good things to see around here. I have an idea, lets walk back to the restaurant where my car is parked and let me drive you to my friend's dacha, he lets me use when he's not in town, where we can have a good walk in the countryside and see the mountains better and the plume now coming out of one of the active volcanoes."

"Sure, that sounds fine with me, but I need to be back to my hotel tonight to get some sleep and be ready to fly at noon tomorrow."

"That will not be a problem Roger, and if you keep taking trips here, I would like to get to know you better."

"Aida, any man would love to get to know a beautiful woman like you better."

"Don't be so generous with your words, Roger. I'm not that pretty and I know it."

"Aida there are many things about you that I like, and I think my overall view from the 30,000-foot level makes me know you are very lovely, and I want to put the nose of my plane down and get to 1000 feet so I can see you better."

"Only a pilot can think of things like that to say."

"That comment shows my thought process, I like to learn about people I become friends with."

"You want to be my friend, Roger?"

"Of course, I would. I would even consider requesting flights here instead of Vladivostok, St. Petersburgh, and Moscow if I knew I was going to spend quality time with a nice lady like you."

"Thank you, Roger, I appreciate those comments."

"My pleasure."

The two walked promptly to Aida's nice BMW, one of the few luxuries she could afford on her disposable income. Using her remote-control Aida unlocked the vehicle and Roger (aka Wilber) instinctively got inside which pleased Aida because she didn't like rookies.

Aida could drive fast because she was FSB. The police were not going to interfere with her work and their license identification system would notify the police officer that's a government operative, disregard. It would normally take the average Russian an hour to get to the friend's dacha from the San Marino Restaurant.

Just like Aida indicated, the landscape in this sparsely populated area was stunningly beautiful with the unobstructed view of the volcanic mountains. The two walked and talked for over an hour about things they each liked including classical music, books, and intellectual growth.

Aida had her own needs. She was reaching the point she wanted to do sex just as much as the men wanted to have sex with her. She was, however, picky and wanted someone special like Roger when the time came. And if Roger turned out to be CIA, she would throw caution to the wind and seduce him like he never felt before and turn him and control him in a deadly game of betrayal. The one thing Aida didn't count on was coming up against someone just as clever and resourceful as Roger, where the mouse turns the pussy cat into a mouse.

"I'm getting kind of thirsty, let's go back to the dacha and get something to drink and relax," Aida said.

"Sounds good to me," Roger responded.

They were soon inside the very nicely decorated dacha that had oil paintings and sculptures that only a wealthy person could obtain.

Flying in FSB jets avoiding airport security, Dmitri could fly back to Moscow

with suitcases full of Chinese Heroin and sell it to his contacts in the Russian Mafia, he sometimes hired to kill people for him and do other nefarious activities.

Wilber (aka Roger) knew whoever owned this place was probably getting his fair share of time with Aida in bed where she was most likely quite capable either as a call girl or an FSB agent. The question he had was, did the FSB have this place wired?

Whether the FSB had the place wired or not, Wilber would perform and enjoy some of the benefits of being behind enemy lines and under covers.

Knowing Roger had wine back at the restaurant, and most likely Cabernet Sauvignons, Aida went over and opened an excellent bottle of Gabrielle Ashley, from Alexander Valley, Sonoma County, California. One of the best vineyards in Napa Valley. She then filled two large wine classes half full and carried them over to Roger sitting on the sofa admiring some of the art works from there.

Aida handed Roger one of the glasses of wine, and said, "I want to make a toast to you."

Давайте выпьем за то, чтобы мы испытали столько горя, сколько капель вина останется в наших бокалах!

{Vyp'yem za to, chtoby my ispytali stol'ko gorya, skol'ko kapel' vina ostalos' v nashikh bokalakh!}

[May we suffer as much sorrow as drops of wine we are about to leave in our glasses!]

Aida and Roger tapped their glasses together and took a deep sip of their wine.

Aida stood up, walked over to the entertainment center and started playing some music. She had listened to this music, Dohnanyi: Piano Concerto No.2 Op.42 a few hours prior while she was brainstorming her plans after she was directed to get ready to check out this American pilot the FSB had not recalled seeing before that was most likely the person speaking excellent Russian to air traffic control on the American Air Freight Aircraft. It would not be the first, nor the last time the CIA snuck in agents into Russia in such a manner. Russians do the same trick.

Aida walked back over to the sofa picked up her glass of wine and said, "Would you mind reclining back on the sofa and holding me in your arms while we listen to this music together?

With the mink coat removed, Aida showed a much thinner top and her nipples were easily observed in the flimsy silk material along with her Areolas that were almost 3 inches in diameter and quite impressive.

While Aida had her back turned towards Roger (aka Wilber), he swallowed an antidote in case she drugged him and was an FSB spy. His billfold was prepacked with all the fake credit cards and identity cards to match his role in this clandestine activity. Wilber would feel the effects of the drugs and know he was drugged but remain lucid and would fake being unconscious as Aida would pilfer through his billfold photographing its contents if that's what her plan was.

Wilber would then play along and set up future rendezvous with Aida on subsequent flights he would not actually make since his only purpose in being here was to enable the CIA scientists to check his poop really good to find the microchip.

Aida's plan was exactly what Wilber suspected but just at the launch point of the drugging something changed. Aida suddenly took take herself out of the spy business for a few precious hours to devour this pilot she suspected was just another innocent bystander in the game of intreague as she chose to begin a tempestuous love affair and dangerous liaison that would rattle nerves in the FSB and the CIA.

Aida didn't want Roger drugged up wondering the next morning if he had happy time. Instead, Aida wanted Roger to remember the sweetness and intensity of it all. If it turns out Roger was indeed a spy, Aida could turn him later if she suspected he was merely a courier and in due time they would discover the mole and deal with that person in the swimming pool or at the crematorium where they interrogated all captured spies.

Aida moved her body around where she knew she could move her head easily to kiss Roger. As soon as his wine glass was empty, she took it from him and placed the wine glass on the coffee table next to her glass she drank out of and turned and kissed Roger in a very subtle manner on his lips.

Aida had graduated with honors from seduction school. She had thousands of practice kisses on short, fat, bald, and ugly stinking men. It was all part of the psychological adjustments. She had psychiatric people who worked for the FSB that were there coaching her, explaining it was merely another form of warfare. Instead of shooting bullets, she was shooting kisses, and she would kill more enemy if she aimed her kisses just right in the most seductive manner.

Aida now demonstrated her kiss targeting not to kill an enemy but instead to enhance her own gratification. She knew that desire was ten times stronger than gratification. They had pounded that into her head repeatedly, thus she knew how to pound it into Rogers little head and to prepare him for transcendence towards the psychological and emotional reaction she wanted because she wanted him jacked up so high his love making would be exemplary.

Little did Aida know; Roger (aka Wilber) had his own training with similar concepts. Not only do female spies seduce males in honeypot schemes but CIA spies often seduce women because it's always best to pick the low hanging fruit and take a circuitous path to the objective. Many a Contessa had fallen for such elaborate scenarios, and Roger had perpetrated the splendor of Casanova when it was materially an advantage to the CIA to do especially if there were no other means to accomplish the mission.

As Aida poured on her charm and her expertise, she got it back from Roger. Aida thought she manifested Roger's reaction, but the master chess player was three moves ahead of her and Aida was falling into Roger's trap just as easily as she thought Roger fell into her ruse.

It seemed like slow motion when the two of them migrated from the sofa to the bedroom and were locked into a physical embrace that let the flood gates of passion furl at one another. Aida had no idea what she was up against, a man with such magnificent control. Roger purposely held back his gratification until he felt Aida was

not capable of having another orgasm without passing out and suddenly gave her the significant sweet surrender of his gratification which induced lingering ensembles of ethereal vibrations.

Just like Aida promised Roger, she dropped him off at his hotel and soon had massive regrets she didn't sleep in his arms that night even if the FSB assholes would be watching her in his hotel room.

When Roger never came back, she knew the truth. It turned out as the FSB suspected, Roger was a spy and that was not his real name.

Aida now understood Wilber, who the FSB informed her his real name, played the game as well as Aida could. Everything is fair in love and war, and Aida understood she was just severely defeated in both love and war.

But the way Wilber (aka Roger) made love to her made Aida think he was doing it in that manner out of some affection for her. Perhaps one day they would cross paths again as it happens in the spy world in a neutral setting like Switzerland or her favorite place, Santorini Greece where she would love to make copious love to him. Then she would sting him like a good Latrodectus would.

***

Wilber O'Toole snapped out of his daydream as the sounds and smell of the helicopter on the top of the office building gave him a dose of reality. Wilber walked over under the propwash and into the Sikorsky S-97 Raider helicopter that featured rotors plus a pusher propeller in the back. The cruise speed for the S-97 was 250 miles per hour. It would not take long to get to Andrews.

Wilber had his suit and sunglasses and that's about it. Anything he needed to support his mission due to the immediate action required, would have to be purchased in-situ.

The S-97 flew directly to the hanger where the GS750 was parked. It would not come out of the hanger until all the passengers were onboard to reduce the surveillance on who was leaving on the jet since there were plenty of spies around.

Several uniformed military people escorted Wilber O'Toole to the entrance on the side of the building and entered a number on the cypher pad and opened the door for him. As soon as he stepped inside there was Tammy, a Nordic blonde with extreme beauty. Tammy was a private person and never entertained any liaisons with military or government employees. Though she did have a slight crush on Wilber and if he made the slightest suggestion, he would discover how fast she would act upon it.

Tammy was waiting for the right guy. Tammy knew she was still smoking hot, and it would only be a matter of time before she hooked some spook like Wilber for a lifelong relationship. Tammy didn't want a neophyte; she wanted a Cowboy like Wilber.

Wilber was smart and never stuck his pen in company ink, but while he was in Petropavlovsk-Kamchatsky, he had to play the role of a good spy would and sacrifice his body for the call of duty. Wilber took sleeping with the enemy to a new level that only a Cowboy would do.

While Wilber was going through debriefings was informed the poop scientists found the microchip and it contained a wealth of intelligence. He also had another interesting surprise. His cell phone had a random beacon that went up to a satellite so the agency could track his whereabouts in case they needed to rescue or disavow him. Just like the FSB/KGB, the CIA also has a few watchers on missions and provide photographic intelligence such as the woman Wilber was with. If he didn't disclose it all he would be hooked up to a polygraph. All his interactions with Aida were disclosed and he in turn was briefed she was an FSB agent and thanks to Wilber going to the dacha they now had another identification and location to where a top- level FSB person hid out with his mistresses from time to time.

Aida was thus a double spy and didn't know it as she provided valuable intelligence and another piece to the puzzle of FSB directorate without placing a high value spy at risk to obtain the same high-quality information.

Likewise, Aida was also briefed on Wilber which the FSB knew a lot about. The way the CIA snuck Wilber into the country was another Intelligence failure of the FSB. Which proves the point even if you know who the enemy agent is, you cannot always prevent the arrival and penetration and damage done. The worst damage is what you do not know they stole. No doubt Wilber O'Toole left Russia with some important information. Just what was it?

In a brief period, the GS750 was airborne and on its way to California. Wilber laid back in his reclining chair and took as much of a nap as he could to help make up for some of his recent sleep deprivation.

Tammy was a smart woman, had dealt with Wilber on numerous occasions and knew once he put on the company supplied sleeping pads that were slightly larger than sunglasses, that meant he did not want to be disturbed, didn't desire coffee, snacks, or conversations.

There were no other passengers onboard thus Tammy grabbed one of her books and reclined in her seat and was soon in another frame of mind as the drama in the Novel now consumed her attention. The pilots had a fresh cup of coffee before takeoff and would be good for a while, but in a couple hours, Tammy would get up, go to the bathroom, tinkle, then make a fresh pot of coffee for the pilots. If Wilber still had on his sleeping face cover Tammy would not disturb him.

Wilber did not stir until they were over central Arizona and then only got up to drain his lizard. As soon as he sat back down in his chair, Tammy asked, "Wilber would you like a cup of coffee?"

"Sure and go heavy on the vanilla creamer."

"Not a problem."

"Wilber was finishing up his coffee as the GS750 started descending from 50,000 feet where the flight had been as smooth as a fashion model's rear end.

Vandenburg vectored the GS750 to 15,0000-foot Runway 30 which is orientated heading towards the Northwest that usually went against the prevailing winds this time of day as the air flow was towards the inland. This is the second longest runway operated by the Air Force.

The jet pulled up to the passenger terminal and after it stopped, Tammy deployed the built-in stairway which Wilber stepped down after saying goodbye to the pilots and Tammy.

A few feet away from the aircraft was an Air Force Colonel Baker who would drive Wilber around the base and to the assembly building where the spacecraft and capsule were all now in the finishing stages of preparing for a launch.

"Hello Colonel Baker."

"Good to see you again Wilber."

"Thank you."

"I was briefed to take you over to the assembly building so you can take a look at things."

"That's right."

"Okay, follow me out of the terminal to my car. The driver is waiting."

In what seemed like a short period of time, the Colonel's car pulled up to the assembly building where they soon were escorted inside.

Work was ongoing, nobody was going to stop work for this dog and pony show. The deadlines were looming. ULA personnel were not panicking, but they knew an awesome amount of pressure was coming down hard from above. It almost seemed like they were being punished for the KH-15 failure. But they didn't view that as their fault since it was government furnished equipment (GFE).

In reality, the KH-15 was Northrup Gruman's tar baby. Another example of the government wanting something yesterday, didn't properly fund it, and changed design criteria mid-stream. Northrup Gruman actually did a great job in building the satellite and if they didn't have a neophyte in the government who always came in at the 11th hour with engineering changes, the KH-15 could have been launched by now.

The assembly building was well lit up at all levels because it was a very tall and heavy rocket assembly. The overhead cranes did a great job of lifting components up to the top of the spacecraft while construction continued. Sometimes there were as many as 200 lifts per day. Time lapsed photography of rocket assembly was an awesome sight.

At this phase of the launch preparations, there were a lot of people around the rocket doing different types of work.

Some of the work was inspectors that did closeout of the rocket body. During the critical phase of the preparations there was almost a two-man rule to prevent sabotage and critical factors not completed before close out. The inspectors had special stickers that went over hex-head screws that locked the access panel to that portion of the rocket with the inspector's stamp and a date/time stamped on it from a handheld label printer. The tamper proof seal would be easily torn and destroyed if anyone attempted to insert a hex-head torque wrench to undo the screw that held the locking mechanism in place so no person could open the hatch and gain access.

If one of the seals were discovered damaged, a full closeout would be triggered after an analysis was done to what level of reinspection was required. Since all access hatches had real time security video on them and a daily log of seal status, the

perpetrator would easily be identified and given the distinct honor of delaying the flight which usually cost him his job and possibly his security clearance, especially if there was no paperwork with re-entry permission.

As Wilber went up the rocket ship in the service elevator and looked at it over good, he could see the myriad of seals and all the camera's focused all over the rocket. The probe space craft was a sight to behold, as it was one of the largest rockets launched since the Lunar Saturn 5 rockets sent man ot the moon.

It did not take a Cowboy like Wilber to figure out the whole ULA group were diligently at work and since nobody approached them or even bothered to look at them, their attention was focused on the task at hand. This is a trait of dedicated people who believe in what they are doing and want it to be a successful launch.

The history of the space program is filled with unscheduled rapid disassembly like a couple space shuttles that were destroyed on takeoff or during re-entry. Space flight is a dangerous business. Space-X and ULA make it look like routine business, but the people doing the work here knew it was not routine business and to have a successful launch required attention to detail, correct interpretation of plans, and astute execution.

"Tell me Colonel, will ULA make the proposed launch date?"

"Wilber, you know there are a lot of people in this business who will not slip a schedule until they do not meet a deadline," Colonel Baker responded in the most serious tone.

"Yea I know, I experience that myself in the past and got numerous ass chewings because a person kept lying, he was on schedule when he and I both knew his schedule was BS," Wilber replied.

"That behavior screws up a lot of schedules because we have to put people on airplanes and fly them out here for various phases of the projects," Colonel Baker said.

"I understand that very clearly since I was a victim in the past when people lied to their management about their schedules. I had to take three trips to the Bay Area to do one job because of that type of lack of management oversight."

"Wilber, I'm not going to do to you what a lot of disingenuous people did to you in the past."

"That's good to know."

"I tell all my managers not to sugar coat it. Tell me how it is. I need the truth, no matter how ugly it might be."

"Yep Colonel, the brutal truth tastes a hell of a lot better than the sour taste left in your mouth after the sugar in the coating is all gone, and reality sits in."

Wilber pulled out a business card out of his billfold and handed it to Colonel Baker.

"Colonel, this is a special number to me. If for some reason you must slip the schedule, call me right away with the reason. I'll have your back and make sure the elephants do not step on you."

"Thank you, Wilber, you have always been an honest broker."

"Colonel that's because I'm one of those Cowboys the agency no longer likes.

They want a Woked up person from Harvard that can dish out the pink Koolaid."

"Thank God we still have a few Cowboys left. Otherwise, nothing will get done."

"It goes in cycles Colonel. From post-Vietnam War to Desert Storm was quite a difference. Then we went back the other way for a while, until 9/11 happened. And since elections have consequences, it seems like the Peter Principal always prevails."

"I'm looking forward to retirement. I'm going fishing."

"Good luck Colonel. I'm happy you will be around to launch this rocket."

"Think it will make a big difference?"

"No, I believe it will be a failure and there were other options we should have taken we'll eventually get around to, but by then we will have wasted precious time."

"You going to stick around for a few days to see what's going on?" "No, you got my business card. I have faith in you will call me if required."

"That I assure you of."

"Would you mind taking me back to the air terminal, the pilots want to know what their schedule is. We are heading back to Washington as soon as I climb aboard that airplane."

"Thanks for coming out here and showing you have confidence in our operation."

"Colonel, I have confidence in you because I know you are a true-blue Cowboy that wears a Uniform."

"I actually appreciate that comment, Wilber."

"Okay Colonel I've seen enough let's go."

***

Wilber was on his way back to Washington and Pat Barton was mildly disturbed that he did not get a phone call that night. He was also quite surprised to see Wilber O'Toole walk into his office the next morning with a verbal status report. "Why didn't you call me?" "There was no status change."

"You expect me to believe that crap? I got people that inform me."

"As of now there are no launch delays. That bird will fly when the Colonel tells you it will."

"With the KH-15 failure and the Vulcan Rocket engine issues, I can't believe this thing will launch on time."

"As you know Pat, I'm not a big fan of this probe method, but I do have faith that Colonel Baker will accomplish it on time. Your problem will be when it doesn't do what you expect it will."

***

Chapter Five

Tangrams Temptations

Due to their locations, Johns Hopkins University, University of Maryland, and University of Virginia Arlington had some interesting government programs.

Intelligence Agencies had labs in all of them. Cloaked in dark secrecy the brilliant researchers.

Some of these men spent some of their time educating the next generation of leaders. But the rest of the time they were lab rats. Eventually some of those lab rats never made it back into the classroom because their tasking was so excessive.

The Fractal group at Johns Hopkins were way ahead of everyone else including Princeton, MIT, Harvard, Cal Tech, Stanford, and UC Berkeley who supervised the Lawrence Livermore Labs. Just like Princeton and Stanford pioneered Wavelet theory, Johns Hopkins secret enclave embedded in a compartmentalized government program were taking fractals to the next level.

As soon as the fractal researchers were brought into the fold and convinced, they would never have to spend another day in the classroom teaching because their research grants allowed the University to hire other professors to take their place, their passions flowed as they chased their dreams.

Then one day out of the blue, NRO brought in some signals to see if the fractal group at Johns Hopkins could piece together a picture of reality.

That's when it all began.

The current distance between Saturn and Earth is the current distance from Earth to Saturn as 1,338,999,202 kilometers. Light takes 1 hour, 14 minutes and 46.9412 seconds to travel from Saturn and to the Earth. It's a long distance away. The Vulcan rocket to get the Venus probe to Saturn as fast as the agency desired would be insufficient. Additional propulsion was installed.

Inside the assembly building the spacecraft took up the maximum amount of room. The assembly building had a unique feature. Part of the area in the middle of the side where the rocket would leave the building on giant electric powered and computer guided treads, a ten-foot-wide section rotated upwards with a cavalier hoist raising it from above giving maximum clearance all the way to the top of the building.

Without the special building lifting rig, the over height of the building would prevent the rocket from leaving when it was due to travel to the launch pad.

The reason why this rocket was such extremely tall was it had a second stage power plant above the third stage main Vulcan thrusters which also had four solid rocket boosters like the Space Shuttle program to provide the additional lift to get millions of pounds off the planet surface.

Once the Saturn Probe rocket reached a critical speed, the first stage and boosters would be jettisoned and land back on planet Earth using flight controls developed and licensed by Space-X.

The second stage power plant had three major devices in it. First it had two small fusion nuclear reactors providing dual backup power for electricity required for the repeater electronics. Signals leaving the probe at a much lower elevation would travel to the mother ship and be retransmitted in a different bandwidth to Earth ground stations that included Hawaii, Australia, Israel, Mid Atlantic, and Florida.

The second device in the second stage assembly is a nuclear fusion rocket engine that was a refined model of such rocket engines built under

Project Pluto designed at the Lawrence Livermore Labs and tested at Area 51 for the SLAM missile President Eisenhower canceled because his liberal brother Milton convinced him the SLAM missile would destabilize the world. That technology remained dormant until the Ukraine war started and Russia started using hypersonic missiles and threatening to use nukes.

The Pluto rocket engine design was miniaturized reducing the size and scale down to almost one fourth of the original design given the code word name Pluto II. The Pluto II rocket engine would continue acceleration of the space capsule and second stage to allow arrival at Saturn in just a few months traveling at super high velocity.

At that point retro rockets would spin the spacecraft 180 degrees and use the Pluto II rocket engine to slow down the craft and place it in orbit around Saturn, then it would deploy the probe that would travel the same velocity at a lower altitude much closer to the planet surface as it did its survey.

When the probe was eventually launched , the initial telemetry would provide breathtaking pictures of Saturn's surface, never seen before. There was a lot riding on this future launch.

***

Chapter Six

Singapore

Xinxin Lin from Singapore, a lovely woman quite sophisticated, lovely, and beautiful with Chinese heritage, had just arrived in Beijing China.

Xinxin Lin enjoyed travel and is a jet setter and had worked as a fashion model. Xinxin heavily involved in Crypto Currency was attending the Crypto Currency event in Beijing China. Xinxin met Wilber O'Toole during the first day of seminars and group meetings. She was always interested in meeting people that knew a lot about trading Crypto Currencies. Prior to this mission Wilber was schooled by PhD economists on many aspects of Crypto Currencies so he would better discover pertinent information at this conference.

Wilber had quite unusual capability being fluent in Russian as well as Mandarin Chinese. Xinxin fluent in Chinese and English had no reason to talk to Wilber in Chinese and they spoke in English and seemed to enjoy conversing. However, Wilber could monitor everything being said by Chinese and Russian speaking people attending the conference.

At this Crypto event there were numerous businessmen from around the world working together to set up a Crypto Exchange and the Chinese are attempting to make Beijing or Shanghai the location of the World's major Crypto Exchange.

Wilber had previously met the Russian FSB (KGB) Aida Abramova in Petropavlovsk because his Alias was a Co-pilot, but he spoke Russian extremely well. Initially, the Russians were still interested in Wilber because of his language skills, so they sent the female spy Aida Abramova after him who attempted to seduce him in a honey pot scheme. During their lover's tryst, Wilber was so convincing he was simply an Air Freight pilot the Russian spy Aida Abramova fell for Wilber's ruse and threw Caution to the wind. After their love making, Wilber left the next day after exchanging his phony business cards with Aida.

Aida Abramova had nothing special to report to her superiors but didn't know the dacha she took Wilber to had hidden cameras and microphones. She thought it was her superior from Moscow's private getaway cabin in the mountains near Petropavlovsk. He of course got to review the surveillance video and saw the two lovers go at it.

Wilber was long gone by the time the FSB (KGB) was able to identify him and discover he worked for the CIA. The Russians of course were wondering why Wilber was in Petropavlovsk. They didn't know that while at the restaurant, he met one of the CIA's spies in the bathroom and was handed a computer chip to swallow. This chip had a significant amount of stolen Russian INTEL taken off a submarine at the nearby base.

Right after Wilber met the beautiful and alluring Xinxin Lin at the Beijing Crypto Currency event, Aida Abramova suddenly shows up.

Aida Abramova, the FSB spy from Russia now knew Wilber is a CIA agent and her handlers wanted Aida to get control of Wilber. The Russian spy Aida Abramova exhibited significant elegance in the way she's dressed for the Crypto seminars. Aida Abramova became quite the head turner for the event.

Xinxin Lin had seen a lot in her days being a sophisticated fashion model and businessperson and got to know Wilber after a couple of days but was vulnerable to his advanced social engineering motives.

Wilber immediately knew he needed a way to throw the Russian Spy Aida off his tail and knew the signals of the fact Aida Abramova probably knew he was a spy, and Wilber was now Aida's target.

Wilber's only recourse was to seduce Xinxin Lin and use her as a chess piece to interfere with Aida Abramova's activities. Wilber remembered how great his former lover from Hong Kong, Monica felt and had started certain feelings developing for Xinxin. Xinxin was equally beautiful to the point she's glamorous.

Xinxin Lin fell for Wilber's ploy and soon is in a lover's tryst with Wilber not knowing she too had the FSB suddenly interfering and attempting to get her out of the way so their agent Aida Abramova could complete the job of "turning" Wilber into one of their double spies.

The Chinese MSS (Ministry of State Security) were of course following the Russian FSB Agent Aida Abramova. They knew Aida Abramova was an FSB agent. Aida didn't know her identity had been compromised because some of her handlers are very sloppy at the way they conducted their business, and it didn't take long for the sophisticated China's MSS agents to detect the entire Russian Spy gang and put them under surveillance.

The MSS recruits' people all the time in situ. They abduct Xinxin Lin and in a private meeting with her explained what the Green Gang of Shanghai will do to her if she does not cooperate and assist them.

At first Xinxin is terrorized and is thinking only in terms of how to escape Beijing and only wanted to just get back to Singapore.

But then the MSS agents explained to Xinxin, "Wilber O'Toole works for the CIA and is using you as a means of throwing off the Russian FSB agent Aida Abramova who's attempting to get to him."

Xinxin didn't want to believe it but quickly learns from the MSS, "We will not let you travel home to Singapore and if you do not agree to do what we tell you to do, we will hand you over to the Green Gang and they will most likely use you in sex slavery." "What is it you want me to do?" Xinxin asked in pure desperation.

The Chinese MSS official simply said, "We want to know exactly what CIA agent Wilber O'Toole is really up too."

"You don't know why he's here?"

"We suspect he is here because America is attempting to sabotage China's efforts in setting up our Crypto Currency exchange?"

Xinxin Lin did not like to be used by anyone and the fact Wilber had made love to her and probably lied to her, upset her greatly, that was her turning point.

The MSS plays hardball all the time, whereas the Cash in Advance people were playing a lot of softball because management was now full of the Pat Barton types.

The Chinese MSS do not leave anything to chance. Now they did the final indoctrination they knew would push Xinxin over the cliff and get her to cooperate.

They played hidden video and audio recordings of this female Russian FSB Agent Aida Abramova approaching Wilber O'Toole and trying to set up a rendezvous for a sexual tryst.

It appeared Wilber was agreeing to meet Aida Abramova only a few hours after she and Wilber had done the horizontal Tango, and Xinxin was utterly stunned.

In her overflowing anger Xinxin no longer felt the urgency to run away back to Singapore. She wanted to hurt Wilber to punish him for what he just did to her.

What Xinxin Lin didn't know nor does the Russians or China's MSS, was the relationship Wilber had with Monica, many years before when he was a very young man, before he got deeply involved in espionage and secret projects.

Xinxin Lin educated in the finest schools of Singapore, also had a British Accent. Almost by a magnificent accident, Xinxin Lin's hair style and accent was identical to Monica and her body was very much similar.

Wilber was slowly evolving in emotional bonding with Xinxin Lin. Wilber was in fact falling in love with Xinxin Lin. Hence his acting according to her thoughts was extremely good. But she was convinced he was faking it to serve the purposes of the espionage he was involved in.

But this wasn't Wilber O'Toole really speaking. The Chinese had altered the sound on the video. Xinxin wasn't hearing what Wilber really said. The voice was contrived completely. So were Aida Abramova's words. Their real conversation was about crypto currency trading, had nothing to do with relationships, even though Aida was going to go down that path as soon as the FSB got rid of Xinxin.

Xinxin Lin had given Wilber her business card when they first met.

Wilber knew how to contact her in the future.

Wilber's handlers discovered the net that Russians and Chinese were getting ready to spring on Wilber, they had to do an emergency extraction.

Wilber disappeared. He didn't show up for a dinner date with Xinxin where the female Russian Spy Aida Abramova was going to confront Wilber and create a scene to scare Xinxin away.

The stage was set. Xinxin arrived at the restaurant. She and Wilber had reservations and she was seated waiting for Wilber who was always punctual. The Russian spy Aida Abramova followed Xinxin to the restaurant table and positioned herself to be able to observe the couple for the big show down.

Wilber had a temporary cell phone the CIA controlled and could self- destruct remotely if required. They monitored Wilber's movements and everything he did including watching his love making with Xinxin with this surveillance device.

Xinxin Lin knew she could contact Wilber on his cell phone and ask why he was late. She felt really mixed up following the MSS orders but at the same time wanted to confront Wilber about his plans with this Aida Abramova woman.

When Wilber was 15 minutes late, Xinxin Lin called Wilber's number which gave the message: "We are sorry the phone number you are attempting to call is no longer in service. Please check your number to make sure you are calling the right number."

Xinxin Lin now confirmed to herself Wilber really was a spy just like the MSS informed her and thus knew he had bugged out. He had used her body and deceived her, and now she was very upset.

Wilber had already put on a sophisticated CIA mask and had departed Beijing on a Rich Saudi Jet on his way to Tokyo where he was put on a CIA private jet and flown back to Langley for debriefing.

After a while, tears started coming down Xinxin Lin in the restaurant. Her Chinese MSS handlers could see she was very upset and knew Wilber had not shown up and observed her attempting to call.

The Russian spy Aida was taking all this in as well and was suddenly highly amused that it appeared Wilber had broken the sweet girl's heart and avoided the snare the MSS were using her to manifest.

Aida suddenly had more respect for Wilber because he had just demonstrated to her he knew his spy craft quite well, and pulled off whatever he was doing here just like he did in Petropavlovsk. What was Wilber really doing in both places?

Thirty minutes after Wilber had not shown up, an MSS agent in a fine suit who Xinxin knew was one of her MSS handlers approached her and said, "Will you please come with me." He could see she still had tears in her eyes.

The Chinese MSS handlers took Xinxin Lin to a secure location and informed her, "Wilber had somehow managed to slip out from under our noses."

Wilber was gone and Xinxin Lin's services were no longer needed, but informed her, "We might want to contact you sometime in the future and utilize your services again and will pay you handsomely for your work."

Xinxin didn't commit and continued to silently weep. Her heart was broken.

The Chinese MSS agents had Xinxin Lin's luggage and had checked her out of her hotel room, and now took her to the Airport where she had first class seat on a Singapore Airlines passenger jet heading back home.

The CIA knew everything. They also knew Wilber was very upset the way this all unfolded, and they briefed him on why they had to do the emergency extraction.

They also knew Xinxin Lin was forcibly coerced by China's MSS, and she was an innocent bystander thrown into the world of espionage.

Wilber stated to his superiors during the debriefing, "I want to take a trip to Singapore and meet face to face with Xinxin Lin and tell her how I really feel about her.

The agency wasn't thrilled with the prospects of Wilber going to meet with Xinxin Lin, but only agreed to let him go if he agreed that a CIA surveillance team went with him and staged themselves to provide logistical support and possibly security if the need arises because they were fearful he would resign his position and management of Solar System Investigations would be extremely upset they lost their spy they loaned to the DD/P, covert ops for the Beijing mission because of his linguistic skills.

Wilber arrived at Singapore a couple days later, checked into a very nice hotel, then took cab and went directly to the office building where Xinxin Lin works.

Xinxin Lin had been down in the dumps upon arrival back from Beijing. Her colleagues were slightly concerned about the melancholy Xinxin Lin exhibited since she came back to the office and didn't want to discuss her experiences in Beijing.

Xinxin Lin had finished a cup of coffee hoping it would somehow alter her mood and allow her to start thinking about business and put all this experience in Beijing behind her.

Suddenly a secretary approached Xinxin Lin's desk and said, "Xinxin there is an American in the lobby who wishes to speak with you."

The last person in the world Xinxin thought would be in the lobby was Wilber O'Toole. Xinxin followed the receptionist to the lobby and there she had a big surprise seeing Wilber standing in the lobby in a business suit.

This truly was an extraordinary event. Xinxin Lin knew exactly everything about Wilber, who he worked for, and here he was right in front of her looking as if he had major concern on his face. It was almost a shocking experience.

"You are the last person in the world I expected seeing this morning."

"We had some unfinished business, and I wanted to personally come here and explain why I could not arrive for our dinner date." Xinxin was speechless. She didn't know what to say.

"Is it possible we can walk somewhere private and talk?" Wilber asked.

Xinxin Lin only agreed because she wanted to hear his flimsy excuse. But she also knew he might be lying. Nevertheless, she wanted to hear it.

"Alright, I'll take you somewhere where we can find private space to talk."

Xinxin led Wilber out of the office building in the central business district and walked up to a cab parked right in front of a bank building next to where Xinxin worked and said, "It's a short drive, but it's too far to walk from here."

"Sure. Wherever you feel comfortable talking to me."

The two were soon in the cab and Xinxin the cab driver looked Malaysian and Xinxin who could speak English, Mandarin Chinese, Malay, and Tamil gave him their destination in Malay, "Take us to the Botanical Gardens."

From the Singapore Central Business District, it was almost five miles to Botanical Gardens and took almost 20 minutes via Zion Road to get there by cab. Per agreement with the CIA, Wilber had an electronic tracker on him in case he managed to lose his human watcher and tracker.

The cab arrived at the Botanical Gardens and the couple exited after Xinxin paid for the cab with a tap on the Taxi computer reader that charged the funds after she agreed to the fee posted.

After the two exited the Taxi, they walked into the Botanic Gardens. There is no fee to get into the Botanic Gardens which is very impressive and one of the benefits of living in Singapore to be able to enjoy such beauty and splendor.

The Singapore Botanic Gardens is a 164-year-old tropical garden located at the fringe of the Orchard Road shopping district in Singapore.

The Singapore Botanic Gardens has been inscribed as a UNESCO World Heritage Site in 2015. The Singapore Botanic Gardens is the first and only tropical botanic garden on the UNESCO's World Heritage List. Today, the Singapore Botanic Gardens is an important botanical institute.

In the company of Xinxin, with exemplary beauty and charm with the backdrop of the many views in the park, created a temporal tapestry in Wilber's mind, knowing how special this woman was. It was almost heart breaking the way their last lover's tryst suddenly abruptly stopped with a very sad ending.

Parts of the park are crowded since it's a popular destination, but there are other areas that have empty and private areas because there is less to see and so much incredible flora elsewhere. The two made their way to one of those private areas where they could talk privately.

"I was wondering why you deserted me after we had established such a lovely affair," Xinxin suddenly spoke.

"I did not desire to leave you. My departure was out of my control and my handlers evacuated me in a very unpredictable manner."

"Yes, I'm well aware of who you are and what you were doing there." "How do you know that?"

"You put me in a lot of danger and didn't even know it." "How so?"

"The Chinese MSS discovered we were lovers and they pressed me into service."

"They were using you as an agent?"

"It was nothing I volunteered to do. I'm pretty sure they would have killed me had I not followed their directions."

"What exactly did they want you to do?"

"I had no way of warning you. They had me wired up and could hear anything I might say to you, and you should know they had video cameras and microphones always on you, Mr. CIA man."

"I realize anytime I'm in China most likely anywhere I go is wired."

"In a way I was glad you didn't show up because I had no way to warn you. But at the same time, I felt abandoned and used."

"I flew all the way here to meet with you, to let you know I did not abandon you, and my life was in danger, I had to leave when I did the way I left."

"So why did you come here?"

"I wanted you to know my feelings and everything I did with you was legitimate. My motives and my evolution into our romance were real. I have deep feelings for you. I did not like way I had to leave you, but since the MSS had their hands on you, I'm sure you realize they are not nice guys."

"I'm quite aware and to be honest I was terrified."

"I'm sorry that I put you into that situation. I did not know that before our scheduled dinner date my cover was blown, and I was only an hour or two away from being detained. You can't imagine what Chinese do to spies when they capture them."

"Yea I know because of how they treated me and their threats."

"I hope you can forgive me for my rapid departure without saying goodbye."

"Nothing to forgive, I understand fully, you were in a bad circumstance and quite frankly the Chinese were astonished you got away."

"What happened to you after I left?"

"When the MSS discovered you slipped out of the country, they packed up my belongings and escorted me to the Airport and put me on a flight to Singapore."

"That's rather kind of them."

"I think it comes down to they are pragmatic and since I was in Beijing representing my company, if bad things happened to me, the company would have filed a complaint with the Singapore Government and the Chinese know their banks here only exist here at the pleasure of our government. We are part of their economic formula."

"You didn't want to stick around for the conclusion of the crypto currency event?"

"No, I was more than delighted to leave and I doubt seriously that I'm willing to go back to China any time soon. I would not feel safe there."

"Xinxin, may I ask you a question?"

"What do you want to know?"

"Is it possible our relationship can continue and grow?"

"Are you serious?"

"Absolutely, why do you think I flew all the way here to see you?"

"Wilber, you are a complicated man. Your situation mildly scares me. I'm not sure that you will be alive a year from now. No doubt you do some dangerous assignments."

"I'm in a different line of work now. That was a temporary assignment and because of what I'm doing now, I'm sure they are not going to risk me getting involved in any more deals with China or Russia."

"What exactly are you doing now?"

"I'm sorry I can't reveal that, but I will tell you I'm not involved in the spy business now, nor do I see them sending me on assignments to dangerous places like China or Russia."

"Wilber, I'm not sure I believe that, nor do you really know if they might need you again to go someplace like Beijing if they need you bad enough."

"My cover is blown in China; they can never send me back there again."

"There are other locations they could send you such as Ukraine or Russia."

"I can't get into what I'm now doing, but it's so important they will not divert me away from that for standard INTEL business."

"We can't do a lot here because as you probably know this place is loaded with Chinese spies because of their banking presence."

"I'm well aware that's why I have a bodyguard over there walking by in the blue polo shirt."

"I could probably fly to San Francisco and a few other places like Boston where we have crypto currency clients to visit you now and then, but if you are serious about a future relationship with me, you are going to have to get out of that line of business and do something else if you expect me to spend a lot of time with you."

"Having dinner here with you is out of the question?"

"There is only one way we can do it today."

"How's that?"

"Room service in your hotel room."

"That we can do."

"Where are you staying?"

"The Fullerton Bay Hotel"

"Lucky pick."

"Why is that?"

"My cousin Idrak is the chief security officer there. He can protect us.

We will not need to dine in room service."

"Can we have the dinner date tonight we missed out on?"

"I'll consider, but first you must tell me the three magic words to unlock my heart."

"That's easy."

"Do you know what the code words are?" "Yes."

"What are they?" "I love you."

"You just let the genie out of the bottle, and you may never be able to put it back."

"There is no reason to put it back."

"What are the Chinese magic words since I'm ethnic Chinese?"

我愛你

"Wǒ ài nǐ." [I love you.]

你確定我是你唯一的愛人嗎？

Nǐ quèdìng wǒ shì nǐ wéiyī de àirén ma?

[Are you sure, I'm your only lover?]

「我以前從未為女人飛過新加坡。 就此而言，幾乎在任何地方。”

`Wǒ yǐ qián cóng wèi wèi nǚ rén fēiguò xīnjiāpō. Jiùcǐ ér yán, jīhū zài rènhé dìfāng."

[I've never flown to Singapore for a woman before. For that matter, almost anywhere.]

"Alright, Wilber. I'll try to work things out if you put forth the effort. But I must tell you now, eventually you will have to get into a new line of work. If we were to have children, you will have to be home most of the time to help raise them."

"After I'm done with this project, I'll seek a new line of work."

"Are you sure?"

"I work for a prick; my days are numbered."

"I'll take you back to your hotel now. I'm going back to my office for a few hours to finish my work for today. Afterwards I will go home and change into something for a special night for you and meet you at your hotel where I know I will be safe," Xinxin said.

"That works for me," Wilber replied.

Wilber knew he wanted to kiss Xinxin that very moment, but even though they were semi-alone in this area, it would not be viewed as proper decorum a Singapore female kissing an American in public. Wilber knew he would have to save that for later.

"Let's walk by the Orchids on our way out of here," Xinxin stated.

"Sure."

Located on the mid-western side of the Garden, the hilly three-hectare site has a collection of more than 1,000 species and 2,000 hybrids of orchids.

As they walked by Burkill Hall, Xinxin said, "Let's go in here for a couple minutes."

"Alright."

Inside the building the display of some of the world's most beautiful orchids created a backdrop and atmosphere that made Wilber enjoy his time with Xinxin. Part of the exhibition located at the back of Burkill Hall, displays hybrids of the most popular VIP orchids. Notable individuals such as Queen Elizabeth, Margarette Thatcher, Masako Kotaishi Hidenka, and Princess Diana are honored by beautiful orchid displays.

Xinxin led Wilber in a circuitous route back out to the front entrance and on the way walked past Eco-Lake where they saw a Cygnus Atratus (black swan).

"I know the name of that swan," Wilber said.

"What's the name?" Xinxin asked with curiosity.

"Pat Barton," Wilber replied.

Xinxin didn't ask any further questions, but assumed Wilber used the name of someone he didn't like such as his boss.

There was several Taxi's waiting out front of the Botanical Gardens who no doubt delivered people here and thus knew eventually they would need a ride back to their hotels or elsewhere.

The couple walked up to the lead Taxi in the line and Wilber opened the door for Xinxin who got in first, then they were driving away.

This Taxi driver was of Chinese ethnicity, so Xinxin said speaking Mandarin, "We are going to the "Fullerton Bay Hotel."

Wilber knew what Xinxin just said and was now wondering if there was a change of plans but before he could ask the question, she turned to

Wilber and said, "I'm going to drop you off at your hotel, then I'll take the Taxi back ot my office." "Alright."

Wilber could see the Taxi driver face in the rear-view mirror. He had a smile that conveyed to Wilber, "You are a lucky dog."

The Taxi driver knew it was not very often he would see an English-speaking person with one of Singapore's most smoking hot women of Chinese descent, in a Taxi who probably got lucky. Wilber startled the Taxi driver by giving him the wink. He knew that would set in thoughts for the rest of the day, because Xinxin looked fantastic in a business suit and had perfume that few could ever forget.

Xinxin lived a complicated life due to her involvement in crypto currency trading. Most likely few other women would have stayed with a dangerous spy under the circumstances. Xinxin by nature of her crypto currency trades was a risk taker, a gambler, and had the sophistication to deal with a leopard who could change his spots to suit the need for the mission.

Wilber seemed sincere enough. But Xinxin knew how to test him and probe deep into his personal life. If he truly meant what he said, he would have no problems introducing her directly to his family. She also needed to know how his family would receive her. If there was no enthusiasm in that regard, it meant it would eventually be a failure so there would be no point in proceeding. There were just too many questions to answer before Xinxin would allow herself to go to the next phase meaning fully giving her heart to Wilber.

Xinxin liked sex. She liked the way Wilber performed and wondered why he was so good at it. Had she known his special training was being used on her, she might have called it quits on the spot. Her other fear was that since it was evident that Wilber operated with aliases and was in fact a spook, was he using his trained talents to snare her for his own enjoyment and nothing more?

Xinxin would be terribly disappointed if Wilber turned out to be someone that was simply using her for his own physical gratification. His strange separation from her in Beijing underscored how Wilber could float in and float out of her life.

Beijing was a disaster for their relationship. Xinxin assumed it was over and she was nothing more than a prop the clandestine operative utilized as part of his cover. But here he was out in open daylight with exposure to the public with some risk since he was now known to be a spy to the Chinese MSS. Xinxin also noted Wilber took a lot of trouble to get here to see her and explain his emotional state to her.

When they were back at the Botanical Garden and Wilber pointed out his bodyguard, that added greatly to the dimension of what Wilber had to do to get here and see Xinxin. It also gave an appearance there was a strong desire in Wilber to go through all this to be with her. Xinxin knew instinctively a handsome guy like Wilber who had the financial resources to chase after her, could easily find quintessential beauties in a lot of other locations.

In Xinxin's mind, Wilber's visit wasn't about sex since no doubt that was something Wilber could arrange with a lot less effort than to travel halfway around the world to experience it with just her. The strong focus Wilber had on Xinxin showed a significant amount of attraction for him.

What does Wilber see in me to do all this? Xinxin asked herself and she answered her own question with the plausible reality:

Wilber is really in love with me. That thought caused Xinxin to have some strange feelings because when you know someone loves you it makes you feel different about life. The human condition then takes on a new life of its own and the reciprocity can be just as strong.

The Taxi pulled into the front entrance arrival and just before the valet opened Wilber's Taxi door, he turned to Xinxin and asked, "Do you still have my phone number?"

"I do, but it stopped working in Beijing."

"That number has been turned back on. Call me when you are on your way, I'll meet you in the lobby."

"Alright."

With the semi-privacy of the cab, Wilber reached over and kissed Xinxin on her cheek in the most sensual manner and whispered something so low in volume the cab driver could not hear it. But Xinxin heard it loud and clear and immediately felt moist and unfurled her passions at Wilber in a quick response.

"I'll get back to you after I make the proper preparations." "Don't torture me by staying away too long," Wilber responded.

"I wouldn't dream of leaving you alone too long, I'll be back in a while."

The conversation was abruptly curtailed when the valet opened the door and Wilber smiled at Xinxin who returned a very sensual smile in a manner she always wanted to do to her lover boy.

***

Chapter Seven

Idrak The Silent Warrior

Because Wilber picked the hotel where Xinxin's cousin Idrak was chief of security, was another one of those lucky events for her life. Xinxin could then conduct herself in a manner she wished and not fear the deadly game of espionage encroaching on her and her lover.

Xinxin would then call her cousin Idrak after she dropped off Wilber and went someplace, she could talk freely. She knew just the place by the waterfront that was empty when no ships were tied up there.

One of the reasons for Singapore preeminence in the world, not just from being a former major British Military enclave, it also guards the entrance to Strait of Malacca, one of the most important shipping lanes in the world.

The Strait of Malacca is approximately 500 miles (800 km) long and the width of the shipping channel that slowly expands to the Northwest varied from approximately 40 miles in the Southeast entrance to 155 mi (65– 250 km) wide at the Northwest entrance.

This critically important shipping channel, between the Malay Peninsula to the northeast and the Indonesian island of Sumatra to the southwest, connects the Indian Ocean with the South China Sea portion of the Pacific Ocean. That is why it's one of the busiest shipping-channels in the world delivering Asian goods to India, Africa, and Europe via the Suez Canal. All the Middle East oil flows on super tankers through this channel heading towards the Pacific Ocean providing crude oil to China, Japan, Korea, and other Asian Nations.

Thanks to Singapore's unique strategic location, there is a significant ship repair industry there with multiple shipyards. Even the U.S. Navy repairs its ships in Singapore. The Fat Lenard scandal racking the U.S. Navy with Dozens of officers being prosecuted stimmed from some of the benefits of senior officers steering repair contracts to Fat Lenard receiving cash and call girls as a bonus in doing so.

It's not unusual to see multiple oil super tankers tied up in Singapore getting voyage repairs. If necessary, they can be drydocked there. What a unique location to have a shipyard halfway between Asia and India for voyage repairs!

Singapore standard of living is on a continuous improvement as the riches associated with a colossal income of being the kings in world shipping repairs at such a unique location.

Xinxin's cousin Idrak was in the security business principally because his father worked for the Malaysian Government who was dealing with the Malaysian communist insurgency led by the Malaysian Communist Party (MCP) that lasted from 1948 until 1988.

The Malaysian Government introduced a successful strategy of fighting the MCP.

It was known as Security and Development Programme, or KESBAN, the local acronym (Program Keselamatan dan Pembangunan), and focused on civil military affairs.

KESBAN constituted the total of all measures undertaken by the Malaysian Armed Forces and other (government) agencies to strengthen and protect society from subversion, lawlessness, and insurgency which effectively broke the resistance.

Undoubtedly the Malaysian authorities found that security and development were the most prudent approaches to combating the Communist insurgency.

The only reason why the insurgency ended was due to the collapse of the Soviet Union which had extended itself too far around the world and as a result became borderline financially insolvent. The communists in Malaysia, though receiving help from China's Communist Party CCP, suddenly had very limited financial support to buy guns and bullets to continue the insurgency and consequently signed the peace deal on the border with Thailand.

Xinxin's cousin Idrak's family moved to Singapore in 1990 because Idrak's father had accumulated a lot of wealth as a paid mercenary and banked most of it. After setting up residence in Singapore, Idrak's father went to work in security for some of the splendid Hotels they had due to their location in the crossroads of Southern Asia and the busiest shipping route in the world through the Strait of Malacca.

Thanks to his British Education in the top schools of Singapore and his father's hands on approach, Idrak became a security official with some of the top corporations that have offices in Singapore. Since Idrak could speak five major languages and was very astute in all manners, he eventually graduated to elite security stature and soon recruited to be the chief security officer for Singapore's Fullerton Bay Hotel.

Idrak was a very confidential person. In the security business where they must be ready to deal with terrorists or unsavory characters, much of what they do and how they do it remains closely guarded. Even the government looks the other way when they know these security people must undertake clandestine measures to neutralize threats to their guests and the hotel.

Idrak knew a lot about his cousin's activities. He also became aware of the MSS mistreatment of her and even though she was far away from where he could lend assistance, it nevertheless upset him. They would regret trying something like that in Singapore because Idrak knew all the top officials in Singapore's Security and Intelligence Division (SID). If for some reason Xinxin became a prisoner in Beijing, there were a number of Chinese bankers in Singapore that could be traded in a hostage swap, and it came very close to doing that.

Because of a few tips and information flowing from SID to Idrak, he discovered his cousin Xinxin was fooling around with a CIA person. Then like all spooks he suddenly disappeared leaving Xinxin in a lurch in Beijing, or so it seemed. And now here he was, with the audacity to stay in his hotel.

When Security monitors who do facial recognition of everyone arriving tagged Xinxin in the cab with the CIA man, Idrak was super animated. It was a surreal moment for him. Idrak didn't know what to do. The man also was seen followed by others so killing him would not be such a simple task, because it was probably the case he was here on a mission. Just exactly what is that mission?

Twenty minutes later Idrak had another rush. His cell phone rang and only a hand full of people had his number, and there she was. Xinxin was calling him! "Idrak?"

"Yes, Xinxin, I was not expecting a call from you. What's up?"

"I need to talk to you."

"Where are you?"

"I'm down at an empty wharf so I can be alone when I talk to you."
"Alright, send me your location."

Xinxin sent Idrak her location via her cell phone app which Idrak put into google maps.

"I'll be there in ten minutes," Idrak said then hung up.

True to his word a black limo pulled up near where Xinxin was standing. Idrak got out of the Limo and so did a couple other men who were obvious hired guns who set up a perimeter to keep their boss and his cousin safe and prevent intruders from getting near to hear their conversation."

"What's up Xinxin?"

"This is kind of complicated, but I need protection." "Why?" Idrak asked.

"I'll lay my cards on the table. This is one of the most important moments in my life and I don't want it spoiled by rotten bastards," Xinxin said.

"What's going on?" Idrak asked.

"In a couple hours I will be arriving in your hotel to meet my boyfriend." Xinxin said.

"Who's your boyfriend?" Idrak asked with a poker face.

"His name is Wilber, and I'm sure with your sophisticated friends at SID, you will probably find out he's a CIA guy," Xinxin said.

"How the hell did you get tangled up with a guy like that?" Idrak asked.

"It's a long story, but he's for real. He flew all the way here to see me to assure me about his feelings and his intentions."

"What are his intentions?" Idrak asked.

"We will eventually be a couple living our lives together."

"Is that so?" Idrak asked.

"There are a lot of things I can't tell you. But trust me he's legitimate, and he has my best interest in mind," Xinxin said.

"How the hell are you going to live with a CIA guy? Idrak asked.

"I'm sure I will live just fine."

You got to know he's one of those here today and gone tomorrow types."

"He's into a new project now where his days as a field agent are over. I asked him to leave the CIA. He said, as soon as he finishes this assignment, he'll find something else to do." Xinxin said.

"Maybe I can hire him to be one of my security guys," Idrak said. "That might be dangerous too, I would prefer he not work in a dangerous situation," Xinxin said.

"What can he do?" Idrak asked.

"My thoughts are that since he speaks fluent Chinese and Russian, he could work for a travel agency. I'm sure there are a lot of things he can do." "Is he financially viable?" Idrak asked.

"He wouldn't be staying in your expensive hotel if he didn't have funds." Xinxin said.

"Yea he's probably like a lot of them made a ton of money doing dirty shit on the side."

"He's a very nice guy. I don't see him as being a nefarious type of person," Xinxin said.

"Since he's CIA that means his middle name is nefarious," Idrak said. "I want you to look at him as family now. That is where we are going with this relationship."

"How long is he going to be staying?" Idrak asked.

"I think his time here relates how I respond to him." Xinxin said.

"What does that mean?" Idrak asked.

"It means he's here for the real event, to plan our lives together. This is real and this is serious. I also know for a fact he loves me," Xinxin said.

"Xinxin, for your own good I need to tell you something." Idrak said.

"What?" Xinxin asked.

"When you went to China, I asked one of my friends in the SID to do a favor for me."

"What was the favor?"

"To keep an eye on you. You were trailed the entire time. We know the Chinese MSS nabbed you and pressed you into working for them."

"You know about that?" Xinxin asked with total shock.

"Yes, I know all about it, and if those bastards had not put you on a plane and sent you home, my SID friends were going to nab twenty Chinese Bankers and use them as hostages until you returned home safely. Had you been killed or severely injured most of them would have been sent back to China missing their dicks."

"What does that have to do with Wilber?"

"I do not like the fact he deserted you in a lurch."

"I must tell you this and I hope you understand. His cover was blown, the Chinese were coming to arrest him. The CIA did an emergency extraction. The Chinese can be very brutal to a spy when they capture them."

"So, you know a lot about what he does?"

"I only know of this incident since I was involved and the MSS wanted to use me to help capture him. I was under a lot of threats," Xinxin said.

"What is it exactly you want me to do?" Idrak asked.

"I want you to keep us safe while he's here so we can have a casual time together and let our future planning flow unencumbered with fear and intrigue," Xinxin asked.

"I'll think about it," Idrak said.

"You know I make a lot of money trading crypto currencies. I will make sure you are well compensated for this. I know you will have to hire people to protect us. I'll do a wire transfer today of a Million $ USD to make sure you have plenty of cash to pay for hired guns," Xinxin said.

"Alright, I'll do this, but I will warn you if he ever mistreats you, I'll make sure he lives to regret it." Idrak said.

"Thank you. I'll be visiting him at your hotel in a couple of hours, no doubt we'll have dinner at the LA BRASSERIE restaurant. If you want, you can come by there and I'll officially introduce him to you. You need to start realizing Wilber is now a family member, my future partner in life." Xinxin said in the calmest fashion.

"If this all happens, he's one of the luckiest guys in the world," Idrak said.

"He does not know how fast I can make money. Yes, he's lucky," Xinxin said.

"There is one thing I want you to do to help me so that I can make sure you are always protected."

"What's that?"

"Here's a tracker. Put it in your purse and keep it close with you so I always know where you are to make sure I have people staged to keep you protected."

"That's reasonable. I hope there's no bug in it because I don't want you to hear our private moments."

"Not to worry, I already know what you are going to do, just like you did with him in the past." Idrak said knowing that if Xinxin realized how much she was spied on, she would feel real crappy.

"Thank you for being so understanding," Xinxin said.

"My father was very attached to his brother, your father. Your family was very special to him," Idrak said.

"Your dad was my kindest relative. We loved all his visits," Xinxin said.

"Do you want me to give you a lift back to your office?" Idrak asked.

"Yes, I appreciate that," Xinxin replied.

Moments later when Xinxin went back to her office, some of her associates noticed an extraordinary shift in her. The past few days Xinxin seemed like she was living in a world of dread. Her trading patterns were sporadic, and she wasn't jovial, they knew something bad must have happened since her trip to Beijing, she wasn't the happy lady they all knew.

When Xinxin came back to the office after leaving with the mystery man earlier, she was beaming and full of smiles. Women have a sixth sense about other women who are having emotional tranquility and a transcendence to a much more pleasurable plateau in their lives.

Xinxin did something nobody expected or predicted. In the span of an hour, she did 60 trades. Her fingers were going to town like a concert pianist on the keyboard. The action was remarkable, and she indeed made a small fortune in the span of an hour. Some of her trading partners wanted to know what she was drinking because they wanted some of it too.

Win or lose, Xinxin was out of the trades before she left the office. Today it was 58 wins and 2 losses. The gains were spectacular, and Xinxin built up enough cash to support trading for several months with all losses. Then suddenly she shut it all down and logged out full of smiles.

Moments afterwards Xinxin received a text message from Idrak, "I received your wire transfer of funds. I appreciate this because it makes it much easier for me to add security staff to handle this situation."

"Alright."

"This will cover it, assuming Wilber will probably only be here a couple weeks." "Alright, please stop by and visit us while we are having dinner."

"I would love to do that so I can look your lover in the eye," Idrak said.

Xinxin was soon home getting ready. After a sprite shower and getting the cologne in all the right places for a happy time later in the evening, Xinxin put on a fashionable dress that went well with the designer high heels she put on. The makeup refresh didn't take long. The biggest chore was to put on that very expensive lipstick that gave her the tantalizing high gloss lips she knew would draw Wilber's lips to her with the hunger he showed the last time they were in a lover's embrace.

Since Xinxin cleared over seven million $$ U.S. Dollars on her sixty trades in an hour, she was going to treat herself with an expensive Limo ride over to the Fairmont Singapore. She had the exclusive Limo Service on her fast dial. She sometimes had to use them to pick up clients at the airport to wine them and dine them before setting them up with Crypto Currencies.

One of her greatest joys was taking their large investments and using them to do "shorts" on the currency. They did not suffer a loss long because when she took her profits, she bought the equal amount which the combination of covering her short and doubling up the shares when she did the transaction usually netted them profits as well. Nothing sweeter than to use other people's money to short crypto currencies and make huge profits quickly. That's another reason why she never held onto a trade overnight when bad things can happen on the other side of the world to see your assets have crumbled by the open of trade the next day.

Xinxin saw firsthand with her friend who traded options with Google stock and suddenly found herself under water by three million $$ USD. She got lucky right at the 72-hour mark, she was able to offload the options and netted a $25,000 profit, but she almost had a nervous breakdown until the planets aligned and she got out of the trade without losing her skirt.

Xinxin was often criticized for her trading style and leaving the trade before the end of the trading session. But she internally smiled when she saw some of the people who criticized her were facing a dilema because their trade went against them after hours.

The Limo Driver texted Xinxin fifteen minutes later saying, "I'm out in front of your building."

"I'm on the way," Xinxin texted back as she was leaving her luxury condo in a very jovial manner knowing she was going to go meet the love of her life.

Xinxin then texted Wilber and informed him, "I'm leaving my home now, I'll be there soon."

Wilber was one of the nicest guys Xinxin met in her lifetime. He was very sweet, which proves you can't judge a book by its cover. Xinxin was no fool and knew beneath the veneer of that sweet personality was a spy and a killer. I wonder how many men and women Wilber's killed. Xinxin thought.

If Xinxin knew the unbridled truth, she would probably say goodbye to Wilber especially if she discovered what he had to do to a couple women. Just like male spies, sometimes a person in the business had to kill a woman for self-protection. It was kill or be killed.

On one occasion while sleeping with the enemy, Wilber and the female spy had just finished having copious sex. The woman got out of bed went into the bathroom to tinkle. Wilber could hear her fire hose running as she didn't bother shutting the bathroom door. Pissing like a Russian Racehorse is what Wilber was thinking about then.

The lovely female Chinese spy Faye Wong who Wilber thought was his lover, came out of the bathroom and there was barely enough light in the room to see what she was really doing. Her purpose of going to the bathroom was to get the very sharp knife and take care of business first. The female spy raised the knife as she approached the bed.

With Wilber's back turned towards the female spy, he could see the faint shadow on the wall and knew the woman was going to attempt stabbing him and most likely the blade was covered in poisons which is often done.

The female Chinese spy Faye Wong who looked like the recording star Jennie Kim's twin sister, didn't know Wilber had a gun with a silencer under the covers and just before she could lurch at Wilber he quickly rolled over and put a couple slugs into her midsection including through the middle of her heart. The woman stood frozen, and, in a moment, blood came out of her mouth, and she crumpled over onto the bed and quickly had no pulse. She was dead.

Wilber soon had an emergency extraction and departed. By the time the authorities were checking the deceased woman holding onto the unused knife in a death grip, Wilber was long gone having been driven to the airport and was soon on a private jet flying out of Vienna that would eventually be landing at Andrews Air Force base.

Wilber would never believe Faye Wong was a spy trying to kill him because of the way she made love. That's how it is in the spy business with deception and betrayal. Female spies are the world's best actors. Taking a load between their legs was no different to them than a soldier taking a bullet on the battlefield. It was mortal combat, and this woman just paid the ultimate price for sloppy execution.

***

Wilber made reservations by the window for a nice view of the harbor. At first the reservationist didn't want to give him such a great table until Wilber said, "I know you are somewhere in the Hotel. If you are willing to meet me in the lobby, I have $500.00 USD in Cash in Advance to help you find me that excellent view."

"Actually I'm 50 steps from the lobby in our reservation room."

I'm out in the lobby wearing a black suit with a white designer shirt. I'm the only person out here dressed like this about 30 feet from the counter, you can't miss me.

"I'll be right there."

In a few minutes, a nice-looking young female approached Wilber and said, "I understand you are having problems with your reservation for dinner?"

"Yes, I'm Wilber who held out his hand to shake the lovely young lady's hand who was suddenly animated by the sexy looking man with a tan and the jaw Hollywood was always looking for."

When they shook hands, the female could feel something in her hand.

She knew what it was. Cash in Advance.

"Wilber, I will be sure and take care of your reservation." "Thank you. What's your name?"

"Wilber, my name is Liu Shishi."

"Did anyone ever tell you that you look like a movie star?"

"No."

"Actually, you do. Go google top Chinese movie stars and you will discover there is one you could be her twin sister."

"That's very nice of you to say."

Wilber then shocked the young lady in perfect Mandarin which she was fluent said,

"如果我要找一個情人，我會爬上珠穆朗瑪峰，去尋找一個像你一樣美麗的女人。"

"Rúguǒ wǒ yào zhǎ o yīgè qíngrén, wǒ huì pá shàng zhūmùlǎ ngmǎ fēng, qù xúnzhǎ o yīgè xiàng nǐ yīyàng měilì de nǚ rén."

["If I were looking for a lover, I would climb mount Everest to find a woman as beautiful as you are."]

Feeling the money in her hand and receiving those special words from the stranger made Liu Shishi suddenly feel especially wonderful tonight and responded:

如果我不是害怕你傷了我的心，我現在就會帶你回家，跟你做愛。

Rúguǒ wǒ bùshì hàipà nǐ shāngle wǒ de xīn, wǒ xiànzài jiù huì dài nǐ huí jiā, gēn nǐ zuò'ài.

[If I were not afraid of you breaking my heart, I would take you home this very moment and make love to you.]

Liu Shishi then promptly turned around and briskly walked to the reservations center where she had other customers on phones waiting for her.

***

Xinxin's Limo pulled up in front of the Singapore Fullerton Bay Hotel and the valet was there to immediately open the door for the luxuriously dressed ethnic Chinese Singapore female.

Xinxin's dark purple dress had two small straps holding up the top. The dress fit her breast size perfectly. The diamond necklace that accentuated the dress was real. Thanks to Xinxin's trading successes in Crypto Currency, she could afford lavish jewelry and dresses.

With a nice slender body, the upper half of Xinxin's dress had fantastic artwork on the fabric giving a unique image. The fashion designer who created this couture dress had a three-dimensional aspect to the fabric in the upper half of the dress above the waistline. Below that was a velvety looking material of the same dark purple.

The brown highlights in Xinxin's hair which could easily be misunderstood as sun bleached hair was the result of British ancestry dating back almost one hundred and fifty years when a Naval Officer married into the family providing that unique DNA that gave Xinxin many generations later, an auburn like hair color even though her facial expressions appeared almost beautiful Han Dynasty like person.

There was no doubt the Valet and the Bellhop were mesmerized by the beauty and the charm of this gorgeous woman who stepped out of an expensive Limo. They had no idea who owned the Limo, but the initial image of the woman getting out of it, left no doubt in their minds she was somehow connected to money.

Due to Xinxin's exquisite beauty and her perfect posterior geometry of the, they could not help but let their eyes follow her into the lobby of the Hotel and their next big surprise happened. There was a very handsome Anglo, either British or American who met the beautiful woman, and it was obvious something was going on after a kiss on the cheek revealed he was waiting for her.

Wilber was wearing a black suit and a white designer shirt for tieless expressions of exquisite male influences showing a little of the chest hair along with the fabulous tan.

"I really like the way you look tonight, Xinxin," Wilber said.

"Wilber, you look so good I would devour you right now, but honestly I'm slightly hungry since I skipped lunch today."

"Let me escort you to the LA BRASSERIE so that we can take care of all that hunger."

Idrak had an alert on his security system for when Xinxin showed up. Her facial recognition was on file and as soon as she walked into the lobby, she was being tracked.

There were four men assigned security of Xinxin tonight. They had cell phones with APPs that had tracker imagery and saw her as well. They also saw the tracker on Wilber with his name tag on the tracker.

All four agents knew where the couple was going since Xinxin informed her cousin Idrak earlier. Two of them were already in the restaurant enjoying French cuisine on Xinxin's Nickle.

"Let me escort you to the LA BRASSERIE," Wilber said.

"Thank you, dear."

* * *

Liu Shishi noticed Wilber had given her $600.00 USD. She felt guilty so she decided she would take $100.00 and give it back to Wilber. She just opened the door out into the hallway to approach Wilber and to her ghast, there he was with that luxurious woman in the purple dress, and they were turning and walking back in this direction.

Liu Shishi stepped back into the office and shut the door and waited for a minute or so and then peaked out the door and saw the couple was past her so she then opened the door more and saw the couple walking along twenty steps away and it was a sight to behold. Wilber was indeed with a beautiful Singapore princess. She knew Wilber must be a special guy because rarely do you see smoking hot Singapore ethnic Chinese women with Anglo's unless they were filthy rich. She knew then she had met a special man, and his words left an indelible mark because of the way he said it seemed so real and sweet. No doubt Wilber was a charmer, and Liu Shishi realized, Wilber had charmed her as well.

Soon the couple entered the fabulous French Restaurant, LA BRASSERIE. The exceptionally beautiful Singapore female maître d' looked at her tablet as the couple arrived. Thanks to artificial intelligence they were already tagged, and the man was a hotel guest named Wilber O'Toole. She didn't notice before, but Wilber had one of the best seats in the restaurant reserved.

Little did the maître d' realize it, Liu Shishi had done her magic in fixing reservations and was so pleased she had done that, not so much for the nice bribe, but Wilber had the graces to be in the company of such a beautiful woman, he deserved a great seat. Plus, Liu Shishi was still feeling nice vibrations from what Wilber gave to her earlier.

Soon they were sitting down gazing into each other's eyes. Wilber knew for a fact he wanted to engage in life with Xinxin. She had touched the fabric of his soul in ways she had no idea how deep and real it was.

Wilber was a world class spy and had been in a few fixes before, just like in Beijing where he made it out of Indian Country, a term INTEL people used for behind enemy lines, with only minutes to spare. It took the utmost critical timing and effort to escape the trap.

The Chinese MSS are excellent and the best spies in the world, including the Blue-Eyed Blonde Chinese the MSS recruits from ethnic Chinese Caucasians that live in Northwest China that are direct descendants of a massive migration with Kubla Kahn when he abandoned Europe because he felt culturally advancing Europeans seemed impossible.

Wilber's assessment: anyone who doesn't respect the Chinese MSS are fools.

They ran these best spies in the world willingly take a bullet for their team.

Wilber hated fighting the MSS because he had tremendous respect and admiration for China. One thing Wilber understood which Pat Barton had no clue of, the Chinese MSS were ALL COWBOYS. They had no girl scouts and were good at what they did. The Chinese MSS didn't pussyfoot around. One of the greatest tragedies

that Wilber felt in the line of duty is when he had to kill his female Chinese MSS agent he was in love with. She was beautiful, resourceful, and intelligent. But she was also a deadly killer, and it was her life or his life. Wilber had no choice when he pulled the trigger with less than a second to live, otherwise.

His last words to her were, "I would love to be your lifetime lover, but I had to kill you."

The look on her face was total disbelief she had been shot. Wilber had great affection for Faye Wong, so his last deed in her life was double edged, he killed her and at the same time had a memory he could never forget. It sucks when you must kill your lover because she's an enemy agent.

Wilber could see light at the end of the tunnel, at least that's what he thought. Little did Wilber realize was, he was soon going to be embarking upon a scenario that would make him wish he was back in the spy business living on borrowed time. Wilber didn't know he was looking at a temporal anomaly. There would be stress and heartbreak in his life. He would have to find the inner strength one of these days, as the odds were piling up against him.

"What would you like to drink," the beautiful Singapore waitress asked.

Wilber was glad something took him out of his flashback to reality. His problem was he simply had experienced too many events in his life and when a person lives nine lives like he has, there was an endless number of memories to sift through and experience when the brain suddenly for no apparent reason triggers such memories like the Chinese MSS spy Faye Wong he knew he had loved but killed.

The paradox of love and murder combined creates interesting memories.

"I would like a glass of Chardonnay," Xinxin replied.

"And you sir?" the waitress asked.

"Just give me a glass of Cabernet Sauvignon," Wilber replied.

"How are you doing today," Xinxin asked after the waitress left.

"I'm enjoying the time because I got to see you again."

"I was quite surprised when you arrived at my office."

"It was something very important to me. I needed to recover the lost time that was out of our control. I'm so very sorry how that all transpired."

"Not to worry there are some things I want to tell you when we are alone."

"Alright, I hope you don't plan on breaking my heart."

"No, nothing like that. But you need to know the rest of the story." "Alright, I'm a big boy, I can take it."

"I'm glad you came back for me. I was crushed when you disappeared, but now I know a lot more about what occurred, I'm of a different mindset."

"That's good to hear I think."

"For you, it is. I don't give my heart out so easily." "I'm sure you do not."

The two sat there engaging in small talk about nothing really important. It was merely the calm before the storm.

Xinxin and Wilber were cut from the same cloth, risk takers. As they gazed upon each other they knew what the other person was really like. Before Wilber came to Singapore, he was thoroughly briefed on Xinxin and advised not to come.

Wilber suspected he knew some of the details Xinxin would soon privately tell him. She was naïve to think Wilber didn't know about the MSS and Beijing. He knew they had fully coerced her before he left. But he also knew it was none of her choosing. She was an innocent bystander thrust into something people in society normally do not experience and hope to hell they never did again.

There was great anticipation as well as desire between the two. The dinner and socializing were merely just milestones in tonight's events that would soon unfold and they both knew it.

Xinxin and Wilber were served their drinks which broke the tension slightly then suddenly, a well-dressed man approached their table. The Maître d' observing all this knew well who this person was, and what he did in the hotel. She had her own dealings with him a time or two.

The man smiled at Xinxin who smiled back and was glad he was here. "Wilber, let me introduce you to my cousin Idrak."

Wilber stood up and held out his hand and said, "It's a pleasure to meet you, Idrak."

"Wilber it's a pleasure to meet you as well. My cousin Xinxin has spoken very positively about you."

"That's nice to know."

"Xinxin is a special woman. For her to be with you makes you special. I know her well and she doesn't suffer any fools. The fact she likes you speaks volumes about you."

"Thank you for the compliment. I'm very fond of Xinxin."

"That I know and to meet you in person is good."

"Would you like to join us?" Wilber asked.

"Wilber, I would love to, but I'm a busy person and I'm actually working now. But some other day we'll get together."

"Alright, thank you." "You are most welcome."

Xinxin was beaming because Idrak was being so kind and courteous. But she also knew Idrak knew a lot about Wilber and by now no doubt had conferred with his SID friends for INTEL on Wilber. And her guess was correct. Idrak now knew his cousin was involved with a heavy-duty CIA person who was in love with her. Her life was now very complicated.

Idrak could tell by the various surveillance videos including the $600 bribe that Wilber was a smooth mover. What does he see in Xinxin? That question was Idraks most profound question.

Idrak would be greatly distressed to see a picture of the MSS spy Feye Wong that Wilber killed. She could almost pass for Xinxin's twin sister and Xinxin could pass for Jennie Kim. If Idrak ever discovered Feye Wong and her history, he would always wonder if that was the reason for the infatuation with Xinxin.

Idrak was soon gone and the two love birds were engaged again with their private parlay of words and a special time together. Wilber wasn't quite sure why Xinxin seemed so calm and almost relieved. Little did he know she just spent over one million $$$ USD to ensure they had safety tonight and no cares of the world.

As Idrak left the restaurant, he smiled at his two security guys enjoying a fabulous meals so that they could be in position to intervene and observe any activity by others that might suggest nefarious activity going on.

The French food was quite appealing and after their meal, Xinxin suggested they go for a walk to help digest the meal and do talking. There was plenty to see near the hotel and good places to walk.

Halfway through the walk when Idrak's security people notified him there was another American that seemed to be tailing Wilber, and showed pictures of him, they were informed. He's Wilber's bodyguard, do not approach him. That's when the security team suddenly started to get vibes this person of interest must be someone of importance. It now dawned on them why Idrak's cousin was interested in the American. Was he a movie star or someone they didn't know about?

After walking around and holding hands, Xinxin surprised Wilber and said, "Us go up to your hotel room and get more comfortable."

"Alright."

In 30 minutes the two were undressed and it was like in the past when they discovered the essence of each other. But this time it was different. It wasn't a causal meeting like before that resulted in a lover's tryst.

Now it was something else because Wilber O'Toole traveled a long distance and went through a lot to get back to Xinxin. She could feel the love. There is a strange magnetism that develops between a couple when they each think they are in love. Just like when two magnets align with their poles properly aligned the mutual attraction is strong.

That strong valence pulled the two together as they transcended into lover's bliss and evolved into that physical intertwine that gave each of them intense pleasure. It was a huge release of cosmic gratification for both. The floodgates of passion unfurled, and the covalent bonding created that tapestry in their minds that almost like out in nature that creates strong actions in wildlife that get males killing each other to fight for the females. The lure and the attraction can be overwhelming.

After a while Xinxin said, "I need to leave soon to protect my reputation. If you want to spend the night with me, you'll have to do it at my place tomorrow. I need to leave you now because I must work in the morning."

"Xinxin I fully understand. Everything is about images. I'll be happy to visit you tomorrow."

"Wilber, thank you for understanding."

Xinxin crawled out of bed and started dressing. After she had all her clothes back on she went into the bathroom and put on some lipstick and pulled a small auxiliary brush out of her purse and reshaped her hair to look as if when she first arrived. Looking at Xinxin now you would not know that just fifteen minutes earlier she was laying in Wilbers arms enjoying every minute of it.

"Alright Wilber my dearest, we'll meet up tomorrow for lunch. I'll try to curtail my day early so we can spend more time together," Xinxin said.

"Thanks," Wilber responded.

Moments later Xinxin was gone. On her way to the elevator, she texted the Limo company to send over a car to pick her up. This time of day the Limo company wasn't serving a lot of customers, so they had plenty of standby transportation available.

Idrak had not left work yet and watched his cousin leave the hotel looking happy and smiling. He knew what most likely transpired. His cousin was blindly in love with a CIA agent who apparently was not alone in Singapore.

Wilber was now the most protected person in the world, being protected by two different sources. Should the Chinese MSS make a move against Wilber while he was in Singapore, they would quickly regret it.

Chinese bankers made a lot of money in Singapore and a Chinese MSS boss would quickly regret screwing up and losing a lot of income. The bankers would have the Green Gang of Shanghai take care of the Chinese MSS official if he did so then make apologies to the Singapore SID, which would not be the first or last time something like this happened.

By the time Xinxin walked to the entrance of the Singapore Fullerton Bay Hotel, the Limo was waiting there and the driver standing by the passenger door opened for her and bowed as she approached. She knew this driver quite well as he had given her lifts many times in the past, including earlier this evening on her way to the Hotel.

Xinxin stepped into the Limo and was on her way home. She was tailed all the way to her apartment building by Idrak's men and if the Limo driver did something stupid, he would be fish food tonight. Singapore organized crime usually liked to grind them up before they fed them to the fishes since it meant more of them would get fed. One of the problems for someone who screws up in an island nation is the ocean usually takes care of the problem.

Once Xinxin was safely home in a high security building most of the security detail went home except for one person who was the night watch keeping the vigilance all night long. Then after Xinxin was at work in the morning, he would be dispatched home to rest well earned.

None of the security detail men were grumbling like times before because they got paid cash in advance. They were making good money and fast because Idrak knew Wilber would not be staying more than a couple weeks, so he had plenty of cash to share with his men who had a growing like for him because he treated them very well over the years and today was another memorable time where he treated them extra well. But they also knew this was a special deal. Xinxin was family and the American was someone special to her.

In the morning Xinxin went into work and by lunchtime performed fifty trades. Xinxin accomplished forty-nine wins and one loss. The loss was caused simply by her wanting to close out her trades early for the day because she wanted to spend time with Wilber. Xinxin's associates were quite happy because between yesterday and today, Xinxin made so much profit, she covered all the group's losses for the entire month and provided gains on top of it.

In two days they crypto currency trading, wonder woman Xinxin was raising eyebrows with her trading prowess. What they didn't know Xinxin was a trading Lioness who could read the charts better than most and make instantaneous decisions and had it not been for the fact she wanted to leave work, she could have hung around for another thirty minutes and not had any losing trades for the day.

If Goldman Sachs knew how good Xinxin was, she would be in NYC right now. Not so much to make them money but to expose her to some of their traders to learn her methodology that worked. Unfortunately, like most Wallstreet firms they didn't realize the finesse was in understanding the charts and knowing precisely when to strike. Waiting for optimal conditions didn't make you money. Xinxin simply learned, deal with what you have, nothing more nothing less, and never put macho into the trade.

Xinxin removed all emotion and acted like a trader should using her intuition and decisive acts that often were minutes ahead of a shift in sentiments and chart actions that resulted. Some people in NYC would trash her for leaving too much money on the table.

But on the other hand, Xinxin always took money off the table except for a few rare instances like today when she had personal matters to attend to. Her lesson to the 800-pound gorillas (wall street) would be, success is the willingness to leave money on the table and leave some action for the other guy.

Get out, take your profits and don't look back at how much you could have made. Because it also meant how much you could have lost. Greedy get killed but pigs get slaughtered. Xinxin was neither greedy nor a pig. She simply executed trades when she needed to do so, period.

Xinxin went home and changed. She thought today she would treat Wilber with a big surprise. Xinxin loved many of the Chinese dresses that were available. South Asia was influenced by Malaysians, Vietnamese, Southern Chinese, and Indonesian styles in prints as well as design of women's clothing.

A beautiful Singapore woman with a tan in a Chinese dress can appear quite beautiful and Xinxin was going to show that to Wilber today. Since she was of Chinese heritage she was proud to wear Chinese styles.

Xinxin had a great appreciation for the fact Wilber took such interest in learning to speak Mandarin Chinese. Even though it was harder for Wilber he could also understand Cantonese quite well enough but could not converse quite as well as he could in Mandarin where he was rock solid. In the case of Singapore, the main Chinese dialect spoken was Mandarin, not Cantonese, even though Hong Kong and Guangzhou were a lot closer.

The short sleave cream color Chinese style dress Xinxin changed into had a beautiful large red flower positioned in the middle of her chest. There was also a large blue flower around the area where her belly button was, then other flowers near the bottom and the sides. The dress was not a mini skirt, but it rode up high exposing a lot of Xinxin's legs.

Xinxin's Chinese style dress came up probably 7 to 8 inches below her crotch. The dress sleeves and the traditional Chinese collar had red trim and a small red bow tie at the top holding the two sides of the collar together. Xinxin knew Wilber would like this dress and when they met at the JAAN restaurant for lunch, she could tell by Wilber's body language, he appreciated what he was looking at.

Yesterday's trades more than paid for the money Xinxin paid her cousin for Wilber's protection. Today's trades paid for a lot more. Xinxin realized she might not have been so eager and excited to do those trades almost in a machine gun style if Wilber had not turned her on so much.

His inspiration really got to her psyche. And it was all because she knew Wilber loved her more than anything in the world.

To have such an intelligent and capable man think so highly of you is a huge motivation. Xinxin's trades this morning proved that. When she left work early, Xinxin's office was on fire. Everyone was so proud of Xinxin for being such a great winner the past couple of trading sessions. Then the rumors started going around Xinxin had a boyfriend in town, and he was a good looking guy.

Just by luck later when Xinxin was at the JAAN restaurant with Wilber, four of the women from the office accidentally went there for lunch around the same time and low and behold halfway across the restaurant was none other than Xinxin dressed to kill and her suave boyfriend and he was looking really good as well, dressed in inspirational clothes, hair style, the tan, the body build, the whole nine yards.

The four women were utterly stunned. There was far more to Xinxin than they ever imagined. If they knew who the person really was and what he did for a living, they would actually be fearful. From a distance they could tell the couple were having a fantastic time together. Xinxin was acting like a woman in love usually does. Her whole focus was on Wilber as if nobody else was around.

After their meals and drinks, Xinxin suggested to Wilber, she take him on a Taxi tour of the area to give him a feal for Singapore, which he readily agreed too. The women had paid for their meals and were mostly finished eating so when the two love birds left the restaurant, they quickly followed them. And to their utter surprise they watched them holding hands and walked up to a cab and got in together.

In an hour every woman in the area of the company where Xinxin worked trading crypto currencies, heard stories and embellishments of the lovely couple.

Singapore is an interesting place. It has an endless city one feels. They drive like British on the wrong side of the road. A lot of money went into Singapore. There was a lot of money earned that went into the city. It goes to show the wealth generated due to its unique location. The British figured out early on to colonize it and make it a major seaport. Singapore remained in British hands until the Japanese conquered it during WW2.

Driving around the island gave Wilber far more appreciation for the people of Singapore. Since Wilber is a train buff, he's aware of Singapore's tremendous rail line construction. Since the 1980's

Singapore went from virtually no rail service to now a network that rivals Tokyo that is growing. Singapore planners put a lot of efforts into making the MRT and the LRT trains.

The MRT trains are standard trains on steel rail. The LRT trains use rubber tires on a ceramic track and are considerably quieter. The LRT trains serve as feeders to the MRT trains. The average daily rail passenger ridership in Singapore was 3.4 million in 2019. Without these trains, Singapore would experience transportation gridlock as there is not enough real estate on the Island to support all the automobile traffic that

otherwise would exist. The MRT and LRT systems are so expansive they have huge coverage all around the island as if they were bus routes.

"Is there anything in particular you wish to do Wilber?" Xinxin asked right after

they passed in view of an MRT train.

"You might think I'm nuts for saying this, but I like trains." "That's not nutty at all, I like trains too," Xinxin replied.

"After we finish this Taxi tour us go ride a few trains, then later today, there is a restaurant in my hotel that has a DJ that plays music. We can get something to eat there, and maybe do some dancing."

"Are you a good dancer, Walter?" Xinxin asked.

"Yes, I took ballroom dancing lessons and used to practice on Sunday evenings at the Alo Wai Swing Dance Club at the Alo Wai Golf Course in Waikiki Hawaii on

Sunday evenings."

"What was that like?"

Typical night there were 300 dressed up women wanting to dance and about 7 guys. They lined up at your table to ask you to dance.

"A charming guy like you probably received some side benefits, I would imagine."

"Actually, there were significant benefits. Women who wanted to dance with me often always invited me over for dinner."

"Did that include some boom-boom time after dinner?"

"There is no way I would touch any of those women because I know if I did they would blab it to everyone and lay claim to me. I didn't want any of them to think they owned me. Plus, I wasn't there to meet them. I just wanted to practice my ball room dancing to get better at it."

"Did you get better?"

"I got so good fifty of them would line up at my table to ask me to dance. The drinks were on the house!"

"You never got interested in any of them?"

"I met two Chinese ladies and their male friend. He was the best dancer I ever saw. I became friends with them because the two women were always the best-looking women there and I secretly watched their male friend to learn his dancing style."

"What were these women like?"

"The woman he danced with most of the time had a tremendous body, and a beautiful face. They were not lovers; just good friends and she loved the way he danced."

"That sounds good."

"The other lady was married to a high-ranking military officer who neglected her. I would never fool around with someone else's wife. But I considered the three of them my friends and we often met at night clubs around Waikiki to dance together. Why spoil a great friendship with romance?"

"I see your point. Are we just friends?"

"No, you and I have gone past that point. We are more than friends. Our friendship is in the rear-view mirror now. We slipped into Romance and took it to another level." "Are you sure about that?"

"Sure, enough to fly halfway around the world to see you, that's how sure I am." "Did you miss me?"

"More than you can imagine. You have no idea the pain I felt in my heart when I could not make our dinner date, because of the situation you know about."

"That reminds me I need to talk to you about my situation when we have privacy.

Don't let me forget."

"Surely I will not."

Singapore has about 280 square miles of land. Guam is about 210 square miles to give a perspective on size. New York City (NYC) has about 472 square miles. New York City has 8.8 million people. Singapore has 5.6 million. So the Density of Singapore is slowly catching up with NYC. Singapore has 20,000 people per square mile. NYC has 29,000 per square mile. The only thing that will hold Singapore back is natural resources which it has very little of and must import practically everything. One could say the same for NYC.

In a couple hours, Wilber said, "This has been an enjoyable experience, but I think I would like to go back to my hotel and freshen up then take you to the bar, night club later."

"Will I look okay in this dress with you?"

"Dear, you will look more than okay. I will be very proud to have you with me looking this nice."

"Thank you Wilber, I like that you enjoy my Chinese dress."

"Xinxin, your dress is very beautiful. It's inspiring."

"Thank you."

***

Chapter Eight

Singapore Delights

In about fifteen minutes the couple were dropped off at the front entrance of the Singapore Fullerton Bay Hotel. Ldrak was notified via artificial intelligence tagging the two, they were in the hotel, and he followed them up to Wilber's hotel room where he figured they would probably soon engage in the horizontal tango. If it were not for the fact Xinxin was his cousin, he would pursue Xinxin and would prefer he was the one knocking the rims off her tires instead of this American.

But one thing that was quite apparent. Xinxin normally did not look all that happy. She acted as if she was bored with life and had no significant interest in anything other than making money. But Ldrak noticed Xinxin was a different woman when she was around Wilber. Wilber affected Xinxin's feelings somehow that seemed to engulf her into a positive valance.

Xinxin now was smiling frequently. She had a major happiness now. It was quite apparent to Ldrak that Xinxin was in love with Wilber. But at the same token, Ldrak's bugs in the hotel room and other things he did, gave him a strong indication Wilber was just as much in love with Xinxin. That strong bond between the two allowed Ldrak to accept the fact his cousin was emotionally involved with a CIA guy.

Interesting developments transpired today while the love birds were out and about. Wilber's bodyguard soon detected surveillance. And soon the bodyguard was quite surprised, the surveillance was coming from two separate groups, unrelated. The bodyguard sent an encrypted message back to Langley Virginia and the watch officer then forwarded Wilber's bodyguard's concern to his superiors who now were looking into the matter.

The bodyguard would have no way of knowing the DD/P had routine secret communications link with a SID agent. There were times when SID and CIA had to team up against international arms dealers that were selling advanced weapons to potential adversaries. In short order, a CIA person contacted his SID connection and discussed the concern.

The SID agent said he would investigate the surveillance because they themselves were interested in who two groups were following Wilber and Xinxin and what were their motives?

Now, Wilber had a third group interested in him. The SID person quickly discovered one of the groups was none other than Ldrak's security team following Wilber around. Soon afterwards, Ldrak received a visitor as to find out why his men were following Wilber around.

Ldrak knew the SID person quite well. They went to school together.

They were friends.

Before the day was done, Ldrak's team working with the SID were identifying the third party. It did not take time for them to figure out who they were because everyone has a price. Including the Chinese MSS station chief in Singapore.

There was going to be a hit or an abduction the following morning. SID and Ldrak's team working together knew who the target was and how they were going to nab him if he went some place where they could abduct Wilber and if not, kill him.

The Chinese MSS now had a good lead that showed them, who was with Wilber O'Toole and thus only had to follow Xinxin to lead them to Wilber.

The following day was a little like the previous day. Xinxin went into work in the morning and did her Lioness trading skills and was so positive because of what was happening in her life with Wilber, she made 55 trades, all winners making some really big gains today which impressed her trading associates. Three big winning days in a row was quite a spectacle to them. Between gossiping women about her love life and her trading acumen, Xinxin was on fire. Anyone who underestimated Xinxin in the past was duly corrected by now.

When Xinxin was ready to meet Wilber again, she called him to let Wilber know she was on her way and to meet her at the front entrance the Singapore Fullerton Bay Hotel. Today Xinxin was wearing black slacks with a white top that had a pattern of black diagonal images in a grid. The long- sleeved top had a black collar and black cuffs that gave off a sense of radiance.

If there ever was a last image Wilber wanted to remember Xinxin by, this was it. She looked not only beautiful, but wholesome. The ambience Xinxin created with her clothes, her makeup, perfume, and smile with her white pearl teeth, made the day suddenly pleasant for

Wilber when he met her standing by the Limo.

"Where would you like to go?" Xinxin asked when they were in the Limo driving away.

"Let's see China Town, then hop on an MRT train for a short ride, then I wouldn't mind visiting the Botanical Gardens again. There is so much to see there, and we only saw a small portion of it."

"Sounds good to me." Xinxin responded then in Mandarin asked the ethnic Chinese driver to drop them off at China town.

In a short period after exiting the Limo, the couple were standing in front of the Buddha Tooth Relic Temple. Xinxin liked the reverence Wilber had towards the Chinese. Based on their conversations, Xinxin knew Wilber had studied Chinese History quite a bit and delved deeply into Chinese literature including the Five Tang Poets, which he made comments about and while they were enjoy the view of the Buddha Tooth Relic Temple.

Wilber repeated one of those wonderful Tang poems that captured the essence of the imagery this temple gave them. Buddhists are the majority religious people in Singapore followed by Christians and others.

Walking around China Town, the Sri Mariamman Temple was soon commented, "The Sri Mariamman Temple sure creates a visual spectacle with lavish decoration and architecture."

"Terengganu Street is another must see tourist spot you must see Wilber," Xinxin said observing Wilber taking it all in.

They just happened to walk by the Chinatown Heritage Center and that captured Wilber's curiosity, so he said, "Let's go in here for a short while." They spent quality time there as well. Wilber felt grateful for all Xinxin was doing for his amusements.

The two then had to walk along the Chinatown Street Market in due time they both felt the need to eat and Xinxin suggested, "I know a restaurant about two minutes away we can walk to if you are hungry."

"Sure, lead the way," Wilber replied.

Xinxin led Wilber to the Fortune Court restaurant [天福阁]

The two were seated, soon receiving hot Jasmine Tea, and looking at the menus.

"Xinxin, what are you considering ordering?" Wilber asked.

"I think I will have the X.O Lobster EE-Fu Noodles." Xinxin replied then added. "Wilber, what are you thinking of eating?"

"I think I'll try the White Pepper Crab. Want to share Stir fried Asparagus with XO Sauce?" Wilber asked.

"Sounds good to me," Xinxin replied.

In due time their orders were served, and Wilber quickly stated, "The taste of the food is excellent."

"Yes, I like eating here now and then Xinxin said."

In a while the male Chinese waiter came by with a pitcher of hot tea and asked, "How's the food sir?"

"Please give my regards to the chef. This meal is utterly outstanding." "He will be happy to hear that," the waiter replied in English with a British Accent.

"How is your Entrée Madam?"

"The food here is fabulous, that's why I keep coming back."

"Thank you for your patronage."

"You are most welcome and please tell the Chef what my friend said for me as well."

"I most certainly will," the waiter replied now thinking this lovely couple who were well dressed would most likely leave him a nice tip. He was not disappointed that the tips exceeded his expectation. Little did he know Xinxin made more profit just this morning than the restaurant would probably in a years' time. She felt quite generous as a result.

The small talk lingered while they were relaxing and drinking their after-dinner tea. Xinxin was surprised when Wilber ordered a shot of Gin and even more surprised when he poured that into his teacup more than half full of tea and took a small bag of Sweet and Low sweetener and added it and stirred it.

"That's a strange drink you made," Xinxin said.

"This drink I created tastes good, and it gives me a kick and a buzz at the same time. Here, try and take a taste of it." Wilber offered.

Wilber handed Xinxin his cup and she tasted it and replied, "Your drink has a nice taste to it, I can hardly taste the Gin.

In my past, I've had to work some long hours and needed a buzz and a way to keep up my vigilance. I was always experimenting with creating new drinks that give me added endurance."

"Why do you need the added endurance?"

"I'll demonstrate that later when we are alone someplace special."
"I can't wait."

"Nor can I. By the way, I texted you more contact information for me besides my phone number which you already have, in the event we are ever separated again unexpectedly, you will know how to contact me. You know my real name but the contact information I gave you is a "John Dunbar." He doesn't really exist but in case the MSS or some other outfit grabs you and searches your cell phone or email accounts they will find that innocuous name. When you read anything from John Dunbar, immediately erase it so you do not leave any breadcrumbs behind for them to dig deep into who you know."

"Then what's the purpose of me emailing John Dunbar?"

"That will give me a signal to contact you. If for some reason I do not reply, do not get upset or depressed. It just means that for whatever reason

I cannot reply at this time. As soon as I can, I will call you on the phone or text you phone."

"Why do I need to do this?"

"It's our backup plan so that our relationship can always continue no matter what issues we run into."

They soon left the restaurant and were at a train station a short while later.

"When I was younger, I used to take the train into work because I lived further away."

"How did you like the commute?"

"It's okay during daylight hours because Singapore police are always nearby. I didn't like taking the train at night."

"Understandable," Walter responded.

"We'll get on the Purple line station here in China Town and switch over to the Orange Line that makes a nice circle around almost the entire city," Xinxin said.

"This kind of reminds me of the Greenline in Tokyo where you can go completely around Tokyo in a giant circle of the city," Wilber said a few minutes after the Orange Line train left the station.

"Are you enjoying the view?" Xinxin asked.

"Actually, I like this better than the Taxi," Wilber replied.

"In 2024 the MRT is going to finish a section in the southern portion of the Orange Line which is referred to as the circle line that will make it a complete circle," Xinxin noted.

"I'm sure the tourists will love that," Wilber said.

"I think the MRT got the idea from the Japanese," Xinxin said and winked. But the Circle Line doesn't have much to see, it's almost all underground. If you want to do sight-seeing, you need to take the East West Line or one of the LRT lines.

"Is there a train that goes by the Botanical Gardens?" Wilber asked.

"Yes, this train goes to the Botanical Gardens if you want to get off there its stop CC19 which is about in another ten stops."

"Let's get out there and walk around."

"There is also the Downtown line that leaves the Botanical Gardens we can take back to your hotel."

When they got off at the Botanical Gardens, one of Idrak's men called him and reported they were at the Gardens and wanted to know if they could take a break and go off and get some lunch.

Idrak had just received a report from his SID friend the American CIA who now had several agents following the couple detected two other groups doing surveillance on them.

"Stay with them closely. Someone is following them besides a couple CIA agents. You may have to do an emergency intervention."

Now Idrak's men were quite animated. They had not detected the CIA guys, nor had they detected the third Party. They suddenly had to look for anyone, including Americans and Asians. This guy must be someone special to be followed around by so many people, the lead security man thought.

Once the two lovebirds were off the Orange-Route train and into the open, Idrak's security men wondered how an Intel Agency would abduct this guy in such a public place. Then it dawned on him: They might just be here to kill him, no abduction planned which means they might kill Idrak's cousin since she would be an eyewitness. The adrenalin started flowing.

The entire security team spoke Malay. That was what Ldrak preferred.

Too many people in Singapore spoke Chinese.

The Chinese spies following Wilber did not speak Malay and had no reason to, but Idrak's men could also speak Chinese and overhear what the Chinese Tourists were saying.

When you know the enemy is nearby that can kill you, there is no vigilance decrement. Everyone is focused and ready to do business.

There was a nice Gazebo along the path Wilber and Xinxin approached and decided to go there sit down and enjoy the sight and talk.

There was nothing on the radar screen, but suddenly Wilber noticed off at a distance his bodyguard flashing a hand signal which meant danger was approaching. Four innocuous Chinese Tourists were approaching from one direction, and they didn't realize the Five Asiatic Tourists coming from the other direction as a threat. They knew there were two Americans nearby that could be trouble but four against two, they liked those odds.

Wilber having a sixth sense did not like people crowding around him and so as the four Chinese Tourists approached, he grabbed Xinxin's hand and said, let's move on and give these people some space. That quick movement saved his life because it put the attackers at a bad angle and as soon as one of them moved towards Wilber, he knew they were trouble and yelled at Xinxin, "RUN AS FAST AS YOU CAN AND START SCREAMING."

"WHAT?" Xinxin asked yelling.

"DO IT AND DO NOW OR YOU MAY BE DEAD SOON!" Wilber Yelled.

In terrible fright Xinxin took off screaming which also threw the four Chinese off guard and suddenly one of them went chasing after Xinxin who was running right at the two CIA guys but had no idea who they were.

The First Chinese MSS agent lunged at Wilber with a knife. He wasn't trying to stab a rookie, and soon realized it would be a tough takedown as Wilber was fighting for his life. It was kill or be killed and Wilber always came prepared for moments like this. He grabbed the man's arm with the knife, not trying to prevent the cut, just delayed it long enough to put his thumb into one of his eye sockets immediately causing him disorientation.

The Chinese men did not see the five guys sprinting to them. The first guy fell in total agony and the other two toting knives now came at Wilber in a cautious manner which delayed them too long and by the time the first man took a swing at Wilber with his knife the second guy was hit in the back by a Taser from one of Idrak's men and soon on the ground shaking as he was getting multiple shots. The guy with the knife going after Wilber suddenly looked down and saw his partner shaking on the ground when he too was hit with a Taser.

Xinxin ran right towards the two CIA men who were quite capable of handling the one Chinese Guy who was almost ready to grab Xinxin when one of the CIA guys put his lights out.

A couple of Ladrak's men ran up to the CIA guys and raised their hands and said, "We are friendlies here to protect Wilber."

Then they yelled at Xinxin who was still screaming, "We are Idrak's security men, you are safe." Xinxin stopped dead in her tracks and turned around and saw her assailant laying on the sidewalk unconscious.

Ldrak's man called him and reported what went on.

Put Wilber and Xinxin in a Limo and bring them back to this Hotel immediately.

"What about if the officials show up, they will be here any minute."

"Get them out of there fast and now."

"Alright boss."

He then turned to Wilber and said, "Ldrak who you met has instructed us to get you and Xinxin into a Limo right away and back to the Fullerton Bay Hotel before the authorities get here."

"Would it be okay if I take those two Americans with me?"

"If it makes you more comfortable, sure. We can handle these guys.

And deal with the authorities."

"Alright let's go get Xinxin, I'm sure she's shook up pretty badly."

Within moments a couple golf carts appeared and Wilber, Xinxin, the two Americans and a couple of Ldrak's men were riding to the entrance of the park. They passed by authorities that were heading towards the altercation and a man lying on the sidewalk with two of Ldrak's men standing over him, still unconscious.

The man who had the knife had a severe trauma to his eye and was taken out in an ambulance.

Once they got to the hotel, Ldrak hustled them into a private room for the discussion.

The two CIA men had already received their instructions. They were to transport Wilber to a safe house, and he would be flown out of Singapore in a couple hours. Room service was already packing up his belongings and in a matter of moments everything he brought with him was packed up nicely ready to depart.

Tears were flowing down Xinxin as she knew the obvious. Wilber was leaving her again in an unscheduled manner. Her only solace was his foresight to send her that special communication link as if he knew something like this would happen.

"I'll contact you as soon as I can. I'm sorry but I am ordered to leave."

"I understand. I probably should never have gotten involved with you in the first place. You live too much of a dangerous life."

Moments later the two CIA men led Wilber to the front entrance and put in an unmarked car being followed by four SID people who were called in to make sure Wilber left the country right away.'

Word had already trickled down Wilber had severely damaged the eye of a Chinese Diplomat and they were complaining directly to the Secretary of State who then had discussions with the DCI, and soon Pat Barton was ready to sanction Wilber for getting him in such a spotlight of having a rouge Cowboy in Singapore damaging the eyeball of a Chinese Diplomat.

Pat Barton had already given Wilber his final warning, so he started administrative actions before Wilber had left Singapore on his way back to Washington. Flying in a private jet with a refueling stop in Honolulu made it a fast trip.

SID people had secretly videoed the incident including sound. Some of Wilber's Cowboy friends found out how Pat Barton was going to get Wilber and before Wilber arrived in Washington DC, through Xinxin, he had copies of all the videos of the poor innocent Chinese Diplomat wielding the knife.

Within hours of arrival since this was such a major diplomatic incident, Wilber was inside the SKIF with the DCI, DD/P, senior diplomat from the state department, his attorney and a couple agency lawyers.

Wilber of course let Pat Barton run his mouth, make all the accusations, vent his pent-up rage and resentment and a long list of Cowboy charges and Wilber didn't say anything, but he kept smiling. That got to the DCI who asked, "Wilber, since this is such a terrible diplomatic incident how the hell can you sit there smiling?"

Now it was Wilber's turn.

"Well sir, this is the first time I've had any communication with my supervisor. You would think he would want to know if there was some sculptitory evidence before he went after me with such outrageous charges and adverse administrative actions."

"What are you trying to say?"

"If Pat Barton wasn't such a dumb ass, he would have discovered the entire incident was filmed by a foreign intelligence agency."

Now suddenly, there was an eerie quiet in the room.

"Would you like me to show you the video before I give it to the Washington Post and write an op-ed about incompetent people like Pat Barton who just damaged the career of one of his most important assets without finding out the facts first?"

"We'll stop you for giving that to the Washington Post."

"Someone else will be giving it to them who you can't stop. Do you want to see the video, or do you want Pat Barton to lead you off the cliff?"

"Show us the video."

The sound, with Xinxin screaming and running and being chased and the Diplomat swinging the knife at Wilber was filmed with a good zoom and lots of fidelity.

When all the videos were ended, Wilber looked at the State Department Guy and said, "You need to show the Chinese Ambassador this video and remind him there are lots of copies of the video in Singapore. I would also estimate, Chinese Bankers in Singapore are now having some issues with the SID."

The next day, after having private meetings with the DCI and the DD/P, Pat Barton, senior member of CIA's Deputy Director of Solar System Investigations was suddenly now required to justify his actions which the DCI, and the CIA's DD/P were frowning upon because it resonated with them that Pat Barton took administrative action against Wilber O'Toole without even first discussing the matter with Wilber. The video made Pat Barton appear to be weak and ineffective. Pat Barton was soon on a short leash himself, but they don't call it "final warning."

After the Chinese ambassador was given copies of the video and warned there were many other copies the head of the Chinese MSS was given her marching orders to stay the hell away from Wilber O'Toole, he was deemed safe for now. But conditions can change, and Wilber knew that.

Only one thing good came out of this and that was internal review of Solar System Investigations wrote Pat Barton an official reprimand and gave him directives on how he would proceed in the future before he attempted any administrative actions against Wilber who had a legitimate legal reason to haul him and the agency into court for defamation of Wilber's character.

In one of Wilber's past missions, he saved the life of an Oil Sheikh's son who was kidnapped by ISIS terrorists that were going to cut the son's head off. Wilber, using unconventional Cowboy methods rescued the son. The agency would never know what all Wilber did because they would never approve of the tactics. Unlike girl scout tactics Pat Barton would use. Wilber simply did what terrorists would do but at a much greater level of destruction. Wilber also illegally hired mercenaries with Cash in Advance black money all spies need for moments just like this they can't let the agency know about.

Sheikh Omar after the incident, gave Wilber his business card with his private line and said, "If there is anything I can ever do for you in the future, please call me."

Wilber was feeling down in the dumps because his lover was too scared to ever be seen in public with him. Then he suddenly came up with the idea. He walked over to his filing cabinet in his home where he kept a lot of business cards from people he met in the past and other contact information such as mercenaries in case he needed them and a few other Cowboys he knew he could count on.

He easily found Sheikh Omar's business card and took it with him over to his comfortable chair and sat down and called him.

After a couple rings, Sheikh Omar answered the phone:

مرحبا، هل يمكنني مساعدتك؟

mrhbaan, hal yumkinuni musaeadatuka?

"Hello Sacrates (code name for Sheikh Omar they agreed on). This is John Dunbar."

"Very interesting to suddenly receive your phone call John Dunbar, I was just thinking of you. How are you these days?"

"Your excellency, you would not believe it, but I got girl problems."

"Really? I got to hear about that."

Knowing his phone could be tapped, John Dunbar gave Sheikh Omar the unclassified version of the story.

"What can I do to help out with this woman?" Sheikh Omar asked.

"I thought of a diabolical plan to be able to spend some time with her where she would feel safe."

"And where is that?"

"I think if I paid you a visit, and asked her to come with me, she would know those people could never get near her."

"Smart idea. My son would really like to see you again."

"I wouldn't mind seeing him too. How's Zayd doing?"

"You have no idea how much you inspired Zayd. He really hits the books hard now and is learning a lot."

"That's good to know that I had some positive influence."

"Wilber, you had more effect on his life than anyone else. He also owes you his life, and he appreciates you more than you can imagine."

"He deserved to live a long life. I didn't like the idea someone thought they could take it from him and not receive any kind of retaliation."

"You left behind a bloody mess that's for sure."

"Sometimes a person has to shoot their way out of a fix."

Sheikh Omar, who is a very brilliant planner, was thinking about how to get Wilber to his estate incognito and came up with the idea.

"Wilber, this is what I suggest. Have your lady friend fly to Paris, spend a couple days there, I'll have security men there to protect you, and then after the two of you

rekindle your romance, my private jet will fly you here. Nobody will know where you went."

"I like that idea."

"How soon do you want to come?"

"My agency has given me two weeks of administrative leave for the goat fawk they caused me, so I cool my jets and they calibrate my supervisor. I can leave now. Let me contact my friend and present her with the plan, then I will call you back immediately."

"Sounds good I will be waiting to hear back from you."

Wilber then called Xinxin. He knew it was about her bedtime, but he also knew she was in emotional turmoil now and the phone call might help.

When Xinxin first saw the caller ID was John Dunbar, she at first didn't want to answer it, but love does strange things to people.

"Hello John, I wasn't expecting to hear from you."

"I'm sorry that I called at such a late hour for you, but I wanted to present a plan so that we could see each other and salvage some of the time that was stripped away from us by those unsavory characters."

"I'm not sure I want to be around you after that incident."

"I have some interesting friends who I helped in the past who want to return the favor. This is what I'm offering. I want you to fly to Paris and meet me there. We'll spend a couple days to unwind and get our relationship on track, then my friend will fly us on his private jet someplace nobody can get to us. You will have more security than you ever experienced in your life. When we finish our time visiting my friend, he will fly us to Singapore where I'll drop you off, then continue back to Washington DC. We can then think about how we can meet in the future in places you will feel safe and comfortable."

"I'll think about it. I'm not going to decide tonight."

"Alright dear, I know you went through a lot of traumas, so that's understandable."

"I'm going to bed now; I already took some sleeping pills and I'm feeling sleepy." "Okay dear, rest well."

When Wilber did not call the Shiekh back for a while he got a text from him, "I know you and she are having deliberations. That's understandable. Send me a picture of your girlfriend. I want to know what the woman you are sleeping with looks like."

Wilber sent Shiekh Omar a picture of Xinxin she didn't know existed his CIA buddy took for him while doing surveillance when she was dressed up very nicely having dinner with Wilber.

A moment after receiving Wilber's text, Sheikh Omar texted back, "She is very beautiful, I'm proud of your taste in women."

"Thank you," Wilber texted back.

Wilber spent the day relaxing, then worked out some, getting in some running. He went down to a gym where his friend ran that did workouts, martial arts training, and boxing.

When Wilber was working on his thumbs the trainer asked, "Why do you spend so much time with your thumbs?"

"You never know when Boshi-ken – (The Thumb Strike) might come in handy. Then Wilber informed the trainer about some of the videos he watched of Kung Fu training at the Shaolin Temple (少林寺; shǎ olínsì) located in Henan Province, China. Some of the applications Wilber observed which caused him to concentrate on his thumbs.

"I have a copy of the popular Novel, The Travels of Lao T'san if you want to read it," Wilber said.

"Do you think I would get much from it?"

"Yes, you would understand why I train my thumbs."

Wilber then went on to discuss a Japanese Martial artist who trained the big toes kick (Tsumasaki geri).

"In 1921, a young Karate master named Arakaki Ankichi was at a bar in Tsuji, the notorious red-light district in Okinawa. He sometimes went to bars to get into fights to practice his Karate. We'll never know for sure if this incident was one of those occasions but one thing, we do now is that while on his way to visit the toilet, Arakaki Ankichi accidentally bumped into a well- known Sumo Wrestler who decided to kick Arakaki Ankichi's ass and threw him in the corridor on the second floor. Although Arakaki Ankichi claims he tried to ignore the man, Arakaki Ankichi was unable to get out of his way and the Sumo Wrestler shoved Arakaki Ankichi down the staircase.

Being in such good physical condition, however, Arakaki was able to roll down the stairs smoothly and avoided injury. The enraged Sumo Wrestler leaped down the stairs and grabbed Arakaki Ankichi by the arm, trying to yank him up to punch his face in. Seizing the man's arm with his free hand, Arakaki swiftly kicked his big toe into the armpit of the attacker, resulting in the man dropping to the ground like a sack of potatoes.

About six months later Arakaki Ankichi was shocked to see a story about the Sumo Wrestler who had died because of injuries sustained by a Karate expert at a bar in Tsuji. Despite the Sumo Wrestler allegedly dying as result from his encounter with Arakaki Ankichi, the police were never called in.

Karate researchers today suspect Arakaki Ankichi' Tsumasaki- geri kick may have caused an aneurysm, which would explain the delayed death."

"That's quite a story," the gym owner said.

When the gym owner saw Wilber was in one of his moods, obviously pissed off, he asked, "Would you like to get in the ring with some of my boxers and work off some of that frustration?"

The gym owner knew Wilber well and his students would probably get the crap knocked out of them, but it would be great training.

"I would but I didn't bring a mouthpiece."

"Not to worry. I have some spares and I keep them in containers full of Listerine, so they are nice and disinfected."

"Alright if you got a mouthpiece to loan me, I suppose I could."

There were five eager beavers waiting to do some work out in the ring including four men and one woman who thought she was one tough bitch. Wilber got a nice thrill thinking about beating her up then having sex with her afterwards. He met a female boxer one time who wanted to do that, and what a date!

With his gym clothes on not really exposing his body, Wilber did not look too intimidating. The cocky young man in the ring waiting for him planned on kicking Wilber's ass in a minute or less was soon in for a big surprise. Wilber wasn't thinking about the young man, his thoughts were on Pat Barton and wished he was in the ring and then the Chinese dude's face he poked came in a flashback, then Wilber went to town. In less than a minute the gym owner was blowing his whistle like crazy and yelling STOP!!!!

The others were suddenly no longer joking and coking as they watched the cockiest SOB in the gym just get the crap knocked out of him in about a minute.

"Remember these guys are students, not professionals!" The gym owner yelled.

"Sorry, I just had a bad memory of a recent event. I'll go softer on the next student."

The next student who was almost as cocky as the first one wasn't sure he wanted to do this, but it was either box the mad man or eat shit from the rest for being a chickenshit from now on. He stayed hoping the owner would blow the whistle quickly.

Wilber was feeling sweaty, so he took of his gym clothes top and set it up on the ropes and turned and faced the loudmouth punk who suddenly had one of those oh my fucking god moments when he saw those six pack abs and what he just had observed.

The owner was not going to let this match go too long if Wilber did not maintain control. He was not disappointed. Wilber danced around like a boxer and laid some powder buff punches on the punk who was exhilarated he was lasting the match and got a good work out on it as Wilber was almost coaching him on protecting himself and laying out proper attack methods.

The woman was last. She attacked like crazy. Wilber knew he could put her lights out in about ten seconds but toyed with her and gave her a good workout. The woman was seriously thinking about inviting Wilber over to her place because she figured he could perform in bed as well as he could in the ring. She knew he purposely didn't hit her hard, but he sent a message to her that she was defenseless against him.

In a way the gym owner was happy Wilber had tamed the first punk who was no longer the boisterous mouth they often had to endure. Just like Wilber knew, one day you will run into someone tougher than you.

After a good workout, and a run, Wilber went home and took a nice long hot bath relaxing and meditating. After the bath and change of clothes, Wilber was snacking and drinking and suddenly he received a text message. It was from Xinxin. Her female emotions were obviously at work because even though Wilber scared the hell out of her, he had one attribute that topped all others, he was actually in love with her. Few women ever meet a man who has such a strong heart like Wilber.

"Alright, I'll go. When will we meet?"

"Try to arrive in Paris in the afternoon."

"Okay, I'll book my flight now. I'll travel light and buy clothes I need there."

"Sounds good to me. Let me know date and time of your arrival."
"As soon as I book my flight, I will text you."

"Thanks."

In thirty minutes, Wilber received the text and saw she would be arriving in Paris in eighteen hours.

He then booked his flight and texted Sheikh Omar who then responded with a text saying he would be there in about 48 hours to fly them to the Middle East, and they would land in the UAE and fly on his personal helicopter to his residence which was out in the desert and highly protected.

Wilber would also be traveling light because he knew when he arrived at Sheikh Omar's mansion, he would be supplied with comfortable Thawb's to wear just like wealthy Japanese supply their guests with clothing that looks like pajamas and house coats and slippers.

Sheikh Omar's four wives would be very interested in Xinxin because she was stunningly beautiful but also full of charm. From past meetings with Sheikh Omar when he met his four wives, Wilber discovered they were well educated in Great Britain and spoke English with a British accent, just like the way Xinxin sounded. They would also put Xinxin in expensive Arabian gowns and watch over her as a distinguished guest.

One of the four wives looked very favorably upon Wilber for saving her son's life at the 11th hour when everyone else gave up hope. All they had to do was call a Cowboy the first time and it would not have had to go to the 11th hour. That's another lesson Pat Barton will never learn. Proceduralized managers cannot deal with chaos and the wickedness of unsavory characters.

One thing that Wilber did not know was when he spent time alone with the young Sheikh Omar's son Zayd smuggling him to safety riding on camels, while they were eating rough around the campfire, talking in general, knowing the boy's father could afford anything, he told him, "If you learn to play the violin, I will visit you to personally hear you play."

Wilber was also the reason why the boy was now an avid reader, reading as many science fiction Novels as he could get. And on Wilber's recommendation had read Asimov's Foundation Series, Heinlen, Bradbury and a host of others. The boy was an intellectual now and his teachers were amazed at his dedication to classwork. His father was also mildly surprised when he requested a violin and an instructor.

A few violinist celebrities were flown in to work with the boy a few times, and the boy after hearing Walter's comments informed his father, "Send me a hard ass Russian instructor, I want the best."

It was rough at first but after a few years, the palace looked forward to hearing the young man, Zayd, playing his violin and after two years was now to the level, Zayd could become a concert violinist.

Young Zayd was thrilled to learn his friend Wilber was soon to arrive to hear him play his violin. His father was very proud of young Zayd who had completely surprised everyone how brilliant he was in literature as well as music now.

Often when Zayd was doing his homework, he had on headphones listening to the great masters. His appetite for learning was strong. Another attribute all this caused was a very humble and polite person. Zayd could think for himself, and his thoughts were the future, and his mind was full of the future. Being the eldest son also put him into a unique situation. He also enjoyed all his time with his father, especially when they went out with their falcon Olimpico to watch it fly.

Zayd was no wimp either. He also exercised, worked out and during those few days alone at night with campfires, camels and near starvation, Wilber told him that he needed to take martial arts training in the future so he would have some means to protect himself.

Zayd had some of the best martial arts instructors from the military visit him and brought other kids along to practice with him. Zayd knew Karate well, understood Wing Chun, and had a lot of knowledge of Kung Fu.

The reunion between young Zayd and Wilber would be a happy occasion. Sheikh Omar knew his son Zayd viewed his father as the most important person in his life, and they had numerous discussions that clearly elucidated that point, but the second person most influential in Zayd's life was in fact Wilber O'Toole. There was no doubt about it.

There were a lot of wealthy Arab men whom Sheikh Omar personally knew and knew their family's well. He knew none of their sons matched Zayd and his future because of what he did and his higher calling to all elements in life. In a way Sheikh Omar was sad because he knew that probably Wilber O'Toole had more influence on Zayd's direction in his life than his own father. But it was all good because in the end it was where Zayd was going that counted. Sheikh Omar owed Wilber far more than what Wilber understood.

Wilber left his CIA phone in a special container under the floor in one of his rooms well-hidden and locked. The CIA's trackers would think he was at home. He took his John Dunbar phone with him, and fake identity created for a John Dunbar for a mission a long time ago the agency most likely forgot about. He had the means of Travel without Pat Barton tracking him and hassling him. Theoretically, he should have contacted a person in the agency to report foreign travel just like he was supposed to report meeting foreigners, but he was so pissed off now, if they yanked his security clearance, he would simply say sayonara, let some Girl Scouts take care of your business. Call me when you realize you need a Cowboy.

John Dunbar took the Acela to NYC and a cab to JFK airport and flew from there to Paris with only carry on with essentials like toothbrush, tooth paste and a change of underwear and sox.

By the time the DCI wanted a private meeting with Wilber he was long gone. It took them 48 hours to find out he was nowhere to be found. Alerts were put out for places like Singapore because they thought that's where he would be heading. Paris was the last place in the world Wilber would go. Finally, when they figured out, he might have gone to Paris based on Airport Security video, he was already on a private jet to the middle east. Wilber had disappeared which added significantly to Pat

Barton's indigestion issues.

The plan worked out well. Wilber and Xinxin rekindled their relationship, with their lover's tryst in Paris completely invigorating their love making and satisfaction with each other.

Xinxin had not had the proper time and place to inform Wilber what went on in Beijing. She knew it would hit Wilber like a ton of bricks to learn she was being used to helping the MSS trap him.

"They were with me all the time and threatening to kill me the Chinese style, choking me to death where I would poop my pants as I was dying." To Xinxin's surprise, it didn't faze Wilber at all.

"Xinxin, you were just an innocent bystander. In the deadly game of the spy business, people like you are coerced into doing things like this. There was nothing you could do about it. You had some very tough bastards that would use you any way they wanted."

"You are not upset with me that I almost betrayed you?"

"I look at it differently. You were not betraying me at all, you basically were a hostage with a gun to your head and you did what they forced you to do. In many cases they make women do far worse than what you experienced. You are lucky you got the hell out of there without suffering too much."

"Maybe that's the reason why I'm having a hard time to adjust to all of this."

"I'm no longer employed against the Chinese and the Russians. They have real spies with real purposes they need to deal with. If they concentrate on me that will open gaping holes elsewhere, they will quickly regret it, because there are others out there just as good as I am that can do them a lot of damage. I think when they no longer see me in action and they must deal with all the other spies in the world, their attention will be focused elsewhere."

Wilber knew better than to stand in line for some venue like the Louve where his picture would be taken and CIA's artificial intelligence reading French security cameras would tag him and start tracking. During the 48 hours of lover's bliss, they spent time either in a taxi or a covered boat or out in the French countryside drinking fine wines and eating wonderful French food. There was plenty to do in 48 hours. As example, the one-hour helicopter tour was nice.

The smartest thing that Wilber did was to pay a Taxi driver a large fee to drive them all day long around the French Countryside. They got to see far quicker than most tourists since the Taxi driver knew exactly the best way to get to and from avoiding traffic jams.

True to his word, Sheikh Omar was on the private jet and while it was being refueled to make sure they took off with a full tank of gas allowing them to fly nonstop to the UAE, there was the pleasant surprise that Zayd was on the plane with his father. This was a special gift to Zayd who had impressed his father for the past couple of years to allow him to travel with him to meet up with his friend so they could talk on the plane.

The seats on the private jet allowed people to face each other as some seats were turned 180 degrees for that purpose.

When they were on the plane flying to the UAE, Zayd was seating directly across from Wilber who was sitting next to Xinxin, and Sheikh Omar was facing Xinxin.

Xinxin had that special sheen on her face women often get after having great sex and gratification.

Zayd and Wilber talked the entire time flying to UAE. Sheikh Omar had a bed further back in the cabin of his private jet and excused himself and said he was very sleepy and went to sleep for most of the trip. Xinxin ended up with her head resting on Wilber's shoulder sleeping most of the time as young Zayd and Wilber got into quite a few different discussions. Zayd, having fully read a lot of science fiction novels, had many questions. Zayd knew that Wilber had the answers to many of his questions, and he was interested in how Wilber thought about some of this science fiction.

As far as Zayd was concerned, Wilber was his best friend in the world and the person who enlightened him the most. Granted he had fantastic teachers, but it was Wilber who steered him initially in the right direction so he could start learning much.

Zayd was a human sponge he soaked up information like few could realize. Wilber in a short period of time assessed Zayd as an intellectual with an IQ quite higher than most people many years older than he was. Through Zayd, Wilber thought there was some hope in the world because in his future with all his future financial might Zayd could help charter a better path for the world.

During the campfire discussions years past when Wilber rescued young Zayd, he asked Wilber, what do you think of Allah and Mohamed?

"It's simple. Allah is God and Mohamed was a prophet."

"Do you believe Mohamed spoke to God?"

Zayd wasn't quite ready for the response but when he heard it, that shaped his opinion of Wilber greatly.

God no doubt can communicate with whomever God chooses. Only God knows why he decided to communicate with Mohamed.

One thing we know is after that event happened, there was a fantastic change in Mohamed who was viewed at the time by the public many years more advanced than his age. Even at the age of 20 Mohamed was deemed so fair and distinguished that often he was picked by both sides in a quarrel to arbitrate issues. No doubt Mohamed had an incredible handle on things."

Zayd really started thinking about Wilber's comments and before he could ask another question, Wilber even transfixed his thoughts even more by a simple question.

"We know that when Mohamed was a young man he was viewed as an intellectual and far brighter than most people. If God was to choose to talk to a person here on planet Earth. Who do you think he would prefer to converse with? A dummy or a brilliant thinker like Mohamed?

"Wilber, I never thought of that before in the way you just explained it. I can now clearly see why God picked Mohamed to converse with."

"As you will discover in your education, there are others who claimed God talked to them. Take for example Moses who received the 10 commandments. And then of

course there was Noah's arch. Its only logical God would speak to man now and then when God feels it's necessary."

"Wilber, do you believe in Mohamed?"

"Why not, he left his mark on this planet and his communications were rather sophisticated for the times back then."

"What should I do about my religion?"

"You have someone close to guide you, your father. When you need answers to religious questions, you should seek his advice. He also can easily arrange for experts to guide you. Keep your mind open to lots of ideas because the universe is huge. We are primativie peoples and have very little knowledge of the universe.

"Scientists seem to think they know a lot about the universe."

No matter how bold and inteligente scientists wish us to think they are, the fact of the matter is, the universe is full of mysteries none of us will know about during our lifetimes.

"Is there alien life out there?"

"I have no idea. I've never met an alien. But I know the universe is huge and I do not discount anything including God creating billions of planets with people like us on them."

"If that's the case why hasn't God informed us?"

"My guess is God tell us information when its apparent we need to know about it."

Wilber liked Zayd. He was so bright and energetic. He would be proud if he were his own son.

Thanks to the fact the plane was registered to Sheikh Omar they were cleared to fly over Jordan and Saudi Arabia so the flight from France to the UAE was almost a straight shot and the weather was cooperating with a nice tail wind.

Even though at times Wilber would like to have taken a nap, Zayd kept them engaged in a pleasant discourse. Time flew and before you knew it the pilot informed the cabin crew to prepare Sheikh Omar for landing and departure from the private jet. Thanks to the routing and the tail winds for part of the flight the flight only took seven hours.

But for Sheikh Omar, it had taken him fourteen hours round trip.

Xinxin was also waking up about the time Sheikh Omar awakened so he could freshen up and take a sprite shower.

Sheikh Omar turned towards Zayd and spoke in English vice Arabic, "Are you enjoying the flight?"

"Yes father, I've really enjoyed my time with Wilber my good friend."

"He's a good friend?"

"Yes, he will be my friend for life. Like you taught me, if you find a good friend feel lucky. I feel lucky."

"Are you saying that just because he saved your life?"

"No father, Wilber goes way beyond that. In the past six or seven hours we had a great discussion, and he clarified a lot of things for me. I know I'm facing a great man who proved he's courageous when he saved my life, but in the past six hours I've learned a lot about him."

"Such as?" Sheikh Omar asked.

"Wilber inspired me in the past for my music education and my martial arts training and now he inspires me even more. I know I will be a better person in life by knowing this wonderful person we are so lucky to have as a friend."

In the past year, Zayd had astonished his father with numerous comments that made him so proud of his son. Sheikh Omar was touched because his son was no fool and an intellectual, he could read a person like a leaf. His interpretation of his observations was astute. These comments from Zayd were quite powerful.

***

Chapter Nine

Dubai

The plane landed and moved into a hanger where the doors were shut before everyone got out of the plane into the Limo waiting for them. Nobody could see who arrived and the windows on the Limo were coated, nobody could see inside them.

The car was soon out of the airport and drove a distance to a waiting helicopter. There was nobody around them as this was clearly an isolated location. Once they were all in the helicopter traveling light it was airborne and flew over Dubai on its way out to a mansion in the countryside.

Sheikh Omar had his own desalination plant producing more water than he needed. The excess water was pumped out to sprinkler heads that were slowly transforming this vast estate into a green zone. From the air, people knew someone wealthy must live there. The added foliage also had a significant impact on the air temperature around the palace. It got warm later in the day and seemed to cool off faster as the sun was setting.

The helicopter landed on their private landing pad a short distance from the mansion, but there were a couple golf carts there waiting to take them directly to the mansion and to shield them from the hot sunlight during the short journey.

The two golf carts pulled up in front of the Mansion and there was the welcoming committee who only stepped outside when they received notice from men driving the golf carts via walkie-talkies.

There were four wives and about fifteen children of different sizes and shapes. It was clear to Wilber that Zayd was older than all the other kids by at least two years or more.

Ahead of the line was wife number one, Emily, which also happened to be Zayd's mother who was so happy her husband Sheikh Omar took Zayd to Paris with him. She encouraged the expansion of the relationship between the two every chance she got to make sure Zayd would one day rule the Sheikh Omar's financial empire and take good care of his mother.

Emily didn't mind if Zayd did to his brothers what everyone knew the young Turks did to their brothers. That was the way of life in the Middle East where the culture was well defined over thousands of years.

When the four wives saw Sheikh Omar smiling the way he was, they knew he was happy. They also knew young Zayd was thrilled to spend time with his idol.

Sheikh Omar was informed by the flight crew how young Zayd had kept Wilber awake talking the entire trip which was okay, but he knew then the poor man needed time to rest.

The plan was they would have a welcoming meal that would no doubt make Wilber sleepy, and they would be taken to the main guest room that was usually reserved for head of states or multi-billionaires, that included private assistants to take care of all their needs. These people men and women were dedicated and had the most important jobs taking care of distinguished guests. The women knew that if the guest wanted to parley with her vagina, it was expected she give it up.

But her pay was stratums above most people in the Kingdom, the price she had to pay to become wealthy at an early age. These women were also gracious Sheikh Omar never wanted to tap on them, so they only had to give it up very infrequently, but knew they had to do it when it really counted.

As planned and predicted, the meal with the entire family was wonderful. The chef was fabulous, the food was great. And as soon as Sheikh Omar saw Wilber yawn a few times he instructed his personal valet to take the couple to their guest room where they could take a nap and a bath or shower later after they had a chance to sleep off some of the jet lag.

Thirty minutes after Wilber swallowed his last bite, he was sound asleep holding an appreciative Xinxin in his arms. Xinxin knew she was a coward and gutless, but she knew Wilber was completely in love with her. She would try to find a way to gather courage so they could have a realistic relationship. But for now, her mind was disturbed because she now experienced two separate scary episodes because of Wilber. She didn't know if she could handle much more before she cracked and had to say goodbye forever.

Wilber was so out of it he slept for twelve hours. Xinxin got up, took care of business, and went out into the outer room of the guest enclosure where she could leave Wilber sleeping and not disturb him. She soon discovered women were there to dress and pamper her. Some of them spoke with a British accent which she liked. They might be servants, but they were well paid college graduates from England though they were Arabic working off their college debts.

These lovely women only had debt to Sheikh Omar who paid for everything. He only stipulated they assist for a few years until they found a legitimate permanent mate, then he would simply thank them for their services and send them away to enjoy their lives. It was all gentleman's agreement. No written contracts existed because in this part of the world a person's promise was more important than any piece of paper.

Some of the women stayed around a lot longer than planned simply because Sheikh Omar made them feel like they were part of the family. In the broader scheme of things, they really were family. Sheikh Omar treated them as if they were part of his own family.

These women felt safe with Sheikh Omar and his four wives. Everything worked to perfection. They all figured out how to make it happen and they were very successful. It was a well-run organization built on family principles. Everyone was treated with due respect and even though in reality there were four families involved from four wives, it truly was one big happy family as each brother and sister viewed each other as a sibling. They were all taught in Muslim and Arab ways. There was no misunderstanding ever.

Every one of them knew Wilber had saved Sheikh Omar's son's life at the 11th hour and they had to flee on camel across the desert in a modern- day rendition of Lawrence of Arabia.

Young Zyad didn't have to embellish anything because anything he was going to cover was already in the press when the police and the government officials arrived too late to save the boy from getting his head cut off by terrorists. They of course were

shocked to see all the dead bodies strewn around with no sight of the boy. They also had no idea how Wilber played into all this. Only one person knew Wilber, the Cowboy, saved young Zyad. Unfortunately, that person died in a mysterious plane crash and Pat Barton replaced him.

There was no traceability to Wilber in the kidnapping rescue. The Arabs were tight lipped and would never discuss it with anyone. That is partly the reason why the CIA had no knowledge that Wilber was now in the Middle East and would never guess he was hanging out with Sheikh

Omar and his family.

Wilber would be smiling if he only knew half the grief Pat Barton was now dealing with. There were a couple interesting questions floating around. One was: Is Wilber O'Toole now hanging out with Edward Snowden? How soon would Russia or China announce Wilber's defection? Everyone has their price.

The only rule Wilber broke was not to inform a special officer he was leaving the country. The only thing the CIA could do to him when Wilber returned was to fire him, which Wilber didn't care now. This latest event with the dickhead Pat, had soured his attitude greatly.

Pat Barton was now learning a big lesson in life. Had he not stepped on Wilber O'Toole's dick the way he did, he would not be having all these meetings with the DCI and DD/P who were quickly forming the opinion Pat Barton was one dumb SOB and how the hell did he get into that position?

That's how it is in Federal Bureaucracies, the peter principal where all the dickheads rise to the top because they are no threat to their superiors. Pick a dumb SOB to be under you and you never have to worry about him taking your job.

After Xinxin was all dressed up in Arabic clothing, she was ushered into the forum where she was suddenly with the four wives who greeted her graciously. Wife number one, Emily who happened to be Zayd's mother was a huge proponent of making this woman feel at home. She had seen firsthand how Wilber had influenced her son and he was making great strides in life in music, literature, martial arts, and making his father happy by the intellectual nature of interacting with his father who received those numerous interchanges with Zayd feeling great pleasure.

The four wives were well educated and since most of them all spoke in a British accent it made the room much nicer conversing with the beautiful Singapore woman who spoke in a manner almost identical British accent.

It did not take the four wives long to appreciate Xinxin who was friendly and full of smiles and very happy to be there knowing she would be safe with Wilber and protected by Sheikh Omar and his family.

This trip was not only a vacation, but it also felt like a relief. Xinxin could visit here with these wonderful and lovely Sheikh Omar wives.

Women are curious as to what the other women do. And after Xinxin informed the four wives she traded Crypto Currencies; they were suddenly enthralled and wanted to know everything about Crypto Currencies.

The wives all had their personal computers, their cell phones, and any modern electronic convenience. During several hours while Wilber was sound asleep and

feeling great, the four wives set up Xinxin with a computer terminal so she could show them the magic of Crypto Currency trading.

Xinxin was showing off just a little, nothing serious and did thirty trades. She had no losing trades, and the four wives were super animated when they saw Xinxin make over a million $$ U.S. Dollars in profit in the span of less than two hours. It was just like magic. Now suddenly, the four Sheikh Omar wives were looking at Wilber in a new light. The fact this gorgeous woman who knew how to make fast money was so in love with Wilber touched them deeply.

Because of their Muslim training and teaching, they believed in manifest destiny and that Allah brings people together for a reason. They knew Allah had brought Wilber into their lives not only to rescue Zayd, but for other reasons and here suddenly, they were seeing more magic with Xinxin. Xinxin soon felt the warmth of the four wives who treated her like she was their favorite sister.

A powerful man like Sheikh Omar leaves nothing to chance. He has bugs, secret videos, and all kinds of spyware all over to monitor his household to make sure nothing exists that should trouble him. Among the staff he also had several well-placed spies who kept him informed.

The four wives learned long ago they were an extension of each other to Sheikh Omar. It was in their best interest to look out for each other as if they were blood relatives along with their children. When they unanimously like something like they did Xinxin, it's quite apparent. Their love and grace were extended to Xinxin who felt warmth, respect, and friendship. It made her trip there even far more satisfying because of this unique atmosphere the women created for her.

When Xinxin eventually left the Middle East and went to Singapore which was a much shorter trip than to Paris, she had no regrets. It was all worthwhile. She also had four new friends and clients! There were a lot of Crypto Currency Reps that would love to have these four clients.

Wilber eventually awakened fully rested but starting to feel some slight hunger. His room servants did what he expected, they bathed him and put him into Arabic clothes including a Keffiyeh head piece and the long Thawb clothing, Wilber looked like an Arab short of a beard. But since he had not shaved in a couple days, the beard was now starting to appear. In two weeks', time when he left, people would not know he was not an Arab.

After Wilber was sporting his new looks, he was escorted into a large room which was the main family gathering room. Between all the sofas and chairs, over forty people could be comfortable in the room if they had guests over, which sometimes happened.

Wilber was escorted to a nice chair in the middle of the room and soon the four wives brought in his princess Xinxin who was now dressed up almost in an Arab attire reserved for such special occasions. Arab women are experts on makeup. The Ottoman Empire was very sophisticated in the way women were portrayed especially to the young Turks. Xinxin looked like a princess some young Turks fell in love with.

Wilber who was already in love with Xinxin felt a rush of enthusiasm like almost never before. The four wives, so enthralled with Xinxin and her magic making money so quickly, did all their tricks to make her utterly seductive to her love. Even Sheikh

Omar was enthralled by Xinxin's looks. He motioned his first wife over so he could whisper something in her ear nobody else could hear.

"My dear I'm so very proud of you for taking good care of my guest. I'm going to reward you later today and make love to you like we haven't had in a long time."

The first wife was suddenly beaming with the rest of the wives wondering what the secret message was all about. So that the other women didn't feel bad at a convenient moment she whispered a sweet lie into wife number two's ear, "Our husband informed me he's proud of our conduct in how we are treating the guests. I'm so happy for the encouragement."

The second wife was then smiling and passed the sweet lie on to number three who then informed the fourth. Life was suddenly wonderful in the mansion.

In short order the entire family was brought in to visit with their guests. This was a very rare occasion. All the children were clean and well dressed for the special occasion.

Their father then stood up and walked out into the middle of the room to address everyone.

"We are very privileged to have our distinguished guest, Wilber O'Toole and his first wife Xinxin from Singapore visiting us today."

Sheikh Omar had no choice but to award the couple a temporary marriage especially if they were to have sex under his roof to make in accordance with Islamic Law, which he graciously did.

"Wilber please stand so all my Children can see you."

Wilber stood and Sheikh Omar said, "Wilber is the person who saved Zayd's life when he was kidnapped by terrorists."

It was suddenly very quiet in the room. Every person listened to Sheikh Omar's words with careful attention.

"A few days ago, Wilber asked to come visit us. We have a special connection to him so I was so pleased he would request such a visit. Most of you do not know it but Zayd's rescue took extreme heroism."

Wilber looked at the large family and could not help but feel their vibrations as they listened to Sheikh Omar.

"Wilber could have easily lost his life saving Zayd, when everyone else gave up saying nothing could be done, out of nowhere came Wilber who confronted me and said he wanted a chance to save my son. How could I say no to him. All hope was given up anyway."

Sheikh Omar knew that when all the fighting was over according to official records there were over one hundred dead men found in the Terrorists hideout. There had been a lot of shooting. There has never been a full NEWS account of what happened. Only a very few knew.

"After Wilber rescued Zayd, they rode across the desert for three days on camels with small amounts of food and a small quantity of water. It took a great man like Wilber to bring Zayd back to us alive."

Sheikh Omar knew after talking with Zayd that during those long lonely scary nights out in the middle of the desert where the two easily could have been killed, they found some dead wood to make a fireplace to warm up. In those nights during long discussions Wilber gave Zayd valuable advice including things about literature and music. Sheikh Omar continued with his discussion:

"Zayd plays the beautiful violin now thanks to his time spent with Wilber. He also reads more books than anyone in his school and is the top student in his class, all because of the influence Wilber O'Toole, his savior gave to him."

"In planning for this trip, Zayd asked me to travel with him to Paris to get Wilber O'Toole because his visit here has to be a big secret because of who he is and what he does for a living."

Sheikh Omar then turned towards Wilber and smiled while he looked directly at him when he said the next statements:

"In preparation for that trip Zayd informed me he wanted to play a violin composition for Wilber to show him that his discussions were not wasted and that Zayd took to heart all his recommendations."

"Wilber, thank you for saving my son. Now my son wants to give back to you what you rightfully have earned. Zayd please come forward."

To the side was a grand piano Wilber did not realize was in the room until the music started playing. For this very special event, Sheikh Omar brought in a concert pianist and paid the fee to the symphony for her next concert in Vienna.

Soon young Zayd and the concert pianist were playing Mozart - Violin Sonata No. 36, F Major.

Wilber listened to a lot of classical music in the past and was astonished how good Zayd performed. Everyone in the room was rather transformed. They had heard Zayd's lovely violin playing in the past, but with the concert pianist adding to the music it truly was a remarkable moment.

Zayd's mother had tears flowing down. She was so moved.

Xinxin was also moved knowing Wilber had made such an impression on the young man to put forth the effort to achieve such a mature interpretation of Mozart's, very eloquent composition.

[Mozart - Violin Sonata No. 36, F Major K. 547 (1788) [van Keulen/Brautigam] - YouTube]

Zayd's Russian violin instructor was there on special invite and warned not to mention anything he heard or saw in the palace. The violin instructor knew how cheap life was in the Middle East and knew better than to blab these remarkable revelations now ongoing.

The instructor was recording in his thoughts any areas where Zyad might need improvement. But for this performance, Zayd wanted more than anything to give something back to Wilber to save his life and giving him valuable advice. This violin sonata with the concert pianist would not be performed today without Wilber's past involvement.

Everyone in the room loved the music in the room and more importantly they were very happy one of their relatives was performing it.

The performance was only seventeen minutes long, seeming like a short eternity, but nobody wanted it to end. Few in the room had ever heard this performance with a piano before. It truly was a unique experience watching Zayd play his heart out to his special friend who he had great fondness for. Their seven-hour conversation on the plane flying here added greatly to the friendship. Zayd knew he had a special friend that none of his classmates had.

The violin instructor knew Zayd made no mistakes, and his delivery was perfect. The pianist also played to perfection and even though the two of them only had a few practice sessions together at a recording studio for strict confidentiality and the big surprise, they were almost like a team of precision.

As soon as the performance ended, Zayd lowered his bow and his violin to his sides and bowed. There was major applause then suddenly Zayd's brothers and sisters ran up to him and threw their arms around him. Zayd had captivated this family audience and his mother had tears streaming. Sheikh Omar, who was a hard man had watered eyes and a couple tears. It was an emotional moment for everyone.

Wilber walked over to Zayd and gave a deep bow of respect. Sheikh Omar watched that closely and observed the great respect this superhero paid to his son. That also was a defining moment in the relationship of the friendship that would last for the rest of their lives.

Sheikh Omar valued Wilber greatly. He understood a lot of things in life and knew about a lot of world events and the skull doggery that went on.

Now it was time for the big feast. Slowly the crowd was moved off to the large dining hall that could easily accommodate one hundred people for grand events. Tables and chairs set up for this private family event easily accommodated everyone. Zayd obviously had to be seated next to his friend Wilber who was seated also next to Xinxin.

Across from Wilber Sheikh Omar sat surrounded by his four wives in pecking order with number one and number two next to him and number three and four outside them. That's how it is in a fully Muslim traditional family. No alcohol, no pork, no divorce, and simply a strong family unity full of mutual respect. Of course, that all worked out to perfection except for the Young Turks of the Ottoman Empire.

On one side of the four wives was the concert pianist happy she would be receiving $100,000.00 for her performance in Vienna and the Violin instructor who just received a huge tip via Paypall to his personal accounts.

The concert pianist immediately took a liking to Xinxin due to her Chinese ethnicity as well as the fact they could converse in Chinese.

The Chinese pianist didn't assume that Wilber could speak fluent Chinese and asked Xinxin in Chinese, "Tell me Xinxin, how is Wilber like in bed?"

Xinxin of course blushed and was astonished by the question but even more astonished by Wilber's response that got her laughing so hard she almost fell over.

「女士，你知道嗎，每次把欣欣輪胎上的輪圈敲掉是我的責任。我們 是在穆斯林國家。我在這裡可以有四個妻子。你願意做我的第二個妻子嗎？ 把你輪胎上的輪圈敲掉嗎輪胎？"

Nǚ shì, nǐ zhīdào ma, měi cì bǎ xīnxīn lúntāi shàng de lún quān qiāo diào shì wǒ de zérèn. Wǒ men shì zài mùsīlín guójiā. Wǒ zài zhèlǐ kěyǐ yǒ u sì gè qīzi. Nǐ

yuànyì zuò wǒ de dì èr gè qīzi ma? Bǎ nǐ lúntāi shàng de lún quān qiāo diào ma Lúntāi?"

[Madam, just so you know, it's my responsibility to knock the rims off Xinxin's tires every time. We are in a Muslim country. I can have four wives here. Would you like to be my second wife and get the rims knocked off your tires tonight?"]

The Chinese pianist was utterly shocked! "You speak Chinese?"

我努力學習中文，因為我對中國的歷史和文化很著迷。 我經常研究中國，包括政府、文化、組織犯罪、孔子、中國佛教、唐詩和音樂。

Wǒ nǔ lì xuéxí zhōngwén, yīnwaèi wǒ duì zhōngguó de lìshǐ hé wénhuà hěn zháomí. Wǒ jīngcháng yánjiū zhōngguó, bāokuò zhèngfǔ, wénhuà, zǔ zhī fànzuì, kǒ ngzǐ , zhōngguó fójiào, tángshī hé yīnyuè.

[I've worked hard to learn Chinese because I'm fascinated about China's history and culture. I study China often including the government, culture, organized crime, Confucius, Chinese Buddhism, Tang Poetry, and music.]

"What Chinese music do you like?"

"There are a lot of great Chinese male and female singers, but I also like Chinese

Classical Music."

"Give me an example."

I found Piano Concerto "The Yellow River"-Poems of Motherland: LÜ Jia, Haochen Zhang and NCPAO quite pleasing."

"May I ask what you learned from Confucius?"

"After reading some of Confucius Analects I discovered I'm merely a Noble Savage."

The lovely pianist smiled broadly because she realized Wilber was so steep in the understanding of many aspects of China. It was no doubt in her mind now why he was with this incredibly beautiful lady Xinxin of Chinese ancestry from Singapore.

"I would agree to your request, but I doubt you would keep me. Plus, with a beautiful friend you have like Xinxin, I know you are just kidding me."

"One never knows. But did you know Sheikh Omar could legally marry us tonight if you were really interested?"

"After hearing a little bit today, I would be too scared. I'm sorry."

"Now you know how I feel," Xinxin said.

The pianist is beautiful, but she also saw Xinxin is an extreme beauty and felt inferior to her because of Xinxin's exquisite attractiveness.

They were soon chatting away in Chinese, but the pianist was now slightly cautious as she now knew Wilber knew everything she said.

Zyad turned into a chatter box, but under the circumstances, Wilber felt obligated to engage the young man whom he had a special bond to due to that hazardous assignment a few years before and was one of his defining moments in life.

"By the way Zyad, I was impressed with your violin performance. It made me quite happy."

Sheikh Omar overheard the comment, and the way Wilber delivered it was convincing.

"Thank you, Wilber, I did that for you."

"I really appreciate that; it makes me feel really good you would work so hard to achieve such a great performance."

"Wilber, I owe my life to you. That performance was to tell you how much you mean to me."

"Zyad if I ever have a son, I hope he is like you."

"Thank you, Wilber, I like that."

"You are most welcome. Thank you for that wonderful performance."

"It was my distinct pleasure, Wilber."

"Zyad, may I tell you something?"

"Sure, Wilber, anytime."

"Zyad, see this lovely lady Xinxin next to me?"

"Yes, she is very pretty."

"I'm in love with her."

"I can see why."

Wilber wasn't looking at Xinxin, but all four Sheikh Omar's wives were, and they suddenly saw Xinxin's crocodile tears. Wilber didn't know he struck a nerve in Xinxin. The four wives had tears in their eyes as well. Sheikh Omar's eyes also watered up a bit. It was an emotional moment for all of them."

None of Sheikh Omar family knew about the recent defining moment in Xinxin and Wilber's lives when they came close to being killed by Chinese MSS top assassins. The fact they gave diplomatic status the person who would kill Wilber underscored how bad the MSS wanted to kill him for retaliation in killing a female Chinese spy Faye Wong sent to kill him with a knife that had a blade covered with a deadly poison.

Sadly, had the Chinese MSS not sent their female spy to kill Wilber she wouldn't be dead now.

The Diplomat would have to learn to live with one eye since his other was permanently dysfunctional.

The other three MSS spies were not so lucky. They were known as illegals in the spy tradecraft. That meant they traveled on fake documents, had no diplomatic protection, and were caught trying to kill two people.

The Singapore Government had no reason to go heavy on the Chinese, but Americans had a few people they wanted to swap. That's how it works. Cash in Advance and prisoner swaps during such auspicious occasions.

One of the tantalizing details the DCI had the DD/P pound into Pat Barton was a couple of their spies were now out of Chinese custody and torture because of a Cowboy.

Pat Barton now was starting to realize he was pissing up a rope if he kept openly going after Wilber O'Toole. He then started thinking about other methods.

As part of the celebration, the pianist was paid a nice sum to play after dinner music and soon performed Chopin Nocturns. Workmen moved the piano into the dining hall while they were all eating. Nobody hardly noticed.

Then they were all in for another pleasant surprise.

In the entertainment industry always saves the best for last.

"Wilber, I'm going to play another song now for you. I want to thank you for all the guidance you gave me during our tip on the camels when we escaped the terrorists," Zyad said.

Zayd, if you perform as well as you did the last time, you will make me very happy."

"I will I promise. I worked very hard on this piece."

"I'm looking forward to hearing you play again."

"Thank you."

Zayd walked over by the piano where the workers had moved his violin. The pianist played a few keys so that Zayd could accurately tune the violin. They then started performing that song no family members would forget. Zayd's performance of Brahms Violin Sonata No. 3 in D minor, Op. 108 was videotaped sound included.

[Brahms Violin Sonata No. 3 in D minor, Op. 108 - YouTube]

This 22-minute performance was slightly more than the previous Mozart performance. Brahms was a more modern composer and this Romantic Period composition had amazing melodies and techniques.

Once again, the family gave Zayd a rousing applause. This was one of the happiest days in Sheikh Omar's life in part for a few reasons.

First, Sheikh Omar's special friend was here with his Asian lover who got to see his son Zayd's spectacular performance, and he knew his son would also have a huge positive influence on all his brothers and sisters. This will be something the family could build upon.

Secondly, Sheikh Omar understood having private discussions with the violin instructor and later the pianist after a couple practice sessions to prepare for the private concert performance, reported his son Zayd by all accounts, was borderline genius.

Zayd had tremendous potential and at his present level of performance, he could wind up performing in concerts in Europe with the best symphonies including the illustrious French Radio Symphony. Sheikh Omar would lease a large aircraft and fly

the entire family plus special guests should his son be allowed to perform at the London Proms, or in the great concert hall in Vienna.

After bowing to the family, Zayd took his violin and violin-bow over to a standby the piano and sat them there and returned to his seat. On the way, his father stood in his path and grabbed him and hugged him and in Arabic said, "I'm very proud of you Zayd." "Thank you, father, for providing me great music teachers to help prepare me."

As soon as Zayd took his seat, all his brothers and sisters approached him and took turns hugging and congratulating him. They were very proud of their brother.

They also looked fondly on Wilber whom they knew saved Zayd's life when he rescued him from terrorists. This also gave them a chance to see Xinxin up close. She is such a beautiful woman; they would never forget her image as the memories were indelibly etched to this wonderful event in their lives.

The pianist played a few more songs one notably Alexander Scriabin Prelude in B major, Op 11 which endeared Wilber and satisfied Xinxin greatly.

At the conclusion of that performance the children were slowly filtering out, some needing to spend time in the bathroom, others simply wanting to play their computer games.

The Asian pianist closed the lid of the piano keyboard and walked over and sat down on the empty seat next to Xinxin. The last person in the world the pianist expected to see was Xinxin, a beautiful Asian lady, dressed in glamorous Arabic attire, that in bygone eras only the Sultan's could afford to clothe their top concubines in.

The women were in discussions again speaking Chinese. From the earlier exchange when she found out the hard way Wilber could understand everything she said, her language was more guarded, and she knew not to discuss certain matters. But if she and Xinxin were alone together the conversation would flourish!

"I'm going to be performing in Dubai in a couple days, I would like to invite you," the pianist said.

"I'm sure we would love to hear your performance; I'll discuss it with Wilber and see what we can arrange."

"I'll invite his excellency, Sheikh Omar and his son Zayd, you all must come." "What will you be performing?" Xinxin asked.

"I'll be performing Shostakovich Piano Concerto No. 2 in F major."

That sounds so exciting, I hope we can attend. After the meal and when everyone was relaxing in the large family room, Zayd approached his father and related the information about the pianist performing in a few days and requested to go see it. Sheikh Omar then had his personal Valet make all the appropriate arrangements. He would take his first wife Emily, Zayd, Wilber and Xinxin to the concert and they would have a private luxurious balcony booth with lots of security.

***

Dubai is now one of the most protected cities in the world because of all the international banking that goes on there. It's where a lot of the Middle East money flows in and out of. Dubai and nearby Abu Dhabi that make up the UAE are the

Switzerland of that area of the world. Abu Dhabi generates the most income for UAE.

Extraordinary deals are made in Dubai, Abu Dhabi, but also in the nearby nation of Qatar. A significant percentage of all new motion pictures are now funded from deals made in the UAE and Qatar as most of the investment capital originates there. Not only does Hollywood finance films there, so do British, French, German, Chinese, Japanese, and Korean film makers seeking investors in the UAE. When a major motion picture takes in a Billion $$ US, a lot of the returns go to Dubai, Abu Dhabi, and Qatar Banks where movie investors conduct their business.

Qatar a has the 4th largest GDP in the world and is the world's largest export of natural gas and the number one emitter of carbon dioxide according to experts. Because of its location directly across from Iran Persian Gulf central coastline, Qatar is in a strategic location to intervene against Iran and has signed military agreements with USA, Great Britain, and France. Wilber spent time in Doha, Qatar in the past and that's where he met up with the mercenaries, he hired to go help free Zayd.

Dubai on the other hand might be in one of the most strategic locations due to its location near the straits of Hormuz and the Sea of Oman.

Wilber O'Toole worked alongside UAE and Qatar forces helping U.S. forces fighting in Afghanistan and Iraq, as well as being an active, SOG expeditionary participant in the Global Coalition to Defeat ISIS, and in operations against al-Qa'ida and their regional and global affiliates.

Qatar hosts U.S. Navy ship port visits allowing for crew liberty and logistics support and resupply. Qatar also provides support to the Combined Maritime

Forces Combined Task Force 152, a multinational naval partnership that conducts maritime security operations in the Persian Gulf.

During SOG missions in Afghanistan, Wilber spent time at Al Udeid and other facilities in Qatar that serve as logistics, communications, and support facilities for the U.S. Central Command (CENTCOM). Wilber participated U.S. air operations deploying from Qatar, flying incognito into countries, including Iraq, Afghanistan, and Syria, while deploying covertly with SOG troops. UAE personnel were valuable translators in these missions. The most important member on the team was the Arabic translator as far as Wilber was concerned. Wilber knew the region quite well.

Sheikh Omar understood he had to protect Wilber, but he also had to protect his own family and had already experienced firsthand what terrorists can do. He took nothing for granted and was always interested in security arrangements.

With the growing beard, the Arabic clothing and sunglasses, nobody would guess it was Wilber with him.

Xinxin wasn't a well-known person, and with her formal Arabic clothing and wearing a Niqāb partial face cover, nobody would recognize her.

This would be an exciting event for Zayd, and Sheikh Omar knew Zayd would want to sit next to his friend Wilber. Sheikh Omar's wife Emily, and Xinxin would sit next to each other. He would sit on one side of Wilber and Zayd would sit on the other side with the women in front of them. Behind them would be servants and security men. It would be a fun event.

*****

Chapter Ten

Olimpico

The following day started out delightfully as Sheikh Omar wanted to take his son Zayd and Wilber to the outdoors with his prize Falcon Olimpico. They would ride Camels about a mile from the home to a nice area that had an escarpment, that allowed Olimpico to see a good distance into the shallow valley below. A Land Rover would follow behind them carrying cages that included the falcon, and a couple rabbits and two houbara bustards in case there were no wild animals sighted.

Falconry is very popular among Arabs in the Middle East. Falcons are treated with great pride and respect. Many Arabs loved raising falcons and hunting game with them. Falconers are often seen on family outings.

Sheikh Omar named his falcon Olimpico remembering a song he once heard in Italy. Olimpico is sometimes Anglicised as "Olympico" and means "Olympian" in Spanish.

Because of a lack of game in this part of the Middle East, many falconers go to Morocco, Pakistan, and Central Asia to hunt. Sheikh Omar, concerned about personal security decided it would be far safer to import animals such as rabbits and houbara bustards and turning them loose on his property.

With his personal desalination plant and ample potable water, several artificial ponds with reeds, pond grass and Poaceae were created next to a private eight-hole golf course providing natural habitat to the animals brought in for the Falconry sport.

Falconry is believed to have started in Central Asia approximately around 2000 B.C., with the steppe people who learned to tame falcons and use them to hunt. Ancient hunters had no guns or other modern hunting tools and depended on hunting dogs and tamed falcons to capture animals.

Falconry also has ancient roots in Japan and the Middle East. Horsemen the Central Asia introduced the sport to Europe.

Genghis Khan's passion was falconry. Genghis Khan kept 800 Sake Falcons and 800 attendants to take care of them and demanded that 50 camel- loads of swans be delivered every week the falcons preferred game animals. Marco Polo reported that Kublai Khan employed 10,000 falconers. The size and scale of that operation suggests part of it was to gather food.

The four men in the Land Rover each had an AK-47 to protect Sheikh Omar but also, they would hold the camels and release the rabbits and houbara bustards when directed by Sheikh Omar.

This was another great moment for Zyad, who the Falcon Olimpico knew well.

Zyad was wearing a long leather glove that had a seven-inch-long padded cylindrical cover over the leather near his hand. The leather portion of it went to his elbow. That large cylindrical padded area allowed the falcon to easily hold on. Zyad carefully reached into the cage and grabbed the leather leash attached to one of Olimpico's legs. Simply by routine activity, Olimpico knew to climb on Zyad's padded area of the falconer's leather glove, and he would be taken out of the cage.

Most falconry gloves do not have that unique padded area observed by many in Dubai. They usually look like extra padded leather gloves.

Olimpico hated being in the cage. He was happy to be joining his friend Zyad because he knew that meant he would soon be hunting.

Olympio's Aviary the falcon was kept in was shaded, large and comfortable. The sanitation of the Olimpico's Aviary was kept up very well, otherwise it would stink badly. Every day when Olimpico was taken out of the Aviary by a handler for exercise, a cleaning team went in and cleaned and if necessary, hosed it down with disinfectant.

Sheikh Omar was standing on the edge of the escarpment with the cages of the rabbits and houbara bustards. Wilber was standing next to Sheikh Omar and watched Zayd approach them carrying Olimpico. Zayd was smiling because this was going to be a very joyous event watching Olimpico climb into the air and attack its prey.

Olimpico was very conscious of strangers. Olimpico had never seen Wilber before and focused all its attention on that direction. Sheikh Omar knew Olimpico would not be ready to hunt for a while until he absorbed Wilber's presence and decided he was not a threat.

Zayd stopped a couple feet away from his father and Wilber.

Falcons, like many birds of prey, rely on their eyesight to find their food. They can smell, but not as good as vultures and other birds that eat the carcasses of dead animals.

Zayd was not going to release Olimpico until his father either observed wildlife through his binoculars or released a rabbit or one of the houbara bustards. Some people would frown upon observing Olimpico killing these animals, but out in the wild, its exactly what they do to survive.

Sheikh Omar knew Olimpico quite well. He knew when the bird was calm and not distracted by strangers. Olimpico was a smart bird and very close to Zayd and Sheikh Omar. Birds have a unique connection with humans at times and are certainly far more intelligent than we give them credit. They have emotions and attitudes that blend into their ultimate temperament. Sheikh Omar understood that when Olimpico observed his actions and Zayd's interactions with Wilber, the bird would soon settle down and slowly lose interest in Wilber and be primed to hunt animals.

Looking through the binoculars there were no animals in sight. For every rabbit or houbara bustard released, Sheikh Omar often released a second one hoping to establish a future population as he terraformed his property thanks to irrigation and land management. Sheikh Omar was not the only person in the area doing this. Other neighbors terraformed their properties as well and the combination of landscaping in Dubai and the other UAE regions, along with efforts by individuals was slowly reclaiming the desert.

People who have never traveled to Dubai or the UAE would be in for an utter shock at the pace of development. It's like building Orange County California on steroids.

Wilber had no idea how well the Sheikh Omar and Zayd knew Olimpico and all the Falcon's behaviors. They understood how Olimpico reacted to everything from distraction by strangers to detecting a wild animal and potential prey.

As soon as the Sheikh Omar was satisfied no wild animals were in the shallow canyon below them and Olimpico was now relaxed and no longer focused on Wilber it was time to start hunting.

They had been through these routines numerous times before. Sheikh Omar had it worked down to a science. He grabbed one of the rabbit cages and carried it down 50 yards down the escarpment into a sandy area void of trees and plants. He then sat the cage down on the ground and opened its door and stood back. The rabbit hopped out of the cage then turned around and saw the human standing there and turned away from it and started running away perpendicular to Olimpico.

Zayd watching Olimpico knew the bird was tracking the rabbit. As soon as Sheikh Omar returned to the top of the escarpment with the group and nodded at Zayd, the boy let loose of the leather leash and catapulted Olimpico into the air.

The falcon Olimpico climbed up into the sky. Falcons will fly as high as 3500 feet searching for prey. Today Olimpico would not exceed one thousand feet because it already knew where the prey was.

Olimpico circled overhead and at the precise moment desired flew down and grabbed the rabbit and killed it within 20 or 30 seconds. Olimpico didn't eat much of the rabbit because it preferred to eat a houbara bustard birds.

Olimpico was trained to respond to Zayd's bird whistle which meant come back, we'll be serving you dinner shortly. The rabbit would be left for critters in the night that would devour it by the following morning, making up part of the new food cycle for this newly developing area of the desert slowly being changed back to the way it was 100,000 years ago.

Just like many times before, Olimpico flew up and landed on Zayd's Falconer Glove.

The houbara bustards were different in they could fly. These were wild caged birds recently captured from a far-off distance and transported here by aircraft to ensure they were healthy and ready to attempt flying for their lives. Launching of the houbara bustards was a two-man operation to achieve the results they wanted. One person would pull the bird out of the cage while the other person would take the cover off its head so it could see and was immediately terrorized by the image it saw being held by a human.

At the proper time determined it was time to launch the houbara bustards, the bird would be flung up into the air just like it was catapulted. The houbara bustards then flew away in fright not knowing where it was but obviously trying to get away from danger. Olimpico saw the houbara bustard flying away and wanted to be released immediately. Zayd knew not to let Olimpico's leather strap loose until he counted to sixty after the others released the houbara bustard because Sheikh Omar wanted Olimpico to work for his prey and go after it with all its might.

Eventually Zayd launched Olimpico, and the falcon took to the sky chasing after the houbara bustard that had a good head start. Birds even when scared do not fly in a straight line, they sometimes circle back looking for the danger to know where the predator is currently located as to know which way to fly to get away from it. All too often all that does for the poor bird is burn up precious time allowing the falcon to catch up.

Today the houbara bustard made that fatal blunder and gave away one third the distance and Olimpico was soon closing on it. Olimpico also climbed to gain altitude because he was going to utilize speed in the attack. Some falcons can go over 300 miles per hour in a dive if they are up high to give them the time in flight to build up speed. The houbara bustards was probably 500 feet in the air and Olimpico climbed to probably 800 feet to the attack altitude selected by it. Everyone knew when Olimpico tucked in its wings it would start a sharp dive and at 300 feet it could gather quite a bit of speed.

Olimpico flew in so quickly the houbara bustard had no time to react and avoid getting hit. Soon the birds were tumbling together as the houbara bustards fought to get away in a useless struggle. This wasn't Olimpico's first rodeo. It had the killing routine down to a science and stabilized the fall down the remaining 500 feet so it would not be a hard impact and the houbara bustard's body cushioned most of the impact to the ground.

The three men hopped on their camels and rode out to where Olimpico was having his meal. Olimpico liked fresh meat. Olimpico did not like stored meat and would only eat it if it got very hungry and the chefs had to prepare it in a special manner to give it a fresh taste, one might say sushi style.

The other rabbit was let go by the pond grass and a grassy area adjoining the golf course. As far as they knew none of the rabbits had survived. Predators got all of them. They were hoping one day, they would be introduced as a species to the area that would enhance the food chain for nature in general.

The other houbara bustard had a lucky day. It lived for another day.

The three stood there and watched Olimpico eat his meal. Olimpico ate very methodically and took its time. Olimpico knew his friends would wait and would not rush it. There was a lot of meat on the houbara bustard. Because they are an endangered species in many areas now. Enterprising individuals operating in the foothills of the Atlas Mountains farm raised houbara bustards and very carefully removed and incubated eggs to increase the population and sold them to people in Dubai as if they were wild animals. They were also doing an amazing job of releasing some of them into the wild to help increase the wild population. The numbers were slowly coming back.

Some claim climate change was killing off the flocks. The truth of the matter is falconry was such a huge sport now, the demand for houbara bustards was increasing at an unsustainable rate. It had nothing to do with climate. Some of the falconers in Dubai with a lot of spare cash actually paid to set up habitat for the houbara bustards. There was a lot of jubilation in 2022 when some researchers claimed the houbara bustards' population was increasing. Those types of statistics were dubious at best.

While the falconers were out enjoying their time with Olimpico, Sheikh Omar's wives were socializing with Xinxin and getting more familiar with Crypto Currencies. When Wilber and Xinxin eventually left the four wives would show Sheikh Omar how much money Xinxin made for them. Xinxin trades for the four wives covered the jet fuel to fly them in for the visit one hundred to one. More importantly, Xinxin brought them up to speed on changing economic developments in the world and how wealth was handled and how people were going about protecting their assets from government confiscation.

The biggest impact Wilber's visit had was his influence on Zayd who didn't slow down one notch on his quest and thirst for knowledge.

Humans have eight major ways we learn according to some experts. One of them happens to be music. Dr. Tomatis the famous French ears, nose, throat doctor who wanted to help children, developed techniques to treat learning disabled children or children with behavior issues using music therapy. Zyad's vast exposure to top-of-theline music and his extremely successful music training did what experts say music does for us. It opens more areas of our brains to allow enhanced learning. That's what Doctor Tomatis banked on in his theory and applications he developed.

Zyad was being psychologically conditioned by music that enhanced all his learning acumen. He was a stellar performer and progressing in ways that made Sheikh Omar proud of him. His attitude and his activity rubbed off on all his brothers and sisters who followed in his footsteps.

Wilber's visit was like a mid-course correction, Zyad's compass was recalibrated and readjusted at a critical moment in time that ensured success. Sheikh Omar recognized that as well.

Sheikh Omar understood no other person in Zayd's entire lifetime helped him as much as Wilber did. Sheikh Omar and Zayd were both eternally grateful to have such a fantastic friend.

The next morning Wilber had been warned ahead of time he would be awaken early allowing them to go play golf before it got too hot. Sheikh

Omar loved playing golf and his friends loved coming over playing golf on his beautifully landscaped private golf course.

Today, it was just the three, Wilber, Sheikh Omar and his son Zyad who was slowly learning the golf game and as his father explained to him in the future, he would be making deals on the golf course. Plus playing golf would give him an excuse to get away from his future four wives to have fun.

In recent years, Syria and Lebanon were such locations where rich Arabs went to have fun, the most spectacular beautiful women on the planet, drugs, alcohol, and in some cases young men. Golf was a conduit to affairs that could not be conducted in Dubai. Such behavior there would not be tolerated. Dubai is much like Japan where authorities will not tolerate nefarious activities.

The golf course is a place where those important discussions can be made. Privacy and security is better than in a SKIF back at the CIA. Now a new scenario unfolded as Sheikh Omar said things, he didn't mind Zayd hearing because he knew his son would fully understand and appreciate it.

Men often do not know how to communicate love for each other. Especially an Arab to an American where the value systems are miles apart. But Sheikh Omar was a very sophisticated and well-educated man spending six years in London getting trained by the best educators in the world. He would now lay out all his cards.

"Wilber, one of the reasons why I wanted to play golf with you and Zayd today is so we could discuss a few things."

"Alright."

"Wilber, you have touched my family like no other. My son Zayd is alive only because of you. He also is a stellar student because of you. He would never have become an accomplished musician without your influence. You defined him as a person more than I have as his father. He reaches for the sky and has a great thirst for knowledge that only comes about when someone special like you comes along in their lifetime. I want you to know Zayd and I love you. You are like my family now. I'm closer to you than any Arab man I know, and I know a lot."

"Thank you," Wilber said not knowing how to respond.

"You have touched Zayd's heart, but you have also touched mine." "Thank you, that means a lot to me," Wilber said observing how

Sheikh Omar's eyes were watering up as if he wanted to cry.

Zayd was not too far behind in sentiments as he remembered when he was in the terrorist camp watching the shootout and people dying just a few years ago. Zayd was an eyewitness to the brutality and viciousness that went on those fateful days.

After the dust settled and Zayd was home with his father, after he was rescued Sheikh Omar asked his son to tell him everything that happened during the kidnapping crisis.

Zayd was already well along in his mental development and thanks to his exceptional education with the finest teachers and tutors available, he could articulate and recreate the images in his mind with great clarity of what all went down without embellishing anything and simply recapitulating all the events including the three-day camel ride to safety.

Zayd was one of those information sources that was golden. The fabric of his story was high fidelity. Any law enforcement agency would love to have such a great witness to lay out the facts so succinctly.

Zayd had never seen some of these weapons used before in the shooting or the sounds they made or the screaming and cussing in the manner that went on during a vicious battle like that. The incredible image he painted for his father was so vivid and real, as if he was creating a holograph his father could see through his fresh memories at the time.

***

Sheikh Omar recalled during his conversation with Wilber how he had asked Zayd, "were you scared when all this was going on?"

"Father, I was terrified. But I knew my fate was sealed there was nothing I could do about it, and I was soon going to be dead going to heaven. But somehow Allah spared my life."

"You must have been a good person. That's why Allah looked out for you."

"I'm very grateful that you gave me English language training so when Wilber approached me and informed me, he was there to rescue me, I was overwhelmed with happiness I had been spared. We were the only two living people left. All the rest were dead including the men fighting with Wilber killing the terrorists.

"How did you leave the compound where the terrorists were holding you?"

"Wilber said to me we were surrounded by a lot of enemy people that would capture us if they knew who we were. Our only way out was riding on Camels he had about a mile away tied up."

"When did all this happen?"

"In the middle of the night. I think the terrorists gave me food and water just a couple hours prior to the battle."

"What happened then?"

"We simply walked to the camels, there was nobody around. Some of the camels carried water. We took them and the two we rode. Wilber told me we had to ride all night long or we would be dead in the morning."

"Did you stop in the morning?"

"No. Wilber said he would tie me up in my saddle so I would not fall off the camel if I fell asleep. He then tied all the camels together in a string and continued. He said we had to keep moving during the day because people would be looking for us and if we were asleep camped out someplace during the daytime it would not appear like we were Bedouin travelers."

"When did you finally stop?"

"Late the next night we found a good area next to an oasis and camped there and had a campfire."

"Wasn't having a campfire dangerous?"

"Wilber said it would be okay to have a campfire because people who wanted to capture us would not believe we had a campfire going or would be by the oasis. Our clothing and attire were filthy and looked like Bedouin travelers."

"Then what happened?"

"We kept traveling. We rested for a few hours now and then, but we moved along smartly."

"Three days after Wilber rescued me, our camel string came into the UAE, and we were soon approached by military people that had UAE and American uniforms."

"How did they find you?"

"Wilber said he called them on his cell phone when he knew we were safe and no longer behind enemy lines."

"Why did they bring you home so filthy?"

"They offered to clean me and Wilber up, but I said I wanted my father to see me like I was so he would know how I looked after escaping."

"Yes, you both were very filthy, but your mother wanted to hug you no matter how dirty you were."

***

Sheikh Omar then snapped back to present reality but was thinking about all that as he continued his discussion with Wilber.

"Wilber, you do dangerous work. We all would be heartbroken if something happened to you."

"I'll be okay."

"I fear your days are numbered."

"Things are changing, I'm not going to be doing clandestine work behind enemy lines anymore. I have other types of work I'm doing now."

"The fact you came here in the manner you did clearly shows the danger you are always in."

"That's only because of recent events."

"Zayd and I do not want to lose our friend. I'm willing to spend the money to get you out of the CIA and let you live a normal life with no danger."

"I need to do something to pay my bills and survive."

"Wilber, I have the financial resources to back any endeavor you chose to make, plus some. Please consider leaving the CIA and keep our family whole."

"Thank you for your consideration, your excellency. I'm into something new now. I'll no longer be in the spy business, nor will I travel to dangerous places."

"What will you be doing so that you do not face dangers of being a spy?"

"Solar System Investigations." "What does that mean?"

"Dealing with UFO's and Aliens."

"Do UFO's and Aliens really exist?" Sheikh Omar asked in total astonishment. "That I do not know, but I intend to find out." "Will you tell me if you find out?"

"Sure, I will call you and ask you to let me go with you and Zyad to watch Olimpico catch its meal."

"Does that actually mean you would come here for a visit?"

"Absolutely, I'm looking forward to hearing Zyad play more violin music."

"Wilber, I will definitely practice and do well," Zyad said. "I know you will. I have faith in you, Zyad."

"Thank you, Wilber."

"What do you say we finish this golf game then go discover what the women have been up to while we were gone," Wilber said.

"Great idea," Sheikh Omar said.

The real names of people like Sheikh Omar are highly guarded terms that are never exposed even for official legal purposes. In this case only the Sheikh Omar's wives knew his real first name and they knew if they ever revealed it they might get their heads cut off.

Wilber knew the secrecy surrounding the first name and said, "Your excellency, may I ask you a question in private, I do not wish Zayd to hear it."

Sheikh Omar was quite taken back by the request and said, "Zayd, stay here so that Wilber and I can walk away where he can ask me an important question."

"Sure father."

The two men walked about 50 yards away knowing Zayd would not be able to hear the question.

Sheikh Omar was now in suspense waiting and wondering why the extreme privacy.

"Your excellency, we are close friends and no doubt one day Xinxin will be my wife and I can tell she is fond of your four wives. We will have a lifelong relationship also because I'm close to your son Zayd and am looking forward to watching him grow up."

"I'm glad to hear that."

"There really can be no secrets between us. Our futures have a great deal of connection for the future. I want to know just one thing which I will promise never to reveal."

"What is that, Wilber."

"What is your first name?"

Sheikh Omar started laughing hard. It was the funniest thing he ever experienced in his lifetime, and he knew a person would have to be there to get the meaning of it. But he also knew Wilber was serious and knew about Arab customs including hiding.

their real first name. They too operated off alias for their own protection."

"My real name is so bizarre nobody would ever believe it if you divulged it."

"I do not plan on divulging it but I wanted to know," Wilber replied.

"My father was a huge Liberace fan and watched his performances often. When I was born, my father gave me my first two names as Władziu Valentino and my middle name is Liberace." Sheikh Omar said.

"That's very elegant. I like Liberace's performances and I watch them now and then on YouTube." Wilber responded.

"I understand why you would feel that way." Sheikh Omar said.

"How so?" Wilber asked.

"I of course was fascinated by the name which I was not informed until I was a teenager. Most people think my name is Ishak which my father spread as a rumor so that nobody would ever come close to guessing the real name." Sheikh Omar said.

"That's very clever." Wilber said.

"My father was a brilliant man. I see a lot of him in my son Zayd." "That's good he passed down good genes." Sheikh Omar said.

"It is. Do you feel better now knowing who I really am? Sheikh Omar asked.

"It makes me feel closer to you. Thank you." Wilber said.

"And thank you Wilber." Sheikh Omar said.

Zayd was observing from afar and smiled when he saw his father laughing and Wilber smiling. That meant to him good things were happening.

Now the biggest event in Zayd's life occurred that utterly shocked him. Zayd had great admiration and respect for his father who had tremendous influence on him.

Suddenly Władziu Valentino (aka Sheikh Omar) grabbed Wilber and hugged him, and they patted each other on the back. Zayd had never seen his father hug anyone before in his lifetime. And they were patting each other on the back and smiling and talking with great affection. This was a joyful moment for the men who were very pleased they had a good, trusted friend. Sheikh Omar understood Wilber quite well because he put skin in the game for his family, putting his life at risk to save his son. Wilber had already proven himself. He was trustworthy and he was not a coward. He would do what is right. No person could ever have such a good friend.

The men soon returned, hopped into the golf cart and drove back to the mansion where they went looking for their women who were also having a delightful time.

After lunch it was time to rest. Sheikh Omar decided he wanted a private meeting with his first wife, who was really the chairman of the board. She called most of the shots. The other three wives were subservient to her, and she could have them flogged if they pissed her off, but that was never going to happen because she was a pragmatic manager.

To the other wives the signal was their husband was going to have sex with his first wife which he did from time to time, at least that's what they thought, but most of the time the private meetings were simply discussions and planning. The first wife was not big on enjoying sex and was glad the three other wives were there as she viewed them as concubines with a title to take care of her husband's sexual needs when she wasn't in the mood, which was most of the time.

The first wife wanted to know why Sheikh Omar sudden urgency to communicate with her was all about. Władziu Valentino (aka Sheikh Omar) was soon confiding in her everything that transpired on the golf course and how it made him feel so happy.

The first wife felt so uplifted by her husband confiding it all in her with total trust, she lost control and started kissing him in a passionate manner. Sheikh Omar felt so emotional by his wife's actions he reciprocated and soon they were rocking and rolling in a lover's bliss like they had not in a long time. The sexual gratification Sheikh Omar gave his first wife Emily was immense. Emily wondered if it had ever been this good before, even when they were younger.

Emily, number one wife, devoured every moment of it and soon had her own pleasant feelings about Wilber, who inspired all this. Wilber and Xinxin were almost like a gift from heaven to her. Emily, the wife number one had never felt so wholesome in all her life, and it got even better when Sheikh Omar suddenly said, "Emily, I love you."

Emily and the crocodile tears started forming. Sheikh Omar was full of surprises today and he just pierced her heart. It was such a joyous occasion!

The time passed as they held each other tenderly. But Emily was the task master and the conductor of affairs. They had a Symphony to prepare for and could not afford to lounge around as there were numerous preparations to make.

This afternoon, they would descend upon the Zabeel Theatre in Jumeirah Zabeel Saray. The Symphonic Middle East (SME) now one of the finest performing entities not only in the Middle East but on par with Vienna, Paris, and the Proms in London, was going to have a terrific performer, including the pianist that was just here performing in the private concert with their son.

The pianist would perform a Shostakovich piano concerto and afterwards the symphony would play Brahms Symphony number four.

The other three wives were not going as it was decided by Sheikh Omar himself to limit the people in their balcony seating to Wilber, Xinxin, Zayd, Emily, and himself. The three other wives were makeup artists extraordinaire and one of them was a fashion designer who had worked in couture in Paris and Milan.

Everyone going tonight would be looking good, but the men would have on Arab clothing as part of Wilber's disguise. Since it was afternoon arrival, he would be wearing sunglasses to hide most of his appearance. With his head cover, and his growing beard, nobody would know who he could be other than he was in the company of one of the Richest men in the Kingdom.

Since there were only five passengers, they flew to Dubai in the Emeriti Sheikh Omar's helicopter, landed on the top of a building, rode the elevator down to street level where several security men were waiting for them with a couple Limo's and took them on a short drive to the Zabeel Theater.

This beautiful venue had a seating capacity of 636 plus the balcony seats added quite a bit more. For these special performances the balcony seats had dividers put up and privacy enhancements for people like the Emeriti.

This was a wonderful night, but Xinxin seriously wished she was holding Wilber's hand. Maybe at the intermission she would ask Sheikh Omar to switch seats with her because his wife missed him and she missed Wilber. Xinxin was brave, it would not phase her in the least bit.

Soon the music started playing and there she was, the lovely pianist that Wilber shocked the day before with his Chinese language skills.

This was good for Zayd because he felt the music and felt attached to the performer whom he played with a couple times. The music was phenomenal. The orchestra had some of the best musicians in the world along with one of the very best pianists.

Zayd was a musical intellectual. He could feel the notes and devour the music. His temporal transcendence super animated him to the extent of watching his Falcon strike a prey seemed lame in comparison. He took in every minute.

Wilber was happy he could enjoy this time and not worry about anything, a shootout, stabbing, poisoning, or other potential deadly scenarios that often bestowed upon him when he least expected.

The piano music component was quite sensational. Shostakovich

Piano Concerto No. 2 in F major has one of the best melodies ever created for mankind around the 9:30 mark. It was so good that Shostakovich should have repeated it a few times. Playing it just once was like dangling eternity in front of a dying person. When that portion was being played, Xinxin was feeling moist and helpless. She wanted Wilber by her side so badly she could almost cry.

The piano concerto is slightly short at 21 minutes, but it does in fact tax the pianist, like Liszt's concerto's so for the sake of the pianist it was probably good to end early. Soon it was intermission, and they were rearranging the stage after a standing ovation and an encore performance. The two women were huddled and talking and when Xinxin informed Emily how much she wished she could be sitting by Wilber.

Wife number one said this, "Go up to my husband and whisper in his ear, 'Emily wants you to sit next to her now'."

"Is your name Emily?"

"Yes, it is, but please keep that confidential."

"I certainly will Emily, then she hugged her strongly. The women appreciated each other."

Sheikh Omar was in for another surprise of his life suddenly.

Xinxin walked up a couple steps as the balcony seats were angled and walked up to Sheikh Omar and whispered in his ear, "Emily wishes you to now sit next to her."

The Sheikh Omar smiled and stood up and walked down the steps and set by Emily and put his arms around her totally not within Arab custom, but he didn't care, he felt invigorated. Xinxin couldn't see it because she was behind Emily, the tears flowing down, it was as if poor Emily had endured a lot in her life being married to an oil Sheikh, was suddenly blessed with this outpouring of affection and true love. She also loved Xinxin more than ever because it was her doings that made all this possible.

Xinxin smiled at Wilber and sat down next to him and cuddled. It was a lovely moment. Brahms Symphony number four made it even better in a few minutes. Young Zayd was getting one hell of an education tonight. And observing his mother and father showing such tremendous affection towards each other warmed his heart. He then loved Wilber even more because he would not have seen any of this without Wilber. Zayd felt he was having a fantastic experience.

The music played on, the Brahms symphony number four was more than delightful as the acoustics were terrific and the musicians were the best in the world. The sound quality for Brahms symphony created temporal anomalies in their hearts and the rest of the concert passed in a majestic fashion that would inspire poets.

About two minutes before the symphony was going to finish, one of the security men walked up and whispered into Sheikh Omar ear and he in turn whispered into Emily's ear and the two stood up and approached Wilber and Xinxin and said, "We must leave now to avoid the crowd."

Wilber, Xinxin, and Zayd stood up and followed Sheikh Omar and his wife out of the venue to a waiting Limo in front.

They were soon on their way to a heavily guarded exclusive restaurant invite only. Sheikh Omar knew the Crown Prince was going to be there, his personal friend. Sheikh Omar thought it would be interesting to introduce Wilber and Xinxin to the Crown Prince. Also, his son Zayd had not seen the Crown Prince for several years. Sheikh Omar knew the Crown Prince would be happy to meet the CIA man who saved his son from terrorists.

During a private time on his golf course with the Crown Prince one day, Sheikh Omar informed the Crown Prince all about his son's ordeal and how he and the CIA agent had to sneak across the desert on Camels for three days. That story warmed the Crown Prince's heart as it was mildly fascinating.

The Crown Prince was expecting Sheikh Omar and his small group and was outside the Restaurant with a dozen well-dressed military people and lots of security all lined up like a formal reception line.

To Wilber's utter shock at the end of the line was none other than John Burkette the DD/P. "I wonder what the hell he is doing here?"

Sheikh Omar surprised everyone that he took Wilber's hand. In the Middle East male friends hold hands out of respect and admiration. This didn't happen with Sheikh Omar very often who never suffered fools. To see this extravagant display in public had a surreal effect on the military people and the security detail. The security detail knew this was the CIA agent who saved Sheikh Omar's son's life when nobody else could place himself in a huge risk situation.

بعد االنحناء أمام الملك: "صاحب السعادة، اسمحوا لي أن أقدم لكم وقال الإلمارات ي

صديقي العزيز ".ويلبر أوتول

waqal al'iimaratiu baed alainhina' 'amam almaliki: "sahib alsaeadati, aismahuu li 'an 'uqadim lakum sadiqi aleaziz wilbar 'uwtul".

["Your excellency, may I please introduce my good friend Wilber O'Toole," Sheikh Omar said after bowing to the Crown Prince.]

When Wilber saw Sheikh Omar bow, he followed suit and held it slightly longer than Sheikh Omar which in the Arabic world shows both men respect.

The Crown Prince, well-educated by the best scholars in the world in social and government affairs, was principally the person behind the incredible transformation of Dubai. He was a visionary and a genius. Everyone who knew him personally knew they had never met any man as intelligent as the Crown Prince who could think twice as fast as anyone.

The Crown Prince spoke with formal British Accent that would be at home with British Royalty. Anyone would think he grew up in London and not out riding camels in the desert and living in tents.

"Wilber, my good friend and Sheikh Omar informed me several years ago everything that occurred and your three-day camel ride across the desert."

"It was an interesting ride your Highness."

"How did you like riding across the desert on camels for three days."

"Your Highness, this might seem kind of strange, but I enjoyed it. I had great company with Zayd, and we had great conversations. The further I got away from the terrorists the better I felt. Aside from the terror of being possibly killed by the bad guys, I can see how a person can fall in love with the desert."

"I think I know how you feel. The desert is a romantic place and gives us memories we cannot get anywhere else."

"That I agree, your Highness."

"Please greet my other guests and thank you for coming."

"It's my pleasure, your Highness."

As Wilber walked down the greeting line still wearing his sunglasses and starting to show a good beard, he received very warm receptions from all the Arabs there. Wilber continued holding Sheikh Omar's hand as the Crown Prince followed directly.behind him and this was never seen before by any of them. But none of them had the rest of the story, but they would soon find out and be even more amazed their spirits were tangling with the spirits of a great man walking before them.

In a few minutes Wilber was standing directly in front of the CIA's DD/P John Burkette who had a smile on his face. This was quite an image. His CIA man was all dressed up like Lawrence of Arabia and probably had similar influence based on what was being observed.

"Wilber, do you realize I did not know you were here until about five minutes before the Limo pulled up bringing you and Sheikh Omar here."

"As you can see sir, I'm enjoying my administrative leave."

"Half the CIA is looking for you."

"I believe you can tell them to stand down now that you have located me."

"Nobody has ever escaped the CIA before in such a clever manner. I must congratulate you for demonstrating our utter weaknesses in the agency."

"I can tell you how to fix it."

"How would that be?"

"Real simple, hire a few more Cowboys and it will self-correct."

"I know what you mean. My father worked with Frank Wizner, Tracey Barnes, Richard Bissell, Desmond Fitzgerald, and a few other Cowboys."

"Then you know."

"By the way, my interest in locating you had nothing to do with Pat Barton's concerns. I need to talk to you soon about Project Solaris."

"I'm always available for you sir, but since I'm on administrative leave, I'm not available for Pat Barton."

"Understand. Enjoy your dinner."

"Thank you."

The Crown Prince overheard the two CIA men talking and the fact the DD/P head of covert ops for the CIA was talking to Wilber in the manner he did clearly underscore the importance of this person. If rescuing the Emirate's son is any indication of the types of things Wilber did, that means he really is an incredible spy. Top notch. The Crown Prince enjoyed being around very special people including the pianist who just performed earlier and would be coming back to Dubai to make a lot of money performing in concerts.

When the Sheikh Omar sent the Crown Prince a copy of the video of his son playing violin with that fantastic pianist, he was very amused. He also received such great remarks about how it was Wilber who inspired his son to learn how to play the violin. The Crown Prince knew the boy had bonded with Wilber, Zayd's personal hero. And now here is his

father showing tremendous appreciation. It also affected the Crown Prince. It's a shame they didn't have more days like today.

The restaurant was reserved for the Crown Prince and his party. People not invited were not allowed near the building stopped by security people a long distance away. The last time Wilber saw so much security was when Queen Elizabeth visited a Hewlett Packard facility in Cupertino California. The Queen wanted to see firsthand Hewlett Packard's revolutionary designs in modern electronics and computers created to take out in the field and drive instrument packages used for very special purposes.

Great Britain needed an infusion of technology. Hewlett Packard would be a part of that, especially when they went into spiral development in fiber optics for military applications. Most of the fiber optic backbone aboard U.S. Aircraft Carriers during the Gulf War was built by Hewlett Packard.

The main reason for going to the restaurant instead of the Palace was simply logistics. It was a short ride via Limo from the concert hall whereas going to the Palace would take a while and require special transportation. This made it easier for the guests. Plus, the Crown Prince liked visiting this restaurant now and then and the chefs were better than those in the Palace. The main difference is due to the patronage of the staff and how they felt the Crown Prince should eat for better health. In the restaurant the Crown Prince could eat whatever the hell he wanted, and nobody would say a thing about it because of the decorum required.

Some Arab dining is on mats next to short tables like many formal Japanese resorts provide. It's a culturalistic thing and part of their living style they felt comfortable doing. In this restaurant they had private rooms set up like that but since the two Americans were present, they picked a private dining room that had tables and chairs; hence they were eating Western style.

The seating had already been arranged and each placemat had a little decorative placemat cards with each person's name.

Xinxin was seated next to Wilber on his left and Zayd was seated to Wilber's right. This was done because Zayd's father explained to his son, "During dinner view of yourself as Wilber's host, even though you will be sitting across from the Crown Prince. It's your responsibility to describe the food to Wilber and Xinxin and answer any questions about the food. In case you do not know the answer to the questions about the food, there will be a Valet right behind you standing to be your advisor to assist you if there is something you do not know the answer."

"Alright father, I will be most proud to assist Wilber and Xinxin."

"Thank you Zayd, you are a great son and you never let me down."

"Father, I hope to always make you happy and proud of my actions."

"Zayd that is what any father hopes from his son."

"I will try my best father."

"Thank you."

"You are welcome, father."

The Crown Prince was sitting directly in front of Wilber so they could look directly at each other while talking. Sheikh Omar was sitting to the Crown Prince's

right, which placed him directly looking at Xinxin. John Burkette sitting to the left of the Crown Prince was facing Zayd directly.

John Burkette the DD/P understood the importance of Zayd. He would one day inherit all the Sheikh Omar's wealth and manage all his affairs. In this phase of Sheikh Omar's life, his focus in life was to train Zayd properly so that one day Zayd could take over and manage the family's fortune which implied also taking care of all his

sisters and brothers and ensuring their success. Zayd already had a lot of observations on him and the UAE desk at the CIA had a group and Zayd was one of their persons of interest because of his future stature in life.

As Wilber looked at John Burkette's poker face, he wondered why he was here. John Burkette had a mannerism to keep important things close to himself. The fact he was meeting with the Crown Prince meant there was something big going to happen.

Sometimes the administration used people like John Burkette as a messenger, a high-ranking trusted official that could be the case. One thing Wilber knew was John Burkette had probably already texted Pat Barton he was going to meet with him in a few minutes after the Crown Prince announced his guest.

But Wilber knew the DD/P wanted to talk to him about Project Solaris which was incidental to his trip here. In a while during dinner Wilber would ask the Sheikh Omar if he would like to play golf in the morning with him Zayd, and John Burke. This might provide a secret conversation and not worry about bugs and other nasty devices that might pick up the conversation.

The Valet standing behind Zayd bent over his shoulder and in a very low voice said, "Zayd, the Crown Prince has asked me to request you do something."

Zayd turned and looked at the Valet speaking Arabic. He responded in Arabic,

"ماذا يريد مني الملك أن أفعل؟"

"Madha yurid miniy almalik 'an 'afeala?"

["What does the Crown Prince wish me to do?"]

I have a pamphlet to give you that covers all the food that will be served. Please inform Wilber he will be served a lot of courses and not to eat too much of each one to make room for many types of food."

Zayd replied, "Alright, whatever the Crown Prince requests, I will try my best."

"Thank you, Zayd, we have faith in you."

"Here's a pen to circle items on the pamphlet that Wilber wants more portions. After he's tasted them all we will give him additional servings of what he liked and how much he wants."

"Alright I will explain it," Zayd responded to the Valet."

The cuisine Wilber will be eating was Arabic and the best. The young Turk rulers and the Persian Kings typically ate similar foods to what would be served tonight.

There would be incredible breads, sauces, and mouth-watering food that would no doubt leave an impression on Wilber as well as John Burke.

The meal would have madrouba, oozie, thareed made with rice, lamb chicken, vegitales, yogurt and spices.

Arabic coffee, pastries, Samosas, Turkish cocktails, Shawarmas, Falafel, and Manakish were also served.

Zayd started realizing he really did have important responsibilities and the way his father looked at him conveyed the unspoken truths: Son this is prime time. You have an important role to play. I know you can do it.

The pamphlet Zayd started reading included writeups of all the food they would be serving tonight. He had a big message he needed to tell Wilber right away:

"Wilber, tonight the restaurant will be giving you lots of samples. Many courses of food, eat lightly on each one of them because more will follow. I have this pamphlet that covers the entire menu of what you will sample. I will circle items on the pamphlet you like and after your taste check, a larger portion will be served with the complete list of items you like."

"All right. Thank you."

"The first item on the list is Shawarma, often a favorite food in the Middle East and the best Shawarma is in Dubai."

"Alright, thank you," Wilber said as a waiter put a food plate with a Shawarma serving on it, down on Wilber's empty placemat after he moved the tent style place card forward.

The Crown Prince, Sheikh Omar, and others informed the waiters what they wanted and didn't go through the taste test as it wasn't necessary.

"Shawarma can be made with chicken, lamb, mutton, beef, and even pork. The most crucial requirement is that it is fatty." Zayd said after reading the pamphlet which had all the talking points written down. Shawarma meat is marinated with a special sauce. Shawarma is typically skewered and cooked over an open fire; we call the cooking process Shawarma."

"This Shawarma tastes pretty good. How long do you barbecue it?"

Wilber asked as he only sampled it per his instructions to make room other dishes.

Shawarma is a dish that needs to be cooked for a long time. This is the key secret to its special taste. But it cannot be left unattended, like other long- cooking dishes. A dish cooked on a direct flame needs to be constantly turned so that the inside cooks slowly.

"As Shawarma cooks, the fat melts and keeps the inside moist, creating a soft, juicy meat. As the top layers are cooked, a thin slice is cut off, leaving the rest to continue cooking. The cut slices lie in a copper tray under the giant cylinder of meat."

"Interesting. What makes the special taste?"

"The marinade for red meat is, of course, very different from that used for poultry. As an example, Lamb or Veal Shawarma in Lebanon is marinated in a distinctive salty water and vinegar. Fresh mint, thyme, parsley, black pepper, white pepper, bay leaf, and nutmeg flavors get thoroughly absorbed into the meat. You will also discover that not all Shawarma is served wrapped in Pita bread."

As soon as it appeared the Shawarma taste test was finished and Wilber was not eating any more, Zayd indicated in Arabic to the Valet to take the dish away and bring the next sample.

A sample of Saloona was served next. "Saloona is prepared with pieces of chicken, turmeric, olive oil, ginger, garlic, onion, chili, many other spices, and, of course, rice is one of our main staples is served on the side," Zayd noted.

The next sample was an Indian food Samboosa, mainly because it was popular in Dubai and the Crown Prince liked it.

Qoozi also called Ghozi, this is a rice-based dish with long, slow cooked lamb with eggs, potatoes, almonds, raisins, and roasted nuts. On the plate was a much larger serving than before because it had a leg of lamb and five different rice types. One of the rice portions appeared normal white rice. The other four rice servings had different colors, textures, and spices. It was also apparent there were five distinct types of rice on the plate including Koshihikari rice, Jasmin rice, Saffron rice, Ponni rice, and Basmati rice.

The next dish served was really the most important one because it symbolized the essence of Bedouin cuisine.

Stuffed camel, as the name might suggest, is a huge meal. It is cooked on a spit over an open fire and is filled with chicken, eggs, fish, sheep, and spices. This meat had an excellent taste and texture to it and Wilber said, "Definitely circle that one, I really like the way this meat tastes."

Shish Tawook was the next sample Wilber was served.

"Shish Tawook contains marinated grilled chicken spread out on a flat bread with pickles and chilis and hummus," Zayd explained.

Wilber tried the sample and shook his head up and down and said, "Yes Shish Tawook tastes excellent as well,"

Falafel, a deep-fried chick-pea patty was served next. "You will never get tired of Falafel as it's so delicious. It usually comes with hummus and vegetables wrapped in thin flat bread." Zayd said.

"Yes, it tastes really good."

Next up was Margooga made chicken broth and meat with vegetables and cooked with a thin bread. "This is a well-known Khaleeji dish. It is also known by different names and can be cooked by various methods. It's a very traditional dish and every part of the UAE cooks it differently." Zayd explained.

"Not bad," Wilber replied after tasting it.

Jarees, a dish of boiled cracked wheat mixed with seasoned lamb was then served next.

"Jarees is a very popular dish in Dubai, especially during Ramadan, at weddings, and big events, basically, on any special occasion."

"It's a has quite a heavy consistency," Wilber noted.

"This is something like Lgeimat is a very common dessert throughout the Middle East, and plays a huge part in Dubaian culture, being found at weddings and tea parties, and it is eaten for breakfast served with tea. Lgeimat is also worthy of offering to guests and is an essential part of Fuwala – the special dishes offered to guests."

Lgeimat seems like a mini donut – it has the same texture and taste," Wilber said. "That's saffron in the small dish to dip it in." Zayd said.

"Alright, thanks." Wilber said.

"Majboos is a mixed rice dish made with rice and meat but can also be served with fish or chicken and even shrimp." Zayd said as it was being served next.

"It has a nice taste." Wilber noted.

"The next dish manakish is Lebanese food the Crown Prince likes that is enjoyed throughout the Middle East. It's a flat bread filled with cheese and cooked in a huge oven. It can also be served with cheese on top and thyme, or thyme and olive oil, lamb meat and hot sauce. It's considered delightful for breakfast and goes well with Karak."

At that time a drink was served that looked like Thai iced tea. "What is this?" Wilber asked.

"This drink is Shai Karak and Barata in a café. It's Originally from India, where it's called Masala Chai. Karak is popular for its unique and strong flavor. It differs from Masala Chai in that it has fewer spices and uses strong black tea with milk and sugar." Zayd said.

"Do a lot of people in Dubai drink Shai Karak?" Wilber asked.

"Most people shopping in Dubai stop for a Shai Karak and Barata in a cafe. It is so popular, anywhere around the Gulf. It is cheap too, and for a little more, you can get a Barata, giving you the full breakfast experience," Zayd said.

"What is Barata?" Wilber asked.

"Barata is a tasty Indian bread which is delicious enough on its own," Zayd said.

Xinxin was tasting the food at the same time and following along all the information that Zayd provided. At this time Zayd took their orders on two similar pamphlets, one with the name Wilber printed on the front cover and the other Xinxin printed on the front cover.

Wilber was impressed with the sophistication the restaurant showed with the printed pamphlets and the sequencing of the food and drink. He then thought, a lot of American restaurants could learn a lot by observing this operation.

The way the Crown Prince and Sheikh Omar were smiling at Zayd, they conveyed appreciation for the way he conducted himself and made their guests more comfortable. They liked the responses that Wilber and Xinxin displayed while tasting and eating the food which was made specially for them since they were considered special guests.

As for John Burke, the DD/P who had often traveled to the Middle

East often, he knew what he liked and ordered accordingly. For the most part, John Burkette ordered about the same as the Crown Prince who had a great evaluation of the foods to pick. The Crown Prince preferred the stuffed Camel, and the Restaurant knew how the Crown Prince liked it prepared including which spices to use.

The meal was soon over, and the dinner party was soon escorted out of the restaurant and got into several Limo's.

The Crown Prince had several professional photographers on his staff who were in the Limos which drove to a spot where they could take pictures of the spectacular Dubai night lights in the background. He wanted some pictures of himself with Sheikh Omar and Wilber standing beside Zayd who had impressed the Crown Prince with his music, his conduct during the dinner party and his general demeanor. Later the Crown Prince informed Sheikh Omar, when Zayd finished college, he would employ him in his administration.

Against the night lights of Dubai, pictures were created of Wilber standing next to some of the richest people in the world looking like a cleaned-up Lawrence of Arabia.

John Burkette really didn't like Pat Barton at all and considered him a flaming asshole, but he was stuck with him. Pat Barton was highly recommended.

In government sometimes people give strong recommendations for people to get them transferred away to somewhere else where they cannot do damage to their organization. Even Wilber had done that with a guy they nicknamed Andy Alphabet who was about the most incompetent person Wilber ever worked with.

Wilber completely lost his respect for Andy Alphabet during an event when Andy said, the people he was working with wanted Wilber to whitewash some discrepancies that needed to be corrected. Of course, Wilber ripped Andy a new asshole informing him, "We are the last line of defense. There is nobody behind us to ensure this crap gets resolved."

Some people in this meeting in a cubicle cleared their throats and nodded their heads towards Wilber conveying look behind you (clear your baffles). Wilber turned around and there was a very senior person in the chain of command standing there smiling. He was happy because he learned a valuable lesson. *Wilber was not the type of person that would take the easy way out and let shit fly.*

The Space Shuttle program had blood on their hands for

Andy's mindsets. Some managers refused to consider important recommendations because he wanted to be a big shot and fly on schedule. That's what gets people captured or killed. Pat Barton was cut from the same cloth as Andy Alphabet.

John Burkette liked to tweak Pat Barton now and then and received a collection of pictures taken against the Dubai nightlights showing great shots of the Crown Prince, Sheikh Omar, his son Zayd, and the modern-day Lawrence of Arabia Wilber. When he was later back in his hotel room, he texted Pat Barton: "Look who I ran into in Dubai."

Within minutes Pat Barton answered and said he had started administrative actions against Wilber O'Toole for leaving the country and going to the Middle East without reporting to his controller he was going on foreign travel.

John Burkette had enough of that asshole and responded, "Just as soon as you send your superior (me) the forms adverse action forms, I'm going to take adverse action against you for interfering with a secret mission. If you have disclosed this to anyone else, you did a security violation.." John Burkette was smiling right after he tapped on SEND.

***

Chapter Eleven

Lawrence of Arabia

The night skyline of Dubai is impressive. The twisted building and the various colors reflecting from the water created a menagerie tapestry that creates a surreal image to anyone. The architects who created this imagery proved one thing. When you have unlimited budgets, and you are not corrupt you can build majestic master pieces. Some people travel to Dubai just to see this image.

Wilber and Xinxin were given electronic copies of the pictures. These were treasures for Xinxin. When she traveled back to Singapore her company would elevate her to the highest stratums. They had a super star and didn't realize it until now. The CEO of the company had SID connections and between the Chinese affair and now Dubai, and four special accounts of Sheikh Omar's wives.

The CEO would never look at Xinxin in the same light. She truly was a remarkable woman. And her mere presence got him excited. But he also knew the reality, this smoking hot woman sleeping with one of the CIA's top spies taking her places to meet the Crown Prince and Oil Sheikhs would never get excited about short fat bald guys. Plus, the CEO knew he had the little dick syndrome.

After the picture session, the Crown Prince said, "Wilber, very few people know the story about you rescuing Zayd. He's my best friend's son. You have no idea what it meant for all of us. Zayd's family and my family were very grateful when you pulled Zayd out of the terrorist camp and brought him back alive. We owe you a lot.

"Your highness, I came back alive to live another day. I did not pay the ultimate price. As Zayd will tell you it was a nasty firefight. I had 12 Mercenaries with me. I worked with these guys often in the past. They truly were great men. They sacrificed their lives so that I could live. I carry a huge burden with me because I caused them to lose their lives."

"I sense how you feel Wilber," The Crown Prince Articulated very respectfully.

"The only thing that makes it all worthwhile and allows me to sleep at night is Zayd was returned alive with no injuries."

"He too could have easily been severely injured," The Crown Prince noted.

"Yes, there were a lot of bullets flying around in the compound. A stray bullet could easily have struck him down. But we had no choice, we were up against some tough guys."

"Wilber, I truly enjoyed my time with you this evening. It's rare that I get the chance to spend time with such an extraordinary person like you and the lovely Xinxin. You have great taste in women."

"Thank you, your excellency. Xinxin and I have experienced a couple ordeals together as well. Without Sheikh Omar's help I could not be with her now."

"Wilber, I'm happy you came to the UAE so you could be together."

"This is one of the most precious times of my life being allowed to spend time with Xinxin."

"I know what you mean, Wilber."

"When you cross the desert on a Camel fleeing from terrorists, you become close to a person like I did with Zayd. He means a lot to me too. He is my friend for life."

Zayd could not hold back after that comment and said, "Wilber you are my friend for life too. As far as I'm concerned you are my brother."

"Thank you, Zayd, I feel the same way about you. Also, when you were playing the violin, you really made me very proud of you. Thank you for doing all that for me."

"Wilber, it was my pleasure, and, in the future, I will arrange for you to hear more."

"I'm looking forward to hearing you play the violin, but can you do me a favor?" "What's the favor Wilber?"

"I would like you to ask the Crown Prince to attend the concert. I would like to hear you perform with the Crown Prince present."

"Wilber, I will ask my father to arrange it."

The Crown Prince suddenly spoke and said, "Zayd, when you decide to do that concert, ask your father to call me and give me the date and time so I can be there to enjoy it and I agree with Wilber."

"Thank you, your Highness," Zayd said.

"Alright everyone, thank you for an amusing evening. It was a very rare pleasure," The Crown Prince said and turned around and walked over to his royal Limo with John Burke, the DD/P following closely behind and soon he and four other Limo's passed off into the night.

The remaining couple of Limos took Sheikh Omar and his group to a nearby location where his helicopter was waiting and took them back to his home.

As they got out of the helicopter, Wilber asked the Sheikh Omar, "Your excellency would it be possible to play a round of golf soon. John Burkette needs to talk to me, and I think your golf course would be a safe place for him and I to have that discussion."

"Wilber my special assistants informed me you need to talk to John Burkette about a serious matter. I know you have important tasks to perform. I will send word to him in a short while to meet us on the golf course in the morning, and the four of us can play together."

"Thank you very much."

Soon Wilber and Xinxin were alone in privacy and celebrating their love with celestial feasts as if they were living on borrowed time. If you knew the world was going to end tomorrow, what would you do? In their transcendence to lovers embrace they answered that question in the most passionate manner.

It was a strange feeling. Almost like a young person's first orgasm. They have no idea what such feelings can manifest when the prolactin, dopamine, oxytocin, and other chemicals the brain produces during sexual intercourse that creates that electrochemical reaction that impacts the emotional center of the brain and the

resulting holographic ensembles, a very small part of the brain produces that is what we call human awareness.

The lovers feast soon manufactured slumber and the two evolved into a different mental awareness as sleep took over their thought process. They were lucky they slept early because early in the morning one of the chamber maids woke up Wilber to get him dressed and out on the golf course.

Soon enough a helicopter landed on the golf course and John

Burkette the DD/P climbed out of the helicopter not dressed for golf. He was here for a conversation and that was it.

Sheikh Omar and Wilber approached and met John Burkette who simply.

said, "Let's go for a little walk Wilber, so that we can have a conversation."

"Your Excellency, please excuse me for a few minutes, I need to have a talk with John Burkette."

"Sure, go ahead, we'll wait here for you." Sheikh Omar said.

The two men walked off and the Sheikh Omar knew that John Burkette was way up in the CIA being the DD/P. John Burkette was one of the most dangerous men on the planet next to Vladimir Putin of Russia. Sheikh Omar realized Wilber was most likely getting a serious briefing. He had no idea it was far more serious.

After they were about 100 yards away, Wilber asked, "What did you want to talk to me about?"

"I didn't agree when the dumb asses sent you to Beijing. I'm not sure why that happened. But it was totally dumb."

"Well, I'm glad it happened that way because of how it allowed me to meet Xinxin and allow me to find someone special for my future."

"That was the only positive outcome from that Pat Barton Goat Fuck," John Burkette said.

"It sounds like you are not a big fan of Pat Barton," Wilber stated.

"To tell you the truth he's dumber than Andy Alphabet," John Burkette said.

Wilber could not help but start chuckling. Then he asked:

"Is that why you wanted to talk?" Wilber asked wondering why John Burkette came all the way here to talk to him.

"No, but I wanted you to hear how I felt about things." "Alright," Wilber replied.

"Wilber when you made your comment about using a submarine on Saturn, I seriously started thinking about what you said."

"Alright, but I felt it might be what we needed to do."

"As DD/P I get to see a lot of things you do not know exist because it really is heavy duty. I know that from time to time we have some pressing issues that take extraordinary efforts like the time you rescued the Sheikh Omar's son from the Terrorists. It truly was a remarkable mission and you never rewarded from it like you should have."

"I received a big award. I'm personal friends with Sheikh Omar and his son. I

like the two of them. That would not be the case had I not been assigned the mission."

"Pat Barton set you up for failure. I'm surprised you came back alive."

"Those Mercenaries that lost their lives didn't come cheap, but they made sure I came back alive."

"Your resourcefulness in that mission did surprise me. But tell me how you paid for those Mercenaries."

"Don't ask, don't tell. A spy sometimes must generate black money funds because there is no other way to recruit and pay for the mercenaries."

"Alright I get it. Now on to the reason why I'm here and the lucky event that brought us together."

"Alright."

"When you brought up the submarine, I immediately went to close friends who helped me a lot in the past."

"Okay."

"I asked them to investigate your submarine idea. And they did."

"That's interesting to know."

"I determined a planet that like Saturn now doing those communications could pose a serious problem for us and it's only a matter of time before the public becomes aware. "

"What do you want me to do?"

"I think the Aliens on Saturn will likely destroy the probe."

"That's what I think too. We are in for a rude awakening."

"When you leave here you will be flying out of here on a CIA GS750 Gulfstream

Jet."

"What about Xinxin?"

"She'll leave with us. We'll stop at Singapore to get her home. Then we'll stop in Hawaii for a couple days, where you will get to meet someone and talk privately with him."

"Any reason why I can't take Xinxin with me to Hawaii? She can fly Singapore Airlines home on a commercial flight from there."

"That would work, save us a stop. The GS750 can easily get from here to Hawaii if we do not make a stop."

"Who am I going to meet?"

"A submarine designer by the name of Pierre Truffaut."

"What's so special about Pierre Truffaut?"

"He's the man who designed submarines for Jacques Cousteau."

"Interesting."

"Let Sheikh Omar know you will be leaving with me in a week from now." "Alright."

The two men walked back towards Sheikh Omar where John Burkette said to Sheikh Omar, "I would have liked to stay and play golf with you, but the Crown Prince is going somewhere with me today for a special event."

"Not a problem, John."

John Burkette bowed to Sheikh Omar, then turned and walked over to the waiting commercial helicopter that had 4 other men inside with machine guns and some high-power rifles and one grenade launcher in case they needed firepower.

The three remaining, Sheikh Omar, Zayd, and Wilber proceeded to play a eight hole golf game.

"Tell me Wilber, how did you like the food last night and what food did you like the best?" Sheikh Omar asked.

"Your excellency, actually I preferred the stuffed Camel the best."

"Wilber, the Crown Prince and I shared your opinion."

"That's good to know."

"Wilber, when you are alone with me and Zayd and nobody is around, I would like you go call me by my real name.

"You want me to call you Władziu Valentino Liberace?"

"You can call me Wladziu or Liberace if it is easier for you."

"I kind of like Liberace, if you don't mind."

"I like it too, call me Liberace."

"Alright Liberace, it will be an honor for me to do so."

"Thank you, Wilber."

Wilber wondered if part of the secrecy of Omar's real name was related to Liberace's sexual preferences, which is contrary to Arab/ Muslim ideals. Liberace was also close friends with several beautiful female movie stars and likely had some happy time with them when he was switch hitting, Wilber thought.

After the golf game, they had a light lunch, and based on Wilber's comments the night before, Sheikh Omar had his chef prepare really nice Shawarma for their meal. He also had fresh fruit and yogurt ice cream and Ghorayeba Shortbread Cookies for dessert.

Even on the golf course they could smell the scent of cooking the Shawarma that permeated the air in a peasant manner.

The Chef had to feed a small army as there were twenty children, that included Zyad. Sheikh Omar was a prodigious fertilizer and up until recently he always had at least one wife pregnant. Sheikh Omar would make the Mormons proud.

Sheikh Omar said to Wilber after they finished eating, "Go take a nap or freshen up for a while, then I'm going to take you on a helicopter tour of Dubai in an hour and half."

"Sounds good."

"If we get time we'll zip down to Abu Dhabi and visit a couple of my college classmates that were with me University of Cambridge."

"I'm sure they would be interesting to meet," Wilber said, and he meant it because it would increase his awareness of the region and may prove valuable in the future.

University of Cambridge is the second-oldest college in England, built in 1209, and provides astounding learning opportunities. The University of Cambridge has one of the toughest admittance policies which helps it maintain its title as the 6th most successful college in the world.

The long list of notable Cambridge graduates includes Sir Isaac Newton, Jane Goodall, Milton Friedman, Charles Darwin, David Attenborough, Alan Turing, John Maynard Keynes, Steven Hawking, Bertrand Russell, Robert Oppenheimer, and Neils Bohr. Hence people that changed the world.

After freshening up with two private toilets they didn't have to wait, Wilber and Xinxin transitioned to a lovely designed and very soft sofa in their suite that had music available, so Wilber started playing some lovely piano music he selected that was performed by an incredible Russian trio, Bel Suono.

The Bel Suono concerts also had incredible singers such as Valeriya (Russian: Валерия). Valeriya is the stage name of Alla Yurievna Perfilova. Also singing with Bel Suono was Polina Gagarina, and Ani Lorak performing with them. Russian Poet Anna Egoyan also reads poems during three musical performances. The music was splendid, and since Wilber knew what she was saying he did quick partial translations for Xinxin who had snuggled up next to him enjoying every precious moment.

Wilber did not quite know it, but Shiekh Omar was watching all this with his security manager including the sound. They were impressed how well Wilber translated the Russian. Sometimes they did transactions with Russians for a variety of reasons such as buying weapons for Arab Groups and others.

"Maybe one day we can benefit by having someone like Wilber on our team we can trust and have better negotiations with the Russians," Shiekh Omar said.

"I'm sorry to inform you, your excellency, the CIA would never let Wilber leave until he retires, and he's still somewhat a young man," The security chief said.

"You are probably right, but I like the positive influence he gives to Zayd." "Zayd is a very sophisticated person for his age," the security manager said.

"He's been through quite a bit more than children ever experience in their lifetimes, especially when he was kidnapped."

"Did you ever find out how they smuggled Zayd out of Dubai?"

"We are getting close to finding out. That's why John Burkette is here visiting the Crown Prince."

"Very interesting," the Security Manager said knowing this was highly sensitive information. He also knew what was likely going to happen. The Crown Prince would do like usually does. Hire guns for hire and take care of business. Most likely the Cash in Advance boys would be the guns. He wondered if perhaps the hired gun was already here snuck in with a very Novel method via Sheikh Omar.

"One thing I like about Wilber," Sheikh Omar said. "What is that your excellency?"

"Wilber always selects great music to hear. I learned a lot from Wilber. Wilber's enriched my life in the way he goes about it. I'll encourage Zayd to keep in contact with him to ask for music selections in the future."

"Are you not worried about the CIA recruiting Zayd?"

"That's possible, but I suspect they would be more concerned about the severe negative repercussions if the Crown Prince discovered they were training spies in the

UAE.

"What if Zayd offered his services?"

"The truly only interface Zayd has to the CIA is via Wilber. Wilber likes Zayd as a friend. I tend to believe Wilber would attempt to prevent Zayd for delving into CIA matters because he wants him to have a good life and help take care of his family in the future."

"You seem to have a lot of confidence in Wilber."

"I've tested him in the past, I know what kind of person he is."

"What kind of tests?"

"When he brought my son back alive with barely a scratch on him rescuing him from the meanest bastards on the planet that made Saddam Hussein look like a saint, I offered him a very large sum of money as a reward."

"Did he take the money?"

"No. He said his expenses were paid for and that his reward was simply seeing Zayd living and returned safely."

"That's amazing. Few men turn down large amounts of money."

"I also offered him two of the top fashion models in the world who would do anything I wanted them to do, because of how I took care of them."

"Did you have sex with them?"

"No silly, I have four wives and all the sex I could possibly want."

"Then what did you do with them?"

"I gave them large sums of money, to simply entertain a few of my guests. They were not required to do sex, but they indicated to me for the kind of money I gave them, they would do it."

"With Wilber?"

"Yes. When I divulged to them, he was a super CIA agent who rescued my son and they saw him swimming in my pool and saw his body, they wanted Wilber."

"Did Wilber enjoy the two women?"

"No, he declined the offer and said, I didn't need to pay him or provide anything. My son living was his payment in full. He was quite happy the two of them were able to come back alive. But I did some investigation with some CIA men who visit the Crown Prince. Wilber had a woman in his life. She was killed but they would not say who it was or how it happened."

The security chief and Shiekh Omar were not privy he killed the woman who betrayed him and turned out to be an MSS spy who almost killed him. The treachery

and the tempestuous relationship that turned into a tragedy because of intreague and betrayal created a barrier to Wibers heart.

Aida Abramova another female he came across was nothing more than enjoying the side benefits of discovering a possible spy. But there was no emotional consequence of that encounter in Petropavlovsk. It was not until Wilber met Xinxin, that a scenario developed the reopened his heart allowing the human condition to flourish when emotional bonds begin.

Xinxin was the victim of sophisticated Chinese MSS agents who know how to play the game better than most. But she too was coerced to produce treachery and that compelling relationship almost turned into a tragedy because of intreague and betrayal.

***

Shiekh Omar decided to allow the lovebirds to hear the Bel Suono concert with the room's spectacular acoustics with its sound system mainly because he was enjoying it as well. As soon as the concert ended, Shiekh Omar said to his security chief, have the Valet get them ready to go out to the helicopter port. I want Wilber and Xinxin dressed as Arabs with sunglasses on.

"Right away, your excellency."

In twenty minutes, the Valet let Wilber and Xinxin out to the helicopter pad that had the engines already running getting ready to take off. Shiekh Omar and Zayd were in the helicopter waiting.

With the way they were dressed, nobody would know they were not Arabs. The disguises were quite good.

The helicopter took off and headed for the center of Dubai. It seemed like it did not take long to get to directly above the Dubai business district off the distance, Wilber could already see the Burg Khalifa tallest building in the world at 828 meters high.

When they got closer Zayd said, "There is a really neat Lightshow at night on the Burg Khalifa."

As they flew around, Zayd gave other information, much of what Wilber already knew but for the sake of informing Xinxin, he let Zayd continue the tour.

The helicopter flew a couple trips over Dubai's palm shamed artificial Islands called the Jumeirah Palm. These artificial Islands were designed to look like a palm tree extending out from the center of Dubai. They soon flew over the far Northwest Apex edge of the Jumeirah Palm to see Atlantis Palm Luxury Hotel Resort. Xinxin made enough money trading crypto currencies to afford to stay there. One day she would bring Wilber back to Dubai just so they could spend a few days at the Jumeirah Palm to enjoy staying at the Atlantis Palm Luxury Hotel

Resort.

"That large building over there is the Palm Tower Building. It has the Aura Sky Pool. That is the World's highest swimming pool on a building at 210 meters. If you swim around the pool, you have a 360-degree view including the Dubai Palm."

In a while they saw the Dubai Fountain, an entertainment location that had food and festivities including Belly dancing.

Next, they flew over the Dubai Marina, Shipyard, with several large ships being worked then off to Dubai Metro and saw some of their new modern trains.

"This is the Dubai Mall. It's the largest Mall in the world. Inside it has interesting things to see, such as the Waterfall, large Ice Rink, and a large Aquarium."

Next, they flew over the Jumeirah Beach Residence, "This beach area is open to the public."

The helicopter flew within a quarter mile from Dubai's Huge Ferris Wheel. "This is the largest Ferris Wheel in the world."

Other landmarks they were shown, some of which Sheikh Omar helped finance, included: Time out market, UMM SEQIUM-2, and the famous Burg Al Arab curved building.

"The Burg Al Arab has a fictitious 7-star rating. Hotels only go to 5 stars. It's built on an artificial Island," Zayd said.

A second palm set of artificial Islands is being constructed down the coastline to the southwest called Nakhlat Jabal Ali. On the Palm branches is Jebel Ali Show Village. They soon flew over Nakhlat Jabal Ali. This second Nakhlat Jabal Ali palm Island structure is 50% larger than the first Jumeirah Palm.

"A third Palm Island structure Northeast up the coast, called Palm Deira is even larger and also under construction," Zayd noted.

"We are now going to fly to Abu Dhabi," Zayd said.

They then flew over parts of the desert watching people in off-road vehicles going out on tourist groups to the Desert.

Wilber suddenly saw they were leaving Dubai behind.

Sheikh Omar could see concern on Wilber's face that was now

sporting another day of beard growth.

Wilber really started looking more and more like an Arab. Another week of beard growth and suntanning and nobody would know Wilber wasn't Arab.

"We are traveling to Abu Dhabi to visit my friends I spent time with while attending University of Cambridge in Great Britain. They are expecting us. They want to meet you."

"It will be interesting to see men with whom you attended University of Cambridge," Wilber said.

"They are very bright men and well educated," Sheik Omar said.

"Knowing people that changed the world that attended the University of Cambridge, I would have to assume, they received an excellent education."

"They are making Abu Dhabi a great place. It shows."

When the helicopter arrived in Abu Dhabi, they received a similar sky tour and there is a lot to see. Abu Dhabi has enormous wealth. The pace of construction seemed rather remarkable and swift.

There are some incredible mansions in Abu Dhabi. It's probably the wealthiest area of the UAE. After getting a look at all those impressive buildings and structures

the helicopter veered off and flew to an impressive home with its own dual helicopter landing pad. There was another helicopter parked on one of the two landing pads.

When the helicopter landed a couple men in formal suits appeared waiting for them. These were not Shiekh Omar's school classmates; they were Valets and security men. Each one had an Uzi machine gun inside and on the backside of the suit they were wearing with 30 degrees C air temperature. It could be worse, it has hit 50 degrees C.

After the helicopter was shut down, and all the passengers departed with the security men, the pilot was escorted to another portion of the mansion. The pilot would be taken to a suite to freshen up, have room service and offered a temporary marriage to a concubine if he wanted.

Valet/security men escorted Sheikh Omar, his son Zayd, Wilber and Xinxin into a large room that appeared to be upwards 100 feet wide with tall 10 feet glass windows that were coated minimize sunlight penetration, almost like sunglasses. And outside was a very long pool with water, no doubt mainly for looks and architecture enhancement.

The large room was nice and cool. One thing Wilber noticed immediately was what appeared to be a Persian rug that must have been at least 80 feet long. That rug alone cost a fortune.

Over to the side was a large grand piano and it appeared to be a Steinway.

Incredible furniture and artwork were in this huge room.

And there the two men were, Sheikh Abdulla, and Prince Bandar, who were quickly introduced by Sheikh Omar.

This Prince Bandar was not related to the Saudi Prince or his family, it was just a coincidence they had same name. But he wished it was because he liked the Prince from Saudi who was a brilliant man and a great thinker.

After the introductions the guests were offered seats in a circular pattern of large, padded chairs and sofas where everyone could see each other and converse.

Wilber quickly noticed the two friends of Sheik Omar they visited, appeared handsome and in great shape in the way they fit their clothes. It was apparent Sheikh Omar's friend had a significant physical fitness regimen.

Sheikh Omar's two friends were sizing up Wilber. They knew he was CIA. They have their own spy networks, and some CIA people have a price too. They had Wilber's dossier. It doesn't really matter what a dossier says, what matters is what they accomplished. And here Wilber was with his personal dedicated disciple, Zayd, who would probably take a bullet for Wilber if Zayd needed to save Wilber's life.

The two sheikhs knew the story full story of Zayd's rescue because they got it from two sources. Omar's version, and another version that came via the terrorists who held young Zayd as prisoner. Not all terrorists died as Wilber thought. A couple terrorists laid unconscious. These terrorists survived their wounds and eventually recovered and informed friends who informed other friends what happened and eventually information like this works its way across deserts and information that is valuable is always for sale.

The terrorists were happy they killed all the mercenaries, but of course were severely aggravated Zayd was rescued and worse yet made it back home safe.

Indirectly the terrorists confirmed everything Zayd informed his father, except there actually these two survivors allowed multi-dimensional reports, how the enemy viewed things.

They of course would never know the identity of who the person was that rescued Zayd. But both sides knew it was a paramilitary operation that took down the terrorists using their own tricks traveling on camels during nights and resting during the days under camouflage tents and attacking late at night when most of the guards were sleeping after smoking quantities of hashish.

Wilber and his mercenaries silently walked and eventually crawled up to the camp area spread-out coming in from multiple directions and converging on the target. The last mile took about thirty minutes because at a half mile they dispersed to come in for the attack and hit the terrorists from the multiple angles. Many of the terrorists were killed sleeping in their tents. The terrorists outnumbered Wilber and his mercenaries ten to one. But with advanced tactics and talent, twelve men took down over a hundred terrorists.

The attack started with simultaneous attacks on a dozen tents and people hitting the building that had over twenty terrorists inside it. The only guidance was don't shoot anyone small, like a child, and they knew the boy was probably tied up and the only risk to him was a stray bullet, therefore the best shooters went into the building with no automatic weapon firing, it was all single shot at a confirmed target.

The tents were another matter. They got hit with grenades and automatic weapons fire. Anyone exiting those tents was struck down by a couple sharp shooters prepositioned for that purpose.

The battle lasted over fifteen minutes and some of the mercenaries were firing their guns knowing they had received fatal wounds and would soon bleed to death. Nothing could save them, so they continued fighting until they passed out due to the loss of blood. The sharpshooters were attacked and managed to take out all the terrorist coming at them, even though they too were being shot full of holes. Gradually as the battle eased off it went down to sporadic gunfire when terrorists exposed their positions.

The very last terrorist killed a mercenary standing beside Wilber. In essence the mercenary took a bullet for Wilber who then shoot the terrorist.

Once the last terrorist was hit, it was quiet. There was no more shooting because everyone was dead except for Zayd who was in a lucky spot protected by boxes of rice and can food ingredients on each side of him. With his night vision goggles, Wilber was able to spot Zayd. Wilber was briefed Zayd cold speak English and went to a British school. That made the conversation easy, as Zayd was less afraid talking to someone in English vice Arabic.

"Zayd, my name is Wilber, I was sent here to rescue you."

"Thank you, Wilber, I want to leave if you can get me out of here."

"Let me untie you and we can go, I think everyone is dead, but we are going out of this end of the building just in case."

Wilber untied Zayd and led him out of the West end of the building, they then ran a circuitous route where the camels were tied up they would ride escaping across the desert.

The next day when the big manhunt started, all the camels the mercenaries rode in on were all let go and wondering helplessly through the desert leaving behind multiple trails that exhaustively delayed the terrorist trying to track Zayd and his rescuers down.

One by one camels were found because they simply stopped walking and sat down on the ground resting. Since Wilber did the smart thing dressed as a Bedouin and kept traveling all during the day, he crossed over other trails where people on camels had passed which further confused trackers, and a sandstorm covered their tracks quite well. Wilber had no problems continuing in the storm traveling via his compass and a beacon he could track with his cell phone application.

The two Sheikh's and the prince had numerous discussions about this event and sitting and talking to the two principal characters Wilber and Zayd had a huge impact on them. Zayd was obviously well recovered from his ordeal appearing quite optimistic.

The three Arab Sheikhs started smoking hashish in water filtered Hash Bongs and water pipes.

Invited to partake, Wilber and Xinxin indicated they were not interested in participating in smoking hashish. Wilber was offered wine and other alcoholic beverages that were normally not allowed in Abu Dhabi, but the super-rich didn't care they had helicopters and trucks to deliver such substances whenever the needed them. Plus, there were several merchant ships that carried stashes of wine and alcohol products to sell or trade for merchandise.

Cargo ships often have 20 staterooms for passengers afraid to fly. The cost is about the same as a first-class airline ticket. Some of those Cargo ships also have female passengers who charge $10,000.00 for sex. Dubai as well as Abu Dhabi have takers for these interesting passengers. Ship visitors sometimes were wealthy Shiekhs and oil billionaires. Why would they visit a ship for sex?

Privacy.

There is no way a local could film them and start to blackmail.

When offered wine, Wilber looked at Sheikh Omar and asked, "Is it permissible to drink wine in front of Zayd?"

Sheikh Omar started chuckling then said, "Wilber when I take Zayd to places like Switzerland and London and have a fine dinner, he and I drink wine together. We usually dressed in Western Business Suits because, I was taught in Cambridge, when in Rome do as the Romans do."

About that time Zayd asked, "Father may I have some wine?" "You sure you would not prefer Hashish?"

"No father I do not like smoking anything."

"In that case yes you may." At that time Sheikh Omar nodded at the Valet/waiter who then poured glasses of a very fine Cabernet Sauvignon that sells for around $2,000.00 in Abu Dhabi. Xinxin received a glass of Chardonay.

The discussions then shifted to a sort of Q & A about the three men together at Cambridge where they all studied for six years obtaining advanced degrees.

"I left Cambridge, and went to Harvard Law School," Prince Bandar disclosed as they were talking about what they learned.

"What did you study, Your Excellency Abdulla?" Wilber asked.

"Wilber, I studied astronomy and received my PhD later from Cornell University."

"That's very interesting, Your Excellency Abdulla," Wilber responded then asked, "Did you apply your degree at any observatories?"

"Wilber, thanks to my association with Cornell, I spent time at the radio telescope in Arecibo in Puerto Rico. Then I was asked to go out to Palamar Mountain in Southern California where Cal Tech and Cornell were working on new revolutionary optical devices that allowed images with more than double the resolution as the Hubble Space Telescope."

"That's rather incredible, Doctor Abdulla. You have had an amazing life and got to see space in a major way." Wilber said and started wondering how Sheik Abdulla would feel about him if he knew he was part of the CIA's Solar System Investigations.

"Wilber, thank you and I prefer the prefix doctor over Shiekh or Excellency."

"Doctor, with your astronomy contributions for mankind, I'm very proud to refer to you as Doctor."

"Thank you, Wilber, that means a lot to me." "You are most welcome Doctor Abdulla."

Wilber was feeling slightly awkward for such a strong exchange with Dr. Abdulla and the Prince Bandar appeared like he wasn't happy he was being trumped by Doctor Abdulla, so he asked, "Your Highness Prince Bandar, what kind of law cases did you perform after you became a lawyer?"

"Thank you, Wilber, for asking that question. As you can imagine, since my stature in life as a prince, I have no choice but to operate at a low level and not expose too much."

"I can see that would be an issue," Wilber said.

"Wilber, your good friend Sheikh Omar was heavily involved in developing the three palm island structures. He was my classmate and best friend in the world. He knew he could count on me. He also knew that based on some of the previous cases I worked on that I'm a skillful lawyer. I have a license to practice law in several countries including Great Britain, France, Switzerland, United States, Canada, Mexico, the UAE, Saudi Arabia, and China."

"China, wow that's amazing." Why did you have to get a license and work in China?"

"Real simple, Abu Dhabi sells China a lot of oil and legal matters often enter the case since there are liabilities especially with Lloyds of London if the super tankers operate in a declared warzone. You can imagine the legal mess that can happen if a shipper declares Force Majeure."

"Yes, I can see that especially right after 9/11."

"Precisely."

"What was the nature of the legal assistance you gave Sheikh Omar?"

"Green Peace and various environmental groups created havoc trying to stop Shiekh Omar from building the Palms."

"What was the basis of their complaints?"

"They claim the construction was creating too much sediment on the Persian Gulf Ocean floor and we were causing too much erosion issues."

"I see."

"I spent a lot of time in court dealing with those matters."

"What's your opinion of the outcome of the Palms?"

"Thanks to the unique location and year-round warm weather makes Dubai and Abu Dhabi ideal locations for beachfront activities. The three Palms increase the number of beaches available far more extensive and will allow a vast increase in tourists. The UAE plans to increase the tourist population to fifteen million."

"Wow."

"Wilber, smart developers like Sheikh Omar were brought in by the government to figure out what the UAE will do after something replaces oil?"

"Think there is something on the horizon that could replace the need for oil?"

"Unfortunately, there is and it's here already and we may have waited too long to move swiftly in the development of the tourist industry to replace income we lose from oil."

"What is it that will replace oil?"

"The world's newest and largest fusion reactor just became operational. Japan's JT-60SA can provide unlimited power. Tesla showed we can have electric cars and trucks. Boeing and Airbus are now designing electric commercial aircraft. The British have developed a commercial electric aircraft that is now starting to sell."

"So, what you are saying is oil is the future buggy whip nobody no longer needs?"

"Precisely. When airliners switch to electric, fuel cell, and Hydrogen, the price of oil will plumet. We will then have an oil glut that will never be reversed."

"I see your point. All very interesting, the kinds of legal work you got involved in."

"Fighting environmental special interest groups is harder than to defend a murder suspect."

"I can sense that. But it looks like you were successful as the Jumeirah Palm is complete and the Nakhlat Jabal Ali is ready for a lot of construction on it. Jebel Ali Show Village construction is well on its way."

"That's true." Also, the third Palm Island, Deira, is built and laid out already. Now it's nothing more than building the structures and the road networks and do the landscaping."

"Have you recorded any climate data to show the impact of the Palm Islands?"

"Yes, the legal matters can get sticky due to international involvement. We have built four new state of the art weather stations and we record weather data every hour of every day. We also get satellite images every day that we collect."

"Any conclusions you have made based on all the imagery?"

"Yes, the area is getting greener, just like Israel that has reclaimed a lot of desert areas. As an example, Dubai Municipality added 1.7 million square meters of green areas in the city in 2018 by planting 44,000 trees. We have started to increase the green area in the emirate, we have exceeded an average of 25 square meters of green area per capita of green spaces in the urban area."

"I noticed a lot of trees flying over Dubai today," Wilber said.

"Part of that development you saw included planting local environment trees such as Ghaff, Sidr and trees that are ideal for the salinity of our soil."

"What about the typical argument from environmentalists about roads increasing local temperatures?"

"We developed and engineered agriculture enhancements' on the sides of the roads and squares throughout Dubai. We introduced for the first-time new trees to withstand the UAE's environment, such as the Boseda and green Cassia trees, which were newly produced in the nurseries of the Municipality. We installed plant walls that prevent the encroachment of sand on the roads," Prince Bandar said.

"I noticed a lot of green when we flew over Jumeirah," Wilber responded.

"Dubai Municipality increased the diversity of horticultural patterns, located along Jumeirah and Al Wasl roads," Prince Bandar said.

"Any other Green enhancements?" Wilber asked.

"Dubai added a significant green area on Airport Road, Nad Al Sheba area and Oud Metha. We put forth a significant effort to increase ornamental plants are found at the intersections of bridges and other areas where it makes sense."

"How about new developments?"

"Property developers in Dubai are encouraged to build green and eco- friendly projects with a growing environmental awareness and rising demand for sustainable living spaces." Prince Bandar stated.

"What are some examples of what developers are doing?" Wilber asked.

Developers are encouraged to incorporate sustainable features into projects such as rainwater harvesting systems, energy-efficient HVAC systems, solar panels, green roofs, standard inclusions to reduce carbon footprints and operational costs.

"How do you measure the extent the developers are cooperating?"

"Dubai Municipality provides certifications to assure buyers and investors of a property's adherence to strict environmental standards."

"That's probably important," Wilber responded intuitively.

"Dubai developers demonstrate their commitment with a program called Leadership in Energy and Environmental Design (LEED) and Dubai's Al Sa'fat helped increase the demand for green building certifications.

"It looks like the UAE spent their money wisely sending you three men to Cambridge because what you brought back with you is all part of this remarkable transformation," Wilber said.

Wilber, for me, Harvard University had a huge impact on my ability to deal with the legal issues of all these urban developments. Without successful legal conclusions, none of this would be possible. Those environmental special interests are very powerful and are well funded by our enemies."

"Such as who?"

"The same people that funded the abduction of Zayd."

Wilber knew he had gone past a point that struck a nerve and realized he should not pursue conversations in the direction they were heading. He was rescued by a pleasant event.

There is a long hallway with marble floors that came into the room. You cannot help but hear people with hard shoes walking down the hallway and the men turned to see who it was. There were several well-dressed young ladies with a couple older women escorts. These were Sheikh Abdulla's family members. The young ladies were stunningly beautiful. Their mothers were blondes from England, and very well-educated Sheikh Abdulla met at Cambridge where they were classmates.

Sheikh Abdulla was now all smiles. He orchestrated this event for the purpose of getting his daughters more interested in Zayd as he viewed a future arranged wedding as probable as that's how families protected wealth through the marriages of their children.

The women approached the men and Sheikh Abdulla introduced all of them and said, "Clara is a pianist, and she has done very well in her musical training. Sheikh Omar sent me copies of a video he made of Zayd playing the violin. My daughter has mastered the piano portion of that Mozart Sonata. She would like to perform it now with Zayd."

"Your excellency, I did not bring my violin with me," Zayd quickly responded.

"Zayd, I realized you would probably not arrive with a violin, so we have a Stratovarius staged next to the piano to play. My other daughter

Anna's violin instructor tuned it moments before you arrived. Its ready to be used now."

Zayd looked at his father who gave him that special look the two knew well that conveyed, "Just do it!"

"Alright, I would be delighted to perform with Clara."

All the adults now smiled as Zayd stood and followed Clara over to the piano and grabbed the Stratovarius and the Arcus Gold Violin Bow. After Clara sat down in a low voice, Zayd asked Clara to play the keys G, D, A, and E as he checked the tuning of the violin. Just like he previously was informed the violin was perfectly tuned.

"You are going to play Mozart - Violin Sonata No. 36, F Major?" Zayd asked Clara.

"Yes, I'm ready," Clara replied.

Clara's perfume and sandy blonde hair with such a beautiful face really put a lot of pressure on Zayd. Her magic now transcended on him, and he wanted to play as good for her as he had done for his idol Wilber.

This Mozart Sonata begins with the pianist and the violinist starting at the same time. Zayd had the violin and bow in position and nodded to Clara who started playing which Zayd synchronized to. In a sense the pianist is the conductor, the violinist uses the pianist as the focal point to play off.

It wasn't Zayd showing off, it was the exhilaration he felt playing with Clara. Her looks and scent from the lavishly expensive French perfume had a remarkable effect on Zayd. Just like before this performance was being recorded by high fidelity video and microphones. After Sheik Abdulla's film editor went through it and repackaged it into an almost commercial product, the video was sent to the Crown Prince who quickly watched it and loved every bit of it and texted his two friends how delightful the performance was and the magic word: BRAVO!

The performance is not long, just 17 minutes, and the two performers interpreted the music with great accuracy and created the sound Mozart intended.

The acoustics in the room, because of how it was designed, gave the audience a significant sound level and a feeling of closeness to the music. This performance was as good as world acclaimed performers would have done. Clara and Zayd performed together as a team, having seldom seen each other and never performing music together before. What they did just now guaranteed they would see more of each other in the future as their parents would influence them to perform at future family gatherings. During these family gatherings the two were allowed to spend private time together with each family hoping they would transcend into a lover's embrace and ensure an optimal coupling for the future.

Clara and Zayd were far more sophisticated than their families understood. They each had their inspiration and future plans. Clara was not necessarily going to spend the rest of her life in the Middle East. Zayd had his own influencer, Wilber. At this point they enjoyed friendship, but neither wanted to go beyond that as it would distract them from achieving their life goals that were still being formulated and they wanted to experience what their parents had done, having their minds altered by the best professors in the world to develop the essential ingredients for future success.

The two finished and Zayd put the violin down on its holder and the bow on its holder and walked back over to his seat. Anna then stood up and walked over and picked up her Stratovarius and Arcus Gold Violin Bow and in about 30 seconds started playing Nicolo Paganini. Caprice No. 24 for violin solo. [Niccolò Paganini - Caprice No. 24 - YouTube]

***

Chapter Twelve

Faye Wong - Dinner Time

Anna's performance quickly gave Wilber flashbacks of his former dead lover, the beautiful and illustrious Chinese spy Faye Wong who attempted to murder him.

Feye and Wilber had just enjoyed an Anna Fedorova performance at the Vienna Symphony hours before that terrible incident.

[Rachmaninoff: Rhapsody on a Theme of Paganini - Anna Fedorova - Live Classical Music HD - YouTube]

The music was lovely, then Wilber and Faye Wong had a splendid dinner and several stiff drinks. Nothing seemed out of the ordinary. Wilber was in love and Faye Wong demonstrated why elegant looking women from Hong Kong are so effective in dealing with Occidental's while making love after the dinner in Faye's hotel room soon after.

Wilber did sense there was something strange going on with Feye, she was lovely and seemed sincere in her lovemaking, but Wilber didn't realize he was making love to Latrodectus, a black widow spider. Then the incident happened, Wilber shot Feye Wong through the heart as she was lunging at him with the knife.

Wilber mildly shook up, got out of bed, turned on the light and checked Faye Wong's pulse and determined she was dead. In the mannerism the knife held in Feye's death grip was situated he could see the blade was coated about two inches around the tip with some type of substance that looked like Vaseline.

Wilber walked over to the hotel's Chester Drawers and on top of it was hotel stationery and envelopes. He grabbed a piece of stationery, walked over, and rubbed some of the substance from one side of the knife blade onto the sheet of paper then carefully folded it up several times then put it in an envelope and sealed the envelope and stuffed it down in his socks when he got dressed immediately.

Shortly afterwards Wilber realized Feye Wong appeared to be nothing more than a Chinese MSS spy operative who he mistakenly thought was his lover in a substantial relationship.

Shooting Feye, drove Wilber into a psychological cyclone. Wilber quickly concluded the name Faye Wong was nothing more than an alias for a Chinese MSS spy. Looking at her documents would serve no useful purpose because they were likely all fake documents like most spy's use. Wilber knew his safety required leaving the hotel immediately.

Wilber left Faye Wong's hotel room and surmised it was probably bugged and even though his gun had a silencer on it monitors might get suspicious and come and check it out. Though they had just had some rip- roaring wild sex, the surveillance team might think they were sleeping. His guess was right, otherwise he would soon be dead.

Wilber traveled light for this secret rendezvous in Vienna Austria. Wilber walked a short distance away and notified his handlers he needed an emergency extraction.

As expected, in fifteen minutes a car pulled up in front of Wilber's location using a CIA tracker APP. Wilber recognized the men in the automobile. Wilber got into the sedan's back seat and was promptly driven to the airport where a private Jet was waiting on standby.

The jet was waiting there because an operation was due to finish at any moment when a spy was scheduled to show up after Wilber finished his rendezvous with Feye and give Wilber some valuable information. The reality is that person was Feye who now lying dead in her hotel room that shocked the maids when they entered the room in the morning and saw Fey and all the blood that soaked into the bed sheets she laid on.

The Vienna police investigators showed up at the crime scene in the morning after the hotel maids called the police and carefully put the knife in a large two-quart zip lock bag to avoid contamination issues. They too could see the knife found in a death grip was coated with something. They found a glass bottle and Q-tips in the bathroom that was used to coat the tip of the knife with Ricin that was mixed with a stabilizer substance giving it an appearance like Vaseline.

All Feye Wong needed to accomplish was penetrate Wilbers skin with the high concentration of Ricin on the blade tip and Wilber would not live to see tomorrow. When the investigators discovered the deadly poison Ricin on the knife blade in the woman's death grip and the two gunshot wounds into the chest and in her heart, they knew this was some type of deadly spy operation. Of course, the Chinese disavowed Faye Wong an Alias traveling with stolen identity.

***

Anna performed the Nicolo Paganini Caprice as good as Sophie Mutter or Hillary Hahn demonstrating she was truly a gifted prodigy.

Anna and Clara were half-sisters, that is why there were two mothers here watching them perform. Anna wasn't interested in Zayd at all, she had her fantasy of one day being with a handsome movie star like Brad Pitt. Anna and Clara got along very well. They were sisters, but they also were best friends.

Sometimes Clara helped Anna practice with sonatas playing the piano portion for her. The violin instructor, a hard ass Russian Igor Luxemburg liked this arrangement since he was not a pianist and would have to bring one to perform the piano accompaniment. The one-hour lessons were taxing for both Anna and Clara who felt Igor was torturing Clara.

Eventually when Anna discovered she advanced rapidly because of the finesse Igor had with training. Her attitude shifted from drudgery to wild speculation on how the violin would open doors for her. Her enthusiasm elevated as she completed more and more complicated violin works. Anna also indirectly helped Clara, who got great benefit out of the training learning the piano portions of the violin sonatas.

After the music ended and all the feelings were greatly enhanced with the Hashish, Sheikh Abdulla was getting hungry and asked his personal valet who stood near him, "Go see if the Chef is about ready to serve us food."

Moments later the Valet returned and reported, "The Chef is ready to start serving appetizers in the dining room."

"Thank you."

Sheikh Abdulla stood up and said, "Alright everyone please follow me to the dining room, I'm getting kind of hungry."

Moments later Sheikh Abdulla escorted his distinguished guests into his fabulous dining hall that could be arranged to handle 100 guests if necessary.

Today the Dining Table had twenty placemats and tent style placemat cards with the seating arrangement already figured out.

Wilber, Xinxin, Sheikh Omar, Zayd and Anna and her mother were sitting on one side and Sheikh Abdulla was sitting next to his two wives and Prince Bandar was sitting next to his wife #2.

Clara was seated directly across from Zayd where they could hold a conversation and since Anna was next to Zayd, Clara could speak to her as well.

There were five waiters buzzing around the table filling water and wine glasses and in some cases delivering tea.

Suddenly a person walked into the room with a large tray and one of the waiters opened a folding table to set the large tray down. That had several dishes filled with Shawarmas on them. These were appetizers to help take care of immediate hunger pains. Waiters picked up those plates of Shawarmas and went around moving the tent placemat card out of the way and sat the dish down in front of each person present. By the time the first tray was empty and removed a second tray was there repeating the process going around the table serving all twenty people and guests.

Besides the eight people that were in the front room hearing the musical performances, more people who arrived now sitting down were being introduced. They were the remainder of Sheikh Abdulla's wives and Prince Bandar's wives that just arrived and were systematically all being introduced to Wilber and Xinxin. The rest of them knew each other and did not require introductions.

All those present knew about Zayd's adventure with an American Spy who was the modern-day Lawrence of Arabia rescuing him in the grips of the enemy the day he was scheduled to get his head cut off.

All those terrorists assigned to kill Zayd instead met their maker and did not receive their 74 virgins as promised by their clerics.

Now was the time the guests were to receive the most astonishing information about the entire ordeal. Sitting right in the middle of the crowd was Wilber O'Toole, the CIA man who saved young Zayd killing over 100 terrorists in the process, placing a huge dent into their organization.

The guests were all dreamy eyed looking at Wilber. And here he was sitting next to Xinxin, a woman with a Chinese name and fully ethnic Chinese, appearing as a Han Chinese, exotic and beautiful. The combination of the Zayd's story and looking at the

sun-tanned man in front of them who could now pass for an Abu Dhabi man with the hair and the beard and extreme handsomeness.

Many of the women present had sisters they wish could become one of Wilber's wives. How many wives did he have now?

In the UAE a woman cannot sleep with a man unless they are married, some of the people present knew Xinxin was Wilber's lover. Hence, he was given a temporary marriage with Xinxin to make the copulating legal according to Arabic laws. Until they had an official permanent unification, the temporary marriage provided the permit to conduct their private affairs in the manner they wished.

Xinxin who was a master makeup artist had herself looking smoking hot, and despite Westerner's misunderstanding of Arab women dress, they indeed could wear quite beautiful clothes like Xinxin was wearing in the privacy of their or their friend's home. Xinxin was the living princess, and her style and grace were infectious.

Xinxin's beauty raised everyone's estimation of Wilber. For him to capture the heart of such a living princess spoke volumes about his human condition and how he interacted with others. Wilber would not be sitting across from two of the most powerful men in Abu Dhabi unless he was someone quite extraordinaire. Wilber's looks, his charm, and his interactions with each of them as the day and evening slowly passed reinforced their first impression.

At the early part of the meal the very large dining hall had more than half of it empty and was now slowly being set up for a small orchestra that was now showing up to perform dinner music and entertainment after the meal. Everyone seemed excited. The musicians were dressed immaculately. This truly was a special event.

Wilber dressed as Lawrence of Arabia fit the evening atmosphere in quite a spellbinding manner. One of the wives present was a Chinese Linguist and fluent in four dialects. Before she became a wife, she was a person used in translation with Chinese businessmen who were heavily involved in a variety of projects as well as international trade. Some of the Arab clothing people wore today was made in China.

This woman was seated in a position where she could talk to Xinxin because she looked forward to speaking with someone in Chinese which she rarely could do now.

"You look lovely tonight Xinxin [今晚你看起來很可愛欣欣]," Sheikh Abdulla's wife and Chinese linguist said in Chinese.

"Thank you very much. You are very pretty as well," Xinxin responded.

The woman thinking nobody else present understood Chinese and said in Chinese, "Wilber looks so handsome. Is he a good love maker?"

Wilber started smiling when Xinxin said, "Wilber is a Chinese linguist, you can ask him in Chinese?"

The woman, born in Great Britain, blue eyed and blond turned bright red with utter astonishment and embarrassment.

Wilber decided to help the woman recover from her blunder and said in Mandarin Chinese dialect:

「如果我沒有一顆善良的心，向她證明我愛她，我就不會和欣欣 在一起。 她知道我的愛是真實的、真誠的。 當兩個人像我們一樣彼此　相愛時，愛情就會像魔法一樣流動，感覺非常美好 。."

`Rúguǒ wǒ méiyǒ u yī kē shànliáng de xīn, xiàng tā zhèngmíng wǒ ài tā, wǒ jiù bù huì hé xīnxīn zài yīqǐ . Tā zhīdào wǒ de ài shì zhēnshí de, zhēnchéng de. Dāng liǎ ng gè rénxiàng wǒ men yīyàng bǐ cǐ xiāng'ài shí, àiqíng jiù huì xiàng mófǎ yīyàng liúdòng, gǎ njué fēicháng měihǎ o.]."

["I would not be with Xinxin if I didn't have a kind heart and proved to her, I was in love with her. She knows my love is real and genuine. When two people love each other as much as we do, the love flows like magic and feels so good."]

Xinxin knew the woman felt so silly for not finding out about Wilber's Chinese speaking ability before she asked such a tumultuous question and decided to respond in a way, she helped reduce the woman's apparent anguish over the embarrassing situation and said:

威爾伯所說的一切都是真的。 我們一起經歷了很多。 我信任他， 我愛他。 祂對我友善而溫柔，並以我想要的方式給予我愛。就像他 說的，感覺就像魔法一樣。

Wēi ěr bó suǒ shuō de yīqiè dōu shì zhēn de. Wǒ men yīqǐ jīnglìle hěnduō. Wǒ xìnrèn tā, wǒ ài tā. Tā duì wǒ yǒ ushàn ér wēnróu, bìng yǐ wǒ xiǎ ng yào de fāngshì jǐ yǔ wǒ ài. Jiù xiàng tā shuō de, gǎ njué jiù xiàng mófǎ yīyàng.

["Everything Wilber said is true. We have been through a lot together. I trust him and I love him. He's kind and gentle with me and gives me love in the way I want it. Like he said it feels like magic."]

The woman quickly recovered her composure and immediately

felt the warmth and friendship from the couple which allowed her to suddenly feel refreshed and no further stress and enveloped a lovely smile. She then spoke in British English, "That is so wonderful to hear. It makes my heart feel good to know you are a lovely couple together."

"Thank you very much," Xinxin responded.

Wilber then gave a bow on his head to show respect and had a lovely smile.

Her husband pickup on some of this would ask her later for the translations but for now decided to ask in Arabic, "Do you like Xinxin?"

"Oh yes, I've quickly determined she's a wonderful person and I'm happy that Wilber, someone who is very close to Zayd and Sheikh Omar, has such a beautiful woman close to his heart." His wife responded in Arabic.

Sheikh Abdulla responded in Arabic, "Yes, I completely agree with you."

Slowly the musical section was completed, and the musicians already fed and given time to freshen up after their meals were ushered into the dining hall where they would soon be performing about twenty feet away from the dining table. There were also five security men in the room packing UZI's in their suit coats just in case one of the musicians turned out to be a terrorist.

The portable Steinway was assembled all during this time. A piano tuner quickly checked it and made any adjustments and then nodded at the conductor and left the room to another room where he and other auxiliary people were staged in case they were needed.

After the musicians were all seated there were four additional chairs set up and soon everyone would know why as four singers well-dressed arrived and took those seats as they would perform individually or as a group on various songs.

Meanwhile the meal was served multiple entrées. The food served that Wilber enjoyed the most included Al Machboos, Khuzi, Stuffed Camel, Al Harees, Tabbouleh, and Saloona.

A couple of the female singers performing appeared like Julia Boutros and Najwa Karam

While the entrées continued to serve the music began. You pay for what you get in the middle east. It's all pay to play. Middle Easterners understand this process quite well. If you spend money at the level the Sheikh Abdulla was to entertain his guests, you get this level of talent that was quite compelling.

The twenty people enjoying dinner were getting their private concert. In a few minutes, Wilber estimated this quality of production was up there with Igor Krutoy, minus the light show. The music sounded impressive and quickly put everyone in a great mood.

The female singers singing Arab love songs, resonated the hearts of everyone, Xinxin included. She did not need to understand the words to know it all meant love and she felt love sitting right next to her. This whole scenario significantly elevated Xinxin's opinion of Wilber. After seeing him in action professionally as a spy and his conduct now in the middle east transfixed her psychology on Wilber who was starting to shape up to be her lifetime partner.

The male Arab singers had impressive voices and range. They too were almost magical. These male singers were as good as Andrea Bocelli, just singing in a different language.

The professional pianist on that portable Steinway as well as the violinist, cellists, base violin, percussionists, flute, and oboe players created an interesting tapestry of sound that created a synergism of musical ensembles adding greatly to the experience. From their advantage point Wilber and Xinxin were facing the orchestra, and the singers were about fifteen feet from them. Microphones were not necessary.

Wilber didn't know this. This show was put on for him. Sheikh Abdulla was spending serious money for his entertainment. That's how Arabs are. When they come across someone like Wilber who put his life on the line to save one of their own, they appreciate it.

These wealthy families are sometimes the victims of terrorists and other types of bad guys. They were vulnerable and had to spend sizeable amounts on personal security. They are probably the most security savvy people in the world because they are close to the action and being by the straits of Hormuz and directly across from Iran creates some perplexing and serious issues.

They also knew more about the incident than Wilber and the CIA knew because there were two survivors and information flowing out about all the human carnage including the one hundred plus terrorists plus the dozen mercenaries who died in that horrific clash. It was a terrible war zone, and the firefight was intense. A lot of lead was flying everywhere, and it seemed like a miracle Wilber made it out of there alive.

The Arabs thought divine intervention and Ala preserved Wilber's life so that he could preserve Zayd's life because maybe Ala had big plans for Zayd.

As one of the security guards said to the other privately watching from afar, "That dude is one bad ass spy." He knew the full story directly from Sheikh Omar himself. He knew Sheikh Omar quite well who was very articulate and never embellished anything and said as little as possible most of the time. He spoke with his pocketbook.

In essence, this performance by the musicians was a celebration for Wilber and Zayd's who traveled across the desert three days and nights on camels. This whole ordeal gave Wilber a greater appreciation for camels. His exposure to the Middle East had a profound impact on his psyche and did a great amount to mold him for his upcoming mission he did not know existed.

Wilber would be the last person in the world to ever think he would be put in that role. But a guy like the DD/P wants to put his very best man on the most important tasks.

In due time everyone saw the female singers were singing to Wilber, there was no mistake about it. They had their special briefing earlier in the day. Their whole purpose in life, being here this evening getting paid as much as they would for a soldout concert in a stadium, was to entertain this one guest Wilber O'Toole. During their special briefings they were shown a lot of pictures of Wilber including him and Zayd as they emerged from the desert on camels filthy dirty in the grateful hands of Sheikh Omar and his wife Emily.

The special video the musicians saw also observed those crocodile tears coming down Emily. Sheikh Omar also had many tears. He had given up all hope he would ever see his first son Zayd alive ever again.

The singers sang their hearts out for Wilber O'Toole because they knew he was a special man who saved an important life in a mannerism where his own life was in severe risk doing this mission, exemplified by the fact every one of the mercenaries he brought with him were left behind dead with severe wounds.

Had Wilber not brought Xinxin with him the two female singers would have offered their bodies to Wilber and given him love that a true hero deserves once in their lifetime for extraordinary valor that is rarely experienced.

Now the guests got into friendly conversations as you would expect at a family gathering where a lot of topics were discussed including the three artificial Palm Island structures built. The three Sheikh's in attendance at the party, financed a lot of the construction.

"Palm Jumeirah, Palm Deira Islands, and Palm Jebel Ali are truly remarkable, but there is one more thing I would do," Wilber said.

"What would that be?" Prince Bandar asked.

"I would build a fourth palm island structure as part of a dome city."

"How would you build it?"

"Same as you have done with the three palms, except this one would be covered by a very large arched dome. The surface of the dome would be solar panels with a lot of glass openings over 50% of the done in a random pattern to let in sunlight during the day. The outside edges would have beach front properties. Lowest level would be roads, parking, transportation (subway trains) HVAC machinery, and all support systems. The second level would be business and habitat. Inside the dome would be high rise buildings. The dome would be built on top of cylindrical pillars to support it. The internal waterways would all be encased in dams and structures to alleviate all forms of erosion, so the environmentalists could not complain. Those in-dome waterways would have boat docks."

"That sounds like an interesting idea," Crown Pince Bandar said. "It would be the first dome city in the world."

"Would it be considered a new city and not part of Dubai?"

"The Dome City could be built Southwest from Abu Dhabi, further down the coast from Dubai where there is more open land."

"What would be the chief advantage of a dome city here?"

"Just like the huge shopping mall in Dubai, nobody would want to leave it because you could maintain the internal temperature at 72 degrees year-round by blocking out half the sunlight and HVAC systems. Individual homes would not need heat or air conditioning."

"I may want to keep in contact with you and discuss this further, the idea sounds very intriguing."

"Prince Bandar, I would enjoy keeping in touch with you and

discussing my ideas about building dome cities. As you grapple with population growth, you could build dome cities in the middle of the desert and pump in sea water for desalination plants creating plenty of water."

"What about greenery?" Prince Bandar asked.

"Since 50% of the sunlight would come into the dome, plants and trees would thrive and help purify the air."

"I like that idea."

"You can put in just as much greenery as now exits at the Palm Jumeirah."

"I suppose we could."

"I would also suspect a lot of sea life would migrate into the dome water estuary's because it would be a lot cooler and better for marine life. You could import some marine life that could not exist otherwise."

"Wilber, you give me a lot to think about. I'm going to have one of my architects make a drawing with your idea. Would you be willing to talk with him?"

"If it would help create a dome city, I would love it too. Especially if you build one out in the desert."

"Wilber, I think I would prefer to build a dome city in the desert first."

"Your excellency, that too would benefit mankind, and it would help you work out engineering principles and not have to develop lessons learned in a tougher environment, such as would be the case with a palm Island structure. But I think eventually you will figure out a palm island dome would be a huge innovation in that it would be creating a city on water."

"Instead of building islands, why not just float the structure?"

"That's an interesting idea and there have been proposals to build floating cities and airports. Hong Kong is an example of a floating city with Sampans, just on a smaller scale."

"I can visualize that. How would a city be built like this?"

"Instead of breaking up single hull oil tankers or cargo ships in a salvage operation, remove the engine room and the super structure.

Move it into position where you want to build the dome city and fill it with sand to sink it at the spot you want it. Take three other ships being scrapped and move them into position creating a rectangle and sink them filling them with sand from the desert.

At the four corners where the noses and rear ends of the ships meet a structure built like build a Mulberry Harbour like they did at Normandy Invasion during World War II, using Phoenix Caissons just on the inside corners where the ships meet that would be fastened to the ships with large steel cables. Phoenix Caissons could also be placed to rim the outside of this structure sunk and filled with sand from the desert. You then end up with a dam that surrounds the site where you build this portion of the dome city."

"Alright," Prince Bandar replied.

"You could then pump out all the water inside this structure and haul in sand from the desert to fill it up. You might want to consider building a temporary railroad from the desert miles out to this construction site coming up from the south where there is vast open desert land with large sand dunes. During this portion of the construction very thick foundations could be created to build the steel rebar reinforced pillars to rise high to support the Dome roof."

"How would this affect the environmentalists?"

Since there would be no dredging involved, they can't complain about increased sediments like they do with the current Palm Islands. Outer portions of the Phoenix Caissons could be built with fish habitats.

"How about the outer ring beach areas?"

"The Phoenix Caissons and the gutted sunken holding the sand creating those large rectangular artificial Islands allows the numerous internal building structures. The very outer ring would then have an artificial beach created. Outside the outer ring built by concentric series of Phoenix Caissons, would have beach, but the inner side would not, it would be solid and part of the artificial island structures."

"What about the beach?"

"You would not want to have a continuous beach. There needs to be water entrances for the internal waterway plus the sea life habitat built."

"That sounds reasonable. How would the beach areas be built which is now part of the Persian Gulf?"

"To build the beach, boulders from a mountain quarry would be brought in to create the first layer of the beach, sloping down into the water. On top of these boulders sand and sea grass would be installed in sections. Hence the sediments put into the water would be significantly reduced."

"What could be the chief complaint of the environmentalists?" "They would claim we are making sea water levels rise." "Seems to me like that's exactly what we are doing."

"Have your architects calculate how much area the Dome City added to the sea level, then dig a huge trench out into the desert where you build a dome city, making an inland waterway. If you have that inland waterway all the way into the middle of the desert, like the Suez Canal, you will have the volume of water needed for desalination and create an artificial freshwater lake in a big hole you create taking out the sand to fill the empty ships and the Phoenix Caissons."

"Sound like I need to hire you as an advisor," Prince Bandar said.

"Your Royal Highness, you do not need to hire me. I will give you my ideas for free. I've done so willingly as to help mankind. You have done exemplary development in the UAE that should inspire the world. You proved by building the Palm Islands that mankind can build magnificent structures if we show the will to tackle the odds and show what mankind is capable of."

"Thank you, Wilber, I do appreciate your comments."

"Sir, I'm not an architect or civil engineer. My expertise lies elsewhere. But based on the Mulberry Harbors and Phoenix Caissons built during WW2, I can visualize how a Dome City could be built on top of a Palm Island Dome City."

"Wilber, I like your idea of sinking ships instead of scrapping them, saves a lot of money."

"Yes, the idea of sinking the empty ships eliminates a disposal problem, and once they water is pumped out of the artificial island created and the hulls are filled with sand and slowly dried out, the steel hulls will last for centuries holding the sand so that

Phoenix Caissons will not have any lateral stress on them."

"Wilber, you also have monetized something we would never think about."

"What's that your excellency?"

"All that sand in the desert is valuable building material and we have plenty of it." "Yes, I agree."

"I have another question if you don't mind?"

"Not a problem sir, please ask."

"What do you think about putting domes over the top of current palm island structures?"

"Your excellency, I think Palm Jumeirah has so much creative architecture designed to be exposed. I would not recommend altering it by putting a dome on top. Palm Deira Islands have not really got to the point where a personality has been developed, it would be a good candidate to put a dome over the top. Palm Jebel Ali has been developed to the point now you are quickly reaching the point where a dome might not be suitable. Plus, since its closer to Abu Dhabi, it might be worthwhile to simply complete the design plan."

"Wilber, you think a fourth dome covered palm island development close to Abu Dhabi would be appropriate?"

"Most certainly, your excellency. I think a dome city could be built atop four island including Al Nouf, Al Ar-Yam, Halat Al Bahrani, and Al Futaisi."

"What about transportation?"

Road and Train tracks could go from the new Abu Dhabi Dome leaving at Al Futaisi Island traveling over Al Hudayrial Island past Kahlifa University where the new four lane road would connect to Sheikh Zayed Bin

Sultan St. (Hiway E10). The new rail line would parallel E10 and follow along to

E12 to make a big loop then back to the Dome City."

"That would be a very ambitious plan."

"The new Dome City call it Abu Dhabi II would inspire the residents of Abu Dhabi and lighting could be put on the dome for nighttime visualization from Abu

Dhabi creating the seventh wonder of the world."

"How about a dome city in the desert?"

"The first dome city in the desert would fit well North of Asab in the large open area between Hiway E15 and Hiway E45."

"Excuse me one moment," Prince Bandar said as he pulled up google maps on his I-phone and started looking at the area.

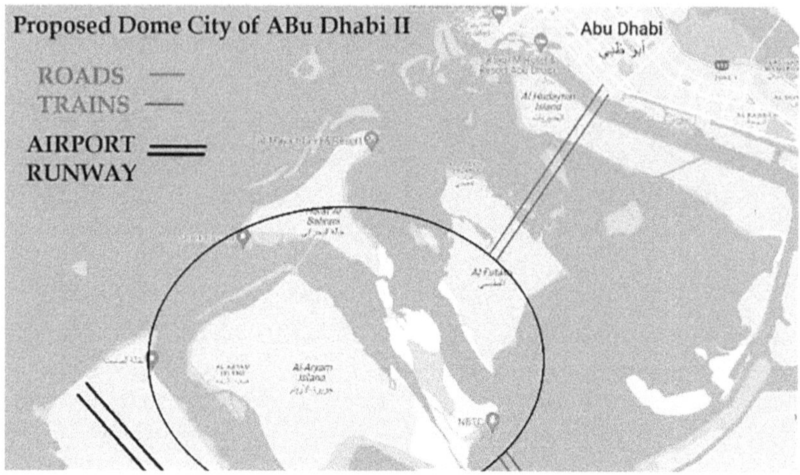

Location of the proposed new dome city Abu Dhabi II

The prince studied the map and said, "I can see where four dome cities could be built east to west of that area. All four dome cities could be spaced equal distance and at the same exact latitude."

"Just think how that would look from space at night, especially if you put a fancy multi-colored light system on them," Wilber said.

"Wilber, you truly inspire me. If you were here all the time, I'm sure we would have never-ending conversations."

"Your Majesty, that is true, and neither one of us would get any work done. That's why it's important I leave!"

The two men smiled, and Prince Bandar was smiling because Wilber was so fun to talk with.

The evening slowly wound down and people started to evaporate. When the three Sheikhs had enough it was time to call it quits. The day was an emotional rollercoaster. But you must experience days like this to remember them for the rest of your life. They were all connected through personal experiences and Wilber and Zayd for even more critical reasons of the past.

***

Wilber, Xinxin, Sheikh Omar, Zayd, and Emily all were escorted to Sheikh Omar's helicopter and flew back to Sheikh Omar's mansion personal landing pad.

There were a few more days of golf and falconing, then it was time to depart.

The night before their departure. The three Sheikhs took Wilber to a special club in Abu Dhabi. Only Sheiks and Princes were allowed in with their special guests, approved ahead of time. Nobody was going to turn down Prince Bandar who was the crown Prince's cousin. The request for the visitor was promptly approved with enthusiasm.

Sheikh Omar took Wilber with him on his helicopter to a high rise building with a landing pad on it. After they got off the helicopter it was required to leave since others were arriving. Sheikh Omar would contact his pilot when to fly back to pick him up and the building administration allowed landing.

This private club was unknown. It was well secluded, and the public would be utterly astonished if they knew what went on in there. But it gave these men most of them related a chance to meet without their wives and have fun. There were many exotic beautiful women there to provide pleasure if required. All the mood modifiers they wanted or needed were there.

Some of the activity was such a guarded secret, the author could not put it in this book for fear for his life.

These close friends all gathered around a rectangular table structure with a large open area in the middle for servants. All the guests sat on the outside with waitresses on the inside to take care of their needs. When the men ordered anything there were three circular areas inside the large rectangular opening with gold railings. The purpose of the railings was soon revealed.

The waitresses, exotic beautiful women would walk over to the gold railings open up what looked like a little gate, step inside and it would drop down to a lower level where she would exit a door that would promptly close. Moments later she would return up that mini circular elevator with the order of drinks, food or in some cases a beautiful woman who would appear, leave the open area at one end of the large rectangular table structure, and walk over to one of the men.

Wilber had a powerful Sheik on each side of him and got a lot of looks even though he was dressed up in Lawrence of Arabia dress. Wilber noticed many guests

were staring at him. He postulated why and could not come up with any real reason for it since his disguise was quite good and now his beard had grown out long enough to look like an Arab Bedouin.

What Wilber didn't know is these men were all well connected at the hip. The men in this room built modern day Abu Dhabi and Dubai. Most of them were genius and well educated in London, Technical University of Munich, Harvard, The Indian Institute of Science, Saratov in Russia, and Paris-Saclay University. Over half of them had PhD's in significant areas of study. They were all in part brilliant men and related to each other through generations.

Prince Bandar ordered for him and Sheikh Omar and Wilber. He knew they had some very special stuffed camel here prepared by the best Chef in Abu Dhabi. Soon each of the three had their personal waiter.

Some of these women reminded Wilber of women he saw in Spain that worked in special bars from Casa Blanca Morrocco wearing see through tops where their areoles and nipples could be seen on very well-formed breasts. There were no women present that were not at least stellar. They all had beautiful faces and bodies. Every waitress was a gorgeous creature and many of them willing to be wife number three or number four.

This club had something highly illegal, alcohol drinks and many men were smoking Hashish in a gold-plated water filter rig. The room was so full of Hashish smoke that even Wilber felt he was getting a buzz off it.

Wilber was quite amused at how well they could make stuffed Camel. The meat not only tasted fantastic, the stuffed Camel melted in his mouth. It was almost as if the event was planned for when the two Sheikh's and Wilber stopped eating.

Suddenly the three circular platforms went down and immediately came back up with three gorgeous women. Wilber was mesmerized. He thought the waitress were beautiful, but these women had eye shadow on and other decorations that created a temporal odyssey like Wilber never felt before.

Momentarily Wilber discovered what their role in life was. The three women were belly dancers. Wilber had seen belly dancers in

Egypt on a mission one time when he was there checking up on four Egyptian nuclear researchers to find out if they were attempting to build the bomb. He found something far more disturbing. They were working with Iranian Scientists. Cash in Advance then happened. Some of those men disappeared. They were part of the ecological food chain of the red sea soon afterwards.

It a short period of time Wilber discovered the three belly dancers were concentrating in the vicinity of where he was sitting. Some of them approached Wilber very closely and they danced like Wilber never could imagine. They danced for several minutes then there was a short break. One of the Belly Dancers approached Wilber and bent over and said in British accent, "Wilber, I have a secret, please come closer."

Wilber moved his head closer so the woman could whisper in his ear, "Wilber, I'm a virgin. I've never had sex before. I'm saving it for a special man. You are a special man. If you want to make love to me tonight, I'll take you somewhere and give my body to you."

Wilber was obviously touched. He knew this was all a setup for him. He turned his face to the beautiful woman and said, "I would probably fall in love with you, and then I would break another woman's heart. I want you to know I do want you very badly but thought of breaking another heart stops me from doing it."

The woman then turned again to Wilber and said, "These wonderful Sheiks can convert you to a Muslim tonight and you can have four wives. I'll be your number two wife."

"Wilber then responded, "I know I want you, but my lover cannot handle such an arrangement. I'm very sorry, but if it doesn't work out with her, can I come back for you?"

"Yes, you may, but don't take too long, okay?"

"I'm always prompt," Wilber said and smiled.

"You are such an amazing man. I think I love you."

"Well, I know I love you, but I can't break another heart."

"Thank you, Wilber. You made my day and made me feel appreciated." "What is your name?" Wilber asked.

"My name is Salma Rachid. There is a famous singer with the same name its strictly coincidental."

"Is she a good singer?"

"She is very good. I wish I was as pretty as she is and could sing like she can."

"Perhaps she's not as good a dancer as you are."

"That's possible, but I know she's tops at whatever she does."

"I'll check out Salma Rachid's music as soon as I can."

"Would you like me to request her music for my next dance?"

"Yes, I would love that. Thank you."

The two smiled at each other and just like on command the music started playing and she started dancing again. It almost seemed like she was drugged. The truth is she was. Her own brain created chemicals such as serotonin at high levels responding to Wilber because she knew his words came from his heart.

There were a few more dances and then suddenly all the waiters and dancers went down the circular elevators, leaving just the men alone. It was now like a secret meeting.

About 20 feet across the room from Wilber was the other side of the rectangular table sections with the huge opening in the middle. When the floor sections came back up sealing in their privacy, one of the men standing directly across from Wilber stood up. There was sudden silence in the room.

"Wilber, I'm Omar's brother. He's my older brother and he taught me all my lessons in life. He's my best friend and guide. Any time I need help with anything I know Omar stands behind me always willing to help and give everything. I could never ask for a better brother."

Wilber listened very carefully because this was an extraordinary revelation that everyone in the room probably knew who he was, which meant his safety now had a lot of risk involved.

"You don't know this, but when the terrorist kidnapped Zayd and were able to escape the UAE which surprised everyone. It was a well- planned event; we had no idea our enemies were so skillful and advanced. No doubt they probably had help from a powerful country. We are one big family. Therefore, Zayd's abduction was quite an ordeal for all of us."

We have a friend, John Burke. We asked him for help. That's how you got involved. We have spies and we had a rough idea where they were holding Zayd. If we did not give into their terms, they were going to cut Zayd's head off that morning scheduled just before you rescued him.

Was that why John Burkette was here? Wilber wondered.

"We know what you and Zayd went through three days on camels escaping across the desert in an epic journey. We also know what the battle was like and how your mercenaries were all killed as well as over 100 terrorists. It was a nasty battle, and you are lucky to be alive. These were some of the most ferocious fighters in the region and very well-paid assassins."

All Wilber could do is sit there and take it all in. He was in a captive audience of very wealthy and powerful men. At least he was on the good side of them.

"From all of us Wilber, thank you. And we are very happy you wanted to come here to visit. It means a lot to us."

Wilber knew he was in a very delicate situation and these powerful men had a long reach. But at the same time, he felt obligated to speak about it. He then stood up, which quickly got all their attention wondering what he was going to do.

"In many cases when I go on assignments, I never know if I was compromised. I had the painful experience of having to kill a woman I thought was my lover who happened to be an enemy spy sent to kill me."

All the people in the room were listening to every word Wilber said.

This was a somber moment.

"When the people I work for and in this case was a man many of you know, John Burkette came to me for a special assignment. I knew it easily could be a goat fuck poorly timed and coordinated. John gave me complete freedom of action including allowing me to hire who I wanted to do the mission." The silence continued.

"I had friends in the business who are hired guns. Mercenaries, it's all about money for them. They were so assured of themselves they thought they could all pull this off and get rich in the process."

"But as you noted we were up against some very tough guys. A lot tougher than we anticipated."

"Now you might ask the question, did I do this for the money?"

"Actually, I get paid a salary. I get paid 25% hazardous duty pay that's all. The mercenaries get paid a hell of a lot more than me. They get paid real money. That's how it works."

"This was really a volunteer mission. I wasn't asked to volunteer, but I understood I had no choice I had to go and manage affairs."

"Now you might want to ask why I didn't turn down the assignment?"

"There were two reasons."

"First of all, I don't like terrorists grabbing people. It pisses me off."

"Secondly, I knew they couldn't send an office warrior to go do this. But I also knew another thing, the chickenshit office warriors were not going to go anyway. A Cowboy had to step up to the plate and do this mission to save a life.

"I never met Zayd before. I never knew who he was before this event. The only plus in the INTEL given me that would be helpful is Zayd could speak English so when the event happened, he would know I was there to rescue him."

"So now you know I only earned my regular pay. There were no incentives. Now you are all probably wondering what I got out of it. There was something more important than money. Zayd is my friend for life now. He's a brilliant person and I like him a lot. He's like the son I never had. He's my blood brother. Zayd proved to me on those three days on the camels he would do anything. I knew I could count on him. The only way we made it out of enemy territory was to stay on those camels and get a lot of miles. I have a huge appreciation for camels now."

"My reward is my friend Zayd is living. Now I know how it was all worthwhile. If I had to do it again, I would be knowing I easily could have been killed since a lot of men were killed in that battle. The enemy is ferocious fighters. Even though they are the enemy, one must respect the martial spirit of such an enemy."

"I have no pleasure in killing the enemy because in reality they too are great men. But it was necessary. Their mistake was supporting Evil which got them killed. They thought they were invincible and had no idea someone else would enter the picture to divert the situation in ways they never imagined. "

Wilber looked around the room and saw those intense looks from all of them. It was a come to Jesus, moment.

Wilber then finished, "Thank you all for inviting me here tonight. I've enjoyed it." Wilber then sat down.

Wilber felt weakness and emotion, but he had his pride and refused to let himself tear up even though he felt it.

There was an awesome quiet for a couple minutes. And finally, Omars brother stood up and started clapping. Just like on cue the rest stood up. Wilber had a standing ovation

from all the richest men from Dubai and Abu Dhabi. No Westerner has ever received this before. This was indeed a singularity.

Wilber stood up and a Sheikh on one side of him grabbed him and hugged him and said, "Thank you Wilber." Then just like clockwork all the men walked around and did the same.

When Omar's brother approached Wilber, he couldn't hold it back. As Omars brother hugged him and felt him weeping he stayed there holding Wilber letting him get past this emotional moment and retaining his dignity. Omar's brother suspected he

knew the hell Wilber had gone through. Shooting your lover who was a spy trying to kill you left deep emotional scars, but obviously there was much more to it. These Arab men were so considerate for Wilber's feelings. Wilber learned a valuable lesson that day. The love and friendship from an Arab are very strong.

It was a night to remember.

Xinxin spent the evening with Omar's wives, and they were all sad she was leaving in the morning. Xinxin had lit up their hearts. They laughed at the Russian incident. All these women knew Xinxin was Wilber's lover and when the Russian incident came up it turned out to be something to laugh about. These were sophisticated European women mainly who chose to hang out with a Billionaire. They knew their lives would be extravagant.

Each of the Sheikh's wives were billionaire so if they left now there would be no regrets as they had the money to buy anything they wanted. But why leave? They had everything they needed and wanted here and since the women shared the sex responsibility equally the Sheikh never wore any of them out. Plus, he truly was a very nice person.

Xinxin's timely arrival alerting them to the world of crypto currency had a profound effect on their thinking. These were intelligent well-educated women and thus benefitted financially by the visit. They would also help their husband who was not savvy in crypto currency.

***

All of Omar's family was lined up by the landing pad to wish off Wilber and Xinxin who they became attached to.

Later Zayd would tell his father how much he appreciated him for bringing his friend Wilber here to spend time with him. It was a successful and enlightening experience for all of them.

The only passengers on the helicopter were Wilber and Xinxin when it took off for the short flight to Dubai's airport. The helicopter requested permission to land at a specific spot which would place it right next to the private jet waiting.

Air Traffic controllers vectored the helicopter to land about thirty yards from the waiting Jet located at one of the private jet facilities. Wilber stepped down out of the helicopter and helped Xinxin out and the pilot carried their small amount of personal items for them to the waiting Jet. By the door to the jet was John Burkette and the smoking hot CIA flight attendant Tammy.

This was the moment Tammy wanted to experience, observing Wilber with his true love. She would discover what kind of man Wilber was with the company he kept.

Even though out in public the Sheikh's wives dress down to show the expected appearance to conform with Arab traditions, in the privacy of their homes to make their husbands happy, they wore very expensive and sexy designer clothes.

Fashion designers working for Couture Houses in Paris and Milon were flown to Dubai and Abu Dhabi to bring samples to these Sheikh's wives and made some serious profits in doing so.

Many of the wives were imported from London, Paris, Vienna, Berlin, Oslo, Stockholm, Warsaw, and St. Petersburg. There was a genetic hybrid society now developing in the emirates. The offspring was beautiful.

The transformation of the UAE was unquestionably breathtaking.

Most Americans don't get it. But the British do because it was one of their former colonies and they still have a considerable influence and a growing relationship.

The clothes that Xinxin wore and a couple changes of clothes the helicopter pilot carried for her to the GS750 jet, cost Emily over $200,000.00 but it was well worth it to Emily because Wilber and Xinxin's presence created a most remarkable and enjoyable period for her like she had not felt for a long time. Also, Emily felt Xinxin's presence was a catalyst for Liberace to recapitulate his love for her.

The DD/P shook Wilber's hand and paid his respect to Xinxin.

Wilber introduced Xinxin to Tammy and said, "This is my special operative. Don't ask any questions." Then he smiled.

CIA personnel were strictly prohibited from flying their bimbos around on CIA jets. Part of Tammy's responsibility as the executive officer and conductor for the Jet, like a purser for an airliner, was to administer all the requirements. She knew Xinxin was Wilber's lover because the DD/P gave her a special briefing and showed her some eye candy on his cell phone.

In no time the GS750 was wheels up climbing to 50,000 feet for a direct flight to Honolulu flying over the Philippines and Guam in case of an emergency.

Since there was only two pilots and four other passengers onboard and very little luggage, the plane was very light and making it non-stop to Hawaii was easy.

It took 12 hours to fly over Guam, and then another 8 hours to Hawaii. When they landed in Hawaii, they had 25% of the fuel capacity remaining.

Honolulu Airport has three areas. One is the normal passenger terminal everyone is aware of. Another is the Air Force base that shares the runway. There is also an air Freight and commercial lease area on the other side of the runway from the passenger terminal. That third area is where they arrived with a Limo waiting for them to drive them to Waikiki where they had hotel rooms reserved at the Royal Hawaiian.

It was late in the afternoon when they arrived having taken naps along the way during their twenty-hour flight, but they were tired. The GS750 got to fully test its sanitary tank overboard discharge in flight a few times because the flight was so long. With such a few passengers there was plenty of water and drinks and snacks for everyone.

John Burkette knew they all needed to check into their hotels and unwind. He had his blonde friend waiting for him in his room she checked in earlier and was waiting on him. Texting him in flight since the CIA jet has satellite WIFI, they had some provocative conversations and the lovely blonde old enough to be his daughter explained in no certain terms what she wanted to do to him. He was more than ready to capitulate to her desires.

Wilber's thoughts were to take a shower, rinse off the middle east, and be down at the waterfront watching the moonlight holding Xinxin in his arms and cherish those rare moments.

It took little time to get ready, the shower felt good. Xinxin had a lot of natural beauty and flew out of Dubai with a clean face and no makeup on.

Since Dukes was located right next to the Royal Hawaiian, after the shower Wilber suggest, "Let's go to Dukes next door and have some drinks and some food and listen to music, then take a walk down the beach."

"I like that idea," Xinxin said.

Tonight, would be a casual night so Xinxin wasn't going to do much to alter her image, but she did a little which multiplied her beauty.

Wilber and Xinxin were soon sitting in at great table with a great view at Dukes, thanks to the nice bribe Wilson gave the Maître d'.

***

About the same time, Sheikh Omar decided to spend a fabulous amount of money to discover what happened to Wilber in Singapore. Everyone has their price, including Chinese spies.

When he eventually discovered what transpired and that SID had videos of the incident, he decided to show the videos he purchased for millions of dollars from SID operatives to Zyad so his son would know his friend indeed was a dangerous spy.

Zyad would view the incident with astute judgement. He already saw Wilber in action during that terrible day when he and a handful of mercenaries freed him from his captors. The only reason why it was just

Wilber and him at the campfire, was the Mercenaries as well as all the terrorists were dead.

Zyad later told his father, "I wish you had shown me this while Wilber was still here."

"How would that have changed anything?"

"Father, you saw the hell that Wilber went through attacked by the four Chinese hit men. When he rescued me, it was far worse. I wish I had known at the time. I would have said my goodbye to him differently."

"I think your goodbye was respectful enough as it was," Sheikh Omar said.

"Perhaps it was and I'm glad I was perceived as the case, but if I had known about this, it would have affected me quite a bit."

"Son, I realize that now. I'm sorry."

"Father don't be sorry; you did Wilber a huge favor. It's clear to me Xinxin is the love of his life. Had you not brought them here, he might have lost her for the rest of his life."

"You are so wise for your age Zayd."

"Thank you, father. A lot of it is because of the time you invested in me."

"I'm glad you feel about it that way."

***

The snacks on the Jet were not food, they did not really constitute a meal, Xinxin and Wilber were hungry and soon were eating the wonderful food Dukes makes.

The music, the food, the Mai Tai drinks, the sunset, everything was perfect. It was the quiescence before the storm.

There were usually three times as many men at Dukes as there were women. Tonight was no exception and Xinxin was eye candy getting a lot of stares.

Some of the horny drunk men looking at her in a lasciviously manner made her feel uncomfortable. She knew they were planning for a walk on the beach. As soon as it appeared Wilber was done eating Xinxin said, "Wilber let's go for that walk now, I don't like the way a couple of these men are staring at me."

When their waitress came up upon them asking if they wanted another drink, Wilber said, "No I just want to pay for our meals now."

"Sure, no problem."

The waitress had a portable device to read a credit card that had a small printer. Wilber tapped his credit card on it and said okay to the tip recommended, and the waitress soon handed him a receipt and the two departed down the stairs that goes directly onto Waikiki beach a short distance away, past Davy Jones Locker that had a reputation because of the swimming pool with the glass window where clientele could observe newlyweds or lovers fooling around in the pool in front of them.

A couple of the drunks from Dukes decided Wilber looked like a wimp and soon followed them. Instead of walking back towards the Royal Hawaiian, they went the other direction and would soon be in an open area where they could see the Hyatt Regency across the street. These two stupid drunks thought they could take down Wilber and grab his woman and drag her into a parking garage in the Outrigger Hotel where Dukes is located where they had their car.

Out of nature Wilber looked around because a real spy could be following him. He always conducted OPSEC and maintained situational awareness. There was a little lighting in the area just enough for Wilber to spot the two men that were at Dukes giving Xinxin the evil eye.

Wilber was now on full alert not knowing what their intentions were. To his utter surprise they suddenly came forward quickly and one of them grabbed Xinxin's hand while the other made an attack on Wilber he soon regretted as the creep was unconscious shortly afterwards. The other guy was dragging Xinxin away who started screaming.

Wilber calmly said, "Let go over her hand or I will have to hurt you punk."

This second guy didn't see his partner was lying unconscious on the beach and concentrated on Wilber who approached rapidly forcing him to let go of Xinxin's hand and Wilber yelled, "Xinxin, run to the street, there should be cops out there."

The man lunged at Wilber and this guy was martial arts trained, so Wilber had a fight on his hands. It was a good match, but the other person wasn't ready to take on someone from the A-Team and soon got his ass beaten.

No sooner than Wilber knocked the creep out the cops were there with Xinxin who found them and brought them back right away.

One of the cops saw a lot of the fighting and he approached Wilber and Xinxin ran up to Wilber and threw her arms around Wilber so the cops knew that was her boyfriend they were going after to rescue.

The two assailants were out cold so the cops called in an ambulance because its possible Wilber might have killed one of them.

The cop then started taking down Wilber's story while other cops were checking up on the two drunks. They obviously smelled like they had been drinking a lot of alcohol.

Wilber had a rule/regulation that if he got into an altercation like this, he had an APP on his cell phone he was required to activate. He then informed the Cop, "I'm a Federal Agent and I am required to report I was involved in an incident. I'm going to take my cell phone out of my pocket and hit an APP so they know I'm involved in an incident."

"Who the hell do you work for?"

"You are going to find out in a few minutes I believe."

"Wilber activated the APP and FBI agents that happened to be down in Waikiki for another investigation, were redirected to this spot on the beach because Wilber's phone had a tracker on it. They also had the person's name "Wilber O'Toole" with instructions to take him to headquarters immediately.

While the cops were doing their business, suddenly a couple men well- dressed came up to the police officer showed their FBI badges and said, "We are with the FBI, we are here to transport Wilber O'Toole."

"That's me," Wilber said.

"Wilber, you need to come with us."

"This is my girlfriend Xinxin, we are alone in Waikiki, she needs to come with us."

"No problem, we have plenty of room."

"Thank you."

The FBI men informed the police officer, "This is agent Porro, he will remain here with you while you deal with these two men on the ground. We'll take Wilber O'Toole's statement in our offices and send it to you. Give agent Porro your email address, and he will get you, our report."

"MayI ask your name again sir?"

"Yes, I'm Special Agent Shannon and this is Agent Broyles."

The two drunks started to regain consciousness but were feeling some pain. By now Wilber had told the two FBI agents who he was, that he worked for the CIA and these two thugs thought they could grab Xinxin and take her away and molest her.

By now John Burkette had been notified and called Wilber. "What happened Wilber?"

A couple drunks accosted me on the beach when I was walking with Xinxin up the beach. One of them physically attacked me while the other person grabbed Xinxin to take her away so they could molest her. I coldcocked the first one who attacked.

me then I got into a fight with the second one and told Xinxin to run to the street, there were usually police officers around there on Kalakaua. She came back moments later with the police who saw me put the other guy's lights out."

"Are you okay?"

"I'm fine but I probably need to take a shower now after working up a sweat."

"Put your phone on speaker phone so I can talk to the FBI agents you are with."

"Sure."

"Hello gentlemen, I'm John Burke, the DD/P for the CIA. Wilber O'Toole who's in the car with you works directly for me. I want you to take him and the woman he is with back to their hotel, which is the Royal Hawaiian. I'll contact the FBI director in a few minutes, and we'll decide how we want to handle the case. But if Wilber is not physically hurt, I just want you to give the drunks a ride home and let them know they fucked with the wrong guy. Next time we'll cut their dicks off."

"Alright sir, we'll do that but before we drop him off, I need to get authorization from my superior."

"As soon as I hang up I'm calling my personal friend the FBI director, you will get your instructions in a few minutes. What's your name so I can tell the FBI director who to direct?"

"This is Special Agent Shannon."

"Thank you, Special Agent Shannon. I want you to know, Walter O'Toole has recently been on some very dangerous missions. He's a national hero. Treat him accordingly."

"Yes, sir I definitely will."

"Thank you. Goodbye."

John Burkette hung up and called his buddy who then had the FBI watch officer at headquarters call Special Agent Shannon out in Hawaii directing them to take Wilber O'Toole to the Royal Hawaiian.

As soon as Special Agent Shannon dropped off Wilber and Xinxin, his boss called him and said, "Shannon, go back to the beach where the police and the two drunks are.

Get all their information then give them a ride home and let them know the assaulted a Federal Agent tonight and we could easily throw the book at them and not to approach Wilber and his girlfriend again or they would be arrested on Federal Charges."

This action was a great segway into events that would soon unfold. Once they were back in their room, Xinxin said, "I heard you mention you were hot and sweaty and needed to take a shower. I need to take one also, let's do it together.

Kissing under the shower water was the perfect aphrodisiac. The two were entranced into a romantic temporal anomaly. But the reality is Xinxin was a coward and could not take much stress. Wilber had no idea how weak she was. She wasn't in for the long haul. She wasn't a soldier willing to take a bullet for the team. Xinxin was making herself a wealthy woman in crypto trading. There was nothing Wilber had to

offer but romance which they soon experienced right after they dried off and looked at each other's nude bodies. Wilber's little head saluting gave Xinxin just the right amount of incentive to initiate physical contact on a theme from Paganini.

It didn't take the two very long to reach the moment of gratification when Wilber's brain was pumping prolactin into his body along with copious amounts of serotonin and vasopressin, creating surreal feelings.

Dopamine and Oxytocin were already pumping in his body during the arousal and quintessential satisfaction of the coordinated emotional transcendence. At that magic moment Wilber said, "I love you."

Xinxin's reaction to those three words was very intense. Xinxin's psychological reaction created a flood of chemicals her brain released into her body, and she started bucking like a bronco with her legs wrapped around Wilber adding significant force to his thrusts. Xinxin's psychophysical response lasted long after Wilber reached a point of quiescence, but he wasn't going to stop until Xinxin reached her climax and released it all which took a while as her mind was out in space like described by the CIA in their Gateway experiments in implementing Hemi- Sync for their spies sent behind enemy lines.

After a honeymoon-like journey to another dimension bathed in love tendrils on a theme from Paganini, the two reached a point of mutual gentle quiescence with

Xinxin's head laying on Wilber's chest where he could gently kiss the top of her head. Xinxin liked this position as she could listen to Wilber's heartbeat and feel those love kisses on her head. She also liked to hold his penis in her hand. It was a strange sensation. She didn't want to let go of it.

Even though most of the CIA's spies ended up killed, at least they didn't suffer as Gateway extinguished all feelings and emotions. Gateway was a good back up for a spy who didn't have cyanide capsules to prevent severe torture leading to death. The best thing to do to brutal son of a bitches that are beating you for information is to die on their hands before they get any useful information out of you.

***

Chapter Thirteen

Submarine Design

Xinxin now had experienced three ordeals with Wilber and two of them he made critical judgement for her safety and stayed behind to make sure she could get to safety. Those drunks attempting to kidnap her had nothing to do with Wilber's line of work it's the kind of crimes that happen far too often because some knucklehead thinks they can do something like this when logic would tell them otherwise.

Wilber had no specific time to wake up in the morning. He was going to wake up when he felt his body said it was okay.

John Burkette also slept in because he had to make a few phone calls and deal with a few people that were not the sharpest tacks on the wall when the matter the night before should have been handled in a much simpler way. The complication came in because the Hospital wanted to get paid for treating the two drunks that Wilber coldcocked. Therefore, it was not until midnight before John Burkette could get some sleep. He wasn't going to wake up terribly earlier. He just like Wilber would wake up when his body said it was okay.

Both men had an issue in the morning that created further delay. It was the essence of being in the company of beautiful women feeling a little froggy wanting some special gratification. They synchronized their little heads into complying with the request. That added another hour delay.

By the time all issues were all taken care of it was already mid-morning. Everyone was hungry so John Burkette contacted Wilber and suggested "Let's get together for Brunch at the Sheraton main building that will be serving for another hour or so." "Sure, we are ready, we'll walk over there now," Wilber said.

In fifteen minutes, Wilber and Xinxin were introduced to the smoking hot blonde Jennifer Thompson, a British fashion model introduced to John Burkette by a high ranking official in MI6 named Hugh Finley.

Finley had been Burkette's friend in the past and on missions together. They spent a lot of time in Hawaii in the past where John Burkette had to deal with that German character who was a great bullshit artist and seldom earned his pay.

The ubiquitous Finley slipped it to John Burkette again. At least he thought he did. Jennifer Thompson was a deep cover MI6 asset, and she got paid under covers pay along with hazardous duty incentives.

MI6 didn't know CIA had a mole working for them. CIA proves time and time; they are just as good as the Russians and Chinese in establishing the price anyone has.

That CIA spy code name Ravik informed his controller who worked directly for John Burke, Jennifer Thompson was an MI6 under cover woman. John Burkette didn't mind because he planned to keep Jennifer Thompson under covers for a long time and knew he would eventually seduce her and turn her into a double spy. There is nothing

sweeter in the espionage business than to use a foreign spy to do your dirty work, ostensibly under covers."

The two couples had a nice brunch that included a couple glasses of champagne. The Dom Perignon helped the Brunch go down nicely.

During the Brunch, John Burkette received a text from Pierre Truffaut asking, "What time do you want to meet and where at?"

"How about 1:30 at the Bishop Museum up on the 3rd floor of the main display building. I want to visit King Kamehameha again." John Burkette texted back.

"That works for me." Pierre Truffaut texted.

"I'm going to bring one of my men with me who will probably be your main interface to the project once we start building this submarine," John Burkette texted back.

"We'll see you then." Pierre Truffaut texted.

John Burkette put his phone back in his pocket and the four continued enjoying the brunch.

Jennifer Thompson, with an alias as a British fashion model, got into countries doing fashion shows. This worked out well because most spy agencies would not think the dumb blonde fashion model was actually a sophisticated spy with tremendous social engineering skills.

Jennifer Thompson was so confident in herself she gladly accepted the task of seducing CIA's DD/P, John Burke. Jennifer Thompson was no different than a lot of women. She enjoyed sex and knew how to not get pregnant and select only clean men with impecable records and stature in life.

Up until now Jennifer Thompson knew she could compartmentalize her emotions. She had no idea she was up against a lethal adversary who knew what her role was. John Burkette also knew that by taking control of Jennifer Thompson's heart and making some promises she could not refuse. That's how it is with deception and betrayal in the spy business.

The small talk lingered until James Burkette announced, "Wilber and I have to go away for a few hours to attend a meeting at the Bishop Museum where we will meet someone to discuss future plans."

"Alright honey, Jennifer Thompson answered to her sugar daddy and sweetheart. "If you ladies would like to go with us and see the museum, you are welcome."

"I was thinking about going shopping and then lay out on the beach in the roped off Royal Hawaiian Hotel Guest area," Jennifer Thompson responded.

"Xinxin, maybe you would like to accompany Jennifer?" Wilber asked.

"I'm a little scared after last night," Xinxin replied.

"I'm a black belt in Karate and also in Taekwondo, I'll be your bodyguard," Jennifer announced to ease Xinxin fears."

"Are you really capable?" Xinxin asked.

"I would not have been as gentle with the thugs last night like Wilber was. When I beat a man's ass, I want him to always remember he got his ass kicked by a female,

and the best way to do that is make sure he loses a testicle," Jennifer stated most emphatically.

"Alright, I'll hang out with Jennifer," Xinxin said.

After freshening up later, Wilber went out to the Royal Hawaiian circular driveway. Moments later John Burkette arrived and handed the Valet Parking person his ticket for his rental car which was brought up to the front moments later.

John Burkette knew his way around Waikiki quite well since he practically lived over there with his chief responsibility of keeping Finley out of trouble for using the term "cocksucker" too often when dealing with marginal performers always bellyaching and watching the clock milking the jobs as long as they could. John Burke's other némesis was German who could never be found and got all hissy pissy when asked for reports.

Even though a lot of the reporting John Burkette had to do in those days was semi-automatic thanks to artificial intelligence and application software that took the data and formatted it and put it in data packages that could be emailed in official reports, and, he had to write a "Quick Look" report giving the sponsors, some idea of WTF was going on.

All too often things were rotten in river city and German was consistently delinquent in inputting his reports forcing John Burkette to hand over the reports to the management team at the 11th hour. John Burkette didn't like operating like that and if he could just replace one dickhead on his team, he would be able to finish the final reports in a reasonable time and spend afternoons down at Waikiki in places like Dukes drinking some good craft beers and looking at the babes on the beach with the slimmest bikini's ever known to mankind.

Some of the females might as well not bother wearing a swimsuit because those one-piece thongs barely covered up anything and surprisingly the modest Japanese tourists wore them too, But the funny thing unlike Americans for a long time Japanese women wearing those swim suits didn't trim their beavers so they stuck out a little. Was that on purpose?

Wilber had spent some time in the Bishop Museum in the past and had a special arrangement visit to the archives in the building they were in where he got to see and photograph several pictures of the Honolulu Trolley System that used to exist, as well as the narrow-gauge railroad, Oahu Railway & Land Company (OR&L). OR&L railroad was very useful during WWII but shut down in the 1950's due to financial ruin caused by storms and the arrival of a lot of trucks to the island taking away a lot of revenue. Also, Buses and Cars damaged OR&L's revenue stream.

The main display building is a modern building with multiple story floors showcasing the Hawaiian Kings family and heritage. If you are interested in Hawaiian History this is the very best place to visit as well as looking at a lot of displays of many generations of Hawaiian Royalty. Another good source is Michner's Novel Hawaii. I would recommend anyone to read Michner's Novel before attending the museum to help make it come to life. Also rent the movie "Hawaii" based on Michner's Novel.

John Burkette led Wilber up to the 3rd floor on the elevator, then got out and walked around looking at the exhibits. There is a large open area in the middle you can look down and see several floors. After they traversed around the third floor, John Burkette spotted Pierre Truffaut and approached him.

"Hello Pierre, good to see you again." "Good to see you as well John." Pierre said.

Pierre was all smiles realizing he enjoyed the income stream from the Cash in Advance boys for projects he worked with John Burkette in the past including building submarines to go deal with Cartel submarines running drugs up to America.

***

The CIA had a very interesting device in their anti-cartel submarines.

Thanks to the underwater cameras and lighting, they would come up behind the drug cartel submarine hauling tons of drugs, shoot a harpoon like device into the propeller and the steel cable part of it would get wound up into the mini-sub's propeller that would usually lock it if not causing major damage to the propulsion train and ending its ability to transit. The CIA mini sub would then come up to its periscope depth and transmit the location via satellite which either US Navy Destroyers or Coast Guard ships would go to.

In some cases, the cartel submarines had very dangerous weapons purchased from Chinese or Russian arms dealers that could damage one of our ships. If they fired on our ships, they soon received deadly return fire that often sunk the cartel submarine killing the crew. And in deep water, the cartel submarine usually imploded. In shallower water Navy Divers would place explosive charges and destroy it and the contents.

Cartels were slowly running out of submarines and figuring out other ways to transport the cargo. Their latest method was drones.

***

Pierre, this is Wilber O'Toole, he is the person you will be dealing with in the future. It was his idea to build the submarine for our purpose."

"Good to meet you, Wilber." "Thank you, Pierre."

"Wilber received a lot of criticism by his office warrior friends who don't know shit from Shinola about this submarine proposal."

"And you think there is some merit in building it?"

"At first I was neutral in my thoughts about building a submarine, but as I reflected on the situation more and more, I realized we have to have a backup plan since I fear their main plan is doomed to fail."

"How soon do you think you need an operational submarine?"

"We want it as soon as possible, but we know there are some very difficult design criteria to deal with and as you discover what it's all about, you might also think it's foolish."

"John, in my experience with Jacques Cousteau, a lot of our ideas started out seeming foolish by our critics until we suddenly had National Geographic with us filming the results."

"That's where we are now, but in days to come when reality hits home, it may be the only way we can achieve what is necessary."

"Is this anything like your anti-cartel submarine chasers?"

"No, we can't talk here. But we can drive down to Pearl Harbor, we have an office there that is cleared for the level of discussions we need to have."

"I'm probably not cleared to go in there."

"You are not cleared, but I am authorized to escort you into the building that has a SKIF."

"Where will this submarine be built?"

"We'll get into all that in the SKIF, but I would assume parts and pieces will be fabricated at a variety of remote locations, and contractors will not know who the other contractors are involved."

"Highly compartmentalized?"

"Yes. You may think we are nuts when we disclose what this is all about. I will say this project will test your faith and make you rethink the universe in a major way."

"I've already started rethinking looking at some of the Webb telescope pictures."

"Beats the crap out of the big bang theory, doesn't it?"

"The problem with the scientists who banked their theory on the big bang, believe we could not see beyond 35 billion light years is how they painted themselves into a corner. I would like to have had a discussion with Steven Hawking had he lived to see Webb telescope images."

"What do you think is the biggest comment Steven Hawking would have said about it?"

"He would say never before had mankind been given the gift of tools to see a God's handiwork at creating new stars like we can now see, even though the events happened billions of light years ago."

He would use the term God even though he was an atheist?" Wilber asked.

"Hawking would use the term God in the context of what most people conceive as the creator of the Universe. Hawking nor can anyone else explain what or how precisely created the Universe," John Burkette added."

The men walked around looking at the exhibits for a short while then Pierre said, "Since we are going to be meeting at Pearl Harbor, I suggest we meet at 9:30 to avoid a lot of traffic, work through lunch if necessary and beat the traffic home."

"Excellent idea," John Burkette responded. Then he added, "Parking is tight where we need to go. Let's meet at the Navy Exchange, which is a short distance away, and we'll drive from there over to the building. At 9:30 in the morning the Navy Exchange parking lot will be empty and lots of room to park. I'll send you a google map place to meet."

"Alright, see you then." Pierre shook their hands and left.

***

Xinxin and Jennifer ended up walking through the Royal Hawaiian Shopping Mall next to their hotel. This was a great place to shop as it had the best of the best on display from everything including fine art to clothing and attire, cosmetics, and various high end fashion stores.

The two women accomplished a lot of shopping and then Jennifer suggested, "Why don't we go back to the hotel now and change and meet out front at the beach and do some sunbathing and get something to drink, I'm thirsty." "Sound's good," Xinxin replied.

In a short while it was apparent Xinxin Lin and Jennifer Thompson were the two most smoking hot women on the beach with their Sheraton supplied sun umbrella and beach reclining chairs. There was a small circular table associated with the sun umbrella they could put drinks and snacks on.

In a brief time, a waiter came and took their drink requests. Xinxin ordered a Mai Tai and Jennifer Thompson ordered a Martini with olives and extra dry, just like the way James Bond liked to drink his.

The white bikini Xinxin was wearing contrasted her suntan and created the essence of grandeur. This was playboy magazine cover quality image. Playboy had not had such an exquisite cover since the famed Cindy Suzuki appeared. Xinxin was up there in beauty and grace as Cindy exhibited if you got to know her. Thanks to her workouts Cindy Suzuki had one of the best bodies on the planet. Xinxin didn't have all those muscles, but she was beautiful in her own way.

Jennifer Thompson's "Victoria's Secret" one-piece strapless black bathing suit contrasted her blond hair and light brown tan greatly. These two lovely women were a magnet to every scoundrel on the beach who would attempt any scheme necessary to enjoy them. And in short order a couple of Azzie dudes appeared laying on the charm. The women were not in any kind of need, having already recently gratified by their lovers, they did not desire no require the services of the young bucks.

While the young handsome men were pouring on the charm thinking they were going to get somewhere with the women sweet talking to them, Xinxin and Jennifer each received text messages and let their lovers. They texted back to let them know they were on the beach waiting.

In due time, John Burkette and Wilber O'Toole walked out onto the beach in very nice swim trunks that accentuated their athletic build. The two Azzie punks had no idea Xinxin and Jennifer's boyfriends had six pack abs.

Not for the sake of looking good but for the sake of staying alive during mortal combat with a lethal adversary where split decisions had to be made, just like in the case when Wilber had to put a couple bullets into Faye Wong, a woman he thought he loved. The betrayal was astonishing.

When Wilber was going through debriefings over the incident that had the added dimension, he had just killed a woman the agency and he thought was his lover and had no idea she was a Chinese MSS spy, it got real dicey for a while.

Furthermore, when lab results indicated the substance Wilber wiped off the knife to bring back to be analyzed was determined to be the deadly poison Ricin, it didn't take a rocket scientist to know very few spy agencies could do an operation like Faye Wong attempted killing Wilber with the deadly toxin such as Ricin.

Assuming Faye Wong's Chinese ethnicity, was a core indicator, it meant that it was a Chinese MSS operation and the recent activity at Singapore's Botanical Gardens showed Wilber was a target and most likely retaliation for killing one of the Chinese MSS super spies Fay Wong.

Another important fact that helped Wilber quickly get over killing Faye Wong was, all she had to do was cut Wilber with the knife to kill him. His instant decision saved his life. Faye Wong was probably one second away from killing Wilber it came very close. Wilber felt it was sad their tempestuous love affair ended on such a low note.

The whirlwind love affair between Wilber and Faye Wong mostly in Honolulu and Hong Kong had been very exquisite. Fay Wong proved she was one of the best actresses on the planet. And as a top spy no different than the famous Russian Spy Margaritta Konenkova who seduced Einstein, using her body in the deadly game of betrayal was no different than Army guys taking a bullet or dropping on a grenade to save a dozen buddies.

The two Azzie dudes that did not have bodies to compete with Wilber and John Burkette were quickly distressed to realize these glamorous women were toying with them, they had bigger fish to fry.

The two Azzie dudes knew it was time to move on, maybe find some Japanese tourists. As soon as they left Wilber and John Burkette laid their towels down on the reclining chairs that had been turned so the Azzie dudes could make their inroads into the lovely women.

In a short while the waiter appeared asking the men if they would like something to drink. John Burkette ordered a craft beer, while Wilber noticing Jennifer Thompson was drinking a martini with olives ordered one on the rocks in a standard drinking glass.

It was a pleasant experience hearing the gentle waves come ashore creating a sound that is sometimes used to treat people having psychological issues. The stochastic resonance that is manifested by wave geometries has a random distribution with a slight resonance that affects the pleasure center of the brain.

The women in the beautiful bathing suits added to the ambience. Xinxin and Jennifer were proud to be with two handsome men that had six pack abs. John Burkette was a little older and didn't quite do the physical regiment Wilber adhered to most of the time was not quite as well shaped, but he was still more charismatic and distinctive than most of the men on the beach.

There was a lot of small talk as they hung out, drank and simply enjoyed the down time. It was the calm before the storm as men with incredible responsibilities were granted this brief time to relax and unwind and enjoy life. Each man needed down time because John Burkette had twenty or more pressing issues all the time day in and day out. There was no escape for him, as he had to receive calls in the middle of the night and make rapid decisions otherwise there was a good chance one of his men would be captured, tortured, or killed. Those timely decisions and directives saved a lot of lives and at the same time meant they did not have to disavow the person.

John Burkette, having his own problem, realized his worst days would never be as bad as Wilber's worst days, especially when he had to put two bullets into Faye

Wong who he wrongly assumed was his lover. Faye Wong is another fine example of the sophistication and abilities the Chinese MSS often used that surprised the Cash in Advance boys when situations like this developed. John Burkette knew how bad Wilber was hurting at the time, and as soon as lab results showed the substance Faye Wong coated the deadly knife with what happened to be Risin, he personally briefed Wilber so that he would get over the melancholy quicker. He recalled the conversation.

"We didn't know who Faye Wong was until just minutes before she tried to kill you. By the time we confirmed she was Chinese MSS, it was right about the time of the deadly incident."

"Faye Wong definitely played a good game. But when I saw Feye coming at me with that knife, my mind told me I had to use deadly force to stop her."

"I know you are taking it hard, but I have the lab report on the substance you obtained from the knife blade."

"What was it?"

"Ricin. Had she just cut you, you would have died quickly."

"This romance lasted quite a while, she was good, I saw no indicators she was an intelligence officer."

"What you didn't know Wilber is we followed her and filmed her working out at the gym. I can't tell you how we know this, it comes from compartmentalized source, Faye was a black belt in Shaolin Kung Fu (Chinese: 少林功夫)."

"I still feel bad about shooting and killing Faye."

There was no way you could have stopped her from cutting you without shooting her like you did. Had you attempted to fight her off, with her martial arts skills, it's a foregone conclusion she would have cut you."

"If she was going to stab me while I was sleeping why the Ricin?"

"The reason why they had her prepare the knife blade with Ricin before the attack, is they knew you could defend yourself and they wanted to make sure she killed you."

Even though people are having a lovely time, their thoughts sometimes drift off in various directions. Xinxin had a taste of what the spy business was like as an innocent bystander and a victim when she was pressed into service by the MSS to betray Wilber. She would never quite understand a lot of their daydreams, from riding camels in the desert like Lawrence of Arabia to killing a Chinese lover who turned out was sleeping with the enemy.

Jennifer Thompson appeared on the outside like a soft peach, full of beauty and glamour, but as an MI6 agent had read Wilber's dossier and knew even more about John Burke. If Xinxin knew just a fraction of what Jennifer knew, she would be heading for the exit and getting a flight back to Singapore. There wasn't much more suspense she could take.

Wilber was quickly learning to take those crumbs of life when he could and enjoy every moment of it, because any day something bad could happen to him. However, he felt gratitude he was now moving up in Solar Systems Investigations and would not be involved in espionage day in day out. Project Solaris needed a Cowboy like Wilber, or they would start to feel the heat of the president when the Office Warriors proved they couldn't handle it.

The afternoon pressed on and the women needed suntan lotion applied. Off to the distance the Azzie dudes watching Wilber help Xinxin with the suntan lotion were started how far up inside her legs his hands want a and when she rolled over on her stomach, he messaged her shaking her body nicely and aroused her.

They then made dinner plans after a couple hours and decided to go rest up and freshen up before they headed out. Xinxin who had plenty of money picked up a couple fabulous garments in the Royal Hawaiian Shopping Center. She was ready to dress for success.

***

The two lovebirds might have slept til morning had Wilber's phone it not been for Wilbers phone ringing. It was John Burkette calling.

"You guys up for dinner?" John Burkette asked.

"Yes, we are but we are not dressed yet," Wilber responded.

"Alright, call me when you are ready. Roy's restaurant is a short walk from here and they have the best food in Waikiki."

"I'm sure that will work out just fine, maybe we can take a walk down Kalakaua after dinner for some exercise."

"Great idea. Call me when you are ready."

Completely satisfied, Wilber led Xinxin into a sprite shower, then casually got dressed feeling rested and satisfied. Xinxin didn't have to do much. Just with her body in such a beautiful dress she purchased today, was more than enough to be qualified as eye candy.

John Burkette and Jennifer Thompson had been doing so much boom- boom lately, they did not need to go at it like Wilber and Xinxin and were not in cerebral declination and were ready for action after a quick round of a journey through their lover's paradise.

They met at the entrance of the Royal Hawaiian by the circular driveway, mainly because it was the most direct route to Roy's over by Lewers Street. The two women walked up front with Wilber and John following behind so the women could talk on the way. Jennifer knew where Roy's was since John took her there often.

The maître d' was a very beautiful Asian lady. She knew Xinxin was wearing an expensive dress because she had her eyes set on it just a couple days ago at the Royal Hawaiian Shopping Center. But it was way out of her price range, and here this gorgeous lady was wearing it. John Burkette had made reservations and guessed about this time; they were all set.

"Do you have reservations?" the maître d' asked. " "

Yes, John Burke, table for four."

The cute Asian maître d' looked down saw the name and crossed it off and picked up four menus and said, "Follow me please."

The four were led out to the Lanai, where they had an excellent table and the ambience for a great dining experience.

The maître d' knew Xinxin paid over $2000.00 for the beautiful designer dress, one-of-a-kind hand crafted and not on an assembly line. She could not resist and looked directly and Xinxin and said, "I love the way your dress looks."

"Thank you very much, I like it too."

"You have a beautiful British Accent are you from London?"

"No, I'm from Singapore, by my friend Jennifer is from London."

"That's right," Jennifer Thompson responded.

With the looks and the accent, the maître d' looked at Wilber who was quite handsome as well and gave him a smile since he was sitting next to Xinxin and it was obvious they were a couple and conveyed in her look, *you are one lucky dog.*

Wilber looked back and smiled and gave those unspoken words, *you have no idea how good it is.*

"Your waiter will be right here."

Soon the waitress appeared who saw John Burkette here quite a bit but also thought she knew the other guy from somewhere.

The ethnic mixed waitress Sandra forgot this gentleman was very close to getting her into bed. They met at the Majestic Black Dragon Restaurant and Nightclub. It was Sandra's night off and was there with her best friend Rachel. Rachel had a good head on her shoulders and always tried to keep Sandra out of trouble. Rachel warned Sandra about this smooth-talking hunk that appeared irresistible moments later when Rachel drug Sandra to the lady's room for some consultations.

Sandra wanted to go for that walk on the beach with Wilber, but Rachel said, "That will result in a trip his hotel room if you leave with him."

During this privacy in the lady's room for a minute or so, Rachel convinced Sandra, "All he wants to do is get your panties off and have his satisfaction with your body. You will never see him again after tonight."

Sandra cowered and soon left with Rachel. Moments after Sandra and Rachel were long gone, Faye Wong slipped in and took over exploiting her target Wilber's little head to start him down that journey in a life scenario he never planned on.

Coming from Hong Kong where she was recruited, Faye knew everything about Hong Kong. She didn't need to fake it and had a lot of legitimate pictures on her cell phone.

The results of Sandra's actions could be taken in one of two ways. Was it the biggest mistake in Sandra's life, or did she escape a heartbreak by the thinnest of margins because Faye Wong was entering the picture and had much more to offer in terms of seduction?

A plane Jane like Sandra could never compete with one of best female Chinese MSS spies who used that pleasant spot between her legs as the ultimate weapon to an unsuspecting enemy.

As Sandra was taking their dinner orders, she was fighting hard to try to remember who the man with the smoking hot Asian lady with an expensive dress was.

Sandra went back to the kitchen with the order and after handing in the order, she grabbed a water pitcher to go out and pour some water for the table while the bartender was getting their drinks together which consisted of mainly wine.

Rachel suddenly entered Sandra's mind. She was mad at Rachel from then on because a couple days later she saw the man with a beautiful Chinese lady. For the next couple of weeks, she saw him again a few more times with that beautiful woman.

Sandra was now bitter at Rachel because she now knew this man was not a hit and run kind of guy. As she went out and poured the water Sandra was mildly irritated the man never looked at her or even wondered who she was. But then again, the way she turned him down with a no-thank-you sealed the deal. Why should he care?

Obviously, the man didn't work out with the eye candy she last saw him with. Will he work out with this woman? Sandra would utterly freak out if she knew Wilber put a bullet through Faye's heart. What people do not know will not hurt them.

Xinxin picked up on the woman staring at Wilber, so she decided to tease her, and she said to Wilber, "Let me whisper something in your ear." Wilber bent his head down so he could hear the secret.

"Darling, I loved the way you made love to me today. My heart is full of joy, would you mind being brave now and kiss me?"

Xinxin a master manipulator in her own right timed it good and had Wilbers lips on her lips just as Sandra was sitting their drinks down. Chinese women usually do not do this in public. Sandra was utterly astonished. She instantly knew this woman received big A from the man she had her chance with, that Rachel blew it for her. What she didn't know was the cruel fact of life. Rachel saved her. No way could Sandra compete with the tempestuous glamorous creature kissing that man, and Faye Wong was even more powerful because Xinxin never had the psychological and spy craft training Feye Wong had.

Before the couple left the restaurant, Sandra would get brave and ask the man what his name was.

The food at Roy's is the best in Waikiki. Any Entrée is a winner. John Burkette knew what he was going to have without looking at the menu, AL FRESCO PRIX FIXE. Jennifer Thompson also knew but she liked the Blackened Island Ahi. And like John told her many times before, we don't have to eat the same thing. Enjoy yourself. It was kind of interesting the Wilber ordered what John Burkette ordered and Xinxin ordered what Jennifer ordered.

Throughout the evening, Xinxin got bad vibes from the waitress Sandra. She was more than happy when they left. But she was utterly astonished when the waitress eyeballed the bill very carefully since Wilber insisted on paying the tab. Now she knew her almost lover's name was Wilber O'Toole. And she also now remembered that's the same name Wilber gave Sandra at the Majestic Black Dragon dance club which Rachel said was an obvious alias.

When she got off work tonight, she would call Rachel and tell her all about it!

***

In the morning the men met with Pierre Truffaut at the Navy Exchange parking lot. He was soon in John Burke's rental car heading for Halawa Drive on Kamehameha Hiway route 99. The five-story brown building that one sees when you turn right on Halawa Drive has no windows. Inside it there is a sign that said, "Lethal Force is authorized against anyone with a visitor badge who is without their escort."

Down the hallway on the second floor about 50 steps is a door that says CIA on it. Pierre was not a US Citizen and had a special certificate sent from Langley required for NOFORN which sometimes happens with British, Norwegian, and others. The only reason why they went in this room was a SKIF. The three went inside the SKIF and shortly Wilber hooked up his CIA cell phone to a cable interfacing with the dumb large screen display.

"Alright Pierre, you can never talk about this to anyone, or it could cost you your

life."

"Understand."

"This information will test your beliefs as a Christian. If you do not think you can handle a significant revelation that may impact your view on religion, I suggest we terminate the presentation now."

"I can handle it."

"Alright. Before we show you the video, I want to tell you what this is about." "Sure."

"We receive alien communications routinely from the planet Saturn. We have no idea who they are communicating with, just that they are involved in high-speed communications to an entity somewhere in this solar system."

"Alright, what does that have to do with a submarine?"

"One of my men is heading up and effort to send a probe there to find out what is going on that planet, but I'm worried it's going to be a failure because the aliens will probably destroy the probe and we'll get nothing from it."

Then what's the submarine going to do for you?"

"We'll get the submarine there so that we can go beneath the surface an explore the uncharted cities that must exist." Wilber then started playing the files Pierre Truffaut would now watch and have his faith tested like never before.

About an hour later after watching the video discussions started on the constraints of the submarine such as submerging into liquid helium and liquid hydrogen.

This was quite a memorable day for the submarine designer Pierre Truffaut. At this point in time, he felt the possibility of such a submarine being built was impossible.

But Pierre Truffaut didn't know a person with a dynamic personality like Wilber O'Toole understood this was their only way of confronting the aliens.

There was much at stake. Who were they communicating with and what were their intentions? Why did they suddenly start broadcasting in such a way Earth could detect them?

Was this part of their plan to draw us in for a meeting? Are they friendly?

After an exhaustive briefing, Pierre wanted to go home and think about it. He would say some prayers and really do some soul searching. It was obvious the CIA had a lot of data. Paul Morgan's data was developed over a lengthy period, so the anecdotal data was very extensive. The details and the information were beyond mind blowing. Perhaps a stiff drink was in order.

They drove back to the Navy Exchange. The rental cops left a ticket on Pierre's car. John Burkette said, "I'll take care of this. Don't worry about it."

John Burkette was good friends with the Admiral who was in command of the combined base Pearl Harbor and Hickam Air Force base.

"Wilber, would you mind driving us back to the Hotel I need to fix this ticket."

"Not a problem John."

"Pierre, Wilber will be in touch with you to set up a facility to do the work. I'm sorry to inform you it will probably be in Vandenburg Base in California. But look on the bright side, you will earn some frequent flyer miles!"

"Alright John. Looking forward to hearing from you."

The men all shook hands and were on the road going in opposite directions.

They barely beat the rush hour traffic, but they were down in Waikiki just as it was building gliding down Kalakaua to the turn off to the Sheraton and the Royal Hawaiian as traffic was building.

They pulled up to the Valet parking attendant in front of the Royal Hawaiian. As soon as Wilber stepped out of the car, the attendant gave him a receipt. Wilber said, "One second please."

Wilber reached into his billfold and pulled out a $20 bill and handed it to the attendant and said, "Have a good evening."

"Thank you, sir, I appreciate this."

"You're welcome."

"Where do you want to have dinner tonight?" John Burkette asked.

"The last time I was here I had a dinner at Ruth's Chris steakhouse, close to Roy's, I would like to try it tonight."

"Sound's good. What time?"

"How about 6:30 P.M.?"

"Works for me, meet you down here then."

"Will do."

In the Royal Hawaiian hotel room Xinxin and Wilber got into a discussion about today's events.

"Jennifer Thompson and I went shopping then we went down to the beach. The two Azzie dudes came onto us again, and Jennifer put them in their place."

"Oh, yea how did she do that?"

"They were getting kind of annoying, and Jennifer said: I know you guys saw our boyfriends yesterday. They are built well for a reason to kick some ass if necessary.

We do not like shrimps with miniature peckers, in fact I'm sure I could kick both your asses at the same time. Now be gone."

Wilber started laughing so hard he almost fell down and Xinxin had to stabilize him, or he would have.

"That's the funniest damn thing I've heard in a long time," Wilber said as he was regaining his composure.

"I saw you in action, so I know all about you Wilber." Xinxin said.

"Really?" Wilber said.

"You know Sheikh Omar's wife Emily knows all the details of when you saved Zayd from the terrorists, she informed me in front of his three other wives on our last night when you went to the special club with the three Sheikhs." Xinxin sid.

"Is that so?" Wilber responded acting in disbelief.

"Emily said everyone attending that special celebration knows all about it because they are all related. Either brothers or cousins." Xinxin explained.

"The cat is out of the bag now." Wilber said in a satire like manner.

"You would be in danger if you went undercover again, right?"

"That's not going to happen, I have a new gig now. That's why I had to go meet a man named Pierre Truffaut with John Burke."

"How did that meeting go?"

"It went well. I'll be seeing a lot more of Pierre Truffaut in the future."

"What's planned for tonight?"

"We are going to walk over to Ruth's Chris steakhouse. It's a half a block from Roy's we went to last night."

"Alright."

"It looks like tonight will be our last night here. I must get back to Washington DC. You can come to DC with me if you want."

"That's okay honey. I want to get back to the office to handle my new accounts."

"Who's the new accounts?"

"Besides the Sheikh's wives, I now have Jennifer Thompson's account." "Interesting." Wilber noted.

"She's been wanting to get into crypto currencies but didn't know anything about it nor did she have anyone she could trust." Xinxin said.

"Why should she trust you?" Wilber asked.

"It's very simple, you work for her boyfriend." Xinxin said.

"I suppose that nails it." Wilber replied.

"It does and now it's time for you to nail me."

"In the biblical sense?"

"Yes Mr. Diabolical, this afternoon I'm your mission and your task is to please me." "I'll do my best."

The two were soon dancing the horizontal tango on a theme from Paganini and Wilber was performing as good as ballet dancer Korotkov Konstantin in the Tchaikovsky Ballet Swan Lake.

The tumultuous allegros played on in an everlasting cascading of ethereal ensembles as Xinxin reached the ultimate physical creciendo, leaving no doubt in anyone's mind as the occupants in the next room heard a woman calling out to God. The husband was about to call the police thinking Wilber was killing Xinxin, but the astute wife schooled him, "If you could turn me on like that man I would be loud too."

And just like she predicted the woman would stop calling out to God as the moment passed and the two snuggled in lover's bliss. This moment put an exclamation point in the relationship. But was it the high-water mark?

After a while, Wilber mindful of the time asked, "Would you like to use the bathroom first before we get cleaned up and ready to go out?"

"Thank you dear, I do not mind at all," Xinxin replied and soon took care of her business.

After a sprite shower Xinxin and Wilber methodically dressed for the special occasion. They wanted to look their best since tomorrow they would have to go their separate ways for a while.

As planned, they met John Burkette and Jennifer Thompson at the entrance to the Royal Hawaiian and walked over to Ruth's Chris steakhouse.

The Chinese maître d' at Ruth's Chris could easily pass for Xinxin's cousin or sister, acted elegantly and graceful.

After verifying the reservations, the charming Maître d' led the four to a table next to the large glass windows allowing them to look out into the courtyard where outdoors dining occurred.

The four all decided on red wine to go with the steaks. Therefore, John Burkette announced, "Let me buy a bottle, we can share." He then selected a bottle of Caymus a California Cabernet Sauvignon. He realized the four of them would devour that bottle and decided he would order another bottle of William Hill California Cabernet Sauvignon just before the midway point of their meal when the first bottle would no doubt be dry.

Soon they ordered. John Burkette and Jennifer Thompson decided on a Porterhouse for Two. The 40-ounce steak was more than they could handle but it's like a filet mignon on steroids. Xinxin ordered the Petite Filet and shrimp. Wilber ordered the Filet.

The meal passed very nicely and predictably they needed that second bottle of wine the waiter was more than happy to serve and could smell a ginormous tip. He

wasn't too far off the mark. As expected, the steaks were cooked to utter perfection and it was a joyous time. The meal finished up and John Burkette grabbed the check and pulled out his credit card and handed it to the nice waiter who promptly came back with the printout. John Burkette was never a cheap Charlie like Wilber experienced with some of his office warrior colleagues.

Worse than that, Wilber observed another department head take the parking receipt off another person's car while going to a meeting in Crystal City next to Ronald Reagan Washington DC airport and putting it on his to avoid paying. The poor dude that lost the parking sticker dumb for putting it under his windshield wiper, no doubt had his wheel locked when he came back to his car. That scumbag department head eventually was forced out over sexual harassment allegations. It's always good for a Cowboy to see an office warrior crash and burn like that.

As the two couples were leaving the restaurant, John Burkette asked, "Do you and Xinxin want to go someplace for a little music and dance?"

"I wouldn't mind," Xinxin quickly answered before Wilber could put forth any negative response.

"Any place you want to go?" John Burkette asked.

"The Majestic Black Dragon is just up two blocks on Lewers Street, let's go see if it still exists," Wilber said.

"Lead the way," John Burkette replied.

Sure enough, the majestic Black Dragon was still there and appeared like nothing had changed. It was slightly early; the crowd had not shown up yet.

The two couples found a nice size booth that had good access to the dance floor and a DJ was already playing music. There were no live bands tonight like there had been almost nightly years ago in Waikiki. Right after they received their first drinks a few showoff couples were on the dance floor. This was typical of Waikiki.

Dancers wanting to practice exotic dances would hit the clubs early before the dance floor had a lot of people dancing where they would have room to do dances like the Tango, Rumba, Cha-Cha, Salsa, and now and then a group would show up doing the Electric Slide.

Tonight was no exception as there were two couples who probably knew each other Salsa dancing.

The four sat there watching the Salsa Dancing while they enjoyed their first drink. The early drinks served were always stronger to help people lose their inhibitions and losen up to get them dancing and enticing other dancers. There was usually a happy hour from 8:00 P.M. until 9:00 P.M. and the early dancers practicing really liked the benefit of cheap drinks and an empty dance floor.

The two women dancers wore ultra short dresses, but they knew their black panties would not show much, but their nice shapes were exposed because their dance moves often exposed a lot. The female dancers were in great shape from dancing often and had no fat on their bodies. They probably worked out at a gym as well.

The male dancers were dressed for success and complimented their dancing partners quite well. It was a team effort, and they were certainly highly skillful, and their dance styles were artwork. After a while the DJ knew he had to clear off the dance floor so that others besides the Salsa Dancers would get out there. The best way DJ's get the showoffs to the sidelines is to play a slow dance.

The song Hometown Glory by Adele started playing. Predictably the Salsa dancers went back to their tables to get a drink.

"I really love this song," Xinxin said.

"Would you like to dance?" Wilber asked.

"I certainly would," Xinxin replied.

DJ's often play two or three back-to-back slow dances to get the romances flowing, especially to couples. Later in the night it would be for the exclusive use of Casanova's to get closer to the female inspiration that captivated their actions.

John Burkette advised Jennifer Thompson, "I would ask you to dance, but there are a lot of people coming in that would hijack our booth."

"That's okay dear, we'll dance when the lovebirds come back."

It was a pleasant sight for John and Jennifer watching Xinxin dance with Wilber. You could see complete satisfaction on her face as Adele's Hometown Glory played on. Just when they thought the romantic episode was going to be truncated with more Salsa dancing, everyone was in for a big surprise watching the beautiful couple on the dance floor that seemed to be a magnet to other dancers, including the Salsa Dancers who could not resist the opportunity to feel their dancing partner in a more inspirational fashion.

The DJ was a smart person and capitalized on the mood shifting the beautiful couple created and slipped in Righteous Brothers - Unchained Melody sung by Elvis Presley in Las Vegas.

[Elvis Presley - Unchained Melody (Rapid City June 21, 1977) - YouTube]

Towards the end of the Unchained Melody when Elvis articulated the I need your love in the high note sequence, there was a compulsive and emotional outpour of Xinxin who reached up and pulled Wilber's face to her and kissed him in the most sensual fashion. Their dancing slowed down to barely recognizable movement, but the kiss was electrifying the crowd, including the two familiar Azzie dudes that came in and spotted them.

Xinxin then pulled back and looked into Wilber's eyes. It was one of those looks he would never forget. And at that point in time the ghost Faye Wong from Wilber's past hit him. Xinxin's face and her sweet appearance was almost a flashback from those days gone past. The tears started to flow. Xinxin thought those tears were all about her. She had no idea the demons Wilber carried in his heart. And when Elvis started singing, "I need your love, emotional tremors were hitting him. Xinxin pulled Wilber back to her closely hugging him feeling his private sorrow that only a spy can feel who shot and killed his former lover.

Xinxin had never felt such strong emotions in her life. She was glad she was leaving tomorrow to go back to Singapore and reflect on all this and get her head together. This was one of those life-changing events, and here she was out on the dance floor feeling the full wrath of that human condition spawned by incredible experiences in life. She should have been wiser to realize it wasn't just all about her. Nevertheless, Wilber's physical reactions, especially when Elvis sang the high notes, I need your love, created a torrent of emotions unequivocally a stratum above anything a person would expect transpire out of such an innocuous activity.

Wilber was eternally grateful the DJ took on high risk to play a third song before switching it back up to regular dance music. This gave him time to recoil from that emotional spike, dry his eyes and regain a quiescent state of mind.

The DJ had quite a repertoire of slow dance songs, and knowing he risked fait by playing a bar clearing song by three slow dances in a row, when many dancers wanted to be swinging or salsa dancing, pulled out a rare gem, When I Fall in Love by the Lettermen.

[When I Fall in Love - The Lettermen - YouTube]

The DJ's risky move proved provincial as at the end of this song, the dance floor was fully packed and the two Azzie's sitting on the sidelines wishing to the Gods they had a crack at Xinxin.

"Let's sit down and enjoy our drinks," Xinxin suggested.

"That sounds good to me," Wilber responded.

John Burkette observing Wilber on the dance floor realized he should give him and Xinxin some space and asked Jennifer, "Would you like to dance?"

John and Jennifer stood up and smiled and went out to the dance floor just as Xinxin followed by Wilber sat down in their seats at the booth.

Alone by. Nicki Minaj was hard to dance to by John and Jennifer, but the dancing showoffs were digging it and moved nicely including a few sexy swings.

[Kim Petras - Alone (Lyrics) feat. Nicki Minaj - YouTube]

Jessie Ware's Pearls played next that seemed to fit John and Jennifer's dance style better.

[Jessie Ware - Pearls (Official Music Video) - YouTube]

Selena Gomez - The Heart Wants What It Wants was too complicated for John, so he said, "Let's sit this one out."

[Selena Gomez - The Heart Wants What It Wants (Official Video) YouTube] "Sure," Jennifer replied.

Xinxin on the other hand, loved this song and asked, "Wilber can we dance to this, please?"

Xinxin is a fantastic dancer, and she had all the moves and she could strut her stuff and in moments was causing temporal turbulence in the little heads of two Azzie dudes that were watching.

Wilber had already enjoyed the celestial feasts with Xinxin earlier, but Xinxin's evocative dancing had the quintessential effects on him as he suddenly re-evaluated, the lack of lust and what happened earlier no longer mattered. It was a new moment filled with electricity by this wonderful lady touched Wilber deeply.

They danced for another hour switching off and on always protecting their booth as it was crowded and full of people who wanted to pirate their booth.

Plus, the vigilance kept people away from drugging their drinks or other nefarious reasons.

The two Azzie dudes came up with a dumb game plan to take the two women away from the dudes. As soon as the two couples walked out of the Majestic Black Dragon the Azzie's followed.

What these punks didn't know is the DD/P never goes anywhere without protection. The DD/P knew the two watchers were always close at hand to intervene in the event of an attempted assassination or other malicious provocateurs actions.

The Azzie's followed the two couples down Lewers Street heading towards the beach and turned left past a parking lot and the pathway to the Royal Hawaiian. That's where they were going to strike the two men from behind, sucker punch them, beat the shit out of them and take their women into the parking structure and enjoy them.

When the two punks started making their bold mood, Wilber heard the fast footsteps from behind and turned. The punks had committed and were coming in fast and suddenly, they heard someone yelling from behind them.

Stop assholes if you know what's good for you. The two Azzie dudes stopped dead in their tracks and turned around watched two men were pointing guns at them.

"Down on the ground face down and don't move or I'll shoot you in you in your dicks, one of the CIA watchers yelled.

The Azzie dudes saw those were real no shit guns pointing at them and were wondering WTF?

One of the watchers said, "John, you and Wilber just continue on, we'll handle this."

"Thanks."

This was a very damaging event for Xinxin. She was just about ready to relax and accept her situation with Wilber, and she had no way of knowing these were just two stupid punks who thought they could beat up Wilber and John and take their women. The punks never stood a chance because Wilber turned around and could offer a lethal response.

As the two couples were rounding a point putting the Watchers and Azzie's out of sight, two Honolulu police officer ran up with guns drawn yelling, "Put the guns down now."

One of the Watchers said, "We are Federal Agents, we have jurisdiction, come put your handcuffs on these lads and we'll tell you all about it."

The CIA man wearing a bullet proof vest was not worried about being shot. Cops always aim for the midsection. He would get some bruises, but the cop would probably lose his job if pulled the trigger.

"I'm putting my gun back in my holster relax. The other CIA man did the same and the cops approached slowly still pointing the guns at them."

CIA watchers who are to protect people like the DD/P also carry an FBI badge so they can deal with dickhead cops they run into now and then who over emphasize their purpose in life.

"Put your guns back in your holsters and we'll show you our badges and you can call your boss and explain to them the FEDs have jurisdiction in this case, as a Federal Crime was occurring which we foiled."

The cops slowly put their guns in their holsters and the two watchers pulled out their FBI badges which the cops knew made this all very serious.

The first cop asked the two watchers, "What's this all about?"

"These two men were about to attack the CIA's Deputy Director for planning, we want to know who sent them."

The cops now knew they had stepped into some really heavy shit, and one said, "I'm calling my supervisor now."

"Good, tell him to send Jim Baccus here right away."

The cop knew who the hell Jim Baccus was, the head of the FBI for Hawaii. He had been to seminars and personally shook his hand.

In short order, Jim Baccus arrived with the cop's supervisor and a dozen other cops. One of Jim Baccus men searched the punks and found their Azzie passports. They were each notified to explain what they were doing and given their Maranda rights.

When one of the punks explained their intentions, Jim Baccus explained they picked the wrong people and were offered the easy way out. They would be escorted back to their hotel, supervised packing their luggage and given a free ride to the Airport to wait to board the next plane to Australia and informed they were put on the Watch List and would not be permitted back into the United States any time in the future.

The two Azzie's actually did commit a serious crime and didn't know it: They destroyed Wilber's future with Xinxin tonight.

What Wilber thought would be a hot steamy evening back in the hotel room captivating the emotions they developed on the dance floor turned out to be something different.

Xinxin was obviously emotionally disturbed.

This event with the two punks threw a monkey wrench into Xinxin's romance with Wilber and she had no idea what that was all about in the altercation earlier. Xinxin went to bed cold as ice and there was no communication. She had completely shut down and turned on her side and refused to look at Wilber.

By the grace of God and perhaps because of some of the alcohol they ingested the two were able to get some sleep. In the morning it was all packing and getting ready to leave. Xinxin didn't feel like breakfast and simply just wanted to get to the airport and as far away from Wilber as possible.

It was silent hell, and it was heart breaking for Wilber because he understood that altercation that almost happened was a game changer. He lost the love of his life due to those two punks. They had no idea the damage they did.

Lucky for them they were in the air on their way to Sydney Australia because Wilber was very pissed off and might have hunt them down and made them pay for what they just did to wreck his life.

Little did Wilber know, the Azzie dudes did him a favor because sometime soon, Xinxin would not be able to handle what was coming up.

Wilber walked Xinxin to the security checkpoint after she got her airline tickets and checked her luggage.

There were no hugs, no kisses, no tears, no nothing. It was an incredible ending.

Wilber wanted to grab Xinxin and profess his love, but he knew she was not in the mood, and it might already be over, so it was probably better to give her space. Maybe she would get her head together and call him soon and work this out.

"Goodbye Wilber," Xinxin forced herself to say. "Thank you for the wonderful time, Xinxin." Xinxin turned and went through the security checkpoint.

Wilber turned around and was heading out of the airport back to Waikiki where he would hook up with John Burkette and fly back to Dulles in a few hours.

As Wilber was walking past the ticket counters to go out and catch a cab back to Waikiki, he passed by two women that seemed to be familiar. One of them was Rachel, the other was Sandra staring at him.

They saw Wilber just moments ago walking Xinxin to the security check point. Xinxin was dressed in one of those $2000.00 designer dresses and looked like a million dollars even though her emotions were bankrupt.

Wilber had a poem he had written to Xinxin and even though he felt the situation was now hopeless based on her behavior, he texted the poem to Xinxin anyway.

The lonely heart that passed to me from far away, When I least expected.

My journey in life has traveled far and wide.

Why would suddenly a princess come to me? I reflected. Beauty and demure as it all unfolded, I still do not know what to make of it.

Why would a ghost from my dream suddenly appear, And be so emboldened.

The mysteries of life we never expect or perceive, How can that be?

As my evolution of thought riddles my consciousness, That I would have enshrined in a bygone era, now perpetuates an expansion of awareness, I need to be careful with a delicate heart.

Is there enough of me left to give?

I can sense the desire of pastural planes and emerald domains, But is it even possible to live?

And if I make the wrong decision, will I crush a heart? Is it not better then to remain apart?

Oh, how much we want to love, Some seek guidance from above, The allegro has just begun, The convolution of destiny reaches out, and I'm floating, looking for landfall. She would want to call, that I am certain. But is there enough left in me?

I want her to feel loved, to feel the ecstasy, the transcendental ensembles of lingering passions.

But haven't I gone down this road once before?

What did I learn?

In due time, Wilber and John were on the GS750 with the adorable Tammy there smiling, knowing these two guys got lucky. How was it, she wondered?

In due course, the Jet was airborne on its way to 50,000 feet enjoying a push from the Jetstream with a speed of 800 miles over ground for over halfway to Washington DC.

The silence in the plane was so deadening, you could cut it with a knife. there was no rancorous exhibit of past tumultuous allegros or anything that would convey the two Cowboys had a good time in Hawaii.

It was a long flight back to Singapore. Xinxin knew Wilber had texted her, but she decided it was over and she was not going to look at it. She did the best she could dealing with the sensation, scared to death out of a love affair. Now she realized when Wilber showed up in Singapore throwing his heart to her, she should have told him to get lost right then and there.

Xinxin was sitting next to a grandmother-like person who was quiet and nice and didn't bug her. She was polite and considerate and Xinxin felt comfort being beside such a person during a crisis in her life.

Because of the sweetness and charm of a grandmother, Xinxin relaxed and took her mind off everything. Her focus soon would be trading Crypto Currencies.

Romance is something she would not engage in for quite some time as she now was emotionally scarred for life.

About an hour out of Singapore after using the toilet and getting ready to get off the plane and get on with her life, curiosity killed the cat.

Xinxin didn't know what drove her to do it, but she opened her cellphone app and read Wilber's text message and the poem. The crocodile tears formed, and she silently whimpered. The nosey grandmotherly type who was well educated in the best British Schools a long time ago eaves dropped on the cell phone text reading it and watching Xinxin's reaction.

She of course had no idea the circumstances, but the poem hit Xinxin in the gut like a ton of bricks. Xinxin now realized the way she left Wilber was despicable. Even though she decided it was over and didn't want to see him again, she should have made a better departure. She could only imagine what she did to Wilber and the tears on the dancefloor said it all, but she didn't know those tears were for another woman, Faye Wong.

***

Chapter Fourteen

Probe Launch

Wilber didn't know it but thanks to his CIA cell phone, they always knew where he was going. He wasn't going anywhere without a watcher, especially since the day on the beach.

The DD/P had a piece of someone's ass because the watcher was out of position when Wilber was attacked on the beach. Had the watchers been in position when the two assailants went after Wilber and Xinxin, they should have prevented any mortal combat. Plus, Wilber should never have encountered Honolulu police.

During the subsequent critique and head shaping the watchers assigned to Wilber at Pearl Harbor went into the CIA's SKIF to explain to them how the Chinese MSS had tried to kill Wilber twice already. They were not there to protect him from two hoodlums but had those men been Chinese MSS there is a good possibility Wilber would be dead now. Their final briefing was, "You need to step up your performance a notch or two."

Unfortunately, the second incident that just turned Wilber's life upside down was probably unavoidable. The two Azzie's looked innocuous until they did something stupid and got themselves on the watch list and barred from visiting America. They also had an Australian welcoming committee, the AIC who did the finishing touches.

Because of the second incident, Wilber's watchers were operating far more aggressively. Their eyeglasses were also cameras the entire area of the fake glasses were camera lenses supplying fantastic resolution video recordings. The nerd-like lenses on the eyeglasses scanned using fractal processes, created a forty-three-millimeter equivalent lenses. Hence much better than the world's best thirty-five-millimeter cameras without a telephoto lens.

Because John Burkette, their bosses-bosses-boss was so aggravated, they had to feed him constant live video so he could check up on them and find out WTF things happened the way they did. The watchers were under a microscope. John Burkette could run a cursor over the video stream and look at any portion of any sources of the video in the buffer that lasted several days.

John Burkette was most interested in the aftermath of the second disaster created by two dumb shit punks who embarrassed CIA officials caught out of position to intervene before it was possibly too late.

Wilber had been very quiet since and didn't want to meet for breakfast. John Burke started watching the video feed and saw the estranged relationship. He knew how bubbly the two had been in total love and now Xinxin was cold as ice. There was no communication. John Burkette, a master social engineer knew the incident with the Azzie punks manifested this behavior change.

The AIC (Australian Intelligence Community) people who met the two punks informed them, they had wrecked the relationship with a highly placed CIA official and they were lucky to be alive and then informed they were on a watch list and would likely be denied travel on any airline anywhere. Their lives were now also changed.

John Burkette looking over the video of Xinxin's departure saw no conversation, no kisses, no farewell, nothing. Just silence. Later when they were on the Jet flying back to Washington, Wilber was silent the entire trip, napped quite a bit and didn't have much to say.

People who had someone abruptly leave their lives understand all this quite well. There wasn't anything anyone could do now. Wilber now knew it was over. Xinxin didn't answer his texts. He had no choice but to start the next chapter in his life.

Xinxin would be surprised. She thought Wilber would pester her and beg her, etc. But he texted her less as time went by.

Life goes on and soon, Wilber was called back off "administrative leave."

Pat Barton kept it up and finally Wilber had enough. He was in the SKIF getting his ass ripped by Pat Barton for leaving the country without contacting his controller.

"Alright Pat, take your final warning and shove it up your ass. I quit."

Wilber stood up and started walking out the door and Pat yelled, "Come back here I'm not done with you."

"Fuck you Pat, I'm done with you."

Wilber went home thinking about his next move.

Pat wrote up Wilber for insubordination and sent his version of the story to John Burke, and the two were soon together in a private meeting with Pat Barton.

"Pat, when are you going to give it a rest?"

"What are you talking about John?"

"Listen you dumb cocksucker I'm your boss, and you continuously piss me off. I'll tell you what we do at the DD/P to idiots like you. I can't fire you, but you sure as hell can disappear. You get Wilber to come back or I'm coming after you."

John Burkette stood up and walked out of the SKIF. He'll give Pat a few days to *unfuck* the situation he created with his vindictiveness towards Wilber.

As soon as John Burkette left the SKIF, Pat Barton was shaking. He heard stories about fratricide within the CIA. He now knew he was on shaky ground and if he pulled any more crap on Wilber, bad things might happen to him. Suddenly Pat Barton became the friendliest SOB in the world towards Wilber. Not because he wanted a promotion. He wanted to stay alive.

For the next couple days, Wilber never answered any of Pat's phone calls. He didn't check out of the organization, he simply walked out of the door.

Pat was forced to do a missing CIA agent report because it was an administrative requirement, that even John Burkette knew was a requirement. But John sent Pat a rebuttal and copied his boss, Brent.

"Listen, Pat, we all know your treatment of Wilber has been deplorable with your final warning BS. An effective manager would have rung his doorbell by now to ask him to come back. Are you effective or are you just an pretender?"

John Burkette sat there thinking because he was not done, he had a few more items to get off his chest and school Pat who had proven to him by now, he's a neophyte.

Pat was now reading the rebuttal email wondering what his next move should be and the next paragraph in John Burkette's memorandum *blazoned* Pat's thoughts.

"Wilber's not missing, he's home stupid because you pissed him off in that ill-advised meeting the way you conducted it. Your actions towards Wilber have been detrimental to the agency." John Burkette elucidated.

Pat was going to complain to John's boss Brent but as he continued reading, he realized he had set himself up for a disaster. John Burkette's next words shook him:

"If I do not hear from Wilber by tomorrow morning, I'm taking administrative action against you and putting you on 30 days of administrative leave to determine if you violated policies by acts and omissions we need to investigate."

Pat realized he had just received John Burkette's administrative enema. But he was no fool and knew a couple of guys in the office that got along with Wilber quite well because they were Cowboys and pulled them into his office for a meeting.

"The reason why I asked you guys to come in here is to give you a very important task that's at the DD/P level of interest." Pat Barton said.

The two men looked at Pat Barton wondering WTF this was all about.

"I admit I truly pissed off Wilber O'Toole. He's an important asset to the CIA and we can ill afford to lose him. I'm going to leave here in a few minutes to go ring his doorbell and ask him to come back to work. If I ring the doorbell, he will likely not answer it. But if you guys come along and ring the doorbell, he will probably answer to give me the opportunity to ask him to come back." Pat Barton explained.

The first man said, "Sure, I'll go with you."

The second man replied, "I'll go with you but the reason why he left here is you have been a total prick to him. Everyone knows it. You need to change your interface methods with Wilber if you expect to retain him as an employee."

"Yes, I realize I need to alter my own conduct, let's go over Wilber's house now."

It was just after lunch and Wilber finished a nice sandwich and was finishing the rest of his beer, he used to wash it down, when the doorbell rang. He walked over and looked at the flatscreen security monitor next to the door and saw Pat Barton who he would not normally answer the door for, but Pat brought along a couple of guys he got along with because they were not office warriors.

Wilber reluctantly opened the door. "What can I do for you?"

"Wilber, I know this might feel kind of awkward, but may we come in for a talk?"

Wilber looked at one of the guys he trusted who gave him a nod like, "It's okay."

"Alright," Wilber said then opened the door up the rest of the way to allow the three men inside his home."

The front room had a couple of sofas and a couple chairs. Wilber said, "Please have a seat.

Wilber was not going to offer drinks because he knew this was not a social call.

The two other men stayed silent Pat Barton did all the talking.

"I realized I rubbed you the wrong way. I was simply trying to follow agency policy and requirements. Perhaps this last time I may have been out of line, and I came over here to personally apologize."

"Alright."

"Wilber, I'm also here to ask you to please come back, we need you."

Wilber's coworker nodded indicating this was the real deal. Wilber read through all this and understood the real unbridled truth, John Burkette probably read Pat the riot act when he found Wilber quit and walked out the door.

Pat Barton is the typical bureaucrat who's the consummate office warrior and never had skin in the game, had no idea what it's like to experience what Wilber had. Wilber knew that had Pat been in that firefight with the terrorists, he would have pissed his pants and cried like a baby.

Wilber understood the real reason why Pat was here. It did not take a rocket scientist to figure out Pat was directed by John Burkette to get him back. Wilber decided it was now time to give Pat some crap like he gave him and simply replied, "After I hear from John Burkette, I'll give you my decision."

Pat understood Wilber was a capable adversary. He just laid down the gauntlet that Pat could not avoid. Pat had no option but to go back to the office and report back to John Burkette, the context of this conversation.

"Alright, I'll let John know. Thanks for letting us talk to you."

The men stood up and Wilber walked over and opened the door and the three promptly left in Pat's automobile.

Pat went back to his office and called John Burkette and reported in. "John?"

"That's me."

"Hi John, this is Pat. I rang Wilber's doorbell and talked to him."

"What was the outcome of that discussion?" John Burkette asked.

"Wilber said he would give me his decision after you talk to him."

"Alright. I'll call him. Meet me in the SKIF in 45 minutes."

"Understand." Pat Barton replied.

DD/P John Burkette, called Wilber knowing the obvious because he had just looked at all the videos. Wilber was indeed heartbroken over Xinxin. Pat was in a way an innocent bystander, but he was also the prick that manifested the situation John now had to handle.

Wilber looked at the caller I.D. and saw it was John Burkette calling. "Hello John."

"Listen Wilber, I'm very sorry the way Hawaii ended for you. I know you are not feeling so happy now, but I need to talk to you."

"Sure."

"Wilber, because of the Chinese situation we must protect you. Those two guys that came up when the punks from Australia attempted to accost us were not there for me. They were your watchers to protect you."

"I see."

"Everywhere you go you should know you are probably filmed."
"Yes, I gather that."

"I know when Xinxin left it was not a pleasant experience for you."

"You can certainly say that."

"I know you are upset because the agency let you down and you have a prick you work for, but I want you to come back."

"I can't work for Pat Barton any longer. I'm willing to work at washing cars for a living if I must."

"Yea I get all that, but you have an important role in Project Solaris."

"Pat Barton doesn't seem to think that."

"Forget about that dickhead. We can rearrange the chess pieces. You have more important things to do now such as interacting with Pierre Truffaut."

"John, I want to help out as much as I can, but Pat Barton just pushed me beyond the limits."

"Wilber, I understand that completely and I've decided to take some actions and rearrange the ORG CHART."

"What does that mean?"

"I knew it was going to come to this and you and I both know that probe isn't going to get the job done. Pat Barton is a fool and will soon learn the error of his ways. The submarine development is where we'll have to go if we want to come to terms with the Aliens on Saturn."

"How are you going to change the organization?" Wilber asked.

"I've redefined and compartmentalized the mission. Project Solaris is now a separate entity and is no longer under Solar Systems Investigations. Pat Barton will continue leading Solar Systems Investigations, but you will be assigned exclusively to Project Solaris which will now come under my direct jurisdiction."

"Alright."

"Because of the compartmentalization, you will be moved out of Pat Barton's office spaces to a new location when you return back to work."

"Where's that going to be?"

"To the Navy Yard in Washington DC."

"Why the Navy Yard?"

"Many Naval Sea Systems Command submarine program managers there. They have a large contingency of logistics codes for operational existing hulls and program management codes involved in New Construction of the new Virginia Class fast attacks and Columbia Class SSBN. We currently own a submarine they operate for us."

"For real?"

"I can't give you the name of it over the phone in case someone has broken into our crypto, but we had another submarine that has been decommissioned and cut up

into millions of razor blades, that has some visibility, due to compromise by spies and some unauthorized books that got published.

"If the program was compromised, then why are we using submarines?"

"Go to Wikipedia and look at USS Parche (SSN-683). We spoon fed the authors of that article disinformation, but it gives you an idea of how we used that submarine that has features we would need for Project Solaris."

"Alright, I'll check it out."

"When you google that submarine, you will be utterly shocked at what has been leaked or put into books. Some of it's true some of it we planted as disinformation to make our enemies keep guessing."

"What's the role of the follow-on submarine?"

"I will tell you this much. It has nothing to do with Russia or China."

"What could possibly be more important than spying on Russia and China?"

"Aliens."

"When can I go in and clean out my desk and move over to the Navy Yard?"

"I sent a team in last night and removed everything out of your office and had it all moved to the Navy Yard to your office in building 28. A few things that could not leave the building due to their classification were destroyed by the SWIPE team.

"What's SWIPE mean?"

"Situation Warrants Item Physical Exchange."

"I suppose it does."

"I'll send you a map soon and all the details. Report there as soon as you can.

"Who do I report into?"

"Your new controller, Jerry Nault."

"Alright."

Let me know an hour before you go there. Someone will be at the main gate waiting for you with a parking pass and escorting you on base. Your CAC card we issued you for access to military installations will get you into the building and into the classified area where your office is located. I'll meet you there after you arrive and introduce you to the staff that has been set up there. This is project Solaris Offices until further notice."

"How does Pat Barton fit into all this?"

"He doesn't. He will be busy with the probe business for a few years until they determine that's a flop and realize we are the only game in town."

"Is there any possibility the weasel will end up over in Project Solaris?"

"He's a few years older than me, he'll retire long before I do. He's not going anywhere near Project Solaris. He doesn't have a good track record."

"Alright."

"But you will have to deal with him one more time, as disgusting as it sounds."

"What for?"

"I've already informed him you have a new role and reporting official as well as controller. But for continuity, he's been ordered to send you back out to Vandenburg during the probe Launch to interface with Colonel Baker."

"Sure, I don't mind that. How soon is it going to happen?"

"You have Colonel Baker's number, get in touch with him and get the nondisclosed date he's holding close to his chest and tell him you want to be out there for the launch."

"Why do I need to be there?"

"Real simple, I trust you. If something goes wrong. I don't want a bullshit artist like Pat Barton feeding me a soup sandwich."

"I have no problems going there. Colonel Baker is a great guy, the best man for the job."

"I agree with you. He's put up a lot of spy satellites for us. The only reason why we have not let him get promoted to General is we need him at his rank doing what he's doing. When he reaches his stress limit, we'll get him promoted to General in a less stressful environment."

"Alright, I'll call you when I'm ready to go in and get situated."

"Thanks." John Burkette ended the phone call.

Wilber had some dry cleaning to pick up. He would wear a suit to work in the morning. First impression is important. His DOD CAC card does not convey to anyone he was affiliated with the CIA.

Also, Wilber's FBI badge was only to be used in an emergency. But he had to pay the price to get that FBI badge. He had to go on some real shitty missions with FBI agents.

The FBI has more dealings with the drug cartels than people understand. DEA, FBI, and Mexican Federal National Police (PFM) often have task forces operating together. Some of those missions required Wilber to jump out of helicopters carrying M16's with bullet proof vests, bullet proof helmet and visor. He fired quite a few rounds. He didn't know if he killed any of the drug cartel people since there were so many bullets flying around. He slept well at night knowing his FBI and PFM buddies were the ones who hit the targets.

Wilber was on Wisconsin Avenue and picked up his dry cleaning. He had two former girlfriends who lived around here, a couple of miles apart. One was a high-ranking executive. She was a knockout gorgeous blonde, but she tried to micro-manage Wilber, so he split with her. Then he met this gorgeous blonde real estate lady freshly divorced. He was in love with her and would have married her. But one month before he proposed to her, she went out with her girlfriend and got drunk and had sex with some dude.

She was an honest person and called Wilber and confessed her sins, hoping it would not sink her ship. Unfortunately, her behavior broke Wilber's heart and he left her ship behind in the sunset in a new chapter in his life.

One cannot permanently delete such memories because of our human condition. They were pivotal events in Wilber's life. He wished he could reach out to the real estate lady and even though it was over, simply tell her, I did love you. He would want her to know she was special to him, and he wouldn't mind giving her a long hug. But that was the past.

As Wilber reorientated his life, he was going to move so that he would never drive-up Wisconsin Avenue again.

Since Wilber was up on Wisconsin Avenue after he picked up his dry cleaning, he decided to go into a Greek restaurant. There is a Greek Orthodox Church nearby where he and his former lover went during the Greek holiday where they cooked lamb on a spit. The crowds lined up. For a while he was in love with her too. She knew he had some incredible tasks he had to do and when she started putting pressure on him, she had no idea the stress he experienced because of his professional tasking would break most men.

One of the last times Wilber saw the female executive was at the American Airlines Terminal in Washington DC crying trying to stop him from getting on the plane. They accidentally met there. She was arriving from a trip, and he was leaving and didn't tell her he was leaving on a long trip, he couldn't tell her about.

Wilber had already decided to end it with the blonde executive who looked amazingly like the beautiful Russian singer Valeriya (Валерия) the stage name of Alla Yurievna Perfilova.

[Валерия — Синица (OST «Я хочу! Я буду!») | Official Video 2022 (0+) - YouTube]

Wilber then he had one of those strange twists in life when he met Faye Wong, another chapter he wished he could yank out of his book of life. Her ghost would haunt him forever. The fact Faye Wong looked like Jennie Kim, made it hard for him to forget her as he loved Jennie's singing.

[JENNIE - 'SOLO' M/V - YouTube]

And now, Xinxin who looked a lot like Faye ran away from him and after several weeks didn't answer his calls or respond to his texts. It was clearly over now. Wilber realized it was time to move on.

Wilber took the Greek food home had a nice meal sat back relaxed and listened to the fantastic singer Polina Gagarina, perhaps the best singer in the world. She was also eye candy. Even though it would be impossible since they lived in two distinct worlds apart, he would love to have a relationship with Polina. But since that would never happen, at least he had the satisfaction of hearing her wonderful singing and watching her in her videos. What an incredible performer, Wilber thought as he listened to this incredible singer Polina Gagarina who resonated his soul.

[.ПОЛИНА ГАГАРИНА - Лучшие песни - YouTube]

Wilber owed Polina Gagarina a great deal of gratitude as she took his mind off all his problems and fell asleep in his recliner where he often slept with a blanket over him after finishing a bottle of Cabernet Sauvignon.

This was another one of those nights as the ghosts of his past slipped away and Wilber suddenly woke from hearing traffic noise outside his home and America waking up. Wilber got up took care of business, made a small breakfast. He was not a breakfast person. Coffee was important though.

After a shower and a shave, Wilber dressed in one of those suits just dry cleaned, got himself together and called John Burkette.

"John I'm ready to go to the office." Wilber said.

"Great I forecast your call and Jerry Nault will meet you at the main gate." John said.

"I thought that was against policy to meet your controller." Wilber stated.

"I'm sending you out against Aliens not Russians and Chinese. Big difference, that restriction does not apply to you." John Burkette responded.

"Alright, I'm ready to leave."

"Good, Jerry Nault will be at the main gate near the gate guards when you arrive."

"Okay, on my way."

"I'll catch up with you later."

Wilber was soon driving on City streets towards the Navy Yard using the Google Navigator with the coordinates for the main gate programmed in.

Wilber was familiar with the route through city streets he had to take and worked his way to the main gate. In part that was thanks to his former girlfriend, the blonde executive who had to go this way often as she worked in Crystal City. This beautiful blonde female executive sometimes had to go over to the Navy Yard to handle contracts as her company sold the Navy a lot of materials.

Wilber's new controller Jerry Nault was standing next to the rent-a-cops (Federal Police). Wilber could see they were a little uneasy, since a 4- Star admiral introduced them to Jerry Nault to explain there were some interesting developments on his base and Jerry was here to bring in the guest and this is his parking permit. Their eyeballs just about bugged out when they saw the expiration date was "indefinite."

Parking on that base is a bitch. If you are not at least a captain forget it. You will pay for parking or get smart and commute. Washington DC has a lot of carpools because of that situation. It's counterproductive because all the office warriors are out the door at 3:00 P.M. And many of them are salaried.

So having office warriors on a salary is a joke if they are hauling ass home at 3:00 P.M. when the design of that salaried position is they should stay to 6:00 P.M. and work like a Cowboy instead of an office warrior, as far as Wilber was concerned.

Jerry Nault had seen many pictures of Wilber because as his controller he was fed all the surveillance videos and his dossier. He knew what his car looked like, what his license plate number was, the whole nine yards. As Wilber's car was nearing the security checkpoint Jerry Nault said to one of the Rent-A-Cops, that's Wilber O'Toole in the car pulling up.

When Wilber stopped in front of the Rent-A-Cop because it was 100% ID check, Jerry stepped forward and said, "Wilber I'm Jerry Nault. I'm going to hop in your car and give you directions to your parking spot."

"Sure thing, hop in."

The Rent-A-Cop working for a contractor agency, said, "Welcome to the Naval Yard, Mr. O'Toole. You may proceed."

As soon as Jerry Nault was in the car, Wilber drove into the Navy Yard.

The Gate Gard knew these two men were CIA as the Admiral explained to him. A lot of interesting things happened at the Navy Yard since NSA was joined at the hip with the Navy.

"You are lucky today, Wilber," Jerry Nault said.

"Why is that?"

"Parking for Building number 28 people is a long way off. Everyone working in Building 28 will be jealous when they find out where your assigned parking spot is."

"How did I rate such a good parking spot."

"You will find out soon your cover is you are the director of Hypersonic Drone Development." Jerry Nault said.

"What the hell is that?" Wilber asked.

"We do not have to put all our warheads on Trident D5 or E6 and soon to be F7 missiles. The Columbia Class will have Drone Cluster launchers that can handle the standard missile or the new Shashka Hypersonic Drones (SHD-8)." Jerry Nault said.

"Shashka Hypersonic Drones" sounds like an interesting name. Where the hell did Shashka come from?" Wilber asked.

"Shashka is the name of a ancient Russian single-edged saber. It's a single- handed guard less backsword."

"Is this for real? Why did you pick a Russian name?"

"Yes, the hypersonic drones are a game changer. The DOD picked the name to send a subtle message to the Russians. They will understand this is directed at them."

"Why Shashka Hypersonic Drone weapons?"

"By implementing the Shashka Hypersonic Drone weapons , we no longer need any Ballistic Missiles that take 15 to 30 minutes to get there and can be shot down, but we'll still have them to complicate the battlefield." Jerry Nault replied.

"Does Project Solaris actually have anything to do with Shashka Hypersonic Drones weapons?" Wilber asked.

"No that's your cover story. You are only here for Project Solaris." Jerry Nault said.

"But that other development will go on?" Wilber asked.

"Yes, it's the perfect setup because they provide all our security for us. Intruders must get through all those nuclear people before they get to us." Jerry Nault said.

"Alright, Shashka Hypersonic Drone development sounds like a good thing to throw people off if they ask questions."

"Nobody but the Navy knows about Shashka Hypersonic Drone development for the Columbia Class SSBN, and they do not want the Air Force to know anything about it." Jerry Nault said.

"Turf Battles?" Wilber asked.

"You got it." Jerry Nault replied.

"My former boss, Pat Barton says turf battles do not exist." Wilber said.

"He must be one dumb SOB." Jerry Nault said.

"He is." Wilber said.

Jerry Nault navigated for Wilber, and they were soon at his parking spot. He didn't know it, but he was in a GS-16 SES parking spot. The SES just retired, which was nice and handy to fit Wilber into his spot.

The parking placard on the spot had license plate number only. There was nothing to indicate who it was or what Wilber did. People handing out tickets for illegal parking would match the placard with the car's license plate number and just walk on past.

Wilber was surprised how close to building 28 he was parking. In Washington DC a good parking spot is one of the more pleasant aspects of life.

Jerry Nault's administrative aide had verified Wilber's CAC card information was programmed into building access and front gate access where the Gate Guard would scan it before allowing him to drive on base.

Jerry had Wilber go in first, and the CAC access worked. There was an elevator, but the stairway was the most efficient way to get to Wilber's new office, so they went that way. Jerry knew Wilber worked out often and would enjoy taking the stairs adding to his daily physical exercises.

The office area they went into had stood up over a month prior and all knew each other and were already busy working and meeting with Navy program managers to get technology from them. The biggest was the super top secret Fusion Reactors NAVSEA-08 developed for black projects including unmanned submersibles that had electric drive from the fusion reactors that also powered all the sensors and weapon systems.

These ingenious robotic submersible devices operated by artificial intelligence were ISR vessels, but they were also nuclear weapon delivery devices in time of war that would swim into a Harbor and fry it in the event of the start of hostilities that would go nuclear.

Since there were no humans onboard and only Artificial Intelligence, when detonated, the structure of the submersible would add to the explosive force as when materials reached a critical temperature via the thermo- nuclear detonation the materials became highly explosive and become part of the plasma created.

None of the people were expecting Wilber. They had no idea Wilber was coming or who Wilber was.

All of them knew who Jerry Nault was. He had his formal introductions several weeks prior. When he walked into the offices with Wilber they were not terribly concerned as the two men walked to the office that was currently not assigned and locked. None of them had been in after hours when the plumbers and the carpenters as they say in the business brought in all of Wilber's stuff and arranged his desk identically to how he left the old Solar Systems Investigations offices.

They went inside and shut the door behind them and then Jerry Nault briefed Wilber on all his tools and facilities available to him. He asked Wilber to log into his computer both high side and low side and make sure he had connectivity and his CAC

card reader on the desktop keyboard read it. He was also asked to check his email to verify all his emails were available and be aware if he had any incoming. Since he had been away from the office for a while, he had a blizzard of email on both low side and high side. His high side access was good for Top Secret.

"I'll let you check some of your emails while we wait for John Burkette to arrive."

"Thanks, I need to check up on a lot of them."

In the typical government bureaucracy, people like Wilber get involved with groups and some of those emails have upwards to 100 recipients. Which means the possibility of a lot of replies to all's coming in. Not all emails need to be replied to, but some people wanted their presence felt and replied but added nothing structurally important to the discussion. Nevertheless, it's like weeds growing you need to cut down or you will soon have them up over your knees.

Pat Barton sent out quite a few emails that instantly pissed off Wilber, none of which he intended on replying to. And suddenly it all ended. Several days before, all emails from Pat Barton ended.

Also, Pat Barton tried to recall some of his stupid emails, but the problem is someone already read them, it was too late.

Wilber could only think, *what a fucking dickhead.* Damn, was he glad to be away from that clown!

And suddenly the good stuff started. John Burkette informed Pat he was sending Wilber out to Vandenburg to monitor the launch. Pat replied he already had people going and Wilber's presence was not desired or required.

"Pat, I'm not asking you to send Wilber to Vandenburg, he's already going under my orders. He no longer works for you; I was merely informing you he was going. Your input on this matter is not necessary."

Talk about bitch slap, Wilber said to himself.

Jerry Nault had already read all those emails and when he saw Wilber smiling, he knew what he had just read.

In a few minutes there was a knock at the door. One of Jerry's assistants said after Wilber opened the door, "Excuse me, John Burkette is in the conference room now and would like you men to join him there."

"Alright thank you," Wilber said. He and Jerry soon went outside the office and led Wilber to the nearby conference room.

This was what you might call an *All Hands Meeting,* in military vernacular. John Burkette was sitting at the end of the conference table and there were two empty seats next to him with placards on them saying Wilber O'Toole and Jerry Nault. Wilber and Jerry took their seats.

John Burkette started the meeting: "Thank you everyone for showing up. As you can see, we have a new person in the Office, his name is Wilber O'Toole. He is a special agent for Project Solaris. He will soon be interacting with all of you, and I want you to know he works directly for me. You will see on the ORG CHART in your briefing pamphlets, there are two people under me that are tied together side by side.

But all of you fall under Jerry Nault. That's because Wilber O'Toole will be busy in various aspects of support for the project and does not have time to handle administrative functions."

"You will all find out soon enough Wilber has a good head on his shoulders and that's why over the years he was selected to carry out difficult projects. His past includes highly guarded secrets, so he's not able to share any details, so do not waste your time asking," John Burkette stated. Then he continued his comments.

"I have some immediate needs for his assistance in Solar System Investigations. Even though his primary focus is Project Solaris, he came from the Solar Systems Investigations group, and they are about ready to launch a probe so he's going to have to spend some time in Vandenburg until that bird flies. Some of you will have to attend meetings for him or go make appointments while he's gone or research information he requests."

"Wilber, would you like to address the group?" John Burkette asked.

"Sure," Wilber said then stood up. His suit was two or three notches in formal wear above what everyone else wore today. He was still in great shape from routine workouts. Everyone eyeballed him as he stood up and saw he had a body that supported a charismatic delivery.

"Like John Burkette said I came from Solar System Investigations and was involved in discovering information that is now the reason why we are all here."

Wilber looked around the room and everyone was focused on him with great interest, especially since he just magically showed up today with little or no warning. A couple women in the group looking for a future mate had significant issues because their clearances were so high, they had to be damn careful with who they dated. That immediately scrubbed about 80% of all the possible men.

Wilber had one experience where one of his prior sponsors was a female. Susan was very pretty, well built and extremely intelligent. No matter how hard she tried in vetting the man she ultimately married, the fact was after they were married and she was pregnant, the agency had to pull her into a meeting and give her the bad news about who she married. It became a huge problem overnight because of the extremely secret project she was a principal manager.

Because of this scandal, Susan was moved out of that position and a male took over. Her life was turned upside down. It was a heart-breaking affair. Wilber felt so bad for Susan and wanted to reach out to her, but he and others were warned to stay completely away from her.

One of the hazards of a high security position was issues like this and our enemies had figured out long ago the reverse honey pot scheme worked just as well.

Wilber had done it himself. His relationship with Xinxin started out that way. He used her, but in the process, he thought he could compartmentalize his heart and his emotions, and he thus became a victim of his own doing. Wilber now felt just as bad as the woman who was on a glide slope probably to a future department head position to find out her new husband and father of her kid created a terrible situation for her.

Susan could not remain married to the guy and keep her security clearance. She was swiftly moved out of her assignment. Her husband discovered how fast he was

out. He wrecked her life and didn't think about the consequences of creating a single mom parent. He quickly disappeared and she annulled the marriage and was thankful the spooks vetted him before they had been married a year making it easy to annul the wedding. When he disappeared, he didn't know he had a child.

Nobody knew what happened to Susan's husband or what terrible things he had done in his lifetime that created this scandal for Susan. But Wilber knew something like this meant one of two things. Either the guy was Mafia and never figured he would be found out, or he was FSB/KGB type. His disappearance was definitely a Cash-In-Advance operation. If he was FSB/KGB, he got traded in a spy trade, if he was mafia, some other mafia dude got paid a lot of money to put him into a tree shredder.

"How many people here know what we are going to build?" Wilber asked.

There were a couple hands raised. Wilber looked over at John Burke who had one of those strange looks on his face.

Not everyone in the room had been briefed and suddenly said, "Only half of the people in the room have been briefed."

"Will they all eventually get briefed?" "Yes, that's the plan."

"May I make a suggestion?"

"Sure, what do you propose?"

"I think they all need to know right now what this is all about and why I'm here. I recommend Jerry Nault get a stack of non-disclosure sheets and have everyone sign them now and after Jerry confirms he has paper for everyone, then I want everyone to know what we will be doing."

John Burke had one of those very painful looks on his face. Wilber just pulled a Cowboy on him like Pat Barton always complained about. But he understood the reality of the situation. The Cowboy understood reality, eventually they all had to be briefed and brought into discussions and involvement. It was a catch-22 issue, but in a moment or so that John Burkette thought about it, he realized the Cowboy was right. An office warrior would have told Wilber to stand down.

"Get the forms, Jerry." John Burkette said.

"Yes sir." Jerry Nault

Jerry Nault stood up, walked over to his office, pulled out the instruction manual and pulled out the master copy of the SF-312 non-disclosure form. He knew how many people worked for him and made that many copies plus a few extras, put the master back in the instruction binder and walked back to the conference room and handed one to everyone and they started filling them out and when complete handed them to Jerry Nault who looked them over briefly to verify the signature and date were on the form.

In fifteen minutes, Jerry Nault informed John Burkette, "Everyone in the briefing has filled out and signed the forms."

"Alright, thank you. Wilber please proceed," John Burkette said.

Wilber stood up and began his briefing. John Burkette had a lot of dealings with Wilber O'Toole in the past and knew he was a charismatic speaker and watching him interface with the Arab Sheikhs cemented his viewpoint.

"Okay everybody. We have a very important task to do this briefing is going to take a little longer than any of you planned." Wilber announced.

Wilber looked around the room and back at John Burkette who had a poker face. But one thing John Burkette knew quite vividly is Wilber's history. "He might have been a Cowboy, but there is absolutely nobody else that would have got Zayd away from 100+ terrorists. He was a man who got things done. Even though he wasn't planning on spending the morning in the Project Solaris offices, this was starting to shape up into a monumental event, his schedule was thus put on hold to let this all unfold and see what Wilber was going to announce and how he was going to conduct himself.

Wilber was now under the microscope. The most powerful people in the government were keenly watching him now with speculation that when they sent the submarine to Saturn, Wilber O'Toole would be the lead for the adventure. It would be an extraordinary and pivotal moment in human affairs and our reality check with the universe.

"We planned for a shorter meeting, but with the changes in the agenda, in 45 minutes we'll take a restroom break and get coffee if required."

Suddenly there were a lot of sour faces in the room. "Everyone please power off your cell phones now."

Wilber looked around the room and watched the cascading movements of complying with the directive. He then asked an important question:

"Even if you have CIA phones, this meeting is now classified TOP-SECRET SCI with designators K, Q, T, W, and Z. So, all phones must be powered off. If any of you do not have those designators in your clearance raise your hands now." Half the room raised their hands.

"I have no choice but to put you people that raised your hands in for a higher clearance. Jerry Nault will get together with each of you when this meeting is over and initiate the clearances. Please do not leave the conference room until all of you without clearances meet with Jerry. Because of the non- disclosures you just signed. You now have provisional clearance. If any of you have any skeletons in the closet and have reason to believe you will fail receiving the clearance, please stand up and Jerry will escort you to the front entrance with administrative day off until we figure out what to do with you. Most likely you will be transferred to another division.

A couple people decided to opt out and stood up and Jerry escorted them to the front entrance of their offices and said, "Enjoy the rest of your day off. Report back here tomorrow. If you think you still want to attempt getting those special designations on your clearance tomorrow, you can opt back in."

The two people leaving were women. Their main reason discovered later was, they realized this project would trap them and the opportunity to meet someone and start a family would be truncated. These women didn't want to go the way that Susan went when her husband was vetted.

When Jerry Nault re-entered the conference room. John Burkette was already happy this was happening because the Cowboy cut to the chase and streamlined the process, they thought would take months before meaningful work could get started.

As soon as Jerry Nault sat down, Wilber stood up again and said, "Alright. Here we go. What we will be doing will require teamwork and more cooperative spirit than you ever experienced in your lifetime."

Wilber looked around the room and saw the intensity on everyone's faces.

"The purpose of Project Solaris is to build a nuclear submarine and operate it on planet Saturn."

There was a small gasp in the people attending the conference.

"In case you don't know it, Saturn's surface is covered with liquid hydrogen and liquid helium. Its bitter cold."

"Now I'm going to tell you something you will not think possible until we do it. Project Solaris will fly five years from today. We must put a date down for everyone to work towards. This will be the greatest challenge since the Manhatten project with similar priorities."

One of the men in the group a former submariner spoke up and said, "Our modern-day Virginia Class fast attack submarines weigh 7800 tons. How the hell are you going to get something so big and heavy to Saturn and safely land it on liquid hydrogen and helium?"

"Great question and while we have this briefing and discussion don't be afraid to ask questions," Wilber responded.

Wilber looked directly into the eyes of the man who quickly thought he was looking at the devil himself when he looked at Wilber, just like Napoleon's Generals did."

"We are going to build modules and fly them to Saturn and assemble the kits there."

The man fearful of the devil looking man had to ask the next question and now considered opting out himself, "What is the purpose of putting a submarine on Saturn?"

"I was going to show all of you a video in a little while, but these two questions have given me reason to jump ahead now and play the video we'll continue discussions after we all see this video together."

A cable was on the table Wilber could hook the miniature USB cable into his cell phone to play the video.

Wilber continued standing but stepped back a few feet to make sure he didn't block the view of any of the people in the room.

The Alien situation on Saturn was discussed first. This special briefing was put together for the President who wasn't considered the smartest tact on the wall, so it went over the detects of alien communications originating from Saturn. Next all the presentations associated with Dr. Morgan were played.

As Wilber gazed out into the room looking at everyone, they all had an Oh My effing God look on their faces.

A few of them now wished the hell they had followed the two women out of the room earlier. But now they were stuck and getting higher clearances and would have trouble sleeping tonight.

Using CIA's artificial intelligence to help him draw an image, Wilber had several images of a modularized submarine basic concepts that Pierre Truffaut, the submarine designer would use to create the actual design.

Everyone including John Burkette was absolutely fascinated. The modularized submarine CGI was so good it would be outstanding for a movie. The CIA CGI boys were the best in the business because they often created fake videos to get to a senator or a congressman, they wanted a few favors from. They also sometimes had to tweak the British or the Germans who were starting to have wavering commitments to special projects.

The CGI imagery looks so realistic even the submariner in the group felt moved as if he were looking at a craft that was already built in total secrecy. The Submariner knew all about a special operations submarine so he knew the kinds of challenges the Cash-In-Advance boys could accomplish, also in a five-year window, with sea trials commencing exactly five years to the date the Submarine's captain had committed to five years earlier.

As John Burkette gazed out among all the Project Solaris staff, he witnessed quite a transformation. He also realized the office warrior Pat Barton would put this crowd to sleep. Wilber in his Cowboy, machine gun style, had them all captivated. He needed their buy-in and Wilber immediately got it.

None of them knew if this gadget could ever come to fruition and a few days ago if someone had mentioned this to them in a conversation, they would have considered it pure fantasy and a pipe dream. But in the context of this presentation, they unequivocally realized this just might be something they could pull off together. A team spirit was formed right then and there, and they all understood the way John Burke allowed Wilber to take control of the meeting, who was the force to recon with, now stood in front of them.

The presentation mentioned electric drive, fusion reactors for power and propulsion, a weapon system with weapons just starting development, sensors, and life support systems. Materials science would take a giant leap forward.

Suddenly the video briefing was over, and it lasted so long it took them up to lunch hour.

"Wilber, I would like you and Jerry Nault to go with me for lunch."

"Sure."

Away they went. Leaving behind an office that now knew what their purpose in life was and no BS story that would slowly turn into reality. They got their marching orders up front. Some were dazzled wondering if five years from now, would really happen?

Wilber knew this would be just as challenging as cutting a submarine in half and adding 100 feet multiplied by a factor of ten. But he also knew one more fact, if they didn't believe it could be done, it would never happen. Just like before there were doubters. They cut a submarine in half and added 108 feet and five years later they were believers going out on sea trials.

"The restaurant I'm taking you, is known to have a lot of FSB spies hanging out there listening to people from the Navy Yard running their mouths. Wilber you might get to see some of your friends if they show up."

"Looking forward to it. Hopefully they do not have diplomatic immunity in case I have to poke out one their eyes," Wilber replied.

Those comments put a smile on John Burkette's face who still remembered vividly how Wilber shoved those charges up the State Department Rep's ass with the SID videos.

The men walked into the establishment after parking nearby thanks to the parking genie being there to grant three parking wishes.

Inside it was already slightly noisy. The long bar had almost all the seats filled. The lunch hour drunks were hitting it hard, then some of them would go back to the Navy Yard and collect their paychecks. They were the consummate office warriors several grades above people doing more important work out in their detachments, labs, and elsewhere. There were a few naval officers with men wearing suits.

These were likely program managers and acquisition managers who were led around by their noses by companies in the past with the names like Tracor, EG&G (formally known as Edgerton, Germeshausen, and Grier, Inc.), that got bought out by URS Corporation.

Tracor was a major player, but EG&G dwarfed them. During its heyday in the 1980s, EG&G had about 35,000 employees. In 2014, URS was acquired by AECOM.

What's interesting about EG&G is they built the nuclear triggers for America's Atomic and Hydrogen Bombs. They had a big affiliation in weapons and worked side by side with companies like IBM who built a lot of sensitive equipment for the military including the SR-71 spy plane, B52 bombers weapon systems, and all the sophisticated sonar processors for American nuclear submarines starting in the mid 1970's, then SUBACS and BSY-1 all revolutionizing undersea warfare.

America took a giant leap ahead of Russia by computerizing sonar processing with the main processing strings controlled by main frame computers stuffed aboard the submarines. There were also mainframe computers that fired and controlled all the weapons. Many YouTube videos show these systems with live video aboard those nuclear submarines.

EG&G had another lesser known role. They helped build Area-51.

Thanks to the table these CIA men were seated, Wilber had full view of the bar. He didn't know which of them were FSB, but in bars all over Washington DC they are frequented by FSB (KGB) agents with recorders going. They learned from experience you never know when a couple guys who think they were alone and talking in code words, that nobody else would know what they were talking about.

Unfortunately, sometimes business must go on there because back in the office are enemies and dickheads that would undermine their decisions and their efforts. Government is full of fratricidal activity. The beltway boys are sharks. A lot of money is at stake. Pat Barton and a couple of his predecessors had their lunch eaten and never could figure out people do not play nice. Adversaries play for their own benefit.

During the cold war, some of the most important decisions were made at the Sports Bar over by Eads Street and 23rd Street in Crystal City. Also, a lot of action happened in another bar back then named Faces. Quite often, Ivan (KGB spies before they became FSB) sat at the bar at Faces and Cash in Advance was sitting just two or three bar stools down. Faces no longer exist nor does the Foxhole.

The Cash in Advance boys were trained to smell Ivan. Ivan (KGB) often had a peculiar smell because of what Ivan ate and the copious amounts of Vodka he/she drank despite guidance not to do it.

Those KGB spies had watchers and sometimes watcher's watcher. When all three were in a bar together it was thick in Ivan smell.

After they ordered their drinks and food, John Burkette said, "We had a very productive morning."

"I thought so too," Jerry Nault added.

"I understand you are going on your vacation in two days, Wilber," John Burkette said.

"It's kind of interesting how time sneaks up on you," Wilber responded.

John Burke was quite happy that Wilber was taking the situation with Xinxin in great strides as well as he did. His command of the meeting during the morning demonstrated he could compartmentalize his emotions. But another factor would be how to deal with Xinxin five years from now when the moment of truth happened. It worked out in the agency's favor as John Burkette realized Wilber would not likely get involved with another woman any time soon allowing him to stay focused on the project and not be distracted by romance.

Wilber soon enjoyed the flavorful Rainbow Trout while John Burkette had the slow roasted lamb in exquisite Balkan spices. Jerry Nault had the Lamb Lasagna. It not only looked amazing it tasted great too. They washed this fabulous meal down with great Balkan wines. The Balkan food in the AMBAR Restaurant was quite good.

The men didn't have much to say. One of the men sitting at the bar was indeed Ivan. His nurd-looking glasses with black rims had a video recording feed to the black box mounted on his back under his suit jacket. It recorded simultaneously ahead and to each side. Since he was facing a mirror on the bar he had three dimensional recording.

Later in the day when Ivan went back to his apartment rented by operatives for him, the recording system fed the video into his cell phone that sent the files up into space via satellite wireless that sent the zipped files to the Lubyanka Building in Lubyanka Square in the Meshchansky District of Moscow, Russia.

The Lubyanka building was originally built in 1898 as the headquarters of the All-Russia Insurance Company (Rossiya Insurance Company), on the spot where Catherine the Great had once headquartered her secret police. Following the Bolshevik Revolution, in 1918 the structure was taken over by the government, for use as the headquarters of the secret police, then called the Cheka that turned into the NKVD, then the KGB, and finally the FSB.

Russians buy technology from everyone. In a way like Bill Gates used to complain there was probably only five legal copies of his operating system in all of China, Russia had similar viewpoint on copyright and in the INTEL business, copyright is the last thing in the INTEL world the FSB would care about.

FSB purchased a single copy of certain AI software that would sift through files and compare images of people filmed at the AMBAR Restaurant in Washington DC and compare them to a database and identify many of the people in the bar. If they couldn't identify them, simply walking out of the restaurant and watching them get into their automobiles and getting the license plate number on their car helped complete the identification.

The FSB had paid operatives in many states to identify the drivers of automobiles. Everyone has a price and some of these DMV people sold out their country for $500. But getting $500 a week helped their income quite a bit, and just like the Cash in Advance people, the KGB did a lot of interesting transactions such as Apple Cards and Stem Cards.

There were often fifty operators at Lubyanka building that worked these networked systems and AI was often used to file and build macros because otherwise it would be laboriously too difficult. When the facial recognition identified someone in the CIA that went to a desk of a person responsible for tracking CIA officials traveling around Washington DC. Within twelve hours that person had a report about the CIA's DD/P having lunch with CIA agents Wilber O'Toole and Jerry Nault. Wilber O'Toole was one of Aida Abramova's responsibilities to track and figure out what Wilber O'Toole was up to.

Back in the office after lunch Wilber met with a couple individuals who had specific tasks. One was a guy working with Naval Reactors at NAVSEA 08 relating to fusion reactors for new stealth autonomous submarines. The military knows the CIA does operations with paramilitary forces and just like the A12 spy plane the fore runner of the SR-71 was flown exclusively by CIA pilots.

The fusion reactors NAVSEA-08 would build for Project Solaris would never be thought of going to Saturn. NAVSEA 08 had qualified submarine officers who did ISR missions and other cold war assignments either as an executive officer or a commanding officer of a nuclear fast attack submarine.

Procurement was starting. Bits and pieces. It would be a 1,000,000-piece crossword puzzle assembled in the harshest environment ever imagined. But they would not reinvent the wheel like a lot of initiatives did. They would use what's available, from display technology used on NASA spacecraft using same display technology in Boeing Jets and new NASA spacecraft going to the Moon and Mars. A sad day in America's history was Wilber would make it to Saturn and start building a submarine before man landed on Mars to start colonizing it.

***

Chapter Fifteen

Probe Adventure

Just like he was warned, a vehicle pulled up to his home and Wilber would not be going to the office. Jerry Nault knew Wilber was on TDY to Vandenburg. Wilber wore a suit as he learned long ago, show up wearing what you wanted to convey especially if you were flying on commercial airliners that lost luggage.

One of John Burke's men was driving Wilber to Andrews where he would get on the Gulfstream 750 and fly out to that long runway at Vandenburg and meet up with Colonel Baker. Colonel Baker had already met Pat Barton's men who were there to inform him they were in charge and Wilber had no authority and was just an observer. But Colonel Baker knew otherwise. John Burkette was sending Wilber to Vandenberg to have his own eyes and ears present to report back the facts and not some BS story Pat Barton would state in the event something went wrong.

Tammy was back and acting affectionate. She already got the story from a reliable source that the situation with Xinxin did not work out and Wilber was once again available. Maybe this is my opportunity to sink my fangs into him, Tammy thought.

The vehicle drove up near the hanger where people were waiting for Wilber. His small travel suitcase had rollers on it, so he simply rolled it over to the door of the hanger and went inside. Tammy was waiting by the ladder of the GS750 as she knew ETA for Wilber.

One of the military security persons entered a number into the cypher lock and after they heard the solenoids click and a sound emitted on purpose, the door opened and Wilber drug his suitcase inside the hanger and walked over to the Jet that had a cargo hold open. Wilber wasn't a sissy and picked up his suitcase and set it inside the cargo hold. One of the ground persons fastened the net over it to lock it in place. There were no other passengers. John Burkette didn't want Wilber traveling with Pat Barton's men. They had no reason to communicate since they were going there for other reasons. One was to CYA; the other was to expose it if things were not done correctly.

There was also a difference in the reception. Colonel Baker was not at the terminal to receive Pat Barton's office warriors. To add insult to injury, they had to get a CIA guy to bring them transportation. By the time these guys were down near the launch pad area, Colonel Baker was not available. The reason? He was at the terminal picking up Wilber.

"Good to see you again Colonel Baker."

"Wilber always good to see you too."

"Thanks, I appreciate that."

"Well, it looks like we are just about ready to launch, weather permitting and no leaks like we had with ULA-66."

"Colonel even though I am no longer with Solar System Investigations, I'll be happy when this bird flies because it's a major distraction for me."

"I feel the same way."

"Do you have someplace we where we can talk as good as a SKIF where nobody can hear us?"

"That I do."

It took a while, but they were soon over by the beach at the edge of the base with a great view of the Pacific Ocean near where the railroad tracks curved and went inland. It was just the two of them and nobody else around.

"What do you want to talk about Wilber?"

"Colonel Baker, I know you asked me to call you Chet when we were alone, but this is official business and quite serious."

"Alright Wilber lay it on me."

"I'm not a big fan of this probe. I know it's not going to last when it gets to Saturn." "What makes you think that?" Colonel Baker asked.

"I'm going to tell you a couple things, one will upset you, but valuable people end up in this situation, and you are extremely valuable to me." Wilber said.

"That's nice to know." Colonel Baker.

"You will probably remain a Colonel a lot longer than you planned and remain here. I need someone like you I can trust." Wilber said.

"Okay cut to the chase, what's going on?" Colonel Baker asked.

"You are going to get an upgrade to your security clearance shortly. You are essential and now I'm going to brief you what it's all about." Wilber said.

"This is mildly disturbing me but go ahead." Colonel Baker replied.

"The reason why the probe is going to Saturn is Aliens are there." Wilber said.

"Interesting." Colonel Baker said.

"They are now routinely communicating. To where we have no idea and to what purpose we also do not know." Wilber said.

"Sounds kind of serious." Colonel Baker said.

"Yes, to the point the President is putting a lot of pressure on the DCI now because he's alarmed this may soon get exposed to the public. He wants to be ahead of the power curve." Wilber said.

"I can imagine so." Colonel Baker responded.

"This is a privileged conversation." Wilber said.

"Understand." Colonel Baker responded.

"I sincerely believe the Aliens will blow up the probe soon after it arrives." Wilber said.

"We would do the same thing if aliens sent probes here." Colonel Baker said.

"You got that right." Wilber replied.

"Pat Barton is a stupid dickhead; he'll send a second probe. Wilber said.

"He's not willing to think there are other alternatives?" Colonel Baker asked then added, "Is there any?"

"There is and we are working on it." "How so?"

"Recently, John Burkett moved Project Solaris out of Sonar Systems Investigations and is now a compartmentalized entity."

"What does Project Solaris do?"

"This is why you will get a higher security clearance and a dozen members of your staff."

"They may not like that. It's an extraordinary hassle especially if they get yanked in for polygraphs."

"I hate to be the bearer of bad news; they will get polygraphed and it's going to happen. If you have people who refuse to go through the process because they are due to be separated from the military soon, then we'll figure out how to transfer them somewhere."

"What about the civilians?"

"That is none of your concern. Cash in Advance has a way of dealing with them. We'll investigate them before we upgrade their clearances, and they will get unexpected reassignment. Some of it will be based on fabrications. We have no choice in this matter."

"It is kind of serious, so I can understand the heavy hand."

"Yes," this is more critical than the Manhatten project according to policy makers."

"I can see that."

"As soon as this rocket launches, the process will begin."

"You stated Pat Barton will likely send up a second probe."

"Yes, just help him get his rocket off with no failures, get it to Saturn so he can learn to deal with reality."

"What's the alternative?"

"We are going to build a submarine on Saturn, and you will be lifting modules to construct on Saturn where we will operate the submarine."

"If they can destroy the probes, don't you think they can destroy a submarine?"

"My guess is they will be curious and wonder. I'm sure they will think it's a surface ship of sort like we have plenty on Earth and they probably know a lot about us."

"No doubt."

"We will get the submarine submerged before they can destroy it. I believe once we are submerged, they will not have the means to attack us."

"What are you going to do with the submarine?"

"We are going to visit their submerged cities and try to communicate with them."

"Okay if all this happens, how does that impact me here?"

"After we deploy the submarine and start operating it, you will be promoted to General and given your choice of duty assignments."

"Well, I already know where I want to go." "Where's that?"

"Hickam Air Force Base in Pearl Harbor."

"That's a combined base now with an Admiral in Charge." "Yes, but the 15th Air Force is still commanded by a General." "Welcome to the 15th Air Force, General Baker."

"Thank you, Wilber, and I want to give you the first invitation to the change of command there when I take over the 15th Air Force."

"General, I would love to be there, but I do not think I can make it."

"Why is that?"

"I'll probably be on Saturn."

"Alright so tell me why I need to remain here?"

"We can't fly a 7,800- submarine from here to Saturn. It's impossible. We'll have to build it there with a lot of pieces. If I'm going to be on Saturn, I want someone here I can fully trust to get all the parts and pieces there."

"Will this ever become public?"

"Probably not."

"I'll enjoy my time at Hickam, then probably retire from there."

"Do you plan on staying in Hawaii after that?"

"Not really."

"Chet, when you retire from the Air Force and if I make it back to Earth alive, I will make sure you have a job at Project Solaris after you retire."

"As a GOV GUY?"

"You can come in as CIA or as contractor. We'll leave it up to you."

"What's the difference?"

"The contractors get paid quite a bit more."

"If that's the case why does a lot of people not quit and become contractors?"

"We do not do it for the pay. We have a higher calling."

"Very interesting concept. Perhaps that's why I always liked you."

"Alright, Colonel Baker. I need to go get a rental car; can you help me with that?"

"Only if you agree to have a beer with me after we get your car." "It will be my distinct honor."

"I know just the place."

"Alright us go do that. Stop by the terminal so I can get my luggage off the Jet and send them home."

"Works for me."

In a while the car was allowed onto the tarmac and drove over to the GS750 because Colonel Baker was driving.

Moments later, Tammy came out of the terminal where she used the ladies' room and got a Starbucks coffee to chill out wondering if they would go home tonight.

Right about the time the car pulled up Tammy walked up to it and asked, "What are we going to do Wilber?"

"I'm going to get my bag out of the aircraft. Colonel Baker is going to drive me to a rental car place, and you guys can fly back to Washington. I think I will be here a couple days at least."

"Sounds good. Nice short trip. I like them that way."

Colonel Baker took Wilber to a car rental in nearby Lompoc, California. "Are you going to get a hotel here?" Colonel Baker asked.

"Yes, I'm going to get a room at the Embassy Suites." Wilber replied.

"After you get checked in your hotel, meet me over at the Solvang

Brewing Company, we'll have a beer there."

"Sure."

"I live not far from the Solvang Brewing Company. I'll drop my car off at home and walk over there."

"Not planning to go back to work today?"

"No, there's a couple CIA men bird dogging me trying to track me down and probably confront me with their BS. They will have to work hard searching for me."

"Good plan."

The men took care of their personal logistics. Chet Baker only had a half a mile to walk to Solvang Brewing Company after he changed out of his uniform into street clothes. Wilber had a mile to walk but he needed the exercise after spending six hours on the jet. Since it was after 3:00 P.M. and the office warriors had already hauled ass to their hotel, Colonel Baker knew he would not be getting very many calls. He also made it clear, any contacts to him concerning the probe launch had to contact the designated Belly

Button Guy for the launch, Dr. Keeney, a former big shot at SWAWAR until he jumped ship.

Dr. Keeney knew that when Colonel Baker left to spend time with a very important CIA man Wilber O'Toole, to hold all calls. Anything short of the missile blowing up on the launch pad, all phone calls would be delayed. Since the Probe boosters would not be fueled up until just before launch, that wasn't going to happen. Empty rockets do not have any serious concerns in that regard, plus all the LOX and fuel tanks were filled with Nitrogen, an inert gas to prevent explosions since this was a high value launch.

Colonel Baker passed by the Maître d' who saw him often knowing he was going to the bar where he usually met defense contractors, senior military, and personal friends.

Fifteen minutes later Wilber walked into the entrance of the Solvang Brewing Company (referred to as the SBC by employees and regulars) and up to the attractive

Maître d' and said, "I'm going to the bar, I have a friend there waiting for me."

"Please enjoy your time here."

"Thank you."

Wilber had changed into street clothes and walking shoes. He was ready to have a few craft beers and would probably eat dinner here at the SBC.

The pretty bartender with a name tag saying Karen asked, "Would you like a drink?"

Wilber quickly looked over the beer menu and said, "I think I will try the Munich Helles Lager; do you have it on tap?"

"Yes, we do." Karen replied.

"Fine that's what I want." Wilber said.

"Coming right up." Karen said.

After Wilber had the satisfaction of a couple drinks of his beer, he then became sociable.

"Looks like you are ready to relax," Chet Baker said.

"Yes Chet, I've been kind of busy lately. I might even sleep in late in the morning.

Anything big scheduled for the morning?" Wilber said.

"No, tomorrow morning will be a good time to sleep in." Chet Baker said.

"Great I could use an equalizer. The plane ride was rough, especially going over the Rocky Mountains, then again later crossing the Sierra's, just could not get any good shuteye." Wilber said.

"So, what's been happening in your life?" Chet asked.

"I thought I met the woman of my dreams from Singapore. But there was an event with me and four Chinese assassins in front of her that freaked her out. Because I poked the eye out of one of them, the agency did an emergency extraction." Wilber said.

"What became of the Chinese dude?" Chet asked.

"Turns out he had diplomatic credentials, and I was suddenly in the shits." Wilber said.

"It seems to me if I remember you are always getting in the shits." Chet said.

"That's what we Cowboys are for." Wilber responded.

"Did the Chinese guy lose his eye?" Chet asked.

"Probably. A couple days later, I had a meeting at headquarters with the DD/P and my boss Pat Barton who wanted to throw me under the bus, and a State Department lawyer that was charging me with misconduct since the Chicoms had launched a major diplomatic complaint." Wilber said.

"You obviously came out of that since you are here." Chet said.

"What my backstabbing boss Pat and State Department guy didn't know is my former girlfriend's cousin is in charge of security for Singapore's number one hotel and he hires SID personnel off hours as security people and pays them well."

"What's SID?"

"Singapore Intelligence Directorate."

"Are they as good as the CIA?"

"Across the board they are better than man of our office warriors who don't know shit from Shinola."

"So how did the SID play into all this?"

"They were following me because her cousin apparently was paid by my girlfriend to protect me. The incident was recorded by secret video with sound. So, I let the State Department guy shoot his mouth off and give me the charges and I responded, "I had video of the incident I'll hand over to news media. I would also then likely have my attorney sue China and the State Department if you do that."

"How did that work out?" Chet asked.

Wilber told the story:

"I have a CIA certified cell phone that can plug into the conference room video system to play for briefings. I then played the video of the incident for the DD/P, State Department Rep, and Pat showing that Chinese Diplomat assaulting me with a knife and one of the assassins chasing after my girlfriend."

"He probably would have killed her except two CIA agent watchers also protecting me because of a recent incident in Beijing China were right where my girlfriend ran when I told her to run and scream. My girlfriend ran past the watchers so did the Chinese assassin and as he passed them, they coldcocked him and knocked him out."

"While this was happening, the Diplomat came after me with a knife all caught on video so I poked his eye out and he fell to the ground in excruciating pain, and the other two assassins came after me with knives but didn't know the SID people were right behind them with Tasers yelling them to put the knives down, plus a few other words I can't say because ladies are present. One of them didn't get the message fast enough and he got Tasered really good."

"This is how you lost your girlfriend?"

"No, while I was put on administrative leave while that incident was being investigated, I took my girlfriend to Dubai and Abu Dhabi and visited a few Sheikhs that are friends of mine and we had a good time.

"We left there flew to Hawaii, where we were assaulted by two creeps who thought they could beat me up and take her to a nearby parking structure and rape her. I sent her to get police help as I started fighting. She ran off and one of them who tried to stop her became unconscious quick, then the other dude who thought he was some kind of martial artist champ came after me and I coldcocked his dumb ass, just before the police arrived."

"That didn't shake her up too much, but she was frightened to be around me thinking this was spy business. Later during that trip, two Azzie dudes came after me and the DD/P

while our girlfriends were with us. That was the deal breaker. She decided she wanted to go back to Singapore and became cold as ice. She's refused to answer my phone calls or answer my texts. It appears it's over with." Wilber said.

"Sorry to hear about that." Chet Baker said.

"I tried to tell her I'm in another type of job now where I would not be subject to espionage, assassinations, or other related events in the future. There was one other event before all this in Beijing China where we first met. She doesn't want any part in any of this. But since I'm going to be very busy for the next five years, it's probably best I'm not having a relationship with a woman now."

"What are you going to do after that?"

"I'm going to retire, find a woman to settle down with and be Mr. Mom if necessary."

"Ah, such a grand plan. What if you stumble across a woman in the meantime?"

"I was trained by my good friend Dexter in SDHNC." Wilber said.

"What does SDHNC mean?" Chet Baker asked.

"It may not be appropriate to say in front of Karen."

"Alright," Chet said and started thinking what the acronym description could be and soon started smiling."

Karen being kind of a frisky woman said, "Hey I'm not a wimp, I want to know what SDHNC means."

Wilber gave her the come to me signal with his finger and she bent over to hear it. Karen burst out laughing and then surprised Wilber, "I wouldn't mind trying an SDHNC. I get off work at 11:00, come by and pick me up."

"Since I'm sleeping in late at my hotel room, I could probably do that."

"Is this for real or are you guys having fun with me?" Chet asked.

Wilber responded and said, "Gentlemen never tell." Wilber then put up a fist with his thumb sticking between two middle fingers on his right hand.

"The benefits of being a regular customer is you get to see all amusing things,"

Chet said.

"Karen, I think I'm going to get an order of wings," Wilber said. "Six or Twelve piece?"

"Give me twelve pieces, I'm sure Chet will help me eat some of it."

"Damn right I will," Chet added.

"Wings coming right up," Karen said.

By the way Karen, this is Wilber my friend," Chet said and followed,

"This is Karen the Aquarian because she didn't like being called Karen the Librarian."

"That's damn right," Karen responded.

"Later tonight I'll explain why I like Librarians," Wilber said.

"Only if you demonstrate your SDHNC is worthy of me," Karen the Aquarian responded."

"I used to in the French Foreign Legion, Dexter taught me well," Wilber responded.

"Wilber is it true what the British SAS said about the French Foreign Legion?" Chet asked.

"Depends on what you are referring to," Wilber answered.

"Something to the effect the French Foreign Legion like to kiss women on the wrong end."

"That we do. It does better preparation for the SDHNC," Wilber said and smiled at Karen the Aquarian.

Wilber also noticed their rouge conversation was starting to influence Karen. Men get "soft offs" while women with really great features start show swelling of certain attributes that give away a signal of subtle arousal.

Wilber then started thinking a tryst with Karen the Aquarian just might do him some good in coming to terms his relationship with Xinxin crashed and burned and is permanently finished. But Wilber is a smart guy and knows women, including an attractive bartender like Karen the Aquarian, probably have some baggage that goes with it which quickly manifested a feeling of killing the deal.

The Buffalo Wings were going down too quickly, and Wilber estimated they might all be gone before he finished his second craft beer, a Central Coast IPA on tap and quickly ordered Carnitas Nachos.

Chet Baker (aka Colonel Baker) knew Wilber was on some serious per diem and had money to burn so he didn't mind him buying all the food and paying for his next drink.

"Were you serious about hiring me when I retire?" Chet asked.

"Most definitely. We have a few places where we could put you then." "Any special qualifications I should work on?"

"Do you know how to speak Russian or Chinese?"

"I've taken Russian and Chinese classes in the past when I was looking at going into the INTEL side of house before I got redirected to launchers. But it's been a while and I have no proficiency."

Я знаю, как можно добиться мастерства. [Ya znayu, kak mozhno dobit'sya masterstva.]

"What does that mean?" Chet asked knowing it was in Russian and recognized a couple words.

"It means I know how you can get proficiency." "Alright, text me or email me your idea."

"I'll send you a free subscription of Rosetta Stone."

"That's very nice of you."

"One of my perks. You can learn Russian and Chinese."

"I'm curious as to why the emphasis in Chinese."

"Real simple. China has 2000 Einsteins. I've personally met some of these men when they attended conferences in San Diego and Cupertino California. Einstein has nothing over them. They are incredible geniuses.

"Are they lapdogs for the Chinese Communists?"

"Chinese Einsteins look at the world differently than most people. They know they are Chinese and live in China, but their viewpoint is humanity. Their brilliance and intelligence are directed to every living person on the planet. Over half of them look beyond the planet and out into space. They can think 1000 years beyond us."

"Does the Chinese government coerce them into cooperating?"

"Sure, their government thinks their actions support their three primary focus." "What is that?"

"Space, Artificial Intelligence, and Robotics." "Interesting. Why is Robotics such a high priority?"

"China has an aging population problem worse than Japan which has a negative birth rate. China plans on dealing with the lack of people taking care of elderly in ten years through the help of robots."

"Personal Robots."

"Yes."

"Will they have that miniaturization of computers to pull it off?"

"China thinks in terms of Sun Tzu in everything they do. Think outside the box so to speak."

"Give me an example of how they would employ Sun Tzu in robotics."

"They would not try to make the robot super smart. It would simply be a dumb terminal. In the home there would be a stationary server or something as innocuous as a laptop computer or even a cell phone that would have all the artificial intelligence processing to run the robot. The robot would have all the sensors such as sight, sound, smell, temperature monitoring, etc. Those sensor readings would be sent to the server via telemetry. It would be no different than controlling your personal drone out at the park on the weekends."

"Do you know for a fact they are doing that now?"

"Sure, the Chinese Einsteins I meet like me because I talk to them in Chinese and I'm interested in things like the 5 tang poets, Chinese Classical Music, Confucius, Sun Tzu, the Ming Dynasty, the Grand Canal, the Chinese pyramids especially the white pyramid."

"What's so special about the Chinese White Pyramid?"

"It's the most heavily guarded place in China. It's guarded better than they guard their nuclear weapons."

"What's the special concern about the Great White Pyramid to have such security?"

"This is the tomb of Emperor Wu of Han (156–87 BC) located in Xingping, Shaanxi Province."

"Why is Emperor Wu noteworthy?"

"The story of Sun Tzu was created concerning him serving Emperor Wu, sometimes referred to as King Wu."

"Whatever happened to Sun Tzu?"

"When King Wu refused to listen to Sun Tzu concerning the Yuan's who were an existential threat, he retired. King Wu gave him a cart of gold bricks and 200 of his best soldiers to protect Sun Tzu. The story goes Sun Tzu traveled across the countryside and every village he visited he gave them gold and paid for all his soldiers food. Slowly he ran out of gold and when his gold was just about all gone, he directed the soldiers to return home. At first, they didn't want to leave Sun Tzu, but he said: As your commander you must follow my orders. I'm directing you to go home now. Take the remaining gold and use it to buy your food on the way."

"What happened to Sun Tzu when his soldiers departed?"

"The story goes, he walked up into the mountains by himself and was never seen again."

"How did Emperor Wu die?"

"Just like Sun Tzu warned him because he had spies (chapter 13), eventually the Yuan attacked and cut his head off."

"Why do you think the White Pyramid is so heavily guarded?"

"I have my speculation, but one day I would like to find out."

"Can you give me a hint?"

"Either his head is missing, or there are Alien Artifacts in it. Why do you think China has space as their #1 priority?"

"Did you ever discuss the Great White Pyramid with some of the Chinese Einsteins?"

"Yes, I did."

"What did they say about it?"

"They said, what happened in the past doesn't matter, we need to focus on the future."

"That's an astute comment."

"Yes, I felt special talking to these men and women. One woman was a rocket designer. She's utterly brilliant."

"I can imagine what it would have been like talking to Einstein."

"Or listen to him play the violin, he was also a violin virtuoso." "I never heard about that." Colonel Chet Baker replied.

"I recently listened to a violin sonatas Einstein performed," Wilber said. https://www.youtube.com/watch?v=MQFmSnG5Ets] { Mozart Sonata in B-flat KV378}

Wilber didn't feel like ordering snack food and eyeballing the menu said, "Chet, if I order that Sampler Meat Plate will you help eat it?"

"Certainly."

"Karen I would like to order that Meat Sampler; can you give us two dishes to share it?"

"Only if you promise to be here at closing time to fulfill your promise to teach me all about the SDHNC protocols."

"You know I just had my heart broken, are you ready to mend my broken wing?"

Chet jumped in and added, "What he said is true."

"I promise to be gentle," Karen the Aquarian replied.

"What if I like it rough?" Wilber asked.

"I'll do boxing with you, if necessary, as long as you promise not to knock me out," Karen replied.

"You are such a brave woman, I would never hurt you," Wilber responded.

"Thank you, I think I like your attitude."

"I definitely like your attitude. If we didn't live in different planets and dimensions, we would be lovers already."

"That's sweet of you to say, but do you really mean it?"

"Confucius says men like me are Noble Savages. I have noble intentions, but at the core I'm still a savage."

"Most men are dogs in heat, I can handle a savage since that's all it seems that I meet these days."

After the meat sampler and a couple more beers, Wilber made the announcement, "Karen, put all the charges on my card. Also, since I'm legally drunk I will not be back to pick you up tonight. We'll have to schedule it for another time when I can legally drive."

"I have to give you credit Wilber you think responsibly."

"I would argue the point since I've not been successful in picking the right woman."

"Pick me so I can help change your odds."

"If I'm alive in five years, I will come back and visit you and determine if we are ready for launch."

"I'll be waiting."

As Wilber and Chet walked out the door of the restaurant, Karen looked down at the printout. Wilber gave her a $100.00 tip. She shuddered. And all the smack he was talking with Colonel Baker was probably close to the truth. She knew Wilber was a special man because Chet did not hang around with losers.

Wilber went back to his empty hotel room. He took off his clothes and only had his underwear on and climbed into the bed. Looked at his messages on his cell phone and as expected, there was nothing from Xinxin. She was fading into his past. She was that special love he would never forget. He felt just as bad losing her as he did Faye Wong. He could never really find the right answers to "why?"

Wilber was by himself. Nobody was going to check up on him. He woke up at 9:00 A.M. and took a shower. Wilber put his suit on and got himself ready including.

wearing Dr. Wang's special glasses that recorded visual and sound automatically to his cell phone.

Wilber left the Hotel in his rental car and drove to Vandenburg.

Wilber's CAC card was nice and handy as it let him breeze through the main gate.

Thanks to his CIA'S GPS APP on his cell phone giving him directions as he drove to Launch Complex 10, he got there very efficiently.

It's amazing how fast ULA can clean up a Launch Complex prior to a launch. They were the master choreographers at getting everything prepared. Everything was checked and double checked and in some cases triple checked.

ULA, comprising Boeing, Lockheed, Northrup Gruman, and others knew the facts of life. A screwed-up launch could be their last launch. The stakes were high and the forecast for the future involved incredible sums of money as the Space Force deployed and new components launched for a space carrier that would be built in the next ten years or less.

Initially that carrier would have 4 squadrons of TR-3Bs then TR-4s came about. Due to delay in funding and construction, TR-5s were about to emerge as well. The forecast is by the time the Space Carrier was ready to deploy, TR-6 would be the space fighter-bomber of choice. TR-6 craft reportedly were designed with 95% anti-gravity capability.

What does that mean?

Gravity can be positive or negative, just like magnetism and electricity. Gravity waves were just as strong as magnetic waves. The main difference is out in space, magnetic drive may not work in many locations. Graviton ships using gravity waves will work everywhere thanks to Newton's laws of every force there is an equal and opposite force.

Wilber wished he could specify graviton drive for the Solaris Mission spaceship, but he didn't have ample time. Currently the plan was to use the nuclear fusion rocket engines developed under Project Pluto in the 1950's. Project Pluto was highly successful but never used because Eisenhower canceled the SLAM missile project on the advice of his liberal brother Milton. Milton convinced Eisenhower the SLAM missile which is the same thing as the modern-day Russian and Chinese hypersonic missiles, would destabilize the planet. Now because of Russian and Chinese hypersonic missiles, some of which were used in the Ukraine War, America is now building hypersonic missiles and will soon deploy them.

There was a second set of security gates to go through to get into Launch Complex 10. Solar System Investigations were very lucky to be able to use Launch Complex 10 needed for such a large rocket because it was reconstructed from a museum into a new launch complex for the secret space program that NASA has virtually no involvement in. Wilber knew some of the details of the secret space program. The biggest revelation is they had already traveled to other solar systems and put people on Mars and the Moon.

Wilber texted Colonel Baker asking, "Where are you now?" "I'm standing about 20 feet from the probe missile."

"I'll be there shortly."

"Good, you will get to see me deal with a couple dickheads."

Wilber went through the turnstile and headed for the rocket in position to launch about 400 yards in front of him. At 400 yards the missile looked huge but as he got closer it got much larger than expected.

The launch pad area was cleaned off. All the extraneous equipment was gone. It looked ready to launch and a lot less people around and an addition security barrier.

At about 50 yards, Wilber could see Colonel Baker and it appeared he was arguing with two men in suits. As Wilber walked about twenty yards from Colonel Baker, it was quite apparent a major argument in progress. The two men in suits had their backs turned to Wilber and didn't know he was approaching.

Colonel Baker saw Wilber and suddenly had a look of relief on his face. He knew these two office warriors worked directly for Pat Barton and they had become a huge pain in his ass. He knew that Wilber would soon intervene, and these big shots would not be so big anymore.

The two CIA men did not turn around until Colonel Baker said, "Hello Wilber how are you doing?"

"Doing great. What seems to be the problem here?"

The two men then addressed Wilber and knew who he was.

"Wilber, this is none of your concern, we'd appreciate it if you please leave."

"Maybe I'll make it my concern."

"You have no jurisdiction over this project."

"Does the DD/P?"

"Suddenly the two men shut their mouths with Wilber's comment."

"Wilber, as you can see, I'm on the other side of the barrier and they are upset I will not let them cross the blue line."

"Are you guys working on the spaceship?"

"No, but we want a closeup look," one of the two CIA men said.

"Why are you attempting to violate rules and regulations?"

"What are you talking about?"

"If you are not part of the launch team you are not allowed beyond the blue line, why were you giving Colonel Baker crap?"

"It's our project, and oversight, we have the right to go check it out."

"No, you do not. I know the rules. I've been associated with ULA and Launch Complex Ten for several years. You have no legal basis to cross that blue line. The blue line is put there for a reason. It has to do with certification and verification. If you cross that blue line, you will trigger a bunch of rechecks and you could delay the launch a week."

"This is none of your business, Wilber."

"Like I said, I just made it my business and if the two of you think you can take me on, I'll be sure and visit you in the hospital."

"I don't think so."

"Do you feel lucky? I wouldn't mind running into Pat Barton if he had to fly out and visit you in a hospital bed."

"Are you threatening us?"

"No, but if you attack me, I plan on hurting you badly. I know I can take on two office warriors."

"We are going to cross the blue line and we don't give a shit what you say."

"Have you ever heard the term REPEL BORDERS?"

"Sure, what's it to you?"

"Because I do not want a week delay in the launch because of your stupidity, I will REPEL BORDERS and you will not make it across the blue line."

"I've had enough of your bullshit; I'm calling Pat Barton right now."

"Good, be sure and tell Pat Barton the DD/P within an hour will be meeting with him and give him some demerits for not properly managing you guys who insist on breaking rules and delaying the launch a week."

As the CIA man was calling Pat Barton who was taking his sweet ass time answering the phone because he was absorbed in looking and talking to his super-hot looking administrative aide. By then Wilber texted the DD/P John Burkette saying he *had a situation at the launch pad with Pat's men and please tell Pat to tell these jokers to STAND DOWN.*

After about 15 rings he finally answered the phone. "Barton here."

The man started informing Pat what was going on and Pat received a phone call from the DD/P.

"Hold on a minute, I got an incoming call from the DD/P."

In a minute or two the DD/P ripped Pat a new asshole and directed him to direct his men to get in their rental cars and leave Vandenburg and to stand down and go back to their hotel rooms until further notice, he was putting Wilber temporarily in charge of that launch."

Pat's hatred for Wilber went up a few notches and he had to eat a lot of crow when he told his two guys, "Alright, understand everything you said. Now what I want you to do is go back to your hotel, then call me from there and we'll discuss it."

The men looked at Wilber with a jaundice in their eye. They felt like kicking Wilber's ass, but it might not be quite so simple especially if the Colonel got involved and told his men to subdue the two men in suits. If that happened, they would be immediately kicked off the base permanently.

"Alright Wilber, we'll take care of you later."

"Is that a threat?"

The man that said that immediately regretted it because he knew he stepped over the line. He also knew Pat Barton was a weasel and would throw him under the bus to protect his own ass. Pat Barton's two men turned and left, clearly unhappy.

As they were past the turnstile and out of hearing range, Colonel Baker said, "I'm glad you intervened. Those two dumb asses couldn't get through their thick heads that since they are not part of the launch team, crossing the blue line would cause us a big delay at the worst time possible."

"Colonel, can you do me a favor?"

"Sure, what do you want?"

"I'm very familiar with the two-man rule and the blue line etc. Can you send me an email and copy John Burkette what delay would have happened if those two idiots had forced their way past the blue line."

"Sure, I can do that."

"This is kind of a timely requirement because Pat Barton will likely start some shit. Can we go over to your trailer now so you can email right away?"

"Sure, not a problem come with me."

Colonel Baker led Wilber over to his trailer that had power hooked up, but communications were wireless because just before launch they would hook up a 18 wheeler tractor to it and take it out past the green line and park it. Colonel Baker slid his CAC card into the laptop and pulled up his outlook account and started typing an email.

The email went to Wilber and copied to the DD/P John Burkette. Subject: Interference and possible cause of delay by two CIA men who refused to adhere to launch controls.

Colonel Baker is a smart man and had the email typed up in about three minutes and had Wilber read it.

"That reads great. Go ahead and hit the send button."

"I hope Pat doesn't call the General on me and screw me up."

"Not to worry, John Burkette plays golf with the Secretary of the Air Force all the time. They are best friends. Your General will get a call from the Air Force Secretary if any bad shit comes down on you. In fact, if the General calls you up and starts chewing your ass, simply ask him, "With all due respect sir, has the Secretary of the Air Force talked to you about this matter yet? He's scheduled to call you soon and inform you about some things you are not aware of."

"Would you like a cup of coffee, Wilber?"

"Sure, just black is fine."

"Coming right up."

Predictably, Colonel Baker's boss, the General called him in about twenty minutes while Chet and Wilber were enjoying their coffee and having a small talk waiting for all the crap to come down.

"Chet?"

"Yes General, what can I do for you?"

"I received a disturbing call from Pat Barton just a few minutes ago."

"I expected you would."

Just as the General started to rip Colonel Baker a new asshole, he did as Wilber suggested earlier:

"With all due respect sir, has the Secretary of the Air Force talked to you about this matter yet? He's scheduled to call you soon and inform you about some things you are not aware of."

Suddenly the General was silent and calmly asked, "WTF is this about?"

"Pat Barton overloaded his ass with his two men here. I'm confident the Secretary of the Air Force and the CIA's DD/P are concerned Pat's men almost delayed us a week by refusing to follow pre-launch rules and regulations. My guess is the Secretary of the Air Force is going to direct you to call me and kick those two guys off the base today." Colonel Baker stated succinctly.

"Pat Barton didn't say anything about that," the General stated.

"I'm sure Pat Barton will be explaining it all to the DD/P John Burkette within a couple of hours. By the way. The DD/P's man is here and is an eyewitness to those knuckleheads that almost delayed launch by a week with a blue line violation they insisted on doing. Would you like to talk with him?"

"No that will not be necessary. Have a nice day." The General said.

"Thank you General." Colonel Baker replied, and the General hung up his phone.

"Now that we *unfucked* Pat Barton men's nonsense, let me ask you Chet, when are we going to launch?" Wilber asked.

"Within 48 hours weather permitting. The launch window starts this evening as we bring in the fuel trucks." Colonel Baker said.

"What's the weather forecast like?" Wilber asked.

"It looks like passengers on inbound flights from Honolulu will get to see the launch from the windows of their aircraft this evening." Colonel baker said.

"That's great, I have a friend down in Santa Barbara who loves to film a night rocket launch. I'll give him heads up that I will call him about 30 minutes before launch so he can get his camera ready." Wilber said.

"Are you going to be here for the launch?" Colonel Baker asked.

"Hell no, I'm going to be drinking craft beers served by the illustrious Karen the Aquarian." Wilber replied.

"You might miss out on fun." Colonel Baker said.

"Call me about 30 minutes before the Saturn probe launches and I'll go outside and watch it. Wilber said.

About that time Wilber's phone rang and it was John Burkette. "Are you some place we can talk?"

"Yes, I'm in Colonel Bakers trailer, just the two of us are here." Wilber replied.

"Alright what all happened?" John Burkette asked.

"Want to hear some good news you can shove up Pat Barton's ass?" Wilber asked.

"Sure, anytime works for me." John Burkette replied.

"You know those fancy sunglasses Dr. Wang fitted me out with when you sent me to Beijing for the Crypto Conference?" Wilber asked.

"Yes, how are they working out?" John Burkette asked.

"Better than you can imagine. I recorded the entire incident." Wilber replied.

"That's great." John Burkette said.

"I'll send the video to you now, so you can put some pressure on Pat and tell him to send his two guys over to Colonel Baker's trailer to apologize."

"I like that idea." John Burkette said.

"John, can you do me a favor?" Walt asked.

"Sure." John Burkette said.

"Call the Secretary of the Air Force you buddy and apologize for the conduct of Pat's two guys and ask him to call the General who Colonel Baker works for and let the General know the CIA men are being sent over to apologize to Colonel Baker for being out of line and almost caused the launch to be delayed a week by their almost Blue Line violation." Wilber said.

"I like that even better." John Burkette replied.

"Thanks." Wilber said.

"Send the video right away." John Burkette said.

"The recorded video with audio will be in your in-basket shortly." Wilber said.

"Great." John Burkette replied.

Thanks to the artificial intelligence on Wilbers CIA cell phone, the files were on their way moments later to John Burkette via email.

Within five minutes of sending the files, Wilber got a text message from the DD/P John Burkette, "This is good shit. I'm going to stuff it right up Pat's ass."

Wilber started smiling and Colonel Baker was wondering what that was all about. Wilber didn't offer any details. Then in fifteen minutes Colonel Bakers phone rang again. The caller I.D. indicated it was his boss the General calling.

"Yes General, what can I do for you?" Colonel Baker asked.

"Thanks for warning me the Air Force Secretary would call me. Also, I want to thank you for the way you handled matters there. We are not going to let the CIA push us around. The DD/P sent me a video and it's clear that you did what you had to do." The General said.

"Roger that." Colonel Baker said.

"One other thing." The General said.

"Yes General?" Colonel Baker inquired.

"In about fifteen or twenty minutes those two CIA men will be visiting your trailer to apologize. Go soft on them. I'm sure they have already been punished enough as it is." The General said.

"Sure, General. The disaster of a week delay has been averted and there is no way my guys will let them cross the blue line now that we are fueling up the rocket."

"Great. Keep up the good work. Its times like this we learn the character of people we work with. I know you are under a lot of stress, but as the video indicated, you handled yourself quite well." The General said.

"Thank you General." Colonel Baker replied.

"I have one question for you if you don't mind." The General said.

"Sure, General I work for you." Colonel Baker asked.

"Who the hell filmed that incident?" The General asked.

"CIA." Colonel Baker replied.

"They ratted out their own men?" The General asked.

"Actually yes. We do have some good Cowboys still left in the CIA. They are not all office warriors." Colonel Baker replied.

"Good job and good luck on the launch," The General said.

"Thank you," Colonel Baker replied.

As soon as Colonel Baker hung up the phone, he turned to Wilber and said, "I like the way you operate."

"I know a lot of people do not appreciate what I do but I know we have serious business all the time here." Wilber said.

"That we do, and I'm glad you get it." Colonel Baker said.

"Thanks. I don't want to be here when the crybabies visit you. I'm going to leave.

I'll see you later, hopefully after the launch." Wilber said.

"Good, thanks for the affirmative backup." Colonel Baker said.

"My pleasure." Wilber said.

Wilber walked back to his rental car. When he got back out onto the road, he passed an inbound car with two guys in suits. One thing Wilber knew was there was no way in hell these two jokers would cross the blue line now because the LOX and liquid methane rocket fuel was now being loaded on the space craft.

Three-man rule now was set due to fueling the rocket and anyone not part of the launch team must stay outside the blue line. The two CIA men would be arrested and handled harshly if they tried to do something dumb and go into that area while they were fueling the spacecraft. That was a big no-no. They would not get near the spaceship that would soon be launched.

Wilber now knew it was simply waiting for the probe to launch, which there was nothing he could do about. He pulled over to the side of the road after he got off the base and called his buddy Grady down in Santa Barbara.

"Grady, this is Wilber. Did you have lunch yet?" Wilber asked.

"Not yet but getting close." Grady answered.

"I just left Vandenburg, I want to drive by your place and pick you and your wife up and take you down to the Santa Barbara Shellfish Company waterfront restaurant at Stearns Wharf." Wilber said.

"That works for me. I'll tell Darlene to get ready." Grady said.

"Great, be there probably about the time she's ready to go." Wilber said.

The lunch was great. Wilber got to check up on his friends and old times in their conversations. Wilber gave Grady a heads up:

"There will be a rocket launch probably this evening and Colonel Baker promised to call me 30 minutes before the rocket launch. I'll call you then."

"Thanks." Grady said.

A while later, Wilber had lunch and a great conversation with Grady and Darlene. Sadly, Wilber had to take these wonderful people back to their home where they were dealing with aging. Going from a vibrant lifestyle as a cross country bicyclist to old geezers has a psychological bearing on them. Wilber was amazed at how much they seemed to have aged in the past 20 years.

It will be a sad day when the former Air Force photo interpreter is no longer with us. He did a lot of exciting things in life such as processing Project Corona Film during critical moments in the cold war. Some of the Top-Secret work he did was just recently declassified.

Wilber went back to his hotel room where he could check his emails on his cell phone or receive phone calls.

It was eerie quiet. No calls and no emails. It seemed like Pat Barton's boys were put in a box and they just got a big lesson. Don't mess with a Cowboy because you never know who he knows.

Colonel Baker was kind and courteous to the two knuckleheads when they showed up to apologize. As they walked to the Colonel's trailer, they saw the red lights flashing and NO ENTRY signs all around the launch pad during fueling the spacecraft. Their desire to take selfies next to the probe missile blew up in their faces. Even Pat Barton would rip them a new asshole if he found out that was what it was about. Office Warrior mentality. Cowboys do not need selfies.

The cordial conversation lasted about fifteen minutes then a worker came up into the trailer and said, "Colonel, we are going to be moving the trailer in a short while and must shut off the electricity. Recommend you finish what you are doing shortly."

"No problem. Go ahead and cut the power and hook up the tractor to move it out past the green line."

"Thanks sir, we are ready to proceed." ULA worker said.

"Thanks for giving me the heads up." Colonel Baker replied.

"You are welcome, Colonel Baker." ULA worker said.

Colonel Baker stood up and said, "I'm sorry gentlemen, we have to leave the trailer they are going to move it for pre-launch."

Colonel Baker then led the two Pat Barton Office Warriors out of the trailer and walked towards the turnstiles as he was now going to drive over to his office and wait for the launch just in case something came up. He would be notified when to go to the bunker where he could watch the launch.

As Colonel Baker arrived at his office informed his secretary and administrative aide Shelly, "I'm going to kick back in my office and relax until it's time to go over to the bunker for the launch."

"Understand sir."

Colonel Chet Baker went into his office and took a quick look at emails. There was nothing important he had to deal with at this moment. So, he rotated back in his nice, padded chair, and shut his eyes and meditated while waiting for the countdown to advance to the point when he must go to the bunker.

Meanwhile Wilber laid down on his hotel bed with his shoes kicked off and rested in a similar manner after setting the alarm on his cell phone for 6:00 P.M.

The probe spacecraft health checks performed by ULA computerized software continued. All the bugs had ostensibly been worked out; all repairs complete all reentry controls certified. Everything administratively was sign sealed and delivered. There was no crew to worry about, just the electronics. Fueling continued all late afternoon. The spacecraft LOX and liquid methane fuel tanks slowly filled up.

Cryogenics were a huge part of the future Project Solaris. Wilber had been thinking about his past when he worked with a Cryogenics corporation starting around 1997 on a special project. The principal investigators from the company were superb. Doctor Bob was probably the smartest scientist on the planet up there with those 2000 Chinese Einstein's. He was a favorite of NASA.

The Project Solaris Submarine (PSS) would become the greatest achievement in Cryogenics in all human development. The nuclear-powered PSS would usher in new science and press the limits beyond anyone's wildest dreams. Operating a submarine in Liquid Helium and Liquid Hydrogen oceans would indeed be the most difficult engineering challenge ever attempted. What was beaten into Wilber's head repeatedly by former Cowboy supervisors, *if you want to succeed start early and work harder.*

Wilber decided to call Dr. Bob. He didn't have his phone number, so he went to the web site and got Steller Cryogenics Incorporated (SCI) contact information.

Wilber is so grateful to have met Dr. Bob in the past who demonstrated a knack for solving problems and figuring out credible designs. If Doctor Bob agreed, he would have the great submarine designer, Pierre Truffaut, contact him and meet and start working together on the hull. No doubt a lot of iterations would be required before a submarine capable of operating in Liquid Hydrogen and Helium was feasible.

"Hello, Bob?"

"Yes, this is he."

"This is your friend from the study we did some time ago, Wilber. O'Toole."

"Good to hear from you Wilber. What's up?"

"You will not believe this but I'm in the submarine design and construction business."

"Nothing surprises me about you Wilber."

"Bob, the reason why I'm calling is I want to steer some work your way if you are not terribly busy."

"Wilber I'm always busy I keep it that way, but depending on what it is I'll squeeze in some time."

"Bob, I'm going to send you an encrypted file. The password to decrypt it and be able to read it is the name of the fractal processing string we developed for our project."

"Oh yes remember that vividly."

"You should be happy to know Lockheed used the imagery those fractal algorithms produced on one of their processing strings developed for the Space Force Strategic Surveillance Initiative (SF-SSI)"

"That's good to know some outfit is using it. The government paid us a lot of money to develop it."

"And as you know under the terms of the contract the government was allowed to give that technology to federal agencies for future projects."

"Yes, I'm aware of that clause but I wish we had not developed it under the Secret Business Initiative Research (SBIR) program. If I had known the possibility of the profits fully owning that research, we should have done it on our own money."

"Well Bob, had you not bid on the contract, you would never have met me or got to see the Dolphin Researchers work on deciphering alien communications."

"That's true Wilber, and the fact is we would never have thought about it on our own. Had you not initiated the project with you SBIR white paper, it never would have been known we needed such tools."

"Take a look at the file I just sent you and let me know if you want in on the project."

"Is this something I will have to bid on?"

"No, it's covered under the umbrella of a black project. It doesn't exist."

"Gotcha."

"Talk to you soon."

"Thanks for the opportunity."

"You are welcome."

The next big obstacle would be materials used to build the hull. No doubt there would be a myriad of components specially designed including hybrid panels made with carbon nano tubes and graphene. But to maintain the structure of the hull a base hull to mount all the hybrid panels would need a material that would not warp from vast temperature changes.

The only thing the inner hull could be in Wilber's mind is Titanium that has a good low temperature performance. Titanium alloys such as TA7 can maintain mechanical impedance at a vast variety of acoustic frequencies and ultra-low temperatures and maintain good plasticity down to minus 253 Degrees Centigrade.

In a past project Wilber was assigned that involved Titanium Dynamics Structural Research Corporation (TDSDRC) located in Los Angeles.

These were the champions in high end Titanium parts used in missiles, F22, F35, B2, and B21 bombers. They also built mounting hardware for American Nuclear Submarines such as outboard foundations and Titanium bottles used to house outboard electronics and fiberoptics network devices reading in sensors and the submarine's sonar cloaking device.

In wartime, just like the Philadelphia experiment, the submarine's sonar cloaking device allows the submarine to disappear. Torpedoes and enemy active sonar and sensors could not detect our submarines when the submarine cloaking device was energized. Hence, Chicken in the White Sea really happened. The Russians still wonder how American submarines snuck into the White Sea!

Wilber still had Gary Knoblock's phone number and called him. "Hello Gary."

Observing the caller's I.D. Gary responded, "Wilber, didn't expect to hear from you."

"Gary, I have a project that will require a lot of Titanium Parts. Are you ready to get rich?"

"Hell, I'm already rich from the last boondoggle you had me work on."

"Gary, you don't know about it because you are not cleared, but those parts you made for us were a crucial item in a very important project that would prevent you from sleeping at night if you knew the half of it." Wilber said.

"I'm glad I do not know, since I like sleeping at night." Gary replied.

"Gary, this project is another hush-hush project and the number of materials you will have to produce are substantial."

"Wilber, I'm sure you will not be needing as many parts as we supply for the F22 and F35 now."

"You might be surprised but they are one of a kind." Wilber said.

"Alright then, what's this about?" Gary Knoblock said.

"I'm going to send you a file and the de-encryption code is your full name followed by pound sign and the numbers 69." Wilber announced.

"Alright." Gary replied.

"Gary, when you open the file, the first thing you will get is a DocuSign document to do an electronic signature, that is a 45-year non-disclosure agreement." Wilber said.

"Okay, I can handle non-disclosure agreements, but when we start machining parts keeping a total lid on it might be impossible." Gary said.

"We have a good cover story which I will tell you about after you watch the video and call me back. That's a one-time view video, once you watch it, the file will self-erase."

"Alright."

"Go someplace private to watch it and wear headphones so nobody else can hear any of it."

"Understand."

"Waiting for your call back."

After the phone calls Wilber laid back on his hotel room bed and relaxed and thought about taking a nap and putting in a time on the alarm function so he would be awake in time to be at the restaurant during the Saturn Probe rocket launch.

Wilber had his eyes shut and was relaxing, almost about to fall asleep when Dr. Bob from SCI called him.

"Hello," Wilber said on his cell phone.

"That's quite a project Wilber. To be honest it sent chills down my spine."

"I would expect it would have. Are you in?"

"Normally I would have turned this down because it is too large and beyond the scope of what SCI is capable of doing, but I see how it is a national emergency with the need just as big as the Manhatten Project is the only reason why I'm willing to get involved."

"Thanks Bob, it's going to take one major effort to pull off." "The public has no idea."

"No, they do not, and we do not think they can handle it." "You are probably right about that."

"Bob, you will be getting a phone call from Pierre Truffaut, submarine designer. He's going to design the submarine hull based on your recommendations of how to build it to operate at extreme low temperatures."

"Probably Titanium is the only metal you can use for the hull." Bob said.

"I agree, that's why I just got off the phone with a Titanium parts construction company that built parts for jet aircraft and submarines." Wilber said.

"I would recommend the hull be covered with another material so that Titanium hull is not subjected directly to the freezing environment." Bob said.

"Good point which I thought of, and I know you know companies that assemble carbon nanotube and graphene devices." Wilber said.

"Yes, several of them." Bob said.

"You will be given a blank check to hire any of those companies you want to provide the carbon nanotube and graphene assemblies and materials for a cryogenic hull treatment." Wilber said.

"No problem but they may start asking questions." Bob said.

This is compartmentalized. They are not allowed to know you are working for us."

"What do I tell them if they start demanding information?" Bob asked.

"We have a good cover story the Navy will allow us to use even without them knowing it." Wilber said.

"What's the cover story?" Bob asked.

"We are building an autonomous submarine." Wilber said.

"Some of the engineers will want to know why we are constructing items with carbon nanotubes and graphene." Bob said.

"If you get pushed hard, tell them it's part of a cloaking device." Wilber said.

"Great idea."

"They will probably want to know how the cloaking device works."

"I'm sure the very mention of a cloaking device will trigger a lot of questions."

"It's all part of the disinformation we must use to misguide the real use. Tell them they are not cleared for direct knowledge of how a cloaking device works and not to discuss it or ask questions about it if they know what's good for them."

"That works." Bob said.

"You will probably get a call from the submarine designer Pierre Truffaut, tomorrow." Wilber said.

"Alright." Bob said.

"A gentleman from my office, Jerry Nault will set up the contracts with you so that you will get paid and can purchase materials as needed." Wilber said.

"That's good to know. This sounds expensive." Bob said.

"All Cash in Advance operations are expensive." Wilber said.

"Alright, looking forward to hearing from Pierre Truffaut. Bob said.

Wilber laid back and continued relaxing and hopefully a nap. He received two notifications on his cell phone via text message stating non- disclosure forms were sent to his email.

That could wait for later, he wanted a nap. But just as he was getting into dreamland and another bad memory of Faye Wong, the phone rang and it was as expected, Gary Knoblock was calling back.

"Wilber, I watched the video, and you probably received the non-disclosure as it said it was sending it to you." Bob said.

"Yes, I saw the message you did the DocuSign." Wilber replied.

"I'm only agreeing to work with you because I'm a patriot, otherwise I would turn you down, because quite frankly this business scared the living dog shit out of me." Bob said.

"Now you know." Wilber said.

"Why do these fuckers in government keep the cover-up bullshit?" Bob asked.

"Want to hear the short answer?" Wilber replied.

"Sure." Bob answered.

"Two reasons. First some of them want to get rich off the alien technology before the public becomes aware." Wilber said.

"Okay, I can see that." Bob said.

"Secondly, highly paid think tanks like the Rand Corporation have advised our government the public cannot handle Alien disclosure. Their *Social Disorganization*

Theory which they advised the government states that *Alien disclosure would set off a serious social disorder with terrible consequences*." Wilber explained.

"What would they do if those Aliens from Saturn suddenly arrived here?" Bob asked.

"Good question. I'm pretty sure Rand Corporation would tell us to go find a bomb shelter to hide in." Wilber replied.

"Alright Wilber, I'm ready to support. Bob said.

"Good, you will hear from a couple of people soon. One is Jerry Nault who will set up contracts with you." Wilber said.

"Alright." Bob replied.

"The submarine designer, and members of his staff will contact you about specific parts they need. Do not assume anyone on his staff is cleared. Just play dumb." Wilber said.

"That I can do." Bob said.

"Alright, talk to you soon and I might even pay you a visit soon." Wilber said.

"Good, looking forward to seeing you again." Bob said.

Wilber then rested again and with no further interruptions was able to catch a nap and as expected his alarm on his cell phone woke him up. Wilber was in his street clothes and needed to walk so he headed for SBC looking forward to seeing Karen.

In less than 30 minutes, Wilber pulled up to the bar stool and was looking at Karen the Aquarian and her smile. She loved those $100.00 tips and suspected Wilber would be back tonight so she dressed in such a way she could show off some of her body when nobody else was around to send a message to Wilber she truly was interested in experiencing an SDHNC.

"Hello Wilber."

"Hello Karen, the Aquarian"

"Wilber, you can call me anything other than a Librarian."

"It's too bad you are not my girlfriend; I would love to call your Darling."

"Wilber, you can call me that anyway, I like it."

"Okay, darling, I'm ready for one of those great craft beers. I'll let you pick one for me."

"Coming right up Wilber."

After Karen served Wilber she asked, "Wilber, where's your friend Colonel Baker?"

"He's going to be busy tonight and in fact in a short while I expect to get a text from him."

Wilber cut to the chase tonight and went right for the gusto and said, "Instead of an appetizer, I think I'm going to have the three-meat sampler with a side of Onion Rings."

"Alright, Wilber."

About then Wilber received the text message, "30 minutes to T-0."

"Karen, hold that food order for 30 minutes, we have something we need to do in 30 minutes."

"Wilber, I'm sorry I can't take off work until 11:00 tonight if you are thinking about giving me some SDHNC you know I want."

"It's something else," After that we can negotiate with a few more beers."

"Works for me."

Wilber knew he would get a text if there was a delay and at the twenty-five-minute mark on his timer he set he informed Karen, "It's time now we need to go outside for about five minutes."

"Sure, the crowd hasn't showed up. I'll have Mary the waitress to take over the bar for five minutes."

They walked outside and soon the sky was getting dark, and Wilber pointed to the Northwest and said, "Look in that direction, you will soon have a surprise."

Two minutes later there was a brightness in the direction they were looking. Soon afterwards they could see the monster size rocket going out into space."

"Wow, a rocket launch. How did you know it was going to happen?" Karen asked.

"I received a text from Colonel Baker about the time I delayed my food order."

After watching the probe fly out into space for a couple minutes, Karen said, "I need to go back inside."

"I'm getting hungry now, I am looking forward to that great meal," Wilber said.

Are we going to hook up later tonight?" Karen asked.

"Karen, you are very attractive, and I know I would enjoy you quite a bit, but I do not do one-night stands."

"That's nice to know. My respect for you Wilber, just went up a notch or two."

"Karen, if I were going to be here for a long time, we could get to know each other better. If you were my girlfriend, I'd take you to the SDHNC Moon tonight and every night afterwards and develop a serious relationship."

"You are a gentleman. I like you."

"Thank you. I really like you too."

***

Chapter Sixteen

Construction and Launch

Wilber was back at his office a few days later in the Washington DC Naval Yard watching developments for all the construction phase of the Project Solaris Submarine (PSS) begin with great speed and determination.

Because of his interest in Solar System Investigations and the Saturn Probe, Wilber continued monitoring it, even though he was no longer involved. He was of course curious as to when it would fail its mission.

The probe was on its way to destiny. Wilber had access to the Saturn Probe data because the DD/P John Burkette tasked him to routinely monitor it. Hence Wilber was spying on the Saturn Probe operation because John Burkette didn't trust Pat Barton and his batch of office warriors.

The telemetry from the Saturn Probe indicated all the background health checks remained consistent with no faults detected. People who studied Saturn were quite happy as they received some of the best videos ever as the Saturn Probe continued to send back a lot of pictures and live videos.

Solar System Investigations had no idea the submarine construction was well on its way. If the probe did everything envisioned, the submarine construction would be halted, and people transferred. Should Project Solaris get shut down, Wilber planned to leave the agency and do something else for the rest of his life because his love Xinxin had been wrecked relentlessly by conditions that manifest in the life of a spy.

Looking back on it, Wilber realized he should have left after the Faye Wong incident. Not everyone gets the chance in life to kill their lover in such a way. Terror and sorrow all combined into the irrational tapestry of clandestine circumstances.

Two submarines were built. Parts of one of the submarines were used as the propulsion and power generator prototype installed in that large new building in Utah sometimes referred to as Area-57. The very large complex was perfect to put the engineering systems prototype since it could be buried amid the sprawling complex shrouded in secrecy full of compartmentalized programs, including some efforts relocated and moved out of Area-51.

The nearby Air Force Base in Utah allowed ease of transportation. The location near a metropolis allowed for the convenience of travelers. Project Solaris had their own machine shop and what would appear like a railroad locomotive builder facility with overhead cranes and heavy lift capability. Every part produced was installed in the Project Solaris Submarine and slowly built with the Genius of Pierre Truffaut.

The sticky point came when Naval Reactors got fussy about delivering the Fusion Reactors in the middle of all this. It simply boiled down to a Four- Star Admiral wanting to be in on the know of what was going on. Wilber figured out how to handle him. He simply would be cleared at the highest levels and when he retired, he could be a member of the team to implement the actual submarine.

The Admiral soon regretted going where he probably should not have as he found himself inside a SKIF in a special meeting with one other person Wilber who by now had slowly received more and more power and authority directly from the DD/P John Burkette who was starting to see this thing was probably really going to come to be. He had to fully back Wilber or it would all fall apart from too many office warriors who had the fantastic ability to fuck up everything they touched.

"Alright Admiral, we normally do not allow the use of cell phones inside the SKIF, and we usually block out the RF signals so that no cell phone or device would work in here," Wilber said during the indoctrination phase.

"Understand all," the four-star admiral responded.

"Admiral, because this is a special briefing, we must give you a non- disclosure document you need to sign. I'm going to deactivate the security device that will allow you to turn on your cell phone and see you just received an email that has the title Project Solaris Non-Disclosure DocuSign. Please open that file, read it and when you are satisfied, select the agree to electronic signature box, then finish."

The Admiral read it, and it was as standard form 312 which agreed to and completed the transaction. What the admiral didn't know was Wilber had just planted an artificial intelligence C-ware on his cell phone and he would be monitored forever by one of the CIA's artificial intelligence projects that was so super-secret that few people below

John Burkette knew existed.

If the Admiral blabbed to anyone in a text or an email, the AI would detect it and he would mysteriously be found floating down the Potamic after suffering a heart attack that can be induced by the combination of an injection and holding his head under water until the heart attack happened.

The admiral electronically signed the DocuSign which Wilber immediately received, and he then said, "Admiral, thank you for signing the DocuSign. I would like you to turn off your cell phone now, and I need to turn the security jammer back on."

"It's off," the admiral said after he powered down his cell phone.

Over the next two hours watching the briefing video quickly made the Admiral regret getting involved. This was probably the biggest mistake in his life.

Being a sophisticated person, the admiral had been involved in Clandestine Activities himself. He fully understood he had already crossed the line of no return when he electronically signed the DocuSign and subsequently watched a major portion of the briefing. He had no way out now. He had no idea how serious this matter was or the ginormous deep state involvement until just now as it raised the hair on the back of his neck.

This was truly a sobering experience for the admiral because it shook the foundation of his belief system because now, he knew the truth and there was no government coverup for him, he saw it all.

The admiral also was advised later during discussions with Wilber about the probe and how Wilber and the DD/P John Burkette expect the Aliens to easily destroy the probe that would not give the President what he needed to know:

Who are these Aliens, what are they doing on Saturn? Who are the Aliens routinely communicating with, and how much about Earth do they know?

More fundamentally the question becomes: What are the Alien intentions towards Earth and why did these communications suddenly begin?

At the end of the briefing and Q & A session, Wilber asked, "Admiral how soon will you approve the shipments of those Fusion Reactors to Utah?"

"Wilber, it's not a far walk from here over to my office since you have a great location here in the Naval Yard. I now understand the significance of all this and will send the approval immediately."

"Thank you, admiral, but please do not forget your personnel are not allowed to know the purpose of the use of the Fusion Reactors and you are required to use the cover story we gave you."

"I get that loud and clear and I understand for their own good it would be best they never know anything about the Project Solaris Submarine."

When the admiral left the SKIF, he had the look on his face someone would have if they just had the most disturbing incident in their life. In a way he did.

***

There were two purposes in building two complete submarines. One was to make sure all the parts would fit seamlessly with the rudimentary construction ability they would have on Saturn in what would be built on an improvised skid with an enclosure that itself was a gigantic innovation. Near a desired landing zone there was a small outgrowth of land that raised up a gentle slope of one of the few areas of the planet that was not covered by liquid helium or hydrogen. This covered skid system would allow them to assemble the submarine, get it functioning then with an ingenious method launch a fully functional submarine and start operating.

Thanks to data provided by the probe before the aliens destroyed it, they had good measurements on the large body of liquid helium they would operate in. They were lucky the Aliens were not situated in the large bodies of hydrogen on other parts of the planet. Helium would be much safer to operate in. Perhaps that's why the aliens are there? Wilber wondered.

The second reason for building two submarines is the fully assembled submarine in what appeared to be a drydock was the prototype to train on. The limited crew could operate the systems using simulators to give them the experience of operating as if it were a real submarine on Saturn.

Elaborate testing was used to determine if the hypersonic devices used for bottom mapping and navigation as well as collision avoidance worked as designed. A very large tank was built that was fully enclosed and could be filled with liquid helium was necessary to test the devices and calibrate them to helium just as if they were operating in salt water in the ocean. Speed of sound in Helium being 973 meters per second (3192.257 feet per second) at zero degrees Celsius. The surface of Saturn is -139 degrees Celsius. So further calculations were needed to get accurate range information on the active pulse returns for the Partial Liquid Lense System that would be the main submarine eyes and ears.

Thanks to miniaturization and state of the art technology, the Partial Liquid Lense System could be built into a small space. By cutting down crew size and automating most features the way Russians did their submarines also allowed greatly reducing crew size.

A 7800-ton submarine was not required. Also, thanks to the small size of the fusion reactors, the engineering spaces were also reduced greatly in scope, so the final design was about the size of a German U212 submarine slightly less than 2000 tons submerged, which also greatly reduced the amount of Titanium needed. The submarine would weigh only seven percent more on Saturn which greatly reduced complicated adjustments for steering and diving and ballasting.

***

The submarine design was well on its way and the hull was in construction when the Saturn Probe began flying around the planet taking measurements and conducting ISR missions. As figured at this distance to the planet's surface, there was such little detail there was nothing gained by the probe, which added great stress to Pat Barton and the cast of office warriors who banked so heavily on the probe obtaining all they needed. After twenty orbits around the planet, no new information had been gained.

Deep penetration of the planet's atmosphere was not planned for weeks, but Pat Barton and his advisors desperately wanted to kill Project Solaris and after a series of meetings including pressing their concerns to the DCI direct going over John Burke's head and thoroughly pissing off John, they did their next blunder.

Instead of a slow descent making multiple orbits around Saturn, they went for the big gusto and decided to get down to low altitudes in just a single orbit after the decision was granted.

Everything was progressing wonderfully. The DCI, DD/P (John Burkette), and Wilber O'Toole were in the SKIF the nucleus of the top

Solar System Investigation principles getting ready to make the case to skuttle Project Solaris which was no longer needed.

There was tension in the air as so much was riding on this probe pass. The probe, now down to 10,000 feet, recorded imagery of Saturn's surface never seen before. It truly was an astonishing jump in science and discovery and just as the probe came over the area near where the alien communication signals originated there was brightness on the screen for about five seconds, then the probe went dead.

Pat Barton with total panic on his face picked up the red phone in front of him that was cleared for TOP SECRET and had a direct connection with mission control located in Sunnyvale California.

Just picking up the red phone receiver automatically initiated the call which gave an eerie alarm in mission control. The phone was immediately answered by Dr. Hicks, the chief engineer for Saturn Probe. The conversation was repeated on small speakers in front of people at the conference table who could hear everything said on the red phone.

"Hello," Dr. Hicks answered in a stressed voice.

Pat Barton recognized the voice and said, "Dr. Hicks this is Pat Barton, what's going on with the probe?"

"Pat, we are not sure, but we are not receiving any telemetry from the probe and it's not answering our queries."

"How long does it take for our signals to reach the probe from Earth?"

"From the current position of both planets it takes one hour, twenty minutes and fifteen seconds for our queries to reach the probe and the same amount of time for it to answer means we will not get a response for more than two hours and forty minutes."

"When was the last time we queried it?"

"We send queries once a minute nonstop, just to keep checking the coms link to make sure it's up. Once we lost telemetry, we immediately started sending the Barking Code."

"What's the Barking Code?"

"It's a command that says we cannot hear you so please Bark a few times. It's something one of the dog owners that works here came up with and it means that if the probe receives the Barking Code, it will send signals out of all its transmitters in sequence and hopefully we'll receive one of them and switch to that alternate channel for primary communication."

"When did you first started sending the Barking Code?"

"Five minutes ago."

"That means we will not hear back for one hour and fifteen minutes?"

"That's correct unless it does a self-initiate if it lost our telemetry to it." "How often do you send the Barking Code?"

"This is considered a potential failure and possibly an *unscheduled rapid disassembly*, so instead of sending the normal minute by minute coms check telemetry we automatically start transmitting the Barking Code sequences."

"What did you mean by *unscheduled rapid disassembly*?" Pat Barton asked.

"It means the craft might have been blown up." Dr. Hicks answered.

"By whom?" Pat Barton asked.

"Who do you think is on Saturn?" Dr. Hicks asked.

Dr. Hicks fully briefed in every aspect of the mission knew the possibility this would happen, and Pat Barton's ill-conceived modification of mission profiles probably pissed off the Aliens, so they destroyed the ship. Had they simply just stuck to the game plan, they might not have destroyed the probe so quickly.

About that time the DCI spoke up. "Pat, hang up the phone, we need to talk about this."

"Thanks Dr. Hicks, I'll call you back later, we are going to have an impromptu meeting now."

After Pat Barton hung up the phone looking like he just saw a ghost, the DCI started in.

"How soon can we get the second probe sent there to verify what we think might be alien involvement in the destruction of the first probe?"

"That depends on if you want to delay the launch of the KH-15 satellite and use its rocket engine."

"I'll have to go over and talk to the Joint Chiefs and get a feel for how desperately they need the KH-15 launched. I'll get back to you on the possibility of cannibalizing KH-15 ULA-97 launch vehicle," the DCI said.

"Okay," Pat Barton replied.

"Let's plan for worst case scenario. I go over and the Joint Chiefs give me an answer that precludes using KH-15 ULA-97 launch vehicle, how long would it take to get another complete probe rocket ready with no cannibalized parts?"

"We'll have to have a meeting with the ULA people and work out the details."

"Alright, ask them to come here like the last time because we have too many people involved that need to simultaneously hear what they have to say and ask poignant questions."

"I'll contact them as soon as the meeting is over."

"Fine. John, I want you and Wilber to come with me back to my office for a sidebar."

"Sure thing," John Burke said knowing they would get there quickly by helicopter, and he would ask in route if they could be flown directly to the Navy yard after their discussions.

Wilber could sense the DCI was not a happy camper. He would have to brief the president today and the outcome of that briefing would be a lot more pressure.

The DCI's office could be turned into a SKIF with the press of one switch on the control panel on his disk under his desktop monitor display. When that happened a blue and a red light each flashed above the door to his office. The door and the walls were also vibrated to make sure listening devices would be blurred in case someone planted one outside the room.

Technicians would immediately come into the room with bug sniffers after everyone was seated and if someone was packing a bug, they would get caught.

That was soon done, and the three men were alone, and the discussion started.

"What do you guys think will happen to probe number two?"

John Burke knew that Wilber had such disdain for Pat Barton likely had a good response and gave him the opportunity to say the obvious.

"Sir I believe it too will have an *unscheduled rapid disassembly* just like probe number one," Wilber offered.

"I tend to agree with you, Wilber. You two are some of my most trusted men, I value your inputs on matters. Even without asking them, I know the joint chiefs desperately want KH-15 launched. How do you see the priority, Probe two or KH-15?"

This time Wilber thought John Burkette should answer this one for both and he already knew what John Burkette was going to say.

"Sir, I think that Probe number two will suffer the same fate as probe number one. As soon as it gets above the alien transmitter site, it will be destroyed," John Burkette replied.

"I tend to agree with you. What do you think we should do Wilber?"

"I agree with what John said. I truly believe we'll have a repeat performance, so if the Joint Chiefs really need the KH-15, they deserve to get that capability since we already know the outcome of probe number two will be identical to probe number one."

Alright, this is what I'm going to do. I'm going to go over to the Joint Chiefs and lay out my cards and tell them I will go along with what they want and I'm sure they will want the KH-15 to launch, that way they will give me affirmative backup with the President when I recommend, we launch the KH-15 ahead of probe number two." DCI said.

"Sounds like a good plan," John Burkette responded.

"I'll give you guys a ride back to the Navy Yard on my way to the Pentagon."

"We appreciate that." John Burkette said.

"One other thing. I'm sure when I brief the President, he's going to be pretty upset and when I tell him the Aliens will likely destroy the second probe, he's going to ask me what our backup plan is. I will mention Project Solaris and offer to have you two guys come to the White House soon afterward to personally brief the president about Project Solaris. I want you guys to put together a good dog and pony show for the President but keep it down to thirty minutes. The President is a busy man," The DCI announced.

"We'll work on that immediately," John Burke said feeling confident he had an illustrious Cowboy working for him who knew the essence of impressing people with videos to make his case.

"Alright, let's go now," the DCI said and flipped the switch that automatically downgraded the posture of the room from a SKIF to just Top Secret-SCI-NORORN.

It was a joyous mode of transportation on the Sikorsky S-97 flying over to the Navy Yard by looking down at all the traffic jams below. It would really suck if they had to wait for a driver and go through that mess to get back to the Navy Yard.

After they got back to building 28, Wilber began immediate work on the Presidential briefing. Using CIA's artificial intelligence, Wilber quickly put together a 30-minute-high level briefing. When he was done with it, he emailed it to John Burkette who then put it on his CIA cell phone to take with him if they were required to go to the Oval Office.

After watching all 30 minutes to censor or critique the video, John Burkette called Wilber.

"Wilber?"

"Yes John, what's up."

"I just watched your 30-minute briefing."

"What did you think?"

"It was so good I thought it was a movie."

"Was it convincing?"

"Wilber, you are in the wrong business. You should be working for Hollywood. It convinced me and I already knew about it. I'm sure the president will feel the same way."

"That's good to know."

"Alright, stand by in case the DCI asks us to attend the meeting."

"Standing by."

"You probably need to hang around to 6:00 P.M. because we might get called in late."

"Not a problem, I'm not an office warrior and 6:00 P.M. is just a good day's work for me."

"Are there very many office warriors working there at building 28?"

"No. Jerry Nault did a great job of screening the people here. Not only did he pick clearable people, but Jerry also checked their work ethics before giving them an invite."

"Sounds like he's a great office manager."

"He is."

"Glad to hear that. I'll call you if we must go to the meeting."

"I'll be standing by."

"Thank you, Wilber."

***

The DCI was wearing a poker face when he met with the Joint Chiefs in a SKIF at the Pentagon.

Most of the admirals and generals did not look happy because they thought the DCI was a proponent of stealing the KH-15 rocket for another classic CIA boondoggle.

Thank all of you for this impromptu meeting on a sensitive subject."

The Admiral a former submarine skipper with brass balls wasn't the ass kissing type. He was full of piss and vinegar started the barrage.

"Sir, we desperately need the KH-15."

"Admiral, you do not agree with placing Solar System Investigation launch in higher priority than KH-15 launch."

"Hell no."

The DCI looked around the long briefing table and could see the venom in most of their eyes and had to ask the obvious question since there was a yeoman over in the corner recording a transcript of the meeting.

"Alright then. Since this is an official meeting and the President may want to read the transcript, I need to ask the obvious question."

The DCI looked around the room and he already knew what the answer would be, but in this business one had to cover their asses because there was a lot of backstabbers close to the President.

"Is there anyone here who disagrees with the Admiral?" It was so quiet you could hear a pen drop in the room.

"Alright then, I will support your viewpoint the KH-15 launch has more immediate vital interest than launching probe number two."

All the Admirals and Generals were suddenly smiling because they had just won a battle with the CIA. And the fact the DCI would back their viewpoint pleased them and conveyed to them, this new DCI was not a goose stepper jumping to the demands of civilians who sometimes have misguided approach to things which often has adverse impact on the military.

The DCI could not openly appear positive with the Joint Chiefs viewpoint, he had to simply come across to the president as someone who respected the joint chiefs' desires, and their viewpoint should receive considerable consideration in this matter.

The DCI being a shrewd operator knew he was in a very opportunistic profile now and then said to the joint chiefs, "I would like to call the president so that all of you can hear in on the conversation and if you have any concerns address it during the call.

The admiral who knew the president quite well said, "That's a great idea and we appreciate you doing it."

"I'm going to turn on my CIA authorized cell phone now and make that call. Any objections?"

There was silence in the room.

The Navy Yeoman hearing all the conversation was truly amazed and this was one of the most interesting meetings he ever attended to take notes and make the official transcript. The Navy Yeoman would receive help that only the Admiral knew of. The meeting was being secretly recorded to make sure they had an accurate transcript. That recording would be destroyed by the admiral as soon as the yeoman gave him a word file of the transcript to ready to approve.

The President saw the caller I.D. was the DCI and immediately answered, "Hello Brent."

"Mr. President, I have you on speaker phone, I'm over at the joint chiefs discussing the probe situation and the KH-15 launch scheduled."

"What did you guys determine?"

"Well, sir, it's a unanimous decision here the KH-15 launch should happen first and the second probe sent later when we can get the rocket built and put on the launch pad."

"Okay, if you agree with the Joint Chiefs, then I will support that decision."

"I do, sir."

"Very well, I want you to come over and talk with me for a few minutes."

"Mr. President, I would like to bring the DD/P and his assistant in Project Solaris, Wilber O'Toole with me."

"Is that the CIA man who rescued the Dubai Sheikh' son from the terrorists?"

"Yes, he is."

"Please bring him, I would like to meet him."

"I'll fly over to the Navy Yard and pick them up. Could you please inform the secret service we are on the way?"

"Certainly. I'll tell them to have you land on the south lawn."

"I appreciate that."

"See you soon." Then the president hung up.

"Okay men and women, it appears we are all set," the DCI said then stood up.

The admiral was the first person to stand and quickly approached the DCI and held out his hand and said, "We appreciate you being concerned about our needs."

"Well, your needs are the same as my needs and I think we jointly know what's more important about this."

***

The DCI was soon on his way to the White House with his two associates and the secret service air traffic controller vectored them into the south lawn where moments before secret service men laid down the three large circular panels that made a temporary landing pad.

Without shutting down the rotors, the three men got out of the helicopter and walked to the side of the lawn where several secret service men were there waiting to escort them into the oval office. The helicopter then took off flying over to an Army base nearby to temporarily wait until called back to pick up the three passengers.

The three CIA men were taken into the building, frisked and had their guns temporarily confiscated after they were asked if they were armed. Unarmed they were ushered into the Oval Office where the Vice President was waiting with the President and the Secretary of Defense.

Have a seat gentleman, the president gestured towards the sofa. "What went wrong with the probe, Brent?

The DCI answered, "We are not sure, we are waiting for the team out in Sunnyvale to give us more details of what went wrong. The probe was function just fine until it flew over the target area, where it suddenly had an unexpected possible *unscheduled rapid disassembly*."

"What you are really saying is the aliens probably blew it up."

The President had his own personal spies and already knew everything the DCI new. He uses people in the NSA to watch the CIA and the CIA to watch the FBI, and the FBI watches the NSA and DHS and gives the president special briefings. Nobody trusts anybody in the spook business. If they do, they are fools.

The people over at Solar System Investigations are not willing to make that call, but the three of us unanimously believe that to be the case."

In case you do not know it, the vice President and SECDEF listened in on your phone call giving priority to the Pentagon over the KH-15 launch. SECDEF has something to say to you."

"Yea Brent, I'm glad how you handled the matter and got Joint Chiefs buy in or buy down on the matter and included the President in on that discussion. It proves you are a straight shooter and look out for the best interest of the United States."

"Thanks. I try to always do my best."

"Okay Brent, what's the plan now?"

"Mr. President, this gentleman is Wilber Otoole who works for John Burkette who you know and early on came up with a plan most of the Solar System Investigation team put down as ludicrous and far-fetched. I saw things differently and so did John Burkette."

"Brent thanks for bringing Wilber over. I wanted to personally thank him for his courageous mission to the middle east to save Sheikh Omar's son. In doing so he greatly improved relations with the UAE."

The president looked solely at Wilber because he read the DCI's report on all that happened including the 12 dead mercenaries that lost their lives to do this impossible mission that nobody else figured could be accomplished. It also sent a message to the terrorists, we can in fact get to you even when you are protected in a country that's our enemy.

"Wilber, you have led an interesting life. Off the record, I don't mind the fact you poked that Chinese Diplomat's eye out. And yes, I saw the SID video."

"Thank you, Mr. President," Wilber said in the humblest fashion.

"Tell me about your submarine idea, Wilber," The president said.

"Mr. President, John Burkette has a 30-minute video that shows the idea and how we are actually implementing it."

"Mr. President, I have the video on my cell phone if I could hook it up to your video monitor and show it," John Burkette interjected.

"Sure, no problem. James, can you help him set it up?" The president asked one of the secret service men in the room protecting the president.

In the overhead of the oval office is a video screen that is hidden and comes down on the wall opposite the sofa the CIA men were sitting at which everyone in the room could see and hear since it had full stereo audio. The secret service man walked over to the sofa area and pulled a cable that hooks up to cell phones for this very purpose and handed it to John Burkette and said, "It's ready to go, all you have to do is plug into your cell phone and start playing the video."

"Thanks."

"No problem." The secret service man said then walked back over to where he was standing.

John Burke plugged in the cable which started playing.

Wilber was looking around the room watching the body language of these powerful men.

The DCI had not seen this video yet to approve it but under the circumstances, this was a crisis and no matter how bad the video might be, it was nowhere near the goat fuck that Pat Barton's people were now doing trying to pressure Dr. Hicks in Sunnyvale to come up with some ridiculous claims of possible atmospheric related demise.

The DCI knew Dr. Hicks refused to play along with the nonsense because the ISR package indicated there was nothing weatherwise out of the ordinary and even though there were high winds on Saturn, the probe had just spent an hour flying through it with no issues.

In bye gone years, it would have taken the CIA a month to put together a video this good. Artificial intelligence was changing many things now including high level briefings that could be built in a short amount of time.

The secretary of defense was utterly stunned that all this was being managed at one of his bases right under the DOD's noses and nobody in the DOD knew about it except a four-star admiral at naval reactors. He was in the video as well discussing some of the safeguards on the fusion reactors.

After the video, the President had a couple questions before they were politely dismissed by, "Your helicopter is arriving to take you back to your offices."

"How long will it before Project Solaris flies?"

"It will be just like the timeline in the window states," John Burkette responded."

"How do you know this thing can work in five years?"

"We've done similar projects in the past, and we deployed them in five years. We have dedicated people; we will get there."

"Alright Gentlemen, thanks for the briefing. James escort them to the helicopter that will be arriving in a few minutes."

"Yes, Mr. President." James said and led the three CIA men out of the oval office where a couple more secret service men were waiting to escort them to the helicopter now landing on the south lawn.

The three CIA men flew back to the Navy Yard where Wilber was dropped off as the two other men went back to CIA headquarters for a private meeting.

The DCI was suddenly appreciative of Wilber who saved his ass. Without the video and Wilber's performance, the DCI might have been fired. But he also helped his own cause by the way he interfaced with the Pentagon, because he bought a lot of points with the DOD who was now suddenly less confrontational with the CIA.

The main purpose of this private meeting was to change priorities. There would not be a second probe attempt. It would be wasting another rocket needed by the military for more pressing issues.

Pat Barton and his cronies would see their project slowly slide off into the sunset. The DCI and the DD/P already understood we had terrestrial threats now pending because of issues in the middle east and Ukraine and China's bold moves.

The Pentagon had launch complex 10 reserved for the next 7 years. There is no slack in the schedule.

Pat Barton's problem if he tried to launch out of Florida, he would have a huge security issue because NASA scientists would be instantly interested and want to know exactly WTF that missile was carrying and if it had juicy tendrils to a classified launch, they would demand even more information.

Launch complex six at Vandenberg ostensibly set up for Space X did have some slack but Colonel Baker who was on the right team would never disclose that to Pat Barton's boys. All those launches to haul Project Solaris components to Saturn would probably leave Launch complex six on a secret deal with Space-X. Another thing was the DCI figured Elon Musk would support the project if there was a little quid pro quo to grease his palms. If Space-X didn't want to launch Project Solaris rockets, ULA would be more than happy. Unfortunately, due to security concerns, Vandenberg was the only location suitable for Project Solaris launches.

***

Chapter Seventeen

KH - 15 Launch

In a brief period, the DCI requested Wilber fly out to Vandenberg to watch the KH-15 launch. The DCI had thoughts that Pat Barton would somehow screw up this launch. Wilber provided the DCI a remote set of eyes and ears and would mitigate a disaster causing delays because Pat was pissed he couldn't grab that rocket to launch another useless probe to Saturn.

Wilber didn't need to do any oversight on Colonel Baker as he had proven his ability. The real purpose of the visit was to give Colonel Baker a briefing on what was to follow and of course to pay Karen the Aquarian a visit for some pre-SDHNC launches.

Wilber was talking with Colonel Baker down near the blue line when a couple men from the NRO approached him. This was their bird and wanted to spend some time with Colonel Baker to get an update on launch status.

"Well as you guys can see, the blue line is set up and we are clearing out the launch pad area of all the support equipment to get it ready."

"Are we confident in the launch date?" One of the NRO representatives asked.

"I'm so confident Wilber O'Toole here sent out by the DCI was invited out to watch the launch."

"You work for Brent?" One of the spooks asked. "Yes, I do."

"What's your capacity in your job?"

"I'm one of the managers in Project Solaris." "Never heard of it before."

"That's good that you didn't, it means we have good security." "What does Project Solaris have to do with the KH-15?"

"It was project Solaris that recommended to the DCI he did not allow Solar System Investigations group to cannibalize this rocket for one of their probes." "You're not on that team?" the NRO man asked. Colonel Baker started laughing.

"What's so funny Colonel? the NRO man asked.

"Well, if you must know Project Solaris and Solar System Investigations do not get along very well?"

Wilber decided to throw some gasoline on the fire and asked, "How did you like it when Solar System Investigations grabbed rocket that was going to launch the KH-15 a while back?"

"It kind of pissed me off," the NRO man said. "Now you know how I feel," Wilber said. "What did they do to you?"

"The manager in charge of Solar System Investigations used to be my boss. It's safe to say, he doesn't like me too well."

"That's good to know you are not part of that squad."

"I was about ready to leave and go over to Salvang Brewing Company.

Meet me over there and I'll buy you a beer."

"Sure bud. By the way, they call me Buster, and this is Brewster."

"What a couple names. It will be easy for me to remember. I'm Wilber O'Toole."

"Alright Wilber, see you over at SBC. We've been there a few times before."

A short time later Wilber walked into SBC and as expected was the lovely bartender Karen the Aquarian. The minute Karen spotted Wilber approaching she lit up.

"Well-well-well, look what the cat drug in," Karen said.

"Hello Karen, as you can see, I couldn't stay away. I had to come see you."

"I'm glad you came back to me."

"I'm going to have a couple friends join me in a short while."

"Sure, not a problem. Why are you dressed up in a suit?"

"I've not checked into my hotel yet."

"Where are you staying?"

"Why would you care?"

"Because I might have to come by your room tonight, since you never show up at closing time."

"I'll believe that when I see it. I'm staying at the Embassy Suites."

Karen suddenly had a wicked grin on her face. Wilber would get the chance to turn her down tonight.

A couple minutes later the NRO guys showed up and sat down next to Wilber at the bar. They also wore suits and Karen knew who the hell these guys were. They came here often.

"Hello guys."

"Hello Karen," Buster said.

"I want to buy these guys a beer," Wilber said.

"Sure."

Karen was putting two and two together. Wilber knew exactly when the rocket launch was a while back and here, Wilber was with two guys she knew that launched rockets. Hmmmm….."

After they had their first sips of their beers, Buster said, "So I take it you do not get along well with the SSI folks?"

"Not at all. Shall we say we are competing interests," Wilber stated. "Does that mean you too plan on stealing our rockets?"

"I promise you we will stay the hell away from launch complex ten."

"That's good to know. Where are you going to launch? Florida?"

"They do not have adaquate security and they have a lot of nosey NASA scientists. I'm sure if we launch it will be over at complex six."

"Heavy lift?"

"Definitely."

"Interesting. Are your offices here at Vandenberg?"

"No, I'm at the Navy Yard in Washington DC."

"I see, a military project?"

"Why else would we be at a Naval Base?"

Wilber could tell these two guys were Cowboys like him and decided to recruit them. He could always use a few more Cowboys, especially for manning the Project Solaris Space Craft and Submarine. Even though he thought the best way to deal with that Admiral from NAVSEA 08 who appeared to be in great shape, was designated to be on the submarine as a crew member and the sub's engineer.

Wilber pulled a couple business cards out of his wallet and said, "If you guys decide you want to get involved in some military launches, give me a call, we might be able to fit you in."

Buster and Brewster took the business cards and handed back one of their own in exchange.

It did not take long to down two beers and Wilber suddenly got a text from John Burkette to call him.

"I'm sorry guys I have to leave, I need to go make some phone calls."

"Nice meeting you Wilber."

Wilber stood up and Karen the Aquarian said, "Don't forget Wilber I'm going to sneak by your hotel room tonight so you can teach me the intricacies of SDHNC."

"I like to take my time and teach slowly and methodically, especially to a new student," Wilber said and smiled then walked out of the restaurant.

The two NRO guys looked at each other wondering WTF is the acronym SDHNC. And of course, they were too embarrassed to ask Karen what something so obvious must be.

Wilber drove a mile up the street and pulled into the hotel entrance parked in a hotel guest parking spot, got his small suitcase out of the back of the car, and went inside and got the key card for his hotel room.

The GS750 had already taken off flying back to Washington, Wilber was going to be here until ULA launched the KH-15 then he would have transportation back to Washington. If the jet was being used elsewhere, he might be requested to fly on a commercial flight back to Washington and out of the black money funds, he would upgrade himself to first class if that happened.

Wilber called John Burkette who quickly answered. "You some place where we can talk?" John asked.

"Yes, I just checked into my hotel room."

"Good. The reason why I asked you to call me is we are going to have a special meeting."

"Back in Washington?"

"No, it will be out West."

"Here where I'm at?"

"No. Brent and I will fly into Vandenberg and pick you up and take you to the location special meeting after you call us and let us know the bird has flown there."

"Sure thing. Can you tell me what this is about?"

"It has to do with Project Solaris and some aspects of it you need to be briefed on that you are not aware of."

"I thought I knew everything that was going on."

"For your own sake, we had to keep some things away from you, that now the time has come you need to be aware of so you can work it into your planning and implementation."

"Alright understand, looking forward to the meeting."

"Thanks Wilber, and oh by the way, the president wanted to give me a prestigious award for the briefing you created. I had to decline since I wasn't the person who prepared it and I told him you prepared it. He wanted me to personally inform you that he's very impressed with you and you have no idea the chord you struck with him. When you rescued that boy from the terrorists, you generated a lot of good will with the president."

"That's good to know."

"This briefing and later discussions with him on your role in Project Solaris are the reasons why we are having the special meeting with you in a few days. You don't quite know this yet, but when you impress the president as much as you have, he grows great faith in you and thus you have opened new opportunities for yourself for your future.

"That's good to know the President likes Cowboy spirit."

"He does and he doesn't really care for office warriors. We'll see you in a few days."

Wilber changed out of his suit into street clothes and was starting to feel hungry. He didn't feel like walking down to SBC, so he looked at google maps and saw a shopping mall not far from the hotel that had some restaurants and fast food and decided just to walk there and get something to eat.

It only took about ten minutes and Wilber walked past a mall area and saw Mi Amore Pizza and Pasta and went in there to try their food.

A waitress by the name of Ami seated Wilber and asked him, "What would you like to drink?"

"I would like a glass of cabernet."

"Is Ballard Lane Cabernet, okay?"

"I've never had it before, but I would not mind trying it."

"Alright, your drink is coming right up."

Wilber spotted Lasagna on the menu and by the time Ami returned with his glass of Cabernet Sauvignon he was ready to order.

"Have you decided what you would like to eat?"

"Yes, I'll have the Lasagna, and when you serve it, I would like some Tabasco." "Sure, not a problem."

Wilber could smell the pizza's cooking and, in a way, wished he had ordered pizza,

but he's always wanting to find good Lasagna and Italian restaurants are generally good at preparing Lasagna.

After a couple glasses of wine and the Lasagna, Wilber went back to his hotel, kicked his shoes off and laid down on his bed just resting. The combination of the wine and the Lasagna soon had Wilber sawing logs with his snoring.

Karen the Aquarian knew Wilber was someone special. Hanging around Colonel Baker and the two NRO guys she saw often meant he was someone a woman should dig her claws into. Karen was a nice girl, didn't sleep around, but saw an opportunity. She had a master's degree in economics and simply preferred bar tending as she was single and lonely waiting to meet a decent guy. It had been a couple years since she last had sex and wasn't in a big rush to get sex from someone that wasn't dear to her heart, and she wasn't going to waste her precious time with a loser.

When Wilber mentioned he was staying at the Embassy suites that was a good omen, because Karen's best friend, April was the night manager for the Embassy suites and they had spent a lot of time together in the past doing whatever they could to get in trouble together, especially when April dragged Karen to the Burning Man Festival.

After Karen closed the bar, she went out to her car, a BMW and drove over to the Embassy Suites and walked up to the counter where April was standing just finishing checking in a hotel guest that was walking away from the counter with his suitcase.

"What brings you here Karen? I don't get off work till 2:00 A.M."

"I'm actually here to see a friend of mine who is a hotel guest."

"That's very interesting. I didn't think you had any male friends lately."

"Not since I kicked Joseph to the curb."

"Yea you had to get rid of that loser, he drained you."

"More than you can imagine."

"Who's your friend staying here?"

"His name is Wilber O'Toole; can you tell me what room he's in?"

"Sure." April did an inquiry on her computer terminal and then said,

"He's in room 222."

"Good. I would stay and talk with you, but I want to see him before he goes to sleep."

"How do you know he's not asleep now?"

"I think he has a hard on because he knows I'm coming."

"So, this is a coordinated visit?"

"Yes, I'm going to have him teach this country girl the intricacies of SDHNC."

"What the hell is SDHNC?"

"Don't ask, don't tell."

"Alright but do me a favor."

"What's that?"

"I know you are a screamer, so please do not wake up the other hotel guests."

"I'll try to be a swallower tonight and not make so much noise." "I know better than that!"

Karen soon left the counter and walked up the spiral staircase to the second floor and walked down and found room 222.

Karent knocked on the door a few times with no apparent answer.

Wilber's AI on his cell phone was programmed to monitor sounds such as someone knocking at the door or someone trying to knock down the door and come in the room for dangerous and nefarious purposes, recognized the knocks on the door and immediately gave a ring tone then said, "Wilber there is someone knocking at your door."

Wilber, somewhat groggy, stood up walked over and looked through the security lens and saw Karen the Aquarian standing there. She was about to leave since nobody responded in the room and suddenly the door opened.

"Hello Karen." "May I come in?" "Certainly."

Wilber of course wanted to know how Karen discovered he was in room 222 but he excused himself and said, "I've been sleeping, and I need to use the toilet for a moment, please make yourself comfortable."

"Alright"

Wilber took care of the business and came out into the room seeing Karen sitting on the side of his bed and not on one of the chairs.

"Tell me Karen, how did you know what room I'm staying in?"

"My friend April is the night manager downstairs; I think she knew I wanted to get some SDHNC training."

Karen was a beautiful woman. She was dressed to impress as she intended to make Wilber's day. She also sprayed on some very exotic French Perfume that supposedly is good at making men's peckers salute.

Wilber sat down on the side of the bed not knowing what to do but he sure as hell felt some arousal and here's a princess wanting to give him something. Wilber's only recourse was to sit down on the bed next to Karen and she immediately started to have physical movement to him that slowly evolved into a firm embrace.

Xinxin still refused to answer Wilber's calls or texts. Wilber slowly concluded it really was over with Xinxin and that relationship was now truncated.

Wilber had not had any physical intercourse since the last time with Xinxin, so his hormones were suddenly racing, and Karen was having a strong effect on him. Wilber finally caved in and said to himself, What the heck, it's time for some SDHNC.

Wilber now reciprocated in the physical embrace and decided to reward Karen for her bravery and as a trained spy know how to kiss women in a way to elevate their emotions which in turn elevated their libido.

In a brief period, they were undressed and fully engaged in a romantic embrace doing the horizontal tango on a theme from Paganini.

Karen soon experienced something she rarely experienced with the few men she had sex with. They were obviously just fucking to get their rocks off. But Wilber was kissing her passionately throughout. Karen was mildly astonished by the way Wilber was conducting himself in such a pleasant manner. It also telegraphed to her; he did have real emotions for her.

Karen's instinct now paid off as she realized this was all true and not faked to get a piece of ass and a one-night stand. There was a lot more to Wilber than she realized, and he was now showing more of it.

Karen didn't realize this was a huge release for Wilber. She didn't know he had been heartbroken over Xinxin and was reluctant to ever fall in love again. Just on a chance encounter here he was engaging in the dangerous passage to the unknown dimension created by a romantic tendril to the heart. People can claim they can control their emotions and not succumb to such perspective until proven otherwise.

Wilber was lucky, he had already had a substantial nap so that in the morning he would not be sleep deprived.

After they both reached the tumultuous allegro and the final crescendo into the transcendence of grand gratification of such rare intensity, they laid side by side facing each other. The lights were on so they could see the full spectrum of each other. It was a unique feeling. Wilber really liked Karen a lot, but he also knew the obvious.

If Wilber allowed Karen to go beyond just some happy time with her, he would be required to inform John Burkette, he had a relationship with this woman that would complicate her life. It would also complicate his life if it turned out she caused some trip wires to be crossed if she had a past like the woman Wilber knew that married the wrong person.

Wilber didn't want to spoil the moment by addressing these uncomfortable details and decided simply to enjoy the moment.

"So, this is what SDHNC is all about?"

"I'll have to give you a briefing on SDHNC as we get to know each other better."

"You want to get to know me better?"

"Karen, you probably don't know this because I never informed you, but I really do like you."

"Well, I like you too."

"I think in due time we'll get to know a lot more about each other."

"Thank you."

"My pleasure."

The two started kissing and hugging and Wilber had not felt this good since he was at the pinnacle of his steamy love relationship with Xinxin. Another chapter in his life was now closed as he would open a new one.

In the days to come, when Xinxin no longer received phone calls or text messages from Wilber, she knew it was over. Did he meet another woman? Xinxin was almost heartbroken to think of such a scenario existed. She hated herself for being such a coward, losing the love of her life because she waited too long to respond.

Wilber felt so good by this transcendence into splendid euphoria Karen caused that he succumbed to sleep. And so did she. But in a few hours because of Wilber's snoring, Karen woke up and knew she had to leave before morning to protect her reputation. She silently got up, put her clothes on without waking Wilber, and left and went home. Her only regret was not getting his phone number before she left, but based on what Wilber said earlier, that was probably coming.

Wilber woke in the morning and wondered if it was a dream but when he found he was not wearing any underwear and all his clothes he was wearing the night before were laying on the floor next to the bed, he realized it did happen. He had fond memories of Karen the Aquarian a true blonde with a nice thick blonde pubis she didn't shave off like most women do these days and lovely breasts any man would love. Up close as he recalled, last night, when they were close and kissing and he could see her lovely face up close, her image truly attracted him. There was a strong motivation to get to know Karen better.

Wilber knew the stakes were high. He didn't want to get involved with someone that would be a security issue. He had friends who were private investigators he used in the past for a variety of purposes, including vetting women before he dated them.

He called up his best investigator who lived in California that would make it easier for him to conduct a private investigation, a gentleman by the name of Javier.

After a couple of rings, Javier answered the phone and found out it was Wilber by the caller I.D.

"Hello Wilber, what's up?"

"I need to hire you to do an investigation."

"Is this one of those Cash-In-Advance investigations?"

"No, its personal."

"What do you want to find out?"

"There is a beautiful blonde woman named Karen with a great body that works at the Solvang Brewing Company as a bartender here in Lompoc where I'm at for a few days that I'm interested in. I need you to check her out and give me a report on who she is and all her personal details, education, boyfriends if she has any, her best friends, and in essence what she is all about."

"Are you serious with this woman?"

"I will be after you clear her and give me the appropriate information that indicates whether or not I should waste my time pursuing her."

"Not a problem, with the information you just gave me I can have a report to you in a couple days."

"Thanks, I appreciate that."

"This is not going to be cheap if I have to do a very detailed investigation for critical factors you need to know about."

"I don't care what it costs. It's my life and my future and I certainly do not want to screw up again with another woman."

"Well, my friend, I hate to be the bearer of bad news, but always prepare to be dissatisfied because you don't really know what a woman is like until you have been around her for a while."

"I'm sure this woman will be fine if you do not find there any skeletons in her closet."

"As you know, I'm good at finding those skeletons."

"Yes indeed."

"I'll get back to you in a couple days."

Wilber was lucky he was in Lompoc. Javier had connections there and would hire a PI he knew to go find out most of the things Wilber needed to know.

One of the mistakes a lot of people make is they leave the license plate holder on their car where they purchased the vehicle. A good private eye knows how to get to a car dealer and with the write kind of bribe get the credit report on that individual if they financed the vehicle.

During test drive of a new BMW, the car salesman was offered a $1000.00 bribe for a copy of Karen the Aquarian's credit report. The good news was this report was only six months old. The information was fresh. That credit report gave Karen's life story and lots of leads to go check such as former employers and residences. Within 24 hours Karen's privacy was thoroughly violated in ways she never imagined. Within 36 hours, Wilber was reading Karen's life story. From the time she was in junior high until she graduated from UC Berkeley with excellent grades and a master's degree in economics.

Also, thanks to nosy neighbors at her current condo and her previous address, a lot of her social information was obtained including finding out about April, her best friend. Then the big whammy was Facebook, Instagram, LinkedIn, and X (formerly known as twitter). People do not realize they are leaving breadcrumbs behind for savvy private investigators to go find, including her former boyfriends and the reason for the breakup.

Some of those people on Facebook got visited and asked questions.

When asked why those questions were being asked, there was a simple explanation. She has a new friend she may be involved with. "We are not concerned about Karen; we are more interested in her friend."

"Why are you interested in her friend?"

"You know some of those rockets they launch at Vandenberg?"

"Yea everyone in Lompoc knows about them."

"He's associated with some of those rocket launches, and we are just checking up on him to make sure he's not involved with the wrong person."

"I can assure you there is nothing wrong with Karen, she lives an idealistic lifestyle, doesn't sleep around and is waiting to meet Mr. Right." The consensus of Karen was utterly outstanding.

Wilber had no idea how lucky he was meeting such an intelligent and beautiful woman. The fact he never tried to get her in the sack lifted her evaluation of Wilber and the way he conducted himself gave Karen great assurances; Wilber was a person worth pursuing.

It so happened 36 hours later was Karen's day off and when Wilber went into the SBC another bartender was there.

"Karen's not working tonight?"

"No tonight is her night off."

"Okay thanks."

Wilber had just seen April at the front desk of the Hotel as he left to drive over to SBC where he was going to give Karen one of his business cards so she could contact him.

Wilber walked up to the cute blonde who by now figured out who he was. "Hello April."

"Good evening Mr. O'Toole, how can I help you?" "Karen said you are her best friend."

"That's probably true."

"This might seem kind of awkward, but I forgot to get her phone number, would it be possible for you to contact her and give her my phone number and ask her to please call me?"

There were no secrets between April and Karen. April knew Karen had slept with Wilber and was touched by his request.

"I would be delighted."

Wilber handed April his business card with contact information on it and went up to his room.

Within five minutes his cell phone rang, it was Karen. "Wilber, April said you wanted me to call you."

"Yes, I assumed you would be working tonight and when you were not there, I wanted to get ahold of you and ask you out for dinner."

"That's sweet of you. What do you have in mind?"

"I have an old friend down in Santa Barbara and I've known him and his wife for quite some time. I want to have dinner with them and introduce you."

"Well sure, I'm not dressed or anything, but give me a while and I can get ready."

Alright call me when you are ready."

"I will, Wilber. And thank you for inviting me to dinner, it means a lot to me. I really do like you."

"You may not believe this, but I think I like you more."

"Don't be ridiculous, you can't possibly like me more than I like you."

"We'll have to trade kisses soon to find out." "I definitely want to do that."

***

Chapter Eighteen

Dinner With Grady

After the conversation, Wilber called Grady to ask him and his wife to go to dinner with him to meet his new girlfriend.

Grady was quite surprised because Wilber didn't have many girlfriends and the few, he did have he kept to himself and never discussed them. He wanted to go to check her out and find out what kind of a woman she was because if Wilber is taking her to dinner and introducing her to his best friends, that means she must be extra special.

When Karen called back, in exchange she gave Wilber her address and he drove over there and picked her up and then drove down to Santa Barbara and picked up Grady and his wife and drove to the Warf to the Shellfish Company restaurant.

Karen looked very pretty and dressed to impress. Wilber's little head was quickly saluting thinking about the amorous activity they would probably engage in later that evening.

When Grady and his wife got into Wilber's rent a car, they could tell quickly there was love in the air with this exotically beautiful woman who would make movie stars like Emily Blunt, Florence Pugh, and Sofia Vergara appreciate Wilber for his fine taste in women because Karen looked just as pretty, they could be made up for a movie shoot.

Grady's wife Darlene was happy that Wilber selected such a fine woman. During the dinner women are nosey. Wilber already secretly knew her life story because he had the file on his cell phone with lots of pictures and links to check out such as all her Facebook posts.

Wilber felt relieved he wasn't stepping into a tar baby which could happen with almost any woman. Everyone has issues including men.

Wilber had to tap on his wife's foot to signal her to stop asking so many questions. But the good news was she got Karen to discuss her education and certain life events and her family.

Wilber was grateful to Grady's wife Darlene because her questions and Karen's answers validated the private detective report, exclusively.

Nevertheless, Karen felt kind of awkward because she knew very little about Wilber. He had not really exposed himself.

Grady's wife Darlene then said, "Let me give you my phone number and if you ever have issues with Wilber, contact me. He's afraid of me so you can assume I'm like the Sheriff and will deal with him harshly if he ever does you wrong."

Grady's wife then handed Karen her business card. Grady's wife Darlene was a real estate agent.

After dinner, Grady's wife Darlene insisted Wilber and Karen come into their

home for coffee and a little music in the background. The coffee stop turned out to be quite reassuring to Karen who was now starting to feel reality unfold that Wilber truly was interested in her to the point he just exposed his best friends and they lived nearby. If she and Wilber became a couple there would be a support structure and family friends to help in times of crisis if they ever occurred,

Time slipped by that evening and Wilber didn't care, the KH-15 launch was not scheduled until the next evening, so he could sleep in late and check his emails later.

Finally, the coffee stop was over, and it was a relatively short drive up to Lompoc and when Wilber pulled up next to Karen's condo she said, "Wilber I think we are getting closer and I do need to protect my reputation. It would be better if you come into my condo to make love to me than to go back to your hotel plus it will save you an extra trip."

"Sure, that works for me."

Wilber knew he had a wet spot in his underwear, Karen had significantly influenced his little head. But she also knew she was very moist and ready to transcend into celestial pleasures.

Wilber knew this was all unplanned and Karen didn't clean her home for him. She was the type of person who liked to have things put away properly, no dirty dishes or stuff laying around. Her condo was nice and clean, smelled fresh, and had a lot of pictures and paintings.

Looking around Wilber could see Karen was a cultured woman and the number of books she had in a bookcase clearly showed she read serious works and didn't dwell on political nonsense.

Karen was well rounded, and Wilber knew all about her academic success because he had her dossier. Wilber was a little surprised Karen chose to be a bar tender over being an economist with her credentials. When they eventually discussed this, Wilber quickly discovered the logical reason. Karen would have to live in a city to be a fulltime economist for a corporation.

Karen made enough money as a bartender to pay for all her needs. Karen was fully independent and because she was an economist knew vividly how and where to invest her money and make it grow. She could in fact be Wilber's future certified financial planner he needed.

Karen's bedroom was totally delightful. It was far better than staying in a hotel. Wilber also knew one thing he should have thought about before now. He didn't use protection and it was possible he could get Karen pregnant. But he didn't mind because something told him she would probably be happy to marry him if that happened. He sensed she was in love with him and in fact she was. No man had ever touched her heart so spontaneously.

The love making began and nobody had to get up early to protect reputations. They fell asleep in each other's arms after splendid euphoria developed when their brains created tri-dimensional ensembles from the pleasure centers of their brains.

At the same time all this was unfolding, Xinxin was slowly decaying. Her love for Wilber had been strong and until the two Azzie dudes freaked her out, she was on a pathway to a permanent relationship with Wilber. Had she just made one phone call

this week, she could have salvaged it. But since she didn't it was now lost forever. Wilber would never be coming back to her.

Wilber's emotions for Xinxin were quickly evaporating and Karen now created a new chapter in his life that gave Wilber great satisfaction. Xinxin had no idea what she lost until months afterwards. Then the roles were reversed.

Xinxin finally got the nerve up to call and text Wilber, but he never responded. It was a bitter moment for her when she realized what she lost. She had no desire to find out what happened because she feared she would discover Wilber had found another lover and the way she crushed his heart the way she left him meant he was susceptible to find the love of another woman. Wilber had never failed to answer or return her calls before now. She knew what had happened. It was a sorrowful day.

The next day, after the two lovebirds woke up, Karen made breakfast for them and fresh coffee that hit the spot. It was past mid-morning when Wilber left Karen's condo as she was going to have to get ready to go to work.

It would be a cheerful day for Karen to know she had a legitimate lover. Wilber said some very sweet things to her during the night in ways few men could express that way. It was sincere, direct, and fully non- ambiguous. It was time for their worlds to obtain the same orbit. Karen knew for a fact a covalent bond between Wilber and her was forming.

Wilber drove back to his hotel, took a shower and changed into his suit and was about ready to leave when the hotel maids showed up to clean his room. The timing once again was perfect.

The launch pad had been cleaned out and the launch team was in the process of moving Colonel Baker's trailer past the green line. Wilber could see fueling of the space craft was in progress and security men were at the blue line to prevent access. They did not have the time to deal with a blue line violation and were in their launch window and barring weather, the bird was ready to fly.

The KH-15 was snugly mounted inside the space capsule that would deploy it. Everything was done automatically with onboard processors. Once the launch supervisor pressed the standby, then launch buttons, the rocket's internal computers would then be given all the authority to complete the launch with all the instructions given to it such as where in space to deploy the KH-15 using all navigation coefficients preloaded to obtain the orbit desired for initial ISR.

Colonel Baker didn't have much time to talk to Wilber, Buster, or Brewster. Wilber understood he was a busy man and asked, "What time have you set for T-0?"

"Right now, it's 18:30 and barring any launch delays will fly then."
"Alright Colonel, good luck."

"Thanks."

There wasn't much that Buster and Brewster were going to do so they went back to their hotel rooms to check their email and relax for the big show. They would return to the base and be at the prefabricated launch blockhouse by 18:00.

By 18:00 Wilber was walking into the SBC to enjoy the company of Karen the Aquarian. Karen was wearing a dark pink top with a black dress, and she had dark pink eye shadow on the lower half of her eye lids designed so skillfully that Hollywood

would be proud. Wilber thought she remarkably looked like the famous Russian singer Alla Yurievna Perfilova (aka Valeriya) when she performed with Bel Suono the triple piano fantastic performers.

Karen was in for a big surprise. Wilber was so touched by Karen, on his way to his hotel room earlier today, he stopped by Lompoc Jewelers and purchased a ring he thought would fit her and a matching necklace.

Wilber had the jeweler put the ring and necklace boxes in a nice design gift bag with handles and then went to another store and purchased a romance card to go with the gift that had an image of "The Kiss." This image was an original oil on canvas painted in 1908 by Gustav Klimt.

Wilber thought if this didn't convey his emotions to Karen, then nothing would. But being an intelligent woman, Wilber knew Karen would most like respond favorably to it.

Inside the envelope with the romance card, Wilber had a copy of his business card, and he did something very dangerous the agency would advise him never to do. He put his home address on the back and on the front, he wrote: "see back."

The Maître d was all smiles because Karen informed her how wonderful Wilber was. She noticed Wilber was carrying a gift bag and would make sure she observed that transaction.

Karen had her back to the bar stools when Wilber glided in and sat down in the middle of all of them. Karen suddenly saw Wilber's image in the bar mirror and turned around and greeted him.

"Hello Wilber. I'm very glad you came here tonight." "So am I."

"I had a wonderful time yesterday and today I called Anna (Wilber's wife) and had a great conversation. You have really great friends."

"Yes, Grady is the best friend a person can have."

"Say Karen there was something I should have done earlier, but I just didn't have time before we went to dinner yesterday. But I took care of it today."

"What's that Wilber."

"Karen, you touched my heart deeply. I've never needed someone so badly in all my life right now. I've gone through a lot and one day I will disclose all that to you. But for tonight, I have something for you that I hope conveys my feelings for you."

Wilber then raised the gift bag and handed it to Karen and said, "I have a little gift for you."

The Solvang Brewing Company Maître d was spying on the couple and heard everything Wilber said then she turned around and saw the transaction.

Karen looked down inside the gift bag and her eyes started watering. She knew it was probably something special, and it touched her like nothing in her life before. She pulled out the smaller box and just as she figured it was a diamond ring. The tears started coming down. She carefully pulled the ring out of the box and slid it on her finger, and it fit perfectly. The crocodile tears were starting to form. Then she picked up the other box and opened it and saw the diamond necklace.

Wilber had spent a small fortune. He didn't care, he could be dead tomorrow.

With the crocodile tears starting, Karen walked around the end of the bar and out to where Wilber was sitting and asked, "Could you help me put this on?"

Wilber put on the necklace for Karen and said, "There you go Karen."

The Maître d could see all those tears and she had a few too. Wilber was full of surprises!

Karen turned around and threw her arms around Wilber and had a romantic sweet, lovely sob. This was one of the best days of Karen's life. But there was more to come. After Karen got control of her emotions she walked back behind the bar and pulled the romance card out and opened it up and saw Wilber's business card with the words, "see back."

Karen flipped the business card around and saw Wilber's home address. This was the real deal. Karen felt lightheaded and wondered if she should faint.

Karen didn't know what to say. Just when she thought her tears were going to dry up, the business card and the romance card took her to the extremes again. A couple customers came to the bar and sat down and were taking it all in, a guy and his wife. They respectfully gave Karen the time she needed. They knew this was a special moment.

Karen grabbed a paper towel she had on a roller to dabble up spills and dabbed her eyes to get all the tears dried up and regained her composure and said to the couple, "I'm very sorry for the delay."

The woman full of empathy was very sensitive said, "That's alright honey, we understand."

Karen quickly provided the couple with their drinks and was now smiling in full blossom. She took the business card and put it in her purse that was nearby and set the gift bag down next to her purse.

Karen then informed the couple, "This is my boyfriend Wilber and the reason why I was the way a little while ago is he just gave me this ring and necklace."

"I would have done the same thing honey," the sweet older lady said. "Thank you for understanding."

"No problem dear."

The woman sitting two bar stools down from Wilber said, "My name is Margaritta, and this is my special love, Albert."

"Please to meet you," Wilber said. "Same to you," Albert responded.

"Do you live in Lompoc?" Margaritta asked. "No, I live in Washington DC."

"What are you doing all the way out here? Visiting your girlfriend?" "At 6:30 P.M.

I will invite outside to see what I do for a living."

"Is it safe to go outside with you?"

"Sure, Karen our bartender will be going with us. But we should go outside around 6:28 to be in position to see it."

Margaritta didn't get it, but Albert husband was smiling. He understood.

Before Wilber could request a drink, Karen had one in front of him that she knew he liked.

Margaritta said, "Karen that is a beautiful ring." "Wilber here is far more beautiful than my ring." "You must like each other," Margaritta said. "Karen cast a magic spell on me." Wilber said.

"And Wilber cast a very powerful magic spell on me," Karen

responded.

Wilber finished his beer and was drinking his second when he looked at the time and said, "We need to go outside now to watch it."

Karen came out from behind the bar, grabbed Wilber's hand and led him out the side entrance that was used by smokers to go out to the smoking area. Margaritta and Albert followed behind.

Two minutes later the ULA launch of the KH-15 happened, and the rocket blasted off into space. KH-15 is a heavy satellite, so the rocket had 2 large boosters the same size as the two space shuttle boosters. Even though the rocket was some distance away, the combination of the three rocket engines gave off enough sound to where they could hear it though it was delayed due to the distance and speed of sound in air.

At about a minute and a half the two booster rockets separated and flew off at angles where they would eventually be flown back to a recovery area. The main booster cutoff happened several minutes later and by now the rocket was traveling at 22,000 miles per hour getting further lift out of the second stage rocket engine.

During this launch, just before reaching the main booster cutoff, the ULA rocket was reaching max Q. The max Q is the maximum dynamic pressure, condition at the point when an aerospace vehicle's atmospheric flight reaches the maximum difference between the fluid dynamics total pressure and the ambient static pressure. This is important because this is the point where forces that could cause the rocket to tip over are the greatest.

After the rocket reaches max Q the forces that would tip it over start declining meaning more control of the rocket begins with a less likelihood of tipping it over and possibly tumbling.

After Max-Q, the force decreases quickly, and the engineers sweat pumps turn to slow speed and they can relax a bit.

"So, you are a rocket guy?" Margaritta asked? "Yes, I have a lot of rocket experience."

"It looks like it's up there, we might as well go back inside," Wilber said.

This was a happy night at SBC.

At 7:15 P.M. Buster and Brewster came into SBC all smiling. "Hello Wilber."

"How are you guys doing?"

"Could not be better, on our way driving here, our boss called

Brewster, I was driving and gave a report the Bird was in place and the cargo was exactly where we wanted to put it and post launch diagnostics indicate no faults. We are already receiving good telemetry of what we are now looking at." "Good to know."

"By the way Wilber, Colonel Baker had a lot of good things to say about you to the General today that made a surprise visit and some Civilians who you probably know."

"Was one of them a guy named John?"

"Yes, it was. I understand you will be meeting them in the morning." "That's affirmative."

"I'm so happy I might have to ask Karen out on a date," Buster said.

Karen heard the comment and said, "I'm sorry, but I'm taken now." She then held out her hand showing an expensive ring. Buster also noticed she had a nice necklace on.

"Who's the lucky son of a bitch?" Buster asked.

"You are sitting next to him," Karen replied and smiled.

"Is this for real?" Buster who had been chasing Karen's skirt for two years asked.

"It certainly is."

"What so special about him?"

"When he taught me how to be naughty with SDHNC, I fell for him." "What the hell is SDHNC?"

"With you being a road warrior, why do not know that acronym?" Karen asked.

Brewster busted out laughing. He got it.

"That's a nice-looking ring, I bet it's expensive," Margaritta said.

Wilber said nothing. He knew love was precious and he had Karen's dossier, she had no idea how much he knew about her. He didn't stumble into this blindly. He kindly reflected how wonderful it would have been to put that ring on Faye Wong or Xinxin Lin. But that's how life is. Life events will throw you a curve all the time.

Wilber, Buster, and Brewster all had something to cheer about. Wilber knew the obvious. Buster and Brewster were unsung heroes. It takes a butt ton of effort to deploy a spy satellite traveling 25,000 miles above the planet to avoid getting hit by a Russian Cosmos 2547 satellite killer.

But he also appreciated these guys giving him heads up that Colonel Baker said nice things about him.

The die was cast. Tomorrow the meeting would change Wilber's life forever. He had no idea how abruptly his whole life would change. The tectonics plates in his life were shifting very soon.

"Karen, please let me order these guys a round of drinks and also for Margarette and Albert."

"No problem honey."

Buster was totally astonished watching all this unfold.

Just after the drinks were served with great efficiency, Colonel Baker walked through the door with John and Brent following behind in street clothes.

Colonel Baker was all smiles. He had just received reports directly from his sponsors in the Pentagon that NRO's KH-15 was functioning perfectly with no faults detected (NFD).

Because of how the bar seating was now, Wilber slid one to the right next to Margaritta and Albert. Colonel Baker slid into the bar stool Wilber moved out of. John asked Buster and Brewster, "Could you guys move down a couple chairs se we can sit next to Colonel Baker?"

"No problem, John," Buster said as if they knew each other well."

Soon they were all lined up with drinks and suddenly bar food started arriving in front of all of them.

"Where did this come from?" Brester asked.

"Your friend Wilber wanted to treat you," Karen lied. She paid for it.

Wilber had that funny look on his face and Karen winked at him to signal, "It's okay honey."

About that time Brent received a text message from the Admiral on the Joint chiefs saying, "We have already received the benefit of today's launch. It's because of you this all happened. You have no idea how many lives you saved today. Your astute judgement that allowed this mission to happen. We do appreciate you."

"My pleasure, but the real hero is Wilber O'Toole who convinced me your project should have priority," Brent texted back.

"Tell Wilber, next time he's in DC, I want to buy him a beer," The admiral texted.

"Nothing better than a beer from an Admiral," Brent replied.

Wilber was luckier than the rest. He was glad he had a two-hour nap today before coming to the SBC. The other men were slowly petering out and after 3 or 4 beers, they slowly eased out and soon it was just Wilber facing Karen.

"It's 10:30 and the place looks dead, I'm going to go tell Silvia I'm leaving early, would you mind coming to my Condo?"

"Not at all."

"How did you get here?"

"I walked I felt I needed the exercise." "Okay give me a minute and we'll leave." "Alright."

The two were soon out the door on their way to Karen's Condo. It was quite an emotional night for them already, but Wilber had been doing some soul searching and as much as he didn't want to do it, he did.

They were soon in bed making love when Wilber decided to do it. There could be no better time under the circumstances when he uttered those important words.

"Karen, I think I'm in love with you."

Karen heard those words loud and clear. The ring and the necklace went a long way to demonstrate Wilber was not BSing her for a piece of ass. A few days later after Wilber left, she had the jewelry appraised and insured and her jaw dropped when she discovered the value. It was totally unbelievable. Wilber had spent some real money

on it. Most brides never get a ring, or a necklace half of this value and they were not even married!"

Those words turned Karen on so much she wrapped her legs around Wilber and bucked him like a bitch in heat. And in just a moment she developed a super orgasm. Many women never experience that in their lifetimes. It's a unique combination of prolactin and serotonin overdose the brain creates, flooding the pleasure center of the brain. It's all in the brain, and not in the vagina as many people think.

Not only was Karen in a temporal psychologically altered state, so was Wilber. All his wounds from Faye and Xinxin were healed. Karen provided the magic band aide that made him whole again and healed the gaping holes in his heart that were now plugged better than a Dutch boy could do preventing a flood.

All Karen could think now as she and Wilber slowly transcended into a post super-orgasmic slumber was, "Where have you been all my life?"

The two did not wake up in the morning until Wilber's phone started ringing. It was John Burkette.

"We are staying in the same hotel as you. We want to meet for breakfast and then go to the meeting."

"I might as well tell you this now, I'm at Karen's condo and it will take me a little to get ready, I'll get there as soon as possible."

"Alright, but you might want to tell her you will not be seeing her for a while, you have a mission to perform."

"Any idea how long it's going to last?"

"It's going to be in phases, and the first one should take one to two weeks." "Alright. I'm getting ready, see you soon." "Is that work?" Karen asked.

"Unfortunately, it is. Would it be possible for us to take a shower and I get ready. I can call a cab if you want."

"That's not necessary honey, I'll take you back to your hotel."

As soon as Wilber got the sticky love residue washed off and felt clean, he was dressed and Karen was not far behind.

As they were leaving, Wilber said, "I may have to depart today. I'm not sure how long I will be gone, but at least one week or two. You know how to reach me. I'm yours now so don't panic if I'm gone a while."

"I like those words, 'I'm yours's now.' I can wait for you. I've waited all my life to find you. Another week doesn't mean anything."

"You have got a great attitude. That will help us deal with my radical schedules at time."

They hopped in Karens car and soon Wilber was back at his hotel walking into the front entrance where Brent and John patiently sat drinking coffee.

Wilber looked fresh as if he didn't need to change so the other two men stood up and said, "We know where a nice breakfast place is, we'll go there." "Do you want me to drive?" Wilber asked.

"No, I'll do the driving so that you and Brent can talk," John Burkette said.

As they were driving to the restaurant about five miles away, semi secluded and off the beaten path, Brent explained things.

Wilber, you are very valuable to us. We have selected you based on the President's comments and concurrence with the Presidential Finding he recently signed that you will be in a Key Role. More important than anything you have ever done in your lifetime.

"What could be more important than Project Solaris?" "We will get to that during the official meeting." "Alright."

"Now I must tell you a few things and please do not get upset with us. You are now deemed essential. You now get the same protection as John Burkette, and I get. You will be followed all the time until you complete the mission. After that, you may decide to retire and spend time with your new girlfriend. Whatever you decide will be fine by us because you paid the ultimate price."

"When did all this surveillance start?" "Long before you flew in here."

"Okay, I figure the business I'm in, that's understandable."

"Now we are going to tell you something you need to know. You are tracked by NSA Prism system. Anytime you communicate electronically with anyone, your oversight reads whatever you say or send."

"I understand, I'm in an important position, we lose privacy."

"Here's an example. We know you hired Javier to create a dossier on Karen. We read it. We are very happy you had the common sense to do that before you got involved with her."

Wilber was utterly astonished but working for the DD/P nothing should surprise him.

"You actually saved us a lot of trouble because for the NSA boys to do what you did, they would have had to get one hundred permissions and it would take months. You did all of that for us in just a couple days. Your information was vetted independently and it's all factual and good stuff. Javier's a good investigator and he left no stones unturned. We have the full picture on Karen now and we are pleased you stumbled across a nice woman to help you get over the Xinxin business. We also know you took it rather hard when you killed Faye Wong. Few men have ever gone through what you have in a lifetime."

"I feel a lot better now after meeting Karen."

"We understand why. She's a well-educated and quality person. You can't go wrong with her. Because we are worried about the tangential effects if something happened to

Karen, she is also protected."

"Sounds like you guys have everything in order." "We work on it."

The men had their breakfast, relaxing and taking it all in as if nothing earth shattering was in the works. They wanted Wilber to relax because soon he would be at the meeting and told what it was all about.

After they finished their breakfast in calmness and a reflective air, they were back in the rental heading to the Hotel to check out and on the way to Vandenberg where a GS750 was waiting.

One of the CIA men who did protection services for Wilber during the night was there early and informed Tammy that Wilber got lucky."

"What does she look like?"

The security guy pulled out his cell phone and showed Tammy a few of Karen's pictures.

"Oh my God she's beautiful. She makes me look like a dog." "She's definitely eye candy."

"I bet Wilber had gotten over Xinxin by now," Tammy said.

"We had to send plumbers into her home so we could monitor what's going on there. I'm sure last night, he completely forgot about Xinxin."

"They were romping and stomping?"

"They both should be movie stars, they are that good."

"I wish you wouldn't have told me that, now I want Wilber!" "I'm available."

"I'm sorry you are not a hunk like Wilber." "I'll work on it."

"You better get busy because he's way ahead of you." "Well as they say, if it's hard, start early."

Moments later when the rental car pulled up to the Jet and unloaded a few pieces of luggage, Tammy had to put on the poker face. But she was happy her comrade Wilber had his Cinderella. Now if he can ever find her shoe again…

Wilber didn't bother asking where they were going because it was out of his control anyway.

From Vandenberg to Area 51 is a short hop when the pilots are allowed to kick it in the ass. When the DCI was aboard the instructions were kick it in the ass and us get there, he had important business to do.

Wilber had been to Area 51 before and had no problems identifying where he was as they came up on Runway 31 heading Northwest.

***

Chapter Nineteen

TR - 4 Check Ride

The GS750 landed and was directed to a hanger where it was towed in with a tug/ tractor. This was a large hanger that three jets could fit in. There was another jet painted black inside the hanger. Wilber had never seen this type of jet before

that looked aero dynamically very sleek.

"What's this?" Wilber asked. "That's a TR-4." The DCI stated.

"Where are we going to have the meeting?" Wilber asked. "Inside the TR-4" the DD/P John Burkette responded.

The three men stepped inside the TR-4 from a special ladder allowing access.

Wilber was quite amazed at the looks internally as it looked very modern.

While the tree men were inside the door was shut so their meeting could be ultra secret.

"By now you probably have a lot of questions Wilber." "I imagine I do."

"The President just gave you the chance of a lifetime." "What's that?"

"You will command the mission to Saturn."

"As in actually traveling to Saturn on a spacecraft." "That's correct."

"Isn't that foolish until we find out how the Aliens will receive us?"

We believe you will be safe as long as you do not fly over the Aliens. You will land a long distance away and be protected by not flying near what is probably a submerged

City."

"How long will the mission last?"

"We expect three months. You will go there, assemble the submarine with some special robotic help then go submerge and travel submerged and find the cities and do an assessment and any ISR you can obtain then come back?"

"Just like that?" "Yes, just like that."

"May I ask why we are in this aircraft vice a SKIF?"

"We want you to experience space flight. In a few minutes you will be leaving with a couple air force officers who will fly you out into space so you can get a feel for it."

"How am I going to explain this to Karen. I don't want to lose her like Faye and Xinxin."

"There was nothing in your power to save Faye. She made a fundamental blunder of trying to kill a CIA agent and paid for it with her life. She didn't love you; she was a good actor and repeatedly lied to you. We have some videos of Faye we never

showed you until now because we felt it would not help your personal psychology if you saw it.

If you want when you get back from Saturn, we'll show you video that will convince you that Faye was an evil person who did all the romance to set you up so she could kill you from orders by her masters. Fay was well paid. She was going to Earn $10 million USD by killing you. She had no feelings for you, but she never thought that you could defend yourself as well as you did.

"I don't need to see the videos. I take your word for it all."

"We are going to open the door now so the pilots can come aboard, and we'll introduce you." "Thanks."

After the door was opened, John Burke signaled to the two pilots waiting to come aboard the TR-4.

The pilots in their flight suits came aboard and were introduced. "Wilber this is Major Barnes, and Major Schmidt.

"Glad to meet you. No space suits?" "Space suits are not required."

Moments later, Brent and John exited the TR-4 and the door was shut and secured making the TR-4 ready to take off.

"Go ahead and buckle yourself into this mission specialist seat. You will soon be able to see outside the craft with these live video display monitors."

"Sure thing," Wilber responded, sad down and plugged in his seat belt and shoulder harness while the pilot and copilot took their seats and fastened their shoulder and seat belts.

Wilber was in for a big surprise. There was no noise.

The craft was pulled out of the hanger by a Tug/Tractor.

In the seat Wilber was sitting at, he had the same video displays as the two pilots. It looked like he was looking outside, but those were camera videos on flat screens. The TR-4 had no windows. The front of the craft was a heat shield.

The TR-4 slowly went vertical and spun around 90 degrees now about 100 feet into the air as it slowly traversed down a ramp then turned on runway 31 heading Northwest.

Wilber could see they were gathering speed at an astonishing rate but felt no vibrations. At the end of runway 31, the TR-4 went up vertical increasing speed as it climbed. Wilber felt no vibrations or sound and the craft soon was on the edge of space and he could see the curvature of Earth. Soon it was getting dark, but Wilber could feel gravity as if he were on Earth.

Looking at all the indicators, Wilber could see the velocity in space. It did not take long before they were traveling at 300,000 miles per hour.

Commander Barnes then surprised Wilber and said, "We are going to use the moon to fling us out in space and speed up.

Wilber saw speed was increasing and the moon dead ahead was getting larger. Fifteen minutes later Wilber observed the speed was now 650,000 miles per hour. It was all surreal to Wilber as this all unfolded.

Now the moon was steadily growing noticeably. In another fifteen minutes, the

TR-4 reached one million miles per hour. To Wilber it almost seemed insane. Within 12 hours he had made love to Karen and was now traveling at one million miles per hour. Now the moon grew in size quicker but seemed to shift to the side because the pilots were going to pass by it at a specific course using the moon's gravity to increase velocity. Eventually it was apparent they were right up on the moon slowly curving towards it.

Major Barnes said, "Not to worry Wilber we will pass five miles from the surface of the moon, here's your chance to see the dark side of the moon the public rarely gets to see."

In another ten minutes the TR-4 was 5 miles above the surface of the moon and curving, but centrifugal force kept it from crashing on the moon.

The calculations were fine-tuned, and the pilots applied maximum propulsion at the right moment and the TR-4 quickly left the moon behind traveling at 1.5 million miles per hour heading for a dot out in space in front of them that appeared to possibly be a star and the speed was increasing and in a few more minutes had sped up to three million miles per hour.

The speed kept climbing and, in an hour, they were cranking along at 80 million miles per hour. Wilber was extremely amazed. He had no idea any of this existed. It was such an exclusive secret space force project. The TR-4 looked a lot like the TR-3B except TR-4 is a planet hopper. Wilber was thinking, maybe this could play into the Saturn mission, especially an emergency extraction.

The TR-4 could be staged in the event such a situation happened. But also, if hostilities started, they could deliver hydrogen bombs come in low skimming over the top of the surface by a few hundred feet and drop the eggs where they needed to neutralize the enemy if it came to such a thing.

The white dot in front of them started growing and in an hour, it was clearly orange in color. It had to be Mars!

Wilber had looked at a lot of pictures of Mars and the great canyon that goes across the equator region is a good identifier. He knew at the velocity they were traveling and the growth in size of the object in front of them in the span of 15 minutes that great canyon should be apparent more spectacular because the planet was rotating at almost a 24-hour period like Earth, Olympus Mons was suddenly coming into view.

Wilber could not hold it back any further. "Major Barnes is that Olympus Mons on the side of the Mars image?"

"Wilber, yes, it is."

Wilber now knew there was call to duty, but this TR-4 might make his trip to Saturn a lot more palatable because he can see this might be a way to get the hell off the planet if bad things happen.

"Wilber, we don't want you to get scared, but we are going to fly by Mars very closely?"

"Not to worry, if you knew how close I came to getting killed in the past, I'm ready if it happens."

"Good philosophy."

It was the most surreal experience Wilber could imagine the Grand Canyon of Mars clearer than he ever saw before. They were coming in fast now and close. Very close. The pilots knew what they were doing. They had trained this in simulator often, they knew what to do like the back of their hand.

The TR-4 got so close to the planet it was only one mile above Olympus Mons passing along the port side of the spacecraft.

Unlike before the TR-4 banked heavily and was now almost upside down compared to the planet and the pilots had maximum gravity applied to the gravity machine a few feet below them in the structure of the spacecraft. The positive gravity pulled the TR-4 in a direction pulling closer to the planet so that they could use the planet to help turn them around without bleeding off too much speed.

Minute by minute traveling at a reduce speed due to the magnetic and gravity breaking caused by the planet, by the time the TR-4 changed its attitude from a bank to what someone on relate to as straight and level flying the velocity was 75 million miles per hour, now heading for another white dot in the sky. Wilber didn't know it, but he was heading home, pointing to earth.

"Wilber is your safety harness nice and tight?" Major Barnes asked. "Yes, it is."

"Keep it that way until we get home." "Certainly."

The speed increased to 100 million miles per hour. The pilots were also executing a high speed test run on the TR-4. This flight had multiple purposes. Wilber had no idea the severely hazardous situation he was in. It seemed all harmless and well designed. But unfortunately, Wilber didn't know all the dirty little secrets and under certain circumstances he could soon be part of a fire ball and his life extinguished promptly.

At 100 million miles per hour Earth came up quickly then the bad news came up.

"Wilber we are going to be slowing soon. It will be painful for about 15 minutes, but if you want to return to Earth alive, it's how we must do it."

"Do what you have to do, I'm along for the ride," Wilber replied.

When the TR-4 was about 100,000 miles from Earth the breaking started. This was another test of the spacecraft Wilber should be glad he had no knowledge of the complications ahead of time. The pilots knew their odds, but they also knew from their special briefing Wilber wasn't a Chickenshit, he was a Cowboy like them. They were proud to die with Wilber if it came to that.

Just like they promised the breaking physiology sucked really bad. But Wilber wasn't going to pussy out like office warriors would, he was going to take it. His great physical condition helped out quite a bit as the TR-4 went into orbit at 30,000 miles breaking and slowing and using 100% positive gravity fields to suck the TR-4 towards planet. Wilber was watching the speed bleed off as well as the distance to Earth shrinking.

Slowly the breaking paid reduced and sum of the terrible feeling lasted 15 minutes and Wilber was drenched in sweat.

After two orbits the TR-4 had slowed to 20,000 miles per hour and continued to decrease.

"Alright Wilber we are going down on the planet now. If we do not make it, I

just wanted you to know it was a pleasure flying with a national hero today. I hope you make it because this country needs you," Major Barnes said.

"Don't worry we'll make it, just think positive," Wilber responded. "I like your attitude."

"I'll tell you a Cowboy story after we land." "Looking forward to it."

Wilber suspected they were going down because it seemed the TR-4 was hotter than hell suddenly. Wilber didn't know it, but the internal temperature reached 150 degrees for a few minutes until the HVAC system was able to remove some of the heat and in five minutes was back to 120 degrees, but it still was hot. But the most important thing was it appeared they made it as they were now over a big ocean.

"Hey Wilber see those small Island on the display?" "Yes, what are they?"

"Those are the Hawaiian Islands."

The TR-4 continued to reduce altitude. And in a brief period, they flew over Point Magu on their way to Area 51. The Altitude was now down to commercial airliner speeds as they slowly went lower, and Wilber could see Las Vegas on the monitor as they curved up to Area 51 following what was probably Hiway 93 for a while.

Soon Groom Lake was ahead of them and in a short period Wilber saw the 17,000-foot-long Runway he was familiar with.

The TR-4 did not land. It followed Runway 31 and slowed down to a crawl and shifted over in front of a hanger and lowered down to ground level right in front of the hanger. A tug/tractor then latched onto the TR-4 and took it into the hanger.

"How was the ride, Wilber?" Major Barnes asked.

"It was an eye opener, but I'm kind of sweaty," Wilber replied.

"So are we. Do you want to know how many times you came close to dying?" "I'm alive so that doesn't matter."

"I wish more people had your attitude Wilber," Major Barnes said. "Thanks."

"Now tell us that Cowboy story."

Wilber then told them about Faye Wong, leaving out most of the details.

"You really killed her?"

"Deader than a doorbell."

"No remorse?"

"When the lab reports came back her knife blade was covered with Ricin, I quickly lost all remorse."

About that time ground support opened the door and the three men exited.

A general and a couple colonels, Brent and John were waiting.

Major Barnes knew they had to go to a debrief and discuss all the technical details, but since he was with this distinguished spy who would likely put his life on

the line and proved to them during the flight, he was not chickenshit, walked up to the General who was standing next to Brent and John and said, "General can I ask you for a favor?"

"Sure Barnes, you earned quite a few favors actually."

"You have no idea how much I appreciate Wilber. I want to take him over to the canteen and buy him a beer."

"The DCI quickly jumped in and said," General we can delay all the debriefings, I second Major Barnes request."

John Burkette who the General worked with quite a bit in the past in his role as DD/P also stated, "General please delay the debrief because I want to buy Major Barnes and Major Schmidt a beer for exemplary support for the CIA."

The general smiled and turned to the two Colonels and said, "Give your data reduction people until tomorrow morning to prepare all the data files for the debrief and critique tomorrow around 9:00 A.M. to give everyone a chance to rest from this arduous mission."

The two Colonels who were always pissed off the Data Reduction people were forced to jump through their asses all the time to create all the eye candy required for the reports supported the notion and one of them said, "General with your permission

I would also like to buy Wilber a beer."

"Alright, us all go over to the Canteen, do we have enough transportation?"

"Yes General, plenty." "Alright let's go!"

On the way to the Canteen the Colonel in charge of the data reduction team notified them, "The debrief has been delayed to 9:00 tomorrow. Put on a skeleton crew to get it done tonight and they can have tomorrow off after the debrief. I'll give them 48 hours so they can go to Las Vegas or Alamo

Nevada to the dude range. Everyone else, I want to invite you to the Canteen to meet our distinguished passenger on the flight."

Moments later the Colonel got a text back: "Colonel, you made the men very happy. This is great news, and we promise you will have great presentations. I personally will stay here and work with the data reduction people to make sure your presentation shines."

"Thank you very much," the General texted back to the head of the DR-BATS (known as data reduction bats because they hang from the overhead getting those reports out)."

From the hanger to the Canteen took about five minutes.

The men all walked into the Canteen and the Irish lady Olivia with very nice breast geometries was there to take their orders and tease them a bit if they needed. She was a fixture at Area 51 running the canteen where men could get coffee or beers when their shifts were over. She was also part of the security apparatus. Operating the canteen was part of her cover. She and the cook were spooks and kept an ear to people divulging SCI information with loose lips.

With Olivia's approval and guidance, they pulled together four tables so the rowdy men could drink beers and relax.

With pitchers of beers and pizzas on the way, the bravado started in. None of these Air Force people had been in the canteen with beers and pizzas on the way with the DCI, DD/P, and a top manager of Project Solaris which they had no idea existed.

The general knew more about what went on than anyone else in the room. The three heroes came close to dying fifteen times. It truly was a miracle they came back alive.

As bad as it might has seemed, Wilber's approach was, he didn't care about "almost." More important is he now knew he had a plausible way home if Project Solaris let him down.

Wilber was enjoying his beer when a pizza was shoved in front of him. Wilber liked Tabasco sauce on his pizza's and saw on a few tables behind him there were Tabasco sauces bottles.

Across from Wilber was an Air Force Officer with a name tag on by the name of West.

"Mr. West can you grab a few of those tabasco bottles behind you for our table?" "Sure, no problem."

All the people attending this impromptu party had a lot of beer and pizza which created great satisfaction. Then about two hours later, John Burkette mentioned to Wilber, "We are going to leave in a few minutes and fly down to Las Vegas to spend the night."

"Alright," Wilber said.

Wilber then stood up and walked over to Major Schmidt and held out his hand and said, "Thanks for the ride."

"My pleasure, glad it all worked out."

"More than what I could ever conceive. But I'm going to tell you this bird we flew in today will probably become part of my future plans."

"Glad to know that. It means more support for the program."

"This little ride today will have a huge impact on implementation. There are some ideas I have I'll soon address with the DCI and the DD/P."

"Good to know."

"You will be seeing me again." "Great."

Wilber then approached Major Barnes and they had a similar discussion.

John Burkette was soon standing by Wilber who knew it was time to leave and they exited the canteen and hopped in a waiting SUV that took them over near the hanger they were at and boarded the GS750 and flew down to Las Vegas.

The crew locked down the aircraft and a couple of SUVs pulled up to the jet the crew and passengers got into that drove them to Ceasars Palace where they would spend the night. The price of their rooms was way above their per diem rate and the DCI said when their travel claims were processed, he would approve the added expenditure above per diem rate due to last minute turn on for the trip, which happens in the CIA often.

After Wilber got to his room, he called Karen to check in."

"Hello Karen."

"Hi Wilber thank you for calling."

"My pleasure."

"I had a couple visitors today before I went to work today?"

"Oh really."

"Now I know how important you are." "What was the visit about?"

"One was a pretty lady from the FBI, the other was a nice lady that works for your agency."

"What did they tell you?"

"After they explained how important you are, they said they had to protect you in all aspects."

"That's how it is."

"They also said because of my relationship with you there will always be someone watching me in case I run into danger."

"I see."

"I've already discovered the surveillance."

"I'm sorry to put you in this position."

"I'm glad you did."

"Why is that."

"They informed me what I already know."

"And that is?"

"You are in love with me."

"And I am happy that I am."

The conversation continued for a while longer, but Karen was at work and said she had to get back to work.

Wilber had just finished up with a conversation with Karen. He knew not to mention his space travel and assumed Karen's phone line was monitored.

Tammy earlier saw Wilber going into the hotel room next to her room and after she took a shower and changed her clothes into something quite a bit sexier left her room and knocked on Wilber's door. She was going to explain, "What happens in Vegas stays in Vegas," then suggest some horizontal tango on a theme from Paganini.

Wilber saw Tammy through the security panel flat screen standing outside his room. He opened the door.

"May I come in I want to talk to you."

"Sure."

Wilber led Tammy into the room and the door shut automatically behind her.

Tammy had never done this before. In fact, she had never slept with Air Force or CIA people. Nobody she worked with knew of any of her sexual experiences.

Tammy walked over and sat down on the bedside facing the big open area of the room. Wilber sat down in a chair facing her.

"What did you want to talk about?"

Tammy pulled up her dress and said, "I wanted to talk to you about why I'm not wearing panties."

"I see."

"I've been wanting to tag you for a while."

"What does tag mean?"

"Get your dick inside me."

"Tammy, I have some bad news for you."

"What's that Wilber? Erectile dysfunction?"

"As you know, I was just getting over Xinxin recently."

"Yes, I'm aware. I know the story."

"People have big mouths, do they not?"

"Everyone except me. If you give me what I want, the secret is safe with me."

"Tammy, I recently met another woman. I've completely gotten over Xinxin."

"That's nice to know, I can help remove any lingering traces."

"Tammy this may be hard for you to believe, but just as much as I was in love with Xinxin, I feel for this other woman."

"You're in love?"

"Completely."

"So, you are not going to take the free gift of my pussy?"

"Sorry Tammy, your timing is off. Had you come to me two weeks ago, I'd be humping you now."

"You can't blame a girl for trying?"

"Not at all, you are my friend. We've been through a lot together."

"That we have."

"I have a suggestion."

"What's that?"

"Let's go see a show together."

***

"I like that idea."

"I'm dressed and can go as I am," Wilber said.

The following day, Wilber was in for a big surprise, he was driven to Nellis Air Force Base. The General he met at Area 51 was there to greet him and John Burkette.

They were taken into a simulator building.

The General said, "I just got here from the debrief, I'll email you a copy of the video on the high side."

"Thanks," John Burkette replied.

"You are welcome, John."

"Anything of importance?"

"Other than Wilber coming close to dying 14 times, nothing major."

"Does the debrief explain how he almost died; I would like to put him in for a medal."

"It certainly does."

"Was this due to poor oversight?"

"No, things happen in space flight we can't predict like a meteorite or a near catastrophic failure of a critical system."

"What was a near catastrophic failure during the flight?"

"During re-entry when the internal temperature reached 150 degrees, the cooling system froze for a moment. But reset codes the inflight computers issued, got it working again just in time."

"What do you mean just in time?"

"The internal temperature would have hit 300 degrees in a couple minutes. Everyone would have died."

"Do you know what caused the problem?"

"Yes, someone illegally substituted a critical component with one that came from China that was a knockoff part and a down level revision and falsely restamped with a later revision part number."

"How did you figure that out?"

"Intel Corporation gave us a back door into the micro engine inside the CPU and we were able to read the serial number of the chip which is a down level revision part."

"I hope you get all the bugs worked out and Chinese parts identified before it flies again."

"We must recertify all the components onboard the TR-4 as well as the spare parts. It will take a couple more weeks before we finish that inspection and correction."

"Are you ready to show Wilber the simulator?"

"Yes of course."

"Wilber this is the simulator for the Project Solaris Spacecraft that will take you to Saturn."

"You built this simulator just for Project Solaris?"

"No, this simulator runs all types of aircraft. One of the reasons why the control panel on Project Solaris Spacecraft is the same glass as you see on a 787 Dreamliner is we build in commonality."

"What about its computers?"

Project Solaris Spacecraft will use computing and networking technology called Time-Triggered Gigabit Ethernet, which will allow Project Solaris engineers to tag different types of data and priorities for data transmissions through the onboard network.

"Give me an example of Time-critical control data," Wilber said.

"Control data relating to vital the navigation and life support - is classified as time-triggered data."

"What's its main purpose?"

"This protocol will enhance bandwidth by message timing arrive at its destination on time."

"What's the computer hardware like?"

Since space aboard the ship is critical and miniaturization necessary, Taipan Computer Company was contracted to build Integrated Modular Avionics already used on aircraft such as the Boeing 777, will make it easier for Project Solaris Engineers to configure the onboard computing for different tasks between missions.

"I thought there was just one mission to Saturn."

"That's true and after its completed, I was advised by your boss that Project Solaris Team will be re-integrated into Solar Systems Investigations. This class of spacecraft will then conduct visits to other planets."

"Multiple spacecraft?"

"Yes, mainly to get your submarine parts to Saturn in an efficient manner." "I see."

"Let me give you an introduction to the simulator." "Sure."

"You can sit in the copilot seat, and I'll be in the pilots chair describing all my actions."

John Burkette sat in an observer's seat next to console operators operating the simulator. Most of it was automatic, but when they deviated from the training package, those people had to manually override some of the control software to allow the deviation that happened to show cause and effect.

The General knew the super spy was a pilot checked out on 747's and recently flew one into Russia. By lunch he figured out Wilber could easily handle the spaceship, especially since they recommended the entire flight be in autopilot.

Wilber didn't have to worry about Tammy trying to get in the sack with him because she flew back to DC the next day with the GS750.

Wilber was informed he would be spending a couple weeks in the trainers and staying in Las Vegas.

"John, I want to fly Karen to Vegas and spend some time with her in my off hours."

"Sure, no problem."

"Thanks."

Timing was good for Wilber when he called Karen later that day. "Hello, Karen?" "Wilber how are you?"

"I'm really missing you. When is your next day off?" Wilber asked. "Actually tomorrow," Karen replied

"Think you can stretch it into 2 days?" "Sure, why?"

"I'm in Las Vegas now. I'm going to send you some ETICKETS so you can fly here and be with me in my off hours."

"Sure, I can do that."

"Just take a cab or limo from the airport to Ceasars Palace. I'm in room 1702. I'll let the front desk know to give you a key, so you can get in while I'm away." "Alright honey, I'll be coming tomorrow." "Thanks." Wilber suddenly felt a million times better.

John Burkette already knew Karen's itinerary since she was being spied on and knew her E-Ticket had her arriving in Las Vegas around 1:00 P.M.

"Wilber, when is Karen going to visit you?"

"Today, John."

"What time is she arriving?" "1:00 P.M."

"Alright send her a text message we'll pick her up at the airport. I want to reward you for almost dying 14 times in your flight."

"I appreciate that, John."

"You've earned it many times over."

Wilber immediately texted Karen, "I will pick you up at the airport, no need to take a taxi."

"Thank you," Karen texted back sitting in the airport terminal waiting on her plane.

With just John and Wilber the SUV had plenty of room for Karen and her small amount of luggage as they met her in baggage claim. The two love birds were deposited at the hotel room in a short time and Karen, though slightly hungry was far more horny than hungry and soon rewarded Wilber for bringing her to Las Vegas. She had on a nice dress with her diamond necklace and her ring, she seemed ecstatic. Wilber was very glad he passed up Tammy's offer because he had saved up a considerable amount of his essence to give to Karen.

The love making was quite magnificent. Karen felt Wilber giving it to her at that special moment that triggered her own instant and expansive gratification. After laying and relaxing in post-gratification splendid euphoria, Wilber asked, "Are you getting hungry."

"Actually I am."

"Let's take a sprite shower and get dressed and get something to eat."

"Sounds good, but don't try to make love to me in the shower I want to get something to eat first."

"Not a problem, you fully satisfied me."

The two were soon dressed and in 15 minutes at the Top of the Word Restaurant at 800 feet with an incredible view. The food was excellent, and the wine hit the spot. Wilber and Karen were out in front of the restaurant down at street level an hour later deciding their next event.

"Would you like to go see a show?"

"Sure, that sounds like a good idea."

"Let's go see Awakening. My friends tell me it's a fantastic show."

"Sure, that sounds good."

After the spellbinding Awakening show was over, Wilber took them back to the hotel room so they could freshen up. He also called the front desk and had them put Karen as one of the registered guests for the room in case she lost a key or needed assistance while he was away at work the next day.

After they freshened up a bit, they were laying together on the bed with their clothes on and Wilber asked, "Is there anything you want to do now?"

"I kind of just want to stay in the room and hang out with you." "That works for me, want to watch some TV?"

"Sure, but I want to get more comfortable if you don't mind."

"No not at all."

Karen stood up and got out of all her clothes except for her panties. If Wilber wanted access, he could just take them off. When Wilber saw Karen was mostly nude, he followed suit and when Karen saw the wet spot in his underwear, she said, "Take them off, they are just getting in the way."

Wilber then did the same for her and the two were nude but went under the sheets as it was a little cool. Karen didn't know why but she suddenly felt like she needed it again and soon hopped on Wilber and proceeded to prepare them for a transition to a different dimension where the pleasure centers of his brain took control of his utter essence.

Karen wanted to please her man and put forth maximum effort and quickly achieved the results desired. Soon they were sleeping fully satisfied and did not wake up until the morning when Wilber's alarm on his cell phone went off. Wilber got up and Karen was still somewhat in a dream state and not fully awake and resisting waking up as she never felt so good in her life.

Wilber had no choice but to use the toilet and grabbed his underwear and when he finished business put it on. Karen soon followed suit.

Wilber had to get ready to go to work and suggested, "Why don't I order room service for breakfast, and then I'm going to have to leave in a bit." "Works for me," Karen said.

By the time Wilber was showered and dressed, room service arrived. Karen had pastry and Starbucks coffee. Wilber had a Starbucks coffee and a breakfast sandwich

including an egg, sausage, and cheese. Timing was good because no sooner than Wilber finished eating, John Burkette called and said, "I'm taking you to a rental car agency."

"Why is that?"

"I'm leaving for Washington this morning, and you will have to have your own transportation to the trainer."

"You are not sticking around?"

"It was a luxury for me to stay gone this long, my deputy is about to go nuts, I need to get back. You can handle it by yourself. You are scheduled for two more weeks of training."

"Can I take a few days off after I'm done with the trainers?"

"Sure, and I bet I know where you are going. Do me a favor, check in with Colonel Baker while you are there."

"I'll buy him a few craft beers."

"Good plan. I'm down in the lobby by the stairway, see you when you get here." "On my way."

On the way to the rental agency, John Burkette said, "I want you to visit Colonel Baker and get the status of his next KH-15 launch. Spend up to a couple days talking to him. This is an official visit, so purchase your airline tickets, rental car, and hotel room on your government credit card. It will save us money by not flying out the GS750 just to pick you up."

"Understand all. Are you going to the trainer today?" "No, you are on your own. Keep up the good work." "I will."

***

Chapter Twenty

Terror In The Casino

As Wilber was traveling to Nellis Air Force Base to the trainer, Karen was getting ready. Room service tray was outside the door in the hallway, she showered went to her small suitcase to put on another change of clothes and noticed an envelope in it with a nice card from Wilber.

Wilber wrote in the open area of the card, "Dear Karen, if you don't know it by now, I do love you. You mean a lot to me. I'll cut my work short today and try to be back around noon time, and we can go for a little drive. I'll pull up in front of the hotel front entrance and call you when I'm near it."

Also was stuffed $2000.00 with another note. "This is your contribution to the casino. Nobody wins, but you have some cash to throw into slot machines. Please leave the CASINO when the cash is gone."

Karen smiled and put the envelope in her purse and continued dressing.

Soon Karen who was looking very sexy for her man Wilber was down feeding money into a slot machine when one of the lecherous stars on the strip approached her. This well-known performer was well trained on seducing women and getting them in the sack. The performer made a bee line to Karen and started laying on the Charm. Karen knew who the star was and felt flattered he was coming on to her. She was then somewhat shocked when he grabbed her hand and started to lead her away from the one arm bandit.

Nobody was going to stop this jerk tugging Karen along and was a mere 50 feet from the elevator where he would soon be enjoying her with or without her permission. Karen didn't know if she should scream, she was in shock. Kind of like how a lamb acts when a lion has it. Just as the star got her to the elevator, two men in suits stepped in front of him and asked, "Where do you think you are taking the lady."

"It's none of your business."

"Oh yes, I've just made it my business. Then, the agent sucker punched the star who was now bent over in paid. The other man also wearing an ear device grabbed Karen's hand and said, "Karen the Aquarian, we are the good guys to protect you. Go back into the casino and act like nothing happened."

Karen went back to her spot at the slot machine where her purse was left as the man dragged her away. Standing there was Casino security all smiles and said, "Karen, we are very sorry for what just happened. We'll make sure he never gets near you again. Please enjoy your time."

The other two bruisers shoved the performer into the elevator and took him up to the top floor where there are penthouses and a special room, they had for 48 hours to protect their special charge. They took the performer into the room and laid some punches in him and said, "If you ever get near that woman again, we'll help you jump out of a window."

"Fuck you," the man said.

One of the men winked at the other and they grabbed the guy and pulled out onto the balcony and had him half over the railing on his way to his death and screamed, "Please don't do this, I'll stay away from the woman."

The man was in pain, they escorted him to the elevator and sent it down to the first floor where hotel security was in position to escort him outside the front entrance with instructions, "Don't come back for the rest of the week. You picked on the wrong woman."

Most women would have freaked out and gone up to their hotel room and coward, but Karen was a tough girl and after the visit from the two women the other day, she knew she was protected and nothing to worry about and stayed and kept throwing money into the one arm bandit. To her chagrin in about fifteen minutes, she won $50,000.00 and started thinking about those three lovely words Wilber said to her as he left that morning. Karen then left the casino and walked through Ceasars Palace that has a lot of neat shops where you can buy some nice gifts. People who hit the jackpot spent a lot of money in these shops.

What caught Karen's attention was a jewelry store with items for men. She started thinking that since Wilber had turned her world upside down in the most pleasant manner, she would dump the entire $50,000.00 she had just won on a ring for him to show him the feelings were mutual.

She went inside the ship where a very well-dressed man and woman were waiting like sharks. They saw the look on Karen's face and knew they would get a sale. Karen knew the rings were probably jacked up quite a bit in price, but she didn't care because this was all lucky money, and nothing associated with her personal budget.

"Can we help you Madam?"

"Yes, I want to buy my boyfriend a ring."

When the two salespeople saw Karens diamond necklace and her ring, they knew there was real money involved and were suddenly more than cordial. On a hunch they took her to the most expensive rings for men in the store locked up in a security display case with bullet proof glass, but customers could see it.

The price tags on the rings were clearly shown as the salespeople didn't want to waste their time showing rings people could not afford. Right in the middle of all those rings was a very nice one with a price tag of

$45,000.00. It looked better than some of the rings selling for $200,000.00, but it didn't have the same central diamond so that's why it was cheaper, but the design was far more attractive as far as Karen was concerned.

"Do you see one you like?"

"Yes, the one right in the middle."

"The sales team knew the woman had seen the price and was likely a legitimate buyer so the salesman unlocked the display case and pulled out the tray so the woman would pick the correct one and keep it simple."

"Could you point out the one in the middle you want?" "Yes, this one."

"Do you know what size you need?"

"The finger he would wear it on is probably the same size as my middle finger." "Alright us size your finger."

After getting the dimensions on Karen's middle finger the salesman said, "The ring is the correct size if it matches your middle finger. If he needs to have it adjusted,

come back and we can have it adjusted in a couple hours."

"Alright can you put it in a ring box for me?"

"Certainly. May I ask how you will pay for the ring?" the salesman asked.

"Cash," Karen answered.

"We are always delighted to take cash," the salesman said and smiled.

Karen didn't look overly rich, though she was smoking hot and had a nice ring and diamond necklace. The salesman learned a long time ago not to judge people because individuals like Karen came in often doing cash deals the public would never assume had a lot of money, especially women from Oklahoma in blue jeans.

When Karen was cashed out of the Casino, they transferred the

$50,000.00 into her ATM account. Casinos have great interactions with banks make it easy.

"I'm going to use my ATM card to pay for it."

"Same as cash that's good for us. We don't get charged a fee like a credit card."

In a brief period, the transaction was completed, and Karen put the ring box into her purse.

"What does your boyfriend do that makes him able to have such a beautiful woman like you?

"He's a very special man. He works with stuff we put out in space." "Really?"

"Want to see a picture of him."

"The woman salesperson said, "Definitely."

Karen pulled out her cell phone and pulled up a picture Colonel Baker gave her of Wilber standing by the KH-15 of him with Wilber, Buster, and Brewster.

"That looks like some pretty serious stuff."

"That's the second launch he was involved in just the last couple of months."

"What's that rocket?"

"I don't know much about it because I don't care about rockets, but you can see in the picture it's a ULA rocket that was launched a couple weeks ago."

"That's very interesting. Are you guys enjoying some time here in Las Vegas?"

"No, he's here working and will pick me up in about a half an hour and take me on a drive."

"Where's he working?" The saleswoman asked. He's over at Nellis Air Force Base," Karen replied.

The salesman got quite interested in this couple all of a sudden. Having worked at Area-51 in the past himself before he retired and bought into this jewelry store, the salesman's cover story was he worked at Nellis Air Force Base. There was no missile stuff done at Nellis. This dude had to be some kind of spook.

After Karen left the store, the man surfed on his cell phone recent ULA launches at Vandenburg and BINGO there it was, a classified payload they would not disclose. He knew damn well what that was, an NRO rocket. And sure, as shit there was a picture of the Colonel in a press briefing with the

ULA crowd who was standing by her boyfriend and two others. Small world we live in.

Karen had about 30 minutes to kill so she continued shopping and went into a store that sold various types of cards from birthday to anniversary to romance. She quickly found one and picked it out and paid for it. The card said, "I love Chocolate, but not as much as I love you." She purchased a nice gift bag with handles to put the card and ring box into.

Karen went to the front entrance of Ceasars Palace and at a concierge desktop, got out the card and pen from her purse and wrote on the card, "My dear Wilber, I do love you. Karen"

Moments later Wilber called and said, "I'm out front."

Wilber pulled up to the entrance. One of the Hotel/Casino security men approached the car on the driver's side and said, "Excuse me sir, but you are going to have to move your car now."

"Wilber pulled out his FBI badge and said, "We have a person under the witness protection program coming to the car now. Be a good sport and open the passenger door for her."

The security guy was about to pitch a fit and tell him to move his car when the two Karen watchers approached him wearing their earpieces wired and walked up to Ceasars Security man who was only doing his job as required, and said, "Excuse me is there a problem."

The security guy could see the two men were wired and stood down his testosterone a notch, but asked, "Who the fuck are you?"

"We are part of his security apparatus; any more questions and we'll have to arrest you."

Suddenly Karen approached the car, and a third man came out of nowhere and opened the door for her and she got inside, and Wilber wasted no time in driving away.

"The third man approached the other two watchers and asked, "Larry are you guys having a problem with this guy?"

"Yes, I think he needs an attitude adjustment."

"I'll call Bob Black and have him talk to him and arrange to give him some conflict resolution training."

"You know Bob Black?"

"Actually I think I'm going to have Bob Black come out and talk to you now."

The third man called Bob and said, "Bob, can you come out to the entrance of Ceasars, we are having an issue with one of your security men."

"I'll be right there."

"Bob will be right here," the agent said.

In less than three minutes Bob Black was hustling out the front entrance of the Hotel/Casino and one of his assistants explained as he was leaving the office what the incident was all about.

"What happened," Bob asked.

"Sir, a car stopped here, and I told the driver to move the car. He then pulled out an FBI badge and said he was here to pick up a person under the witness protection program, which I thought was BS and we had a confrontation about the time these men showed up."

"Roger, if that was an FBI man picking up a person in the Witness Protection Program, don't you think you should have handled it differently?"

"Bob your man came very close to getting arrested for interfering with the witness movement," One of the three men said.

"Roger, do you remember the man in the car?" "Yes, I do, it's not likely I will forget him."

"The next time you see him, walk away from him, and if you have a problem with him, you personally come see me before you do anything, do you understand?" "Yes, I do sir."

"Good."

Bob Black turned to the third agent and said, "Phil, please come with me, I need to buy you a beer."

"Sounds good."

"Phil and Bob Black headed for the front entrance, leaving the three men behind."

After the two were inside Ceasars, Roger asked the guy who gave him the shit, "Are you guys hired dicks?"

"No, we are Cash in Advance." "What's "Cash in Advance?"

"Next time you see Bob Black ask him," The man said and turned around and walked for the entrance with his partner."

Neither Wilber nor Karen was uptight. In fact, they were very happy.

Karen decided to wait until they stopped some place to give Wilber his present. In due time they were approaching the Boulder Dam. Wilber pulled over to an observation point at the Bridge Overlook on Nevada 172 paralleling US Hiway 111, and stopped the car and they got out.

[111 (number) - Wikipedia]

Wilber walked over to the edge of the viewpoint with a spectacular view to take it all in. It's one thing to have such a view, but its another to be here with a woman you are in love with.

"Come over here a second," Wilber said with a nice smile.

Karen approached and Wilber held his two arms out for her. Karen was suddenly feeling special. Wilber pulled Karen closer and gave her the most romantic kiss he learned in Spy school. Most women would salivate to experience such an elegant kiss. Karen's heart was delicately purring in response, she truly was Wilber's kitten.

The kiss lasted a short eternity. It was the most romantic kiss Karen experienced in her lifetime. And to add to the drama significantly Wilber said, "Karen, my sweet love, I cherish you."

The tears suddenly came down the sides of Karen's face as Wilber has once again shot cupid's arrow through her heart. But she had something important to do and pulled herself together to do this most majestic action of her life. Never did she ever think she would spend almost $50,000.00 on a ring for a boyfriend. It seemed almost impossible. But Wilber was Mr. Impossible, he was always coming up with surprises when she least expected.

"Wilber, I have something for you."

Karen reached inside her purse and felt the ring box and pulled it out.

"I love you too." She then handed Wilber the ring box. He took it and opened it and was almost floored. He knew instantly it was a very expensive ring. Even the ring box came from one of the most expensive Jewelers in the country that handled high end clients. He knew vividly because he purchased a ring for Faye Wong there. That also created almost choking nostalgia. He too suddenly had tears forming. No woman had ever done something so special for him. The fact a poor bartender spent such a vast amount of her life savings money on a ring for him articulated the significance of her motive that was genuine and real.

Wilber stared at the ring until Karen snapped him out of his temporal anomaly and said, "Please try on the ring to see if it fits."

Wilber carefully pulled the beautiful ring out of the box and put it on his ring finger. It fit perfectly. He promised himself he would never take off that ring to his last breath. The splendor of the ring demonstrating the depths of Karens emotional appeal and her charming mannerism, drugged Wilber's consciousness during one of the greatest moments in his life.

"I don't know what to say Karen. I'm not sure I've ever felt this way before. My knees are weak, and I feel like a little boy."

"Wilber, you are a man's man. The FBI and CIA woman disclosed a lot about you to me. I know that eventually you would open up and tell me about it when the time was right, but I know all about Xinxin and Faye Wong. You have been hurt very badly in the past. You have a broken wing, and its my job to fix you."

"Karen, you have helped me out a lot more than you know. You gave me a reason to keep living. Before I met you, I was willing to go on a dangerous mission and get killed just to end it all. But now I want to live."

"I want you to live as well so we can be together."

"Karen, I may have to go away for three or four months, can you handle that?"

"The two women who talked to me for several hours which forced me to call in work late, explained that would happen. I'm good with all that. I'll be okay. You are worth waiting for."

"After I finish this mission, I'll never do it again."

"Wilber, sometimes in life we must answer to a higher calling. You can't give up what you do because it's so special just to make yourself feel like you would be doing a better job taking care of me. I'm a big girl. I've been by myself most of my life. I can handle it. If you must go on a mission, just go. I'll be here when you get back."

"But what if I get killed?"

"Eventually we are all going to die. You need to dare to live." "You're serious."

"Wilber that ring shows how serious I am."

"You have no idea how much better that makes me feel. It's like you took the weight of the world off my shoulders."

"Wilber when you come home with another broken wing, I will be here to heal you."

"I believe that."

"Wilber I'm getting hungry all of a sudden, I didn't have lunch."

"Where would you like to go?"

"Since I have to leave in the morning, so I'll be back in time to got to work, I want to go to a special place."

"Do you know where that is?"

"Yes, the Top of the World Restaurant again. I want to see the view and feel you at the same time."

"We can do that."

***

Chapter Twenty-One

Prototype

The Navy pioneered the concept of prototype with its nuclear reactors. The entire first crew of the nuclear submarine Nautilus (SSN-571) went through nuclear power school and spent time at a prototype learning how to operate the nuclear power plant. That included Torpedomen (TM), ICmen (IC), Sonar Technicians (STS), Electronics Technicians (ET), etc.

Shortly afterwards, the Navy realized having all those forward personnel only clogged up the nuclear power school pipelines and prototypes and with a growing number of submarines on the agenda, it was a foregone conclusion they needed to save all the seats in nuclear power school for people that would be assigned to operate the nuclear power plant.

Perhaps because people who were former nuclear trained people, the decision was made to have a prototype. The Admiral from Naval Reactors was almost insistent upon it for good logical reasons. Wilber thought the Admiral's recommendations were sound and convinced John Burkette to endorse the Admirals plan, but added, "We

need to have a prototype for the entire Project Solaris Spacecraft." "We can do that," John Burkette responded.

The IBM facility built at Manassas Virginia was placed there for the location making access to Washington DC on route 66 much easier at least for a couple decades until traffic patterns got out of control.

IBM sold that facility to Loral who resold it two years later to Lockheed Martin after doubling their money. Since, IBM tried to buy it back for ten times the amount. Lockheed has a money maker and responded, "Нет, спасибо (no thanks)."

Wilber had been at that facility when he was on the SR-72 program that replaced the SR-71 and first flew in 1989. Wilber was part of the group that put in block 5 and 6 upgrades to the SR-72 just five years before he met Feye

Wong. Wilber liked the area and knew there still was some open area further North by Middleburg.

Wilber knew how things worked. If they disclosed the location the price of land would skyrocket. He had his own money as well as some black money to play with. He went out and drove around and found a couple significant properties for sale. The owners thought they would make a killing selling on speculation of urban growth and Lockheed people from Manassas and people in DC wanting to live further out in the country.

The land was sold for double the rational cost. Wilber didn't care. By having someone close like Karen who was savvy as an economist, she would buy one property, and he would buy the other with his money. The property Wilber bought would be for their home with some decent property around it to raise horses if they so desired. The other property Karen would sell to Project Solaris for the price she paid so nobody could say there was an insider business going on.

The land purchases happened very quickly, and the former owners were leaving the property where the Project Solaris Prototype Spaceship was to be built for the last

time when they saw the new owners driving onto the property with a fleet of construction equipment following behind including trailers for the construction boss and his team.

The former owners waited until the last large truck passed them moving onto the property and they made a quick U-turn and drove back in over to by the car the new owners arrived in.

The former owner approached Karen and her boyfriend Wilber and asked, "Are you guys building a subdivision? I've not seen any zoning permits."

"The government is taking over the land, they completed their environmental impact statement weeks ago, but they had to wait for the new owners and the contract before they could proceed."

"You should have disclosed this. I might take you to court and sue you?"

"Don't you think you should sue the rightful owner?" "Isn't that Karen?"

"No, she just signed the documents. She sold it to the government. The only reason why we are here is to give copies of the documents to government officials who will be here shortly."

"You probably made a killing I imagine."

"There is a confidentiality clause in the transaction, I'm sorry we cannot comment."

The previous owner utterly disgusted that he got taken advantage of walked back to his car and left the property.

He wasted no time in hiring a lawyer who came back to him and said, "It's fully legitimate and you have no legal recourse. I'm ending my involvement with you. I'm not going to charge you for legal services and advise you to drop all matters relating to that property."

"How come I can't sue them over this?"

"Sure, you can sue anyone, but you have no idea who you are messing with, my advice to you is forget about it. You received double what land sells around here. Count your blessings."

The attorney walked away and would no longer talk to the man.

In due time the area was fenced in with 8-foot-tall chain link fences with razar wire at the top. Full-time security was there. Construction started on a large building. Most of the Project Solaris Spacecraft Prototype was built below the surface with massive amounts of concrete.

The new building had huge access doors and two overhead cranes that ran on rail tracks. This was two buildings in one where nobody from the outside could see what was going on indoors. Thanks to a substantial amount of black funds, lack of money never held up any part of the prototype construction. Six months to the day of groundbreaking, the twin reactors powering the mockup were ready to start providing power.

The cyclonic propulsion thrusters could not be installed so they were replaced by simulators. Real thrusters organized and a partial prototype was built near area 51

so that real power runups could be done. Between the prototype in Virginia and the partial prototype in Nevada, complete space training was accomplished.

Within weeks after startup during a maintenance period at night, the umbilical cord to the thruster simulator was disconnected and the remote direct link between the Project Solaris Spacecraft Prototype and the real thrusters started functioning.

The final crew size determined was six. All six would be involved in the submarine construction on Saturn and three would go to sea on the submarine. The other three would remain at the base camp and be prepared to do emergency communications that were drilled as part of various scenarios exercised.

***

It was suddenly a sad day at SBC as Karen worked during her last day there. Wilber asked her to move in with him in his home back in DC and she would be the house watcher in his absence. That simplified the security arrangement as they only had to protect one location. Plus, perpetrators would be nuts to try nefarious activities near where Wilber lived. There were cameras everywhere. Wilber wasn't the only person protected. Other high ranking government officials and diplomats lived close by.

Wilber suggested to Karen to delay the wedding until he came back from his mission in case something happened, but to protect her interests they would secretly get married. She was thrilled with that idea. Then he really got her excited. "We'll have the formal wedding at our new home across the street from the prototype."

"What's going to become of the prototype?"

"It's going to end up like other similar secret projects, it will be cut up into millions of little pieces and disposed of."

"What about the building and everything else?"

"All that will be demolished and disposed of. The landscape will be restored like what it was before they built the prototype."

"Will the government sell the property?"

"Definitely, they eventually do not want any visibility to the sight."
"Who do you think would buy that property?"

"My guess is that is a prime location for Chet Baker to move into."
"You mean Colonel Baker?"

"Yes."

***

Time flew and Karen thought she was pregnant a few times, but it was a false call, which made Wilber happy knowing he would be back from the mission before such a thing really happened.

"Wilber had to make more trips out to Nellis Air Force Base for training. On one of those trips, Brent, John Burkette, and a female Tammy didn't know were on the GS750 flying into Las Vegas. Tammy and the plane were sent home and not scheduled to come back for a week. Wilber had multiple tasks to do.

Shortly after the four drove off in an SUV from McCarren Airport, out on the Freeway Karen took off the mask.

The security guy Roger was out in front of Ceasars Palace main entrance making idiots move their cars when the SUV pulled up. Oddly before the SUV pulled up three guys who looked familiar wearing suits and an earpiece with a wire running to it came out of the front entrance and stopped a few feet from Roger who was instantly agitated because Bob Black ripped him a new asshole over these three goons. He also knew the bulges in their suits were probably Uzi's.

The SUV stopped in a spot that said no stopping and no parking. The doors suddenly opened, and Wilber got out to help unload their luggage. Roger came up from behind him and didn't see his face and spoke, "Excuse me sir but you must move your car now."

Without looking back Wilber said, "I'm sorry I'm not moving it until I'm done unloading. That sent a subtle message to Roger that pissed him off and he approached Wilber with hostile attention as if he was going to make him regret those words. He tapped Roger's back and planned to sucker punch him when he turned around. About that time someone tapped Roger on the back. It was all three of them.

"What the fuck do you think you are going to do Roger?" That diverted Roger's attention so when Wilber stood up and turned around to face him, he could protect himself as good as any spy could.

Roger turned back towards the man and there he was smiling at him.

Brent and John approached Wilber and came close to him. One of the three men said, Roger, let me introduce you to the Director of Central Intelligence Agency.

Bob Black suddenly flew out the front door of Caeser's Palace and ran up to Roger almost in full panic and said, "Roger, I just sent you a text informing you we had a super VIP arriving, didn't you get it?"

Roger pulled his cell phone out of his pocket and there the text was sent five minutes ago when Roger was being distracted by another person.

"I'm very sorry sir, I was handling a matter then this car pulled up. I missed the text."

Wilber knew he needed to save Roger who would likely be fired, said, "It's not your problem Roger. As soon as I get done parking the car, I'm going to come get you and buy you a beer."

"I'm sorry sir, but I'm on duty."

"Roger, go have the beer with him, I'll handle this and bring someone else in until you are all done." Bob Black said.

"Looks like we are all unpacked Roger, I have VIP parking right over there, I'll be back shortly."

"Nobody budged until Wilber came back with a wicked smile on his face."

Karen, can you get a bellhop and get our luggage up to our room, then come down to the bar, and have a beer with me and Roger."

"Alright honey."

Wilber slapped Roger on the back and said, "Us go have that beer, Roger."

Bob Black made a couple phone calls and suddenly several bellhops with carts appeared. Another Hotel employee came out and handed each of them key cards for their rooms.

Where is Wilber O'Toole?" the employee asked. "He's with me."

"And who are you?"

"I'm registered as Karen O'Toole. Tonight, it will be official." "Congratulations Karen," The hotel employee said and handed her a couple room keycards.

Everyone went up to their rooms but did not stay there as they were all curious what would happen between Wilber and Roger.

Since Roger had his CIA phone with him, he was easily tracked. Plus, a couple of the CIA protective services guys were at the bar sitting next to him in case Roger had some strange notions of taking on a world class spy. They were not there to protect Wilber. They were there to prevent him from killing Roger if a fight erupted.

"Here's to you Roger." "Thanks."

"Roger, just remember, as shitty a day you may have their could be worse," Wilber said.

"What could be worse than almost getting fired. You probably saved my job," Roger said.

Roger, you met the DCI and the DD/P for the CIA earlier. The two guys on my left work for them as well. We have all had bad days, trust me about that. But I'm going to tell you about my worst day to put it into perspective, okay?"

"Sure."

"I was in love with a Chinese lady, Faye Wong from Hong Kong. I thought she and I were getting married. We were in love, and we fucked like rabbits. She was the brightest spot in my life. I didn't know she was a Chinese spy sent to kill me. We just finished fucking and she went into the bathroom to pee. I probably would have fell asleep and she would have succeeded but when she pissed it sounded like she was running a fire hose it was that loud and it woke me up."

"Sounds kind of disgusting."

"Yep, Faye could have at least done the decency of shutting the bathroom door," Wilber said.

"No kidding," Roger said feeling suddenly less stressed.

"But lucky for me that fire hose piss sound kept me awake and alive." "How so?"

"I was fully awake, and she came out of the bathroom with a knife. I saw her shadow raising the knife to stab me I grabbed my gun that had a silencer I had under my pillow and put two bullet holes through her heart. I killed her." "God damn!" Roger said.

I was rather shook-up if you can imagine gut up and turned on the light and there, she was holding that knife in a death grip. I noticed the front two or three inches of the knife had something on it that looked like Vaseline. I got hotel stationery and rubbed one side of the knife on the paper and folded it up and put it in an envelope and stuffed it in my sock. That substance covering the knife blade was a Ricin compound, one of the most deadly substances known to mankind."

"No doubt that was an attempted assassination," Roger noted.

"This was her hotel room. I walked out of the hotel a couple blocks and made a call for an emergency extraction. I've had a few bad days too my friend."

"Thanks for telling me that Wilber. It brings a whole new dimension to my thoughts. I was out of line, I'm sorry."

"Don't worry about it, Roger. I know you got a tough job. You must deal with a lot of assholes day in and day out, so forget about it."

"Sure."

"Roger, you seem to be a nice guy. May I ask you for a favor?" "Anytime."

"In a while I'm taking Karen through an Drive Through Elvis Wedding chapel to get married. I want you to come with me and be my best man, since I do not have one here for me."

"Yes, I would be more than happy to do that."

Roger and Wilber were so focused talking to each other, they didn't see Brent, John, and Bob Black approach them who heard everything. John Burkette was pleased how slick Wilber handled this situation.

One of the men sitting next to Wilber cleared his throat and nodded to the sudden visitors. Wilber looked up and saw all the men smiling.

Before anyone could say anything, Bob Black said, "Roger, I want you to go with Wilber to his wedding to add protection to make sure he gets there and back safely. This is a Ceasar's Palace official movement."

"Yes Sir, I will be most happy to do so."

"I'll contact Mr. DeAngelus to have him provide the Ceasars Palace Limo to go there because I suspect there will be several people that will want to go along." "Bob, I like the way you operate," Brent said.

"Brent, I was SOG and a few of your Cash in Advance guys rescued me in Laos, consider this a payback."

"Paid in full," Brent said. Karen suddenly showed up.

"Everyone, Karen and I need to go up and change our clothes, we'll be back in five minutes to go."

"Karen us go change, wedding's going to happen now."

"Alright dear."

As they were walking past the Jewelry store where Karen purchased her ring the two salespeople were there. On a hunch, Karen said, give me just one minute.

She walked into the store and the two people remembered her vividly and had some conversations about Karen.

The woman had a name tag Sofia and Karen said. "Sofia, I'm going to get married we are going up to our hotel room to change our clothes. I do not have a bridesmaid because this is a secret affair. I'll pay you $5,000.00 if you will come with us and be my bridesmaid at an Elvis Drive Through Wedding Chappel."

Sofia was the salesman's girlfriend and the thought of her earning a quick $5,000.00 he said, "Sofia, go with her and do it, I'll handle matters here."

"Alright Don."

"We'll come back in about five minutes and grab you. Can you go get me a bucket of flowers?" Karen asked then handed her $500.00 and said, "This should cover it."

"Sure, there's a flower shop not far from here, I'll be back in five minutes with lots of flowers."

"Thanks."

The two went up and changed. Wilber put on a black-tie suit and Karen had her beautiful white wedding dress. Wilber spent a lot of money buying for this trip.

"You look so beautiful Karen."

"I'm only beautiful because you love me and make me bloom. Us get going!"

Just like they promised they were back at the Jewelry store in about Five minutes. And there was Sofia with a basket full of the best beautiful flowers sold in Ceasars Palace. Sofia was dressed up very nicely as she was always selling high end rings, and she herself was a head turner.

The three descended back to the bar where everyone was waiting, and they all sighed when they saw the three.

Bob Black immediately said, "I've been informed the Limo is right out the front entrance, and if there is enough room I want to go too."

They all squeezed into the long limo with no problem.

Occasionally the Elvis Pressley Drive Through Wedding Chappel gets a Ceasar's palace limo driving up. They also have an indoor chapel when there are too many people in a Limo like today and the receptionist advised them, "I think it would be better if you all came into our Chappel and did it there."

"I agree, Karen quickly said. Everyone exited the Limo that waited for them because the driver knew Bob Black was running the show for this VIP couple.

The forms were easy. Karen had been advised by Wilber to bring her

I.D. with her for the paperwork. The company copied their I.D. and put it on the marriage application since the current information was correct and all they had to do is sign the official document with real ink and it was done. Legally they were married but they wanted the ceremony, and there was an onsite ordained minister who could

legally perform the Christian wedding. If they wanted a Muslim, Jewish, Buddhist, Hindu, or Shinto wedding they would have to make a reservation in advance.

The ceremony was quickly over and they all piled back to the Limo and Wilber made the announcement, "I would like to invite all of you to the Top of the World Restaurant to help us celebrate."

Everyone agreed to go and as Bob Black got out of the Limo he informed the driver;" I will call you when to come back and pick us all up."

Wilber and Karen were lucky they did this at such an odd hour because it was at a time of day when the restaurant only had half the tables filled with customers. The big crowd would not arrive for an hour and a half.

The Maître d' was quite happy to see such a large group show up which immediately filled a bunch of those empty tables. All the customers were happy to see a woman in a wedding dress with such a handsome man in a black-tie suit. Karen and Wilber were a handsome couple.

The Maître d' was brilliant and quickly seated them in a circular distribution putting the bride and groom in the middle so they could effectively communicate with their friends.

It was a joyous occasion that tested the Dom Perignon reserves of the restaurant.

As to not waste space there were going to be four seats at the bride and groom's table. Wilber insisted Roger and Sofia be those two since they fulfilled the role of best man and bride's maid who also carried the basket full of beautiful flowers up to the restaurant.

One of the waitresses figured out real fast how to handle the flowers. She moved the table away from the window a couple feet and put a servers table next to the window and the basket of flowers on it which created a splendid backdrop for the lovely couple.

Bob Black, Brent, John Burkette and Brent's personal bodyguard sat at the next table. At the table behind Wilber's back were other protective agents.

One of them volunteered to take all the pictures.

The meal and the ambience felt supreme. Sofia soon discovered all the men wanted her. She never felt so good in all her life. She didn't realize she had huge appeal. Some of these guys were sweet talkers and she felt strange vibes from Roger and saw him often back at Ceasars.

John Burkette who looked favorably on Walter, said, "Excuse me I need to use the restroom."

John went to the toilet as he really needed to go but he had other plans. He walked up to the Maître d and asked, "See the groom, isn't he handsome?"

"He certainly is sir."

"See our table next to him with the distinguished looking gentleman?" "Yes sir."

"He's my boss who is in charge of the CIA." "For real?"

"I work for him directly and the groom works for me, understand?" "Yes sir, I do."

"Here's my credit card, can I trust you with it?" "Why" "I want to pay for all this."

"No problem, sir, let me swipe it now and I'll give your card back to you. When you get ready to leave, I'll give you a printout of the charges."

"Thank you. Here's a handling fee for assisting me." John Burkette handed the Maître d' a $1000.00. which made her day real fast."

She knew his name was John Burkette since she read his card and handed it back to him.

When John Burkette walked back to his table, the Maître d' asked one of the waiters, "Please cover for me, I need to go talk to the Chef."

"Sure."

The Maître d' walked back to the Kitchen and walked up to the Chef and asked, is there any way you can produce a wedding cake?"

"Not really but if you need one, I can send one of my cooks to go to a cake store and bring one back."

"How long would that take?" "Probably 20 to 30 minutes."

"Good, here's $600.00 go send them now. We have a wedding couple, and they certainly are VIP's, and this might be in the News Papers tomorrow."

"He's on the way." "Thank you."

As the Maître d' was leaving the kitchen she overheard, "Rascal, come here I have an important task for you."

The Maître d' knew she just gave away $600.00 but it's money she wasn't planning to have and knew that money would be spent better elsewhere because she knew those were amazing men out there. Since her husband was former special forces guy, she knew what these guys did for their country. The guy with his bride probably did some big shit if his boss is paying for all this. It would be a way of showing her appreciation for American heroes. She knew later when she informed her husband, he would be proud of her because he was old school and her personal hero.

The night unfolded; the meal washed down with Dom Perignon was such a delightful experience. Roger sat there feeling special being invited into all this and Bob Black was very appreciative of Wilber for "grooming" Roger who had a lot of potential. He knew this would be a pivotal moment in Roger's life.

When they were all done eating it was time for dessert.

When the waitress came out to ask what they wanted for desert instead she said, "Karen and Wilber, this is a special night for you, so we have a little surprise for you. None of your friends will be offered a dessert menu because we have made all the appropriate arrangements."

One of the customers in the restaurant worked for the Las Vegas newspaper and knew he knew one of those men and surreptitiously took some photographs. He then sent them to the late-night squad at the Newspaper then handled late breaking stories to still them in the paper which finalization was about an hour from now.

In his text he asked the research associate, "Who is the guy in the middle with the purple tie?"

Within five minutes thanks to the newspaper's artificial intelligence identification software the answer was: "That's the director of the CIA and the man with the blue tie sitting near him is John Burkette DD/P for the CIA. When and where the hell was this photo taken?"

"It's right now at the Top of the World restaurant."

"The Editor needs to know this hold on you might have an assignment really quick this is a major story."

The research associate knew the best stories always came in late, Murphy's law.

Moments later the Editor for the paper approving tomorrow's copy, came on the phone. "This is a rather incredible opportunity. I want you to bird dog that celebration, get all the data you can, come back to the office and we are holding the paper until you write the story. Keep it to 1000 words. I'm telling the layout people to move stuff around in the paper. This will be headline news."

Nobody would ever think about Nefarious activity at a Wedding Celebration. Some things should be off limits. However, Newspapers, Politicians, and Spies hold nothing sacred.

The reporter shot up a bunch of pictures with his cell phone and was texting them like crazy. Activity at the newspaper was ablaze. Then the crown Jewell was exposed!

As they brought out the cake, the DCI stood up and said, "Ladies and gentlemen, I'm very pleased to be here tonight with one of my employees. He's an untold American Hero and has done a lot of things

I could tell you about, but then I would have to kill you. But some of the unclassified things I can tell you is he was a principal figure at some of the rocket launches at Vandenberg, and just on one incident alone he helped prevent a delay of nearly a week of an important launch. I wish we had more people on the team like him. His boss who works directly for me is here tonight. John, would you like to say anything? "Sure."

John Burke stood and said, "I'm most fortunate to have Wilber O'Toole work for me. But more importantly a man like Wilber who gave so much for his country in the past under very dangerous circumstances most of you are unaware exists we keep from you so you can sleep at night. Most importantly is a man like Wilber needs a person in his life to make it worth living and to enjoy the fruits of life after some of the most hazardous scenarios that ever existed. He truly is the reincarnation of Tracey Barnes, Frank Wisner, Richard, Bissel, and Desmond Fitzgerald who paid a similar price.

Wilber is not finished yet, but he has the lovely Karen to keep his keel level so that he is able to continue doing things that may never be known but I assure you has a huge element in your security. I'm so happy that such a distinguished person was able to meet such a high caliber woman like Karen that makes his life whole. Karen, thank you very much.

Hearing all this coming from two top CIA managers and after hearing Wilber's story that had a huge impact on Roger along with the invitation to the wedding, created a permanent bond between Roger and Wilber. Roger then stood up and said, "Ladies

and Gentlemen, Wilber is a class act, I will vouch for him, may I propose we cut the cake for this lovely bride and groom.

The Chef and his top three associates were there in the VIP attire they changed into to go meet such elegant guests. The chef stepped forward with a cake knife and asked, "Sir may I have the honor of cutting the wedding cake for you?"

The Las Vegas News Paper reporter was at work in a major way. He was taking more pictures and cranking out a 1000-word story.

It was a joyous time and eventually it was over. There were a lot of smiling faces including the reporter who promptly made his way to the News Paper building with an incredible story.

This came out the next day. The DCI, DD/P, and Wilber were not terribly uptight about it since Wilbers days of operating as a spy were over. The last thing in the world you want the enemy to know is the next of kin (NOK) for a spy who operates behind enemy lines. Spy agencies have spent vast amounts to get a NOK list. One of the mission impossible movies was about such an event.

The Las Vegas newspaper delivered to the FSB a treasure. And soon the artificial intelligence at the FSB computers sent Aida Abramova a copy of the newspaper report and other information they dug up on her person of interest responsibility (POI).

In due time Project Saturn was compromised by someone in Solar System Investigations. Aida Abramova now had new instructions from her superior Dmitri Vasilyevich Bortnikov. She was to use the Karlov Group for deep penetration of Wilber O'Toole.

In Dmitri's final instructions to Aida during a weekend at his dacha in Petropavlovsk, he said, "The last time you had sex with Wilber O'Toole you did it for self-gratification and you blew your mission. In Beijing you did not operate effectively, and I know why."

"Why do you think I wasn't effective in Beijing, Dmitri?"

"Aida, you were having sex with Wilber O'Toole in less than six hours after you met him. You dilly dallied around in Beijing for three days giving the Chinese time to get to him first and they crossed the trip wire and Wilber was evacuated. Had you had sex with Wilber within six hours in Beijing, he would not have been in bed with that woman from Singapore. This mission is very important and requires extreme endeavors."

"If you are thinking what I'm thinking you want me to spread my legs for Wilber right away, may I remind you he's a newlywed with a pretty wife who looks better than me. The honey pot scheme is not going to work with Wilber."

"You have to take ultimate measures and that's why I'm giving you the Karlov

Group for logistical help and unprecedented ability."

"They may not be enough this time."

"Look they outfoxed MI5 and MI6 and accomplished one of the most important assassinations in the history of the KGB/FSB."

"I think they got lucky; their target was a dumb person who let his guard down because he thought he was safe because he was in London."

"Precisely the same setup with Wilber O'Toole. He will think he's safe too because he's very close to the support apparatus of the CIA."

"But he will be a hard target."

"So were Aldrich Ames and Robert Hanssen." "What is my main purpose in this operation?"

"We want to know more about Project Solaris and when it's going to deploy."

"No martial sanctions against Wilber O'Toole?"

"Absolutely not. He's a good friend of the DCI and the DD/P. If we kill him, we will lose 100 agents overnight. I know how John Burkette operates. He would carry out a vendetta and if he discovered you were involved in killing Wilber O'Toole, he would chase you to the ends of the Earth just to have the satisfaction of watching you have a painful death like being fed alive to starving hogs."

"Yea I've read some of his sadistic shit."

"He likes to send a message, that's why he sent me a video of Nadezhda Plevitskaya being fed to hungry hogs after we assassinated his best friend."

"Wilber is a very talented Spy. I can't go to America as an Illegal. I need to have Diplomatic Credentials because this could all unravel very quickly when you are up against someone like Wilber O'Toole."

"The Karlov Group will be traveling as Illegals what makes you so special?"

"Project Solaris could be so important that Wilber O'Toole would go to extremes. If I'm an illegal, the best way for him to handle me would be the same thing he did to his pretty Chinese girlfriend Feye Wong. If Wilber killed a diplomat, he knows he would be in a world of trouble. He might get me kicked out of America in 72 hours after mistreating me, but at least I know I would be going home alive."

"I'll have my boss talk to Sergei Lavrov about getting you diplomatic credentials. But I must warn you, that you will probably be called into his office and explain what you are going to do and what possible issues you will create with your activities."

"I really do not know what I'm going to be doing yet or how I'm going to accomplish it. Some of it will have to be developed In-situ."

"You know a few things you will be doing such as attempting to meet Wilber O'Toole and find out about Project Solaris. You can simply state sensitive sources and methods for this mission cannot be discussed, otherwise the support group will not cooperate if they know anyone outside the Karlov Group knows anything about the mission."

"If I mention Karlov Group, he might think we plan on assassinating him."

"You have to predict what he will ask, and if he gets into that type of questioning, you need to assure him assassination is off the table because he's close to the DCI and the DD/P and the retaliation would be swift and brutal to the point it could cause an actual war."

***

Chapter Twenty-Two

Lubyanka Room 444

The next morning, Aida Abramova, and Dmitri Vasilyevich Bortnikov were flying to Moscow and in twelve hours arrived at the Lubyanka Building and to meet with Dmitri's boss, Vladimir Osechkin a senior member of the Federal Security Service of the Russian Federation, FSB; (Федеральная служба безопасности Российской Федерации, IPA: Federal'naya sluzhba bezopasnosti Rossiyskoy Federatsii).

Note: IPA is sometimes written API, is the International Phonetic Alphabet that allows people interested in Russian to be able to pronounce the words. This is sort of like Pinyin in Chinese and Ramanji in Japanese.

Dmitri Vasilyevich Bortnikov led Aida Abramova up three flights of stairs to the fourth floor where Vladimir Osechkin's office was located. At the doorway had what looked like a bookcase with plastic bags and a large sign that said:

«Положите обувь в эти полиэтиленовые пакеты и оставьте здесь, если она не чистая».

«Polozhite obuv' v eti polietilenovyye pakety i ostav'te zdes', yesli ona ne chistaya».

["Put your shoes in these plastic bags and leave here if not clean."]

There were several chairs to sit down on for shoe removal and replacement. VIPs were given slippers, especially on a wet and snowy day.

If one walked up this expensive carpet with muddy shoes, they would quickly regret it because the office holders on this floor would not tolerate a person making a mess on what is considered the most important carpet in in KGB/FSB directorates due to its history and longevity.

This magnificent hallway with extremely beautiful and expensive red carpet has the KGB's emblem in several places as well as some

Historical Russian depictions of successful espionage.

The two knew where they were going and walked past the receptionist who knew Dmitri Vasilyevich Bortnikov quite well since she had spent some time in the sack with him. She also had reason to believe based on Dmitri's reputation the woman with him flagged on her computer terminal via facial recognition, Aida Abramova, most likely worked for Dmitri sometimes on her back. She had no idea how close to the mark she was because Aida had some snail tracks in her panties.

The two walked halfway down the hallway and opened the door to room 444. Inside the office was a secretary and a couple of people working in the outer office near her.

Above and behind the secretary was a plaque that had a painting of an ancient man with a group of soldiers and said in the description below it: "444, Attila the Hun establishes his residence along the Tisza River (modern Hungary) and plans the coming campaign in the Balkans."

The beautiful blonde secretary Svetlana knew Dmitri and Aida had an appointment and said, "Let me see if Vladimir can see you now."

Vladimir Osechkin could be on the phone or doing something he didn't want to be disturbed. So, Svetlana walked over and tapped three times then opened the door to his office. The three taps were a code she personally was coming to ask a question or inform him of some important event." "Please come in," Vladimir said.

"Sir, Dmitri Vasilyevich Bortnikov and Aida Abramova are here to see you."

"Please escort them in."

Svetlana opened the door completely and turned to Dmitri and Aida and said, "Vladimir Osechkin is ready to talk to you, please come into his office."

The two went inside and were quickly seated in front of Vladimir Osechkin's desk. Svetlana closed the door giving them privacy.

"I read your email Dmitri and I want to hear from Aida why she thinks she needs diplomatic immunity?"

Dmitri nodded at Aida to give her the signal to begin discussing it. "Sir, Wilber O'Toole knows me quite well. In fact, we had sex together.

I was quite confident when he saw me at Beijing, he fully knew I was FSB and probably knew it while he was in Petropavlovsk.

"Why do you think that?"

"Right afterwards meeting him in Beijing, the CIA did an emergency extraction and one of our spies stated because I blew his cover to the Chinese."

"Why did you have sex with him? Was he your lover?"

"No, it was a standard Honeypot scheme, but for whatever reason he was there, he left abruptly and never came back. I'm sure he was there for nefarious purposes."

"Do you have special feelings for Wilber?"

"No, I would put a bullet in his head quickly if required."

"The Karlov Group is not going to be happy if you go in with diplomatic credentials and they have to go as illegals."

"They do not have to know, and I prefer they do not."

"That means you will have to travel there alone so they are not around to see you present your credentials as required."

"I'll slip into the United States via Canada a few days ahead of them so they will not see any of that."

I must go see Sergey Viktorovich Lavrov to authorize this. The United States limits the number of diplomats we can send and have reduced the numbers." "Is there a problem with that?" Aida asked.

Giving you diplomatic immunity means a Russian diplomat who is probably essential will have to be recalled and that will curtail whatever important assignment that person is doing, so I can tell you this will probably go over like a lead balloon."

"What if he doesn't approve it?"

"Be prepared to go in as an illegal if necessary."

"You should know if I go in as an illegal that will severely restrain my area of operations and conduct."

"Contact me after 4:00 P.M. I'll have his answer then." "Certainly."

"Also send me a list of actions you will likely do if given the diplomatic immunity."

"Yes sir, I will email you shortly."

"Before you too go, there is one more thing we must do."

Vladimir opened his large desk drawer and pulled out a bottle of Kors Vodka and three ventage Russian Cut Crystal Shot glasses. He then filled each and handed one to Aida, then another to Dmitri and said a toast:

" Это тост за двух великих шпионов, которые так много дали своей стране. Желаю вам жить долго и процветать."

{API: "Eto tost za dvukh velikikh shpionov, kotoryye tak mnogo dali svoyey strane. Zhelayu vam zhit' dolgo i protsvetat'."}

["This is a toast to two great spies that have given so much to their country. May you live long and prosper.]

This was a ceremonial toast, not socializing. All three drank the Vodka in one swift swallow. Aida and Dmitri put their glasses down on the table then stood up and left the office to go to Dmitri's home to shower, get cleaned up and await their instructions.

***

The prototype training was quite extensive. The 4-Star admiral convinced Wilber to get several of his men cleared for Project Solaris so they could create meaningful scenarios in the training scenarios. Just like the first Nautilus crew, everyone was trained in all aspects of the submarine because they truly had to help each other operate and if necessary, repair it if it were a repairable situation. Otherwise, the Project Solaris personnel deployed would simply die on Saturn doing an unsuccessful mission.

The submarine could easily accommodate all six Solaris Submarine people, but Wilber in private meetings with the DCI and DD/P convinced them a good possibility existed the submarine could be attacked and destroyed, so there was no point in killing everyone. He felt better knowing half of them would be left behind at the base camp to communicate with Earth to give reports if there were such combat.

Suddenly Wilber and one other were being sent to Las Vegas again to spend time in the trainers. This was probably decided too late as reality set in, what would happen to the project if something happened to Wilber. He too needed a backup. The man selected by joint decision of the DCI, DD/P, and Wilber was definitely Cowboy Quality.

Ian Monroe, who had the nickname Snoopy, would soon be Wilber's shadow.

Karen was a little disappointed when Wilber said, "On this trip, you cannot come with me. There are parts of this operation Project Solaris would not want you to know about, but since you are now my wife and an intelligent woman who I know can keep her mouth shut, I'm going to now reveal why you can't come with me on this trip."

"Alright honey."

"We will not spend all our time in the trainers at Nellis. We will spend over half of it at Area 51 and will be stuck up there for three or four days."

"I've heard some interesting things about Area 51. Does this have something to do with Aliens?"

"I can't tell you anything about that at all. But after I go on the mission, while I'm gone you will be visited by those two women again and they will disclose some of it to you."

"Alright Wilber I appreciate being informed why you will be gone a long time."

"You are bound to secrecy even though you are not a government employee. At some point in time, you will understand more about why I went to Area 51."

"Okay dear, I really hope you stay safe. If I lost you, it would break my heart."

"I feel the same way about you, Karen."

Karen grabbed Wilber and wrapped her arms around him and hugged him firmly for a long time. Words were not necessary. Wilber kissed Karen on the top of her head like he usually did.

The next morning Wilber and Snoopy flew directly to Area 51. This was another reason why Karen could not come along.

Snoopy didn't know what he would be doing. He soon spent a lot time in the Trainers at Nellis lately and also a lot of time in the Prototype that was now up and operational, learning more from the NAVSEA-08 admiral than anyone else in his entire life. Snoopy had great admiration for those gold dolphins as it represented the admiral and what he experienced in his lifetime.

In the prototype sometimes to motivate the students the instructors give anecdotal information about scenarios they experienced in the past. The admiral was full of sea stories and had no problem giving one every single day. As a nuclear fast attack submarine officer, the four-star admiral participated in hair raising missions and what was drilled home over and over was Murphys Law meant bad things always happened at the worst possible time you had to recover from.

Snoopy had a lot of charisma and was laying on the charm onto Tammy on the flight to Area 51 while she was facing Wilber and Snoopy who had a direct view up her crotch with her short dress, Tammy caught Snoopy in the process of "snooping" she decided to play with him and made sure he saw more than he bargained.

During the height of the flamboyance, she then gave a salvo to Snoopy.

"Snoopy, I can tell you one time I was dressed up smoking hot with no panties on and went into Wilber's hotel room lifted my dress and offered it to him. He turned me down without blinking an eye. Unlike you, I will spread my legs for Wilber if he ever asks. You will have to work hard for it. Are you willing to put forth the effort

required?" Tammy said with a big smile as to convey, come get it big boy if you are man enough.

Snoopy was quiet and no longer engaged in eyeball liberty for the rest of the flight.

The two were directed to wear comfortable clothes and suits were not necessary for this trip. Wilber suspected he knew what they would be doing, but not quite as much as he figured.

It did not surprise Wilber when they pulled up next to the hanger with building number 28 painted on the front of it.

They each had a small bag with necessary items for the trip and one change of clothing.

Tammy had the ladder down and their small bags out on the tarmac within a couple minutes after the jet stopped near the side of the building. The pilots were told to wait in case something went wrong, they would provide transportation Wilber and Snoopy down to Las Vegas for the night. If that happened, they would be on a Janet flight in the morning. EG&G, now part of AECOM.

EG&G started Janus Airlines back in the days when it had 35,000 employees to haul scientists to Area 51 every morning and return them in the evening.

The fleet's "Janet" call sign is said to stand for "Just Another Non-Existent Terminal or "Joint Air Network for Employee Transportation".

These scientists that flew on Janet flights every day were family people and it would be impossible and impractical for them to live near Area 51, hence Janet Airlines was necessary. The Janet jets were easy to spot leaving Las Vegas McCarren airport because they had no Airline Markings and only an orange stripe running from the front all the way to the rear along the length of the Janet 737-66N aircraft. EG&G had a fleet of eleven 737's that were eventually upgraded to 737-200's by trade-in.

Janet flights also took people from Burbank near Lockheed's Skunk Works existed. A lot of the special planes tested at Area 51 were designed at Skunkworks including the TR-4.

Janet flights also landed at Vandenberg. There are a total of six destinations. The focus cities were Las Vegas, Tonopah Test Range , and Homey Airport (aka Area 51).

The Tonopah Test Range is also designated Area 52. Tonopah Test Range is located about 70 miles (110 km) northwest of Groom Lake, the home of the Area 51 facility.

Area 52 is actually more important than Area 51 since it stockpiles a portion of the United States Department of Energy nuclear warhead storage.

An Airforce pilot who Wilber knew quite well, Major Barnes was there to meet them.

"Welcome back Wilber. Please come with me."

Major Barnes led Wilber and Snoopy to the side entrance of building 28 and entered the cypher lock and opened the door for Wilber and Snoopy.

About ten feet into the hanger Snoopy had one of those come to Jesus' moments. Major Barnes, Ian Monroe, my partner has the call sign we all call him,

"Snoopy." "Please to meet you Snoopy," Major Barnes said without skipping a step and led the two men to the open door of the TR-4.

When they arrived near the ladder Major Barnes turned around and said, "Snoopy, Wilber has already had his check ride in this aircraft, but since you are his official backup, we have to indoctrinate you." "I see."

"We are going to take you for a ride now. This is my co-pilot Major Schmidt. Nobody has as many flight hours in this plane as Major Schmidt. He is a test pilot in the TR-4 program.

"Interesting. Is this plane designated TR-4?"

"Yes, it is a TR-4. Let's get aboard so we can get the mission underway."

Major Barnes walked up the stairs with Wilber and Snoopy following behind, then Major Schmidt went up the stairs and closed the door of the TR-4 and sealed it shut with an interesting looking crank that was also a torque wrench built into it.

The TR-4 felt slightly cramped, but it had more room than an A6 Intruder and behind the rear seats was a small water close/toilet which Major Barnes pointed out since this would be a longer flight.

"Wilber, since you are a seasoned veteran, can you make sure Snoopy is fastened in properly for takeoff."

"Not a problem, Major Barnes."

Seconds later the flat screens in front of Wilber and Snoopy lit up. Together these flatscreens created a composite image giving a forward look at the present time showing the hanger doors opening which gave significantly increased brightness.

***

While Wilber was halfway to Area-51 on the GS750, the Doorbell rang, and Karen looked through the security monitor. There were three women. The first two she met before working for the FBI and the CIA and this time another nice-looking lady.

Karen opened the door because she knew these women and said, "Hello."

"Karen, may we come in and talk to you."

"Sure, come on in," Karen said then held the door open for them and closed it when they were all inside.

Karen led the three women into the living room that was now in far better condition than when Wilber lived alone. Karen was the quintessential organizer and Wilber quickly learned the best thing to do is to stay the hell out of her way.

"Please have a seat," Karen said.

The FBI lady responded, "Thank you."

The CIA woman who interfaced with CIA's HR Office was the key spoke person and she started explaining immediately.

"Karen, the reason we are here is for a couple of reasons."

Karen listened very intently knowing the kind of business her husband was in.

"You and Wilber were recently married. When that happens, our employees fill out paperwork for their next of kin."

"I see," Karen responded not knowing what was going to be presented. She expected a few surprises since three women arrived.

"Wilber also select benefits packages for you and as such, you will soon receive documents in the mail such as your health and dental cards. You will also be notified of other benefits, and you are Wilber's designated beneficiary.

"Understand," Karen replied.

"You are on his insurance policy designated recipient now so if God forbid something happens to Wilber, you will receive the insurance payment as well as his Thrift Savings Plan which is part of his retirement.

"That makes me feel slightly better," Karen said.

"The good news for you is Wilber has always maxed out his contributions so that his Thrift Savings Plan balance has grown substantially. His investment strategy has been phenomenally successful and the areas he picked grew quite a bit over the years.

"That's good to know."

We know you are an economist and maybe in the future you can help him in that regard and make it even better.

"I will certainly try to help him."

"Wilber is no fool and understood there was always a potential something fatal could happen to him so he took out the max coverage on his insurance, so that if something happens to him, you will not have to be concerned about income."

"I'm happy to know that too."

"Karen, Wilber is a very special person to the fact the President of the United States informed the DCI his amount of appreciation for what Wilber has done for his country. He took on very high-risk projects in the past and I know you were fully briefed on Feye Wong and Xinxin. You know Wilber taking Xinxin to Dubai to visit the son of the Sheikh who he saved in a heroic mission and freed him from a sizeable terrorist group when everyone else gave up all hope."

"He's never talked about his past, without you informing me I would not have known."

"Wilber tends to keep a lot to himself probably for good reason. That's why we are here today."

"Understand."

"When Wilber left on that mission to save Sayd who is Sheikh Omar's son, he was given less than a 50 percent chance of living. Quite honestly many people did not think he would pull it off and when he did, he got the attention of the DCI who knew how special Wilber is."

"I know he's special."

"The reason why we told you about Faye Wong is you needed to know what you were getting into before you married Wilber."

"I understand how horrible he felt after that. I think I saw him cry one time and I think it was about that."

"Karen, you also needed to know Wilber has suffered greatly in the past for other reasons. When Xinxin left him, she broke his heart, but he picked himself back up and marched on smartly knowing he had a contribution to make. We three women know you were Wilber's salvation."

"Well, he touched my heart in a very gentle and sweet fashion."
"Now I'm going to introduce you to the third member of your support team, Doctor Shirley. She will be available for you at any time. She's fully briefed and knows all what Wilber does. She is also a person who observes him from afar looking for warning signs where we might have to intervene in case, he is having serious issues. But now she has a new

assignment."

"What's that?"

"You."

Karen was slightly rattled by that comment and Dr. Shirley could see her body language exposed what seemed a gigantic emotional tremor.

"Is there something bad I need to know about," Karen asked now thinking they might be here to give her some heart-breaking news.

"Karen, there is no bad news now, but we must be prepared in the future in case there is. That is why we are here today to explain you have a support team to reach out to. Here's my business card," Doctor Shirley said as she handed Karen her business card.

"Okay."

"Call me any time day or night if you need my help." Doctor Shirley said.

Karen noticed the business card indicated Dr. Shirley was a licensed psychiatrist. The firm Doctor Shirley worked for that contracted her to the CIA was very prestigious. "Alright, is there anything else I need to know about?"

"Don't try to contact Wilber today. You will not be able to reach him. He's heading on a mission today that he can't tell you about. He will be incognito for several days. Send him loving text messages, but we recommend you don't send questions like, "Why have you not answered my text?""

"Alright."

"He will not be able to receive your texts where he is going, but when he gets back, he'll be joyful that you sent them."

"Thanks for the heads up. He's a great guy and I can patiently wait for him."

"Karen, in the future, Wilber will be going on a long mission. You will not be able to contact him for several months. We are your support team. If you feel down in the dumps call us."

"Alright, I appreciate that."

"I also want you to know the DD/P John Burkette made it a requirement that Wilber's paperwork be completed, submitted and finalized before he left on this mission such as a will and power of attorney. If Wilber dies, you have exclusive power

of attorney. Here is a copy of that power of attorney," The CIA HR representative said and handed Karen the copies.

"It's kind of amazing he took care of all this before he left."

"Yes, it goes to demonstrate what you mean to Wilber, the FBI lady said.

"There are no more preparations or actions required by anyone at this time to protect your benefits package since its all now activated." The CIA's HR lady said.

"That's good to know," Karen said.

Should something bad happen, all the portions you need are in place and we will be available for you to get VIP access to those who would disperse funds or take any appropriate actions to ensure, it all works out promptly for you."

"Thank you."

"I gave you my business card the last time we talked but I've updated it with some new information," The CIA HR lady handed her business card to Karen.

"Thank you I appreciate all this."

"Do you have any questions, Karen?" the CIA lady asked.

"No, I have all your phone numbers I can call or text you if I do." "Alright Karen, we are not going to take up any more of your time today. You know how to reach us." "I do, Thank you."

The three women stood up and soon they were in their car and driving away.

***

The TR-4 left the hanger but this time it did not go out into space the same way it did on Wilber's previous trip. There is an extension of Homey Airport (aka Area 51) runway 31 that goes off into the distance for emergencies.

Today, Major Barnes flying at 100 feet like on the last flight continued at 100 feet altitude the full length of the runway 31 emergency extension reaching Mach two then maneuvered pointing the nose of the TR-4 vertical.

With the initial velocity the TR-4 hit 10,000 feet very rapidly. Another amazing fact was no sonic boom. People working at Area 51 quickly lost visuals on the TR-4.

Snoopy was utterly amazed and when the display shifted showing the horizon so the passengers could see the flight perspective, it quickly started getting dark and they could see the circumference of planet Earth.

"Welcome to space." Wilber said. "This is amazing," Snoopy responded.

Wilber pointed to the speed indicator on the flat screen which Snoopy soon observed, realizing they were accelerating, and he was now traveling much faster than anytime in his life or ever expected.

The white spot ahead of them was clearly the moon, Snoopy thought.

As they continued to accelerate, the moon got larger quicker and at 600,000 miles per hour it grew rapidly.

Initially the moon was centered on the display but as it grew it slowly shifted to the right as the pilots were navigating to fly around the moon and use it to fling them to Mars and gain velocity in the process.

The resolution of the surface of the Moon steadily got better and soon looked like a close-up NASA photograph. Passing within 5 miles of the Moon made it appear to fly past quickly during the maneuver where the pilot went 100% maximum force on the gravity machine which allowed the gravity of the moon to help change course, but due to the speed the centrifugal force soon caused a departure from the moon and pointed them on a new heading directly at Mars. Just like before they reached 100 million miles per hour as they passed by Mars and changed course again.

Project Solaris Spaceship would follow this same course which Wilber and Snoopy observed and would practice later in the trainer at Nellis Air Force Base.

The most hazardous part of the trip before they arrived near Saturn would be the penetration of the asteroid belt. The toroid-shaped solar system's large asteroid belt region spanning the space between the orbits of the planets Jupiter and Mars centered around the Sun and would be the most hazardous portion of the journey. Once the TR-4 transited past Jupiter's orbit the asteroids thin out and it becomes increasingly safer.

One of the situations they could not avoid was using radar for collision avoidance. They knew there was great possibility the Russians or the Chinese would pick up the TR-4's navigational radar signals. There was no way around it. And as they assumed they would have many close calls and could collide with a dark asteroid in the shadows of others.

A traitor at Area-51 disclosed the passenger list for the GS750 that arrived at Area 51. Because Wilber O'Toole's name was on the passenger list, Russian FSB (KGB) artificial intelligence immediately sent that arrival information to Aida Abramova who had just received her Diplomatic credentials.

Kosmos 2558 a Russian Spy Satellite sent up to trail USA 326 filmed the GS750 landing, an officer leading two men into the hanger, and the TR- 4 leaving a few minutes later.

Aida Abramova immediately contacted Dmitri Bortnikov and said, "I have an emergency authentication request."

"What for?"

"Wilber O'Toole was on a GS750 passenger list that landed at Area 51 today by the American's top-secret hanger building 28 by Area-51's Homey Airport runway 31. The Satellite image from Kosmos 2558 shows two men in street clothes following a pilot into building 28. Kosmos 2558 and a few minutes later video recorded a new TR-4 left the hanger and flew out into space. I think Wilber was on that TR-4. The GS750 soon departed with no passengers. He had to be on that TR-4."

"What does this have to do with Project Solaris?" "This could be part of Project Solaris."

"Okay I will contact the photo interpreters. Send me the serial number for the Kosmos 2558 images you have.

"You will have them in a few minutes."

"Thanks."

"While Aida was waiting for Dmitri to call her back to confirm one of the two men who went into the hanger was Wilber O'Toole, she received more startling information. Russian receivers picked up an American Radar near the asteroid belt and initial signature components compare favorably to the new TR- 4 radar they had intercepted testing very recently.

This was an extraordinary finding. This is the first time in history where a military radar was flown through the asteroid belt. What are they up to? Aida wondered?

When Dmitri called her back about seven minutes later, he said, "The photo interpreters with the help of AI and thanks to the oblique angle were able to confirm that was indeed Wilber O'tool and another CIA man named Ian Monroe entering building 28."

"Thanks for the confirmation.

"Also, later reports indicate nobody leaving building 28 after the TR-4 left and the GS750 departed Homey Airport (aka Area 51) with no passengers on the manifest."

"That means Wilber and Ian left on the TR-4." "Most likely, yes."

"I've completed missions before with far less anecdotal evidence."

"That Radar must be the TR-4 which means it can travel extremely fast."

"I'm going to contact Vladimir Osechkin this situation needs higher priority and more logistical support."

"I have a hunch. That TR-4 will return like it has on previous missions that Wilber was probably involved in. That could be a day or two from now. When he gets back, no doubt they will spend some time in Las Vegas going to debriefs over at Nellis Air Force Base. I want the Karlov team sent to Las Vegas to put up a net and find Wilber."

"How will we know he's coming back?"

"Really simple. The pilots of the TR-4 will have to turn that radar on again to get through the asteroid belt when they return. When they do it will confirm everything and help establish a timeline of when to expect them to arrive at Area-51."

"Makes sense."

"One other important satellite support we now need. We need Area 51 covered around the clock until the TR-4 returns so we can confirm who's on it."

"Let me check to see what we have available."

Moments later Dmitri called back and said I have three satellites lined up that will give us overlapping coverage, Kosmos 2561, 2562, and 2567. Vladimir Osechkin just sent the request to Sergei Surovikin and received an affirmative response and assigned those three satellites."

"I thought Sergei Surovikin was sacked?"

"Officially he was sacked for window dressing over failures in Ukraine. But he's still on the job and told to keep a low profile."

We need to move the Karlov group to Las Vegas as quickly as possible to set up the video net with Realtime satellite feed.

Just as Aida anticipated as soon as the TR-4 made it through the asteroid belt, they shut down their radar, but they were going in a straight line now traveling at approximately an astonishing 200,000 miles per hour.

***

Chapter Twenty-Three

Blue Beams

Aida Abramova was on a flight to Las Vegas in the USA with her diplomatic immunity. Since she was arriving at an American City, someone from the state department would meet her at the airport and officially recognize her credentials.

The State Department Representative made a subtle inquiry, "May I ask as to the purpose of your visit to Las Vegas?"

"To see some shows and take a little vacation, before I travel to our embassy in Washington DC."

The paper trail had been created, Aida Abramova was now a fully legitimate diplomat and there was nothing the State Department could do without risking the expulsion of their own critically needed people in Moscow. But the State Department knew she was probably arriving for clandestine reasons associated with Nellis and Area 51 nearby.

Dmitri texted Aida a while later, "The TR-4 is heading right at Saturn." The FSB had just within the past few days discovered America and Norway were looking into Alien Signals coming from Saturn."

"That's very interesting," Aida texted back.

The chips are now starting to stack up. Wilber O'Toole who previously made love to Aida was turning out to be one of the more interesting persons she met in her lifetime.

Aida was suddenly getting a lot more visibility in Moscow as Vladimir Osechkin was quickly learning she was the brains behind figuring all this out.

The fact Aida personally arranged for the Karlov group, an elite Russian spy group utilized for most important special operations to now be on their way to Las Vegas to find Wilber was rather daring and astute.

Because Aida speculated Wilber would show up and acted on it, would soon place Aida as one of the top spies of all time, up there with Margarita Konenkova who seduced Einstein and a few scientists at the Princeton Center for Advanced Studies, according to J. Robert Oppenheimer.

If Wilber showed up in Las Vegas real soon, that would put the highlight on Aida like she never knew possible. All her days of dreaming about an assignment to Moscow were about to come true.

Furthermore, Aida wasn't going to be stuck on the first and second floor of the Lubyanka building with the border guards, nor on the third floor with all the mundane agencies dealing with the rest of the world. She was going to end up on the 4th floor where the elite spy controllers like Vladimir Osechkin had his office.

Aida's days of forcibly sharing her body with foreign spies to seduce them in honeypot schemes would soon be over. Up on the fourth floor as long as she didn't

screw up, Aida would be able to live a normal life, find a husband, start a family, and have an insane income like all the 4th floor spy controllers received.

Now the big question was, what exactly was Wilber going to be doing on Saturn?

After Aida got through the McCarren Airport, Aida was on her way in a Limo to Ceasars Palace. In the past CIA people stayed there and, on a hunch, Aida thought that's where they would find Wilber when he returned to planet Earth.

In due time Aida was up in her hotel room reading more text messages getting a full report on Saturn and the TR-4. The TR-4 went into orbit traveling perpendicular to Saturn's rings.

Then something very interesting developed. The TR-4 was shot at by a blue beam of sort according to the Russian Space Force closely observing it was a miracle the TR-4 crew made it away from Saturn alive. Imagery shows the blue beams chasing the TR-4 taking evasive courses. A few minutes later Aida received videos via satellite to her special FSB phone that was significantly altered just like Wilber's phone was. She was a traveling ISR person recording all electronic emanations deemed important.

Watching the video Russia astrophysicists were able to provide real time from Kosmos 2571 was truly remarkable. Aida could not help but hope Wilber survived. She had secret feelings for Wilber and wished the situation was different where they could be lovers.

Wilber was on the first spaceship to be fired on by Alien Forces. Of course, Aida knew the Americans would cover this all up and it would never see the light of day.

Aida knew the TR-4 episode was creating quite a stir in the Kremlin, and it probably would have a huge impact on the relations with the Americans because maybe instead of fearing each other we should start fearing what we just saw on Saturn?

Thanks to Major Barnes supreme piloting and as a combat veteran he applied lessons learned and pushed TR-4 propulsion to the maximum extent and knew as he got around the curvature of the planet those beams could not hit him. He slowly walked the problem around the planet until he reached an exit point and headed straight out into space in constant acceleration. The bonus was Major Barnes navigated the TR-4 right at the asteroid and debris field.

When they were clearly safely away, Major Barnes asked, "Tell me Wilber, what did you think of all that?"

"It sucks because I have to go back soon."

"We got some good intel including the declination of the beams that you can put in your planning to avoid them."

"Yes, that definitely was one of the elements of it I carefully observed."

The Russians were tracking the TR-4 with their new state of the art satellite that was put up for space warfare. They constant positional awareness where the TR-4 was always on its return trip. And just like Aida figured when it got to the debris field it turned on its radar which was duly intercepted and tracked. She received all those reports. Now the last piece of the puzzle was to watch Wilber get out of the TR-4.

Twenty-Four hours later an empty Janet 737-200 passenger jet pulled up near building 28 duly noted by the Russian Space Force and it had not taken on its passengers. They were all still in the terminal quarantined and not allowed to look outside with the shades covering the windows which was standard for up-posture events.

The TR-4 came down and landed in front of building 28 near a Janet Boeing built 737-200 Jet. The two Janet pilots were cleared to see the TR-4 as they see much quite often.

John Burkette was there to meet them and said, "We are going to fly down to Las Vegas on this Janet jet and get a rental car."

"Not a problem but I'm not feeling right. Can you do the driving."
"Sure, not a problem."

"Tomorrow afternoon as soon as you feel up to it, we'll go to Nellis for a debriefing."

"Sure."

Wilber turned around and Major Barnes was standing there to talk to maintenance personnel and for someone to open the hanger doors and tow the TR-4 into the hanger.

"Major Barnes, you did a hell of a job on the mission. One day soon I will wish permission to buy you a beer," Wilber said.

"Wilber, you earned a beer I need to buy you one. We'll hook up and buy each other beers."

"Thanks, I appreciate that."

The men walked over and climbed up the stairway to the Janet Boeing 737-200, while the TR-4 was towed into the hanger and then building 28 hanger doors shut.

The Janet Boeing 737-200 taxied down to the terminal for boarding all the scientists going back to Vegas.

A couple scientists who were accustomed to sitting up front in seats started pitching a fit about these smelly jerks sitting in their seats. One of the crew members who saw these guys get out of the TR-4 sitting next to the DD/P of the CIA approached the disgruntled passengers and said, "Excuse me Doctor Fairbanks, you need to find another seat, or I'll put you off the plane and you will get to spend the night here."

Doctor Fairbanks partner shoved his buddy to the back, and they got two seats side by side in the middle of what they called the cattle car as it had workers of all stratums of life.

The three amigos didn't have much but carryon and were the first off, the plane and first at the rental car agency getting an SUV.

In due time they were at the VIP parking at Ceasars Palace and Mr. Black and Roger were there to meet them including handing them the keys to their hotel rooms.

John Burkette was going to leave them alone thinking they probably needed a rest, which they did. Wilber's biggest chore was to take a good dump on a comfortable toilet and a Hollywood shower next.

Wilber knew his clothes smelled really bad by now, so he took the clothes he wore and put them in a laundry/dry cleaning bag with the paperwork the hotel provides to say how many garments and how to clean them such as dry cleaning or laundry. By the time he came back from Nellis the next day those clothes would be ready to be changed into and he expected to spend several days in the trainers in Nellis.

With fresh change of clothes on, deodorant, and cologne, Wilber was feeling hungry and decided to go down to the hotel bar restaurant he went to the last time.

Thanks to the FSB's great artificial intelligence, Wilber was detected and Karlov group agents were now looking for Wilber. The net closed in on Wilber and while he was eating his meal at the bar, a couple of Karlov agents were now in surveillance mode on Wilber. These guys' surveillance was excellent as Wilber did not detect their surveillance. They had a team to track Wilber and each team member would follow him a short distance before the relay was passed on to the next agent which allowed them to follow him to his room without creating curiosity. Some of the Karlov agents are women, specifically picked to blend in.

Wilber was back in his room answering Karen's texts, but he did not call her because it was late at night in DC and didn't want to wake her up. When she woke up in the morning, she would see all his texts and be happy.

Just as Wilber was going to go to sleep, there was a knock at the door. He figured it might be Snoopy or John Burkette, so he got up walked over and looked through the eyepiece and there was no other than Aida Abramova. Once you have sex with an enemy spy that looks like Aida, you will never forget her for the rest of your life.

Wilber knew that before he opened the door, he needed to go back to his cell phone and the special app he pressed alerted the CIA he was being approached by an enemy agent which set a lot of wheels in motion.

Because Wilber's cell phone had his GPS coordinates, CIA protection group personnel staying at Ceasars Palace knew exactly where he was. Help will be on the way shortly in case needed. He put his cell phone under the mattress in case this was going to turn into a struggle the sound would be recorded but the enemy would likely not look for his cell phone if it wasn't out in the open.

Wilber then opened the door right after Aida knocked one more time knowing Wilber was in his room because surveillance never lost track of him. "What can I do for you?"

"I would like to come in and talk to you for a few minutes."

"I'm married now, so I don't think its possible for us to get it on."

"That's okay I still want to talk to you."

"Alright come in." Wilber only let her in the room because there would be a backup in five minutes, and he wanted to know why Aida's surprise visit, and how the hell she found him.

Aida had her game plan worked out. She knew Wilber was an ultra-dangerous spy and had killed women before. She took a chair as far away from him as possible so he could not lunge at her when she pulled out her gun with a silencer.

"Tell me Wilber, what were you doing on that TR-4?"

"I do not know what you are talking about."

Additional Russian Spies were to come into the room because they had a hotel maid's room key and the hotel maid was tied up, gagged, and stuffed into an empty room. These Russian spies were listening to the Audio coming from Aida's listening device waiting to hear Aida's question to come into the room.

Wilber heard the door open and was starting to stand up when Aida said, "Sit back down Wilber," and noticed she was pointing a gun at him. As a trained spy, Aida no doubt knew how to shoot that gun. Wilber slowly sat back down on the bed and five Karlov Group men came into the room all toting guns.

Wilber knew he was in a trap and there was nothing he could do until Calvary showed up in about five minutes.

"Lay down flat on your back on the bed in the middle," One of the Karlov Group Spies said.

Wilber had been through training and his guidance was just comply especially if you know the calvary was on the way, however behind enemy lines, you make your own decision because you are screwed, might as well take a couple with you before they kill you.

With his arms and legs spread they were quickly handcuffed to parts of the bed. He was now in a very vulnerable position with nothing he could do about it. Since there were plenty of guns on Wilber, Aida put her gun back in her purse and pulled out a stiletto.

She walked over to Wilber and said, "You know Wilber, I always liked you and when you made love to me in Russia, I enjoyed every minute of it. I still think I love you." Then Aida unzipped Wilber's trousers and pulled out his manliness and started squeezing it to case an erection so there would be plenty of it when she cut it off, if required. She spat on her hand and started masturbating Wilber to get him all jacked up and nice and hard and if the other men were not in the room with her, she might have performed fellatio on Wilber and possibly hopped up on him and caused an orgasm, the last one before losing his penis.

Aida then flipped the blade on the stiletto out and said, "Wilber unless you tell me what I want to know I'm going to cut off your penis. What were you doing on the TR-4."

"Aida, I would love to tell you, but something tells me you would not believe it and you would think it was farfetched."

"Tell me Wilber and If I think you are lying, I will cut off your penis which is nice and hard now and you will probably bleed a lot.

"You might as well start cutting because you will not believe me."

"Wilber you never know, I might just believe you."

"You will not believe this but since you are going to cut my dick off, I don't care.

I went to Saturn."

"You know what Wilber; I actually believe you."

Aida closed the stiletto knife and put it in her purse then put Roger's penis back in his pants and zipped up his trousers.

"Wilber, why did you go to Saturn?"

"There are Aliens there and the CIA is worried they may be a threat to this planet."

"I see. Were they trying to kill you with the blue beams."

"Seems to me you already know a lot about this. If that's the case, why are you hassling me?"

"Wilber, I just want to fill in the blanks. I also think this is a serious issue and your government should start talking to my government about it, because America might not be able to handle it alone. Russia probably needs to team up with America on this matter."

"You know what Aida, I totally agree. And I think Russians deserve to know about what's happening on Saturn."

Wilber, since you are a reasonable person, I'm going to tell you some things I know about and I want you to ask only, why?

"Alright Aida."

"Why are you building a submarine?"

"You know about that too?"

"I know you are going to tell me why, so I'm going to help you now. I believe in quid pro quo."

"Okay, how are you going to help me?"

"One of my sources works high up in your Solar System Investigations. He betrayed your country. He was easy to recruit."

"Why are you telling me this?"

"I suspected you and I would be having this discussion because you are a reasonable person."

"Again Aida, you will think this is a BS story, but it's true. We are going to assemble that submarine on Saturn so we can submerge into liquid Helium on the planet and go under and find this alien civilization.

"Wilber, your cooperation in this matter will go a long way towards helping to improve relations between our countries. It's a shame you got married, I kind of want to enjoy you tonight."

"Aida, if you had come to me two months ago and offered to defect, I would be married to you now."

"Are you serious Wilber?"

"Quite serious and since we'll be working together convincing our governments, put down the guns and take these handcuffs off."

"Wilber, you had no idea how much I want to send these guys out of the room with those hand cuffs on and show you how much I can please you."

"If my marriage to Karen doesn't work out, we should get together."

"Okay guys put away your guns and take off his handcuffs."

"Soon the handcuffs were off, and Aida turned to the Karlov Group Russian Spies and said, "You guys go back to your rooms, I'll need to report into Moscow in a big report soon, but I want to talk with Wilber alone if you don't mind."

The men slowly put their guns away and took off the handcuffs and left the room wondering WTF was going on.

About that time the Delta Force guys were at the end of the hallway, but the Russians passed them so casually, they missed their targets.

They too had a hotel master key card and entered the room guns drawn to find Wilber calmly sitting with a woman.

Wilber calmly said, "The incident is over, I handled it."

"Everything is okay Wilber?"

"No, I have a lot to think about and I do appreciate you guys coming to rescue me because 15 minutes ago I thought I needed your help."

"Who's the woman Wilber?"

"Go ahead and tell them Aida."

"I'm Aida Abramova, I'm a Russian Diplomat, and I like Wilber."

The entire incident was recorded on Wilber's cell phone including discovering they had a spy over at Solar System Investigations. Wilber's cell phone was already streaming live audio because he hit the panic button and until he ended it, the live streaming audio would continue.

Wilber then said, "I'm stressed about the near loss of my penis by this lovely spy and need to unwind, I'm going to take her down to the bar and buy her a drink. Those of you who want to have a drink with me are invited. Also let John Burkette know I will not be waking up too early in the morning. I need a good equalizer sleep."

Moments later the room was empty and most of them were heading for the bar, some could not go with how they were dressed in combat fatigues and carrying M16's.

Aida was being watched by a watcher and a watcher-watcher. Aida sat on a bar stool next to Wilber and on the other side of her was none other than Bob Black.

They had a couple glasses of wine and Wilber said, "I'm sorry Aida I'm exhausted. You know what I've been through so I must say goodnight to you."

"Wilber before you go, let me give you a hug for old time's sake."
"Sure."

Aida gave Wilber a passionate hug, and before Wilber could stop her, Aida grabbed Wilber and kissed him on his lips.

"There is nothing better than sleeping with the enemy if you are a single man." Wilber said then continued, "Karen is in my heart now. Back in Russia I liked you a lot and I wished there we could come together. Now that's not possible, but never forget I like you."

"Wilber, you have no idea good that makes me feel. I think you will be proud of me tomorrow if you knew what my report will say."

"Aida, you are a very smart lady. I know what you are going to say and what needs to be said. I hope you are successful with your boss."

"Thank you, Wilber."

Wilber then reached to the side of Aida and kissed her on the ear and said, "I will never forget you. When I made love to you it was extra special. I just lost my lover a short while before we met in a nasty situation. You helped me more than you can imagine."

Wilber felt Aida's embrace strengthening, he knew he struck a chord with her because Aida knew all about Feye Wong, so she knew everything Wilber was telling her was indeed true.

Wilber continued with his whisper looking as if it was just an extended embrace and possibly some love words giving to Aida.

"Even though my time with you in Petropavlovsk was short, it was magnificent," Wilber said in the most affectionate manner.

People get recruited in the most bizarre ways often. Wilber took his shot he knew he had a 50/50 chance to find out who the mole was.

"Who is the traitor at Solar System Investigations?"

Aida shifted her body and pulled away from Wilber and gave him a tremendous smile as if there were amorous words just spoken. Her watchers knew that had to be the case and would not be shocked if she was soon in his hotel room carrying out a lover's tryst and recruiting him.

Aida pulled Wilber close and kissed him and put lipstick all over his ear in doing so replied, "Pat Barton."

They now went their separate ways and Wilber sincerely believed he would never see Aida again for the rest of his life.

"Moments later he was back in his room setting the slide bolt and intrusion alert system on his cell phone pointing at the door via one of the side cameras. He went to the toilet to urinate and saw the lipstick smeared all over his ear. He regretted having to wipe it off with a wet towel, but it was necessary. He then placed his gun and silencer attached under his pillow and went to sleep.

At 9:30 his phone rang. It was John Burkette calling via his CIA phone in a scrambled setting which alerted Wilber the conversation was encrypted.

"I got a full report from the audio recordings off your cell phone. Normally I would be very negative about what you told the spy, but since she had your dick in her hand and was going to cut it off if you didn't cooperate, you probably had to do what you did."

"Sure, the next step after cutting off my dick would have been to kill me. I had to cooperate to save my life.

"Some situations we cannot resolve, it's really up to the agent to determine what their recourse would be. I can't fault you since it sounds like the whole business was already compromised."

"It was. So, there was no reason to give up my life for something they already know about."

"I'm going to call Snoopy soon and take you guys to breakfast."

"John, there is something else I need to tell you."

"What is it?" John replied.

"I'm sure my watchers reported to you I was kissing Aida on her ear and saying Amorous words."

"Yes, that was one of the highlights of the report."

"I felt I had reached an accord with Aida and decided to probe her and find out if she would give me some critical data. That's what that was all about."

"What exactly is the data."

"When she kissed me and left the lipstick on my ear, she told me who the traitor was that disclosed Project Solaris."

"Whom might that be?"

"Pat Barton."

"Amazing."

"Pat Barton sold out his country for pussy and a good time."

"She is beautiful and irresistible, and we know you sampled it too."

"I thought you would like to know."

"Thanks, great thinking on your part. We will not be able to openly prosecute him without exposing some of the weakness in our organization, we'll have to handle it in another manner."

"Such as?" Wilber asked.

"Pat Barton just earned a free extraordinary rendition trip to Dubai."

"Why Dubai?" Wilber asked.

"Sheikh Omar owes me a few favors. Seyd isn't the only problem we had to take care of for him. We also had to save Emily." John Burkette said.

"Amazing. What's Sheikh Omar going to do?" Wilber asked.

"Sheikh Omar has a few young Turks that work for him, they sometimes must deal with situations such as environmentalists and human rights activists. Having him floating down the Potamic might get the FBI involved. This way there will be no traces of his departure."

"How will you do the rendition out of the USA?"

"A wealthy Saudi owns a private runway for his personal jet out past Warrenton Virginia. I'll have Pat drive himself out there to grab a money shipment coming in on a private jet. Pat will think he's getting a cut of the black money for delivering it to me. When they escort him into the hanger to pick up sacks of cash and bit coin tokens, I'll be there to meet him with and ask him personally why he betrayed us."

"Then off to Dubai?"

"Yes, Seldon, Castaldo, Romano, and Scheuer who are my confidants on the extraordinary rendition team will fly Pat to Dubai on the Saudi Sheikh's private jet and be handed over to the young Turks who like to sodomize men they torture."

"Sounds like a plan."

"Wilber, the young Turks will extract a confession out of Pat, but I hope your information provided by Aida isn't disinformation to harm one of our agents."

"John, I'm sure you heard on the recording a lot of data that indicates the Russians know quite a bit. It must be an insider. If you want personal confirmation, I'll ask Aida to go to brunch with just you and me."

"Okay set up the meeting."

***

By now Aida had personally talked with Vladimir Osechkin who then talked with Sergey Lavrov who had a keen sense of history and a huge number of interactions with the U.S. State Department and private meetings with American Presidents.

Aida was asked to remain in Las Vegas and contact Wilber to inform him, there were good developments underway, and his government would soon be contacting him about all this.

Just as Wilber was about to call the hotel operator to ring Aida's room, he heard the knock at the door. He walked over and saw Aida was in the hallway.

Wilber opened the door and Aida was all smiles and said, "Wilber may I talk with you for a few minutes?"

"Sure, come on in."

Wilber, with his phone set on clandestine recording mode before answering the door, wanted to hear what Aida had to say before he invited her to Brunch.

"What do you want to talk about?"

"Wilber, I knew when I made my report it would have huge implications. And it has already. From the highest levels of the Russian Government, our meeting here has been discussed."

"Alright."

"I was instructed a short while ago to remain here until further notice and to inform you that your government would be soon contacting you for further instructions."

"Alright."

"Maybe you and I can spend some leisure time together since I'll be here for a while."

"Aida, you are tantalizingly beautiful, and you know how much I would love to make love to you, but because I'm a married man now, can we keep it at the friendship level only?"

"Whatever you want Wilber, but I want you to know you can have my pussy any time you want it. Don't be afraid to ask."

"I understand that Aida and you don't know how much willpower I have to use to avoid doing it."

"You are a strong man Wilber, very few men have as good self-control as you do."

"I was about to call you and invite you to brunch and introduce you to my boss, the DD/P, John Burkette."

"I would be delighted to have brunch with you two guys."

"Okay I'll call John now to let him know you are going to brunch with us."

Wilber and Aida were soon down by the passenger pickup area in front of the hotel/casino and Roger was there directing traffic and getting the public in and out of the casino in a very efficient manner.

"Hello Roger, let me introduce you to Aida." "Hello Aida. Is Aida someone you work with?"

"No, she's a Russian Diplomat."

"That's interesting."

Aida decided to give Roger an emotional inducement, "Roger it's nice to meet you. Wilber and I used to be lovers, but he kicked me to the curb and married Karen."

"I'll be more than happy to take any of Wilber's leftovers."

"Who knows Roger, you might just get lucky because sometimes I get hornier than Catherine the Great was."

Roger's head was in cloud 9 now not believing something like this would ever be possible. He was quickly rescued by John Burkette who had Snoopy with him. He wanted Snoopy to see who Wilber passed over for Karen.

"Aida, this is my boss John Burkette, and this is the person who went with me on the trip you know about. You can call him Snoopy, that's his call sign."

"Pleased to meet you both," Aida said, looking like spitting image of the beautiful singer Polina Gagarina a few years ago with the same hair style.

[ПОЛИНА ГАГАРИНА - Лучшие песни - YouTube]

Aida was now in a target rich environment and knew her success as a spy was growing quickly.

The four were soon on their way to Boulder City to Iconic Southwest Diner where John Burkette liked eating. This downtown diner is a Boulder City Institution.

Wilber knew they could discuss what Aida would say to convince John Burkette her information was golden. John Burkette was driving, Aida was in the front seat with him.

"Aida, John would like to know about you and Pat Barton."

"Sure, no problem. I seduced him and blackmailed him afterwards."

"That's how you found out about Project Solaris?"

"Yes, plus a few other things like his failed probe attempt."

"Is there any way you can provide us something that clearly shows him being compromised?"

"Yes, I have videos with audio, give me an email address and I'll send it to you. Also give me a mailing address and I'll send you something that will absolutely confirm everything."

"What's that?"

"I have a small refrigerator at the Russian Embassy to store biological samples for honeypot schemes. I have a bottle that has a substantial Pat Barton's sperm deposit he put into me. You can confirm the DNA. Give me an address to send it, and I'll send it there."

"I assume you know where Wilber lives?"

"Most definitely, I thought about ringing his doorbell and tell the lovely Karen how lucky she is and inform her that if she ever breaks up with Wilber, he will be my man."

"Will you be going to Washington DC on this trip?"

"I was heading there today but I was redirected to stay here a bit and be a messenger for you. The minister of foreign affairs of the Russian Federation, Sergey Lavrov is now personally involved in this Project Solaris business and will be meeting with your Secretary of State to discuss it."

"What do you think they will be discussing?"

"Based on my report that came about because of my discussions with Wilber, our government views this to be an opportunity for our countries to work closer together and be less confrontational."

"That's good to know," John Burkette responded."

"After that is all said and done, and they finish discussing the business I will be given directions and most likely be sent to Washington DC next week or earlier."

"When you get to Washington DC, could you take some specimens to Wilber's home. I'm sure he would like to introduce you to Karen."

"I would be delighted," Aida said with a wicked smile on her face.

Wilber had a funny look on his face. He would no doubt have to disclose to Karen his sticky relationship between Aida and him.

Shortly after, the group pulled into Boulder City Iconic restaurant and local Institution, Southwest Diner.

The four were soon enjoying Chicken fried steak, Pot roast, Chili rellenos, and Meatloaf. Aida, Snoopy and Wilber washed the food down with Bloody Mary's and Margaritta's. Unfortunately, John Burkette was stuck drinking coffee because he was the designated driver. Plus, he wanted to keep all his senses and awareness sharp being that he was with an enemy spy.

Aida had her Watcher and Watcher-Watcher following her around and if for some reason they lost her, the GPS tracking device in her purse would alert them to where she was, so they could trail her loosely and not give away they were following. They would be asked where

Aida was located in case Moscow wanted to confer with her.

Right about the time John Burkette finished eating the last of his meal his phone rang. It was the DCI, Brent calling.

"John, I understand you are having a meal with the illustrious Russian spy Aida Abramova, Wilber, and Snoopy."

"That's correct."

"The debriefing at Nellis has been canceled. A GS750 is coming your way, and this might seem kind of bizarre, but you will be bringing Aida Abramova, Wilber, and Snoopy with you. Aida will be informed by Vladimir Osechkin, she's to fly back to Washington with you. The plane will arrive in four hours. Aida will be bringing her personal security detail of two men with her on the plane. Their names are Boris Melnikov and John Cairncross".

"The second security detail guy has an unusual name for a Russian."

"It's probably an Alias."

A short while later the four were back in Las Vegas in the hotel packing up and checking out when the plane informed the CIA via Tammy, they were an hour out of Las Vegas. Aida and her two bodyguards received their new tasking and because of the limited seating in the SUV, Boris Melnikov and John Cairncross followed behind in a Taxi. The elite Russian Karlov group, were on flights back to Mother Russia via Paris.

There is an airport gate near where the Janet jets park temporarily manned by CIA security members today who opened it for John Burkette allowing him to drive right on the tarmac near the spot the GS750 would stop to pick up passengers. Since they flew out with just six passengers on board, refueling wasn't necessary as they had plenty of fuel and expected help via jet stream.

As they arrived at Andrews Air Force Base there was a Soviet Consulate car by the hanger to pick up Aida and her protective agents. The limo also had a high-ranking Russian Diplomat Vladimir Chikov who John Burket had to greet for reasons of Diplomatic Protocol. Wilber and Snoopy remained waiting with John Burkette when the three would be flown by helicopter to Langley in a short while.

Aida met Vladimir Chikov who would later shower her with praise privately. After John Burkette finished a friendly exchange, Aida spoke in English, "Deputy Secretary Chikov, I would like to introduce you to an extraordinary man who really is responsible for all of this, Wilber O'Toole."

Wilber smiled and moved his hand forward and shook Vladimir Chikov's hand.

"Wilber O'Toole, since you are a highly placed deadly spy, I know quite a bit about you. You have led an impressive career. Few spies have ever gone where you have and done what you did. But the one thing I personally know about you, is you have done more positive things for improvement of relations with Russia, since Bill Clinton took office."

"Thank you for the kind words, but I do not think I deserve them."

"Wilber, you do and even though you are a serious adversary, the fact is you are also a very beneficial person. Speaking on behalf of Russia, I want to thank you for bringing about such a positive outcome on this Project Solaris."

"You are most welcome, Deputy Vladimir Chikov."

With those words the Russians piled into the 2012 Zill Limousine that still looked new and were on their way to Massachusetts Blvd, next to the Naval Observatory at their newer embassy. This six-door limousine is powered by a 7.7-liter fuel-injection 400 horsepower gasoline engines, connected to a 6-speed

automatic transmission. With the ability to go 125 miles per hour, the Zil Limousine also had Armor-plating.

Aida didn't get much of a debriefing since she sent most of the real-time information, including videos to Vladimir Osechkin. Most of her time at the embassy was receiving praise from high-ranking Russians for her slick handling of affairs. Aida realized she probably earned her spot on the fourth floor of the Lubyanka building.

The president was in serious discussions with the secretary of state because the Russians had already pitched their plan to the Americans.

"They want to send a person along on Project Solaris."

That put a heavy burden on the president and soon John Burkette was giving Wilber the bad news.

"I'm being forced to send a Russian along to be part of the Project Solaris Submarine mission."

"What will we do with that person?"

"Hate to be the bearer of bad news, but, that Russian will soon be entering prototype training and classroom training about the submarine's construction."

"Where will that Russian get the submarine construction training?" "Out in Utah where you six cosmonauts for Project Solaris practice building that submarine using robotic help, just like you will on Saturn.

The submarine was being built just like it would on Saturn. Most of Saturn's surface is covered by liquid Helium and Hydrogen. But there are a few rocky outgrowths far enough away from the blue beam weapon they would use to assemble the submarine and deploy it from there.

Aida found out about the plan to send a Russian to go with the Americans to Saturn. She immediately contacted Vladimir Osechkin.

"What can I do for you Aida?"

"I heard you are in the selection process for a person to go with the Americans to Saturn."

"Yes, that's correct."

"I think the most important person to send would be a spy."

"That's what I'm thinking too."

"I want to go; I want to be that person."

"Are you serious?"

"Wilber O'Toole is going to oversee the mission and effectively the captain of the submarine. Nobody knows him better than me."

"That's true especially since you had unprotected sex with him."

"Can you pass on my request?"

"Actually, I like this idea. I think in a few months with you on Saturn, Wilber will lose his will power and you can tag him and turn him."

"I do not think it will take a couple months. I think I can seduce him in a couple weeks."

Four hours later Aida was informed she was chosen to go on the mission. Aida was very happy because this meant her career in the FSB would be a historical event for all of Russia as well as mankind, the first female directly involved attempt of contacting Aliens living in our solar system.

Aida went to the special refrigeration unit that stored evidence used in coercion such as DNA samples of Pat. She pulled out Pat's samples and took a Q-Tip and dipped it into the slimy substance. Aida then took the Q-Tip and placed it inside Zip-Lock bag and put on a stick-on white label she could write on with a sharpie. Aida took the sharpie on the countertop used in handling refrigerator contents and with the sharpie wrote: Pat Barton's DNA sample taken September 4, 2023.

Aida then took a Taxi to Wilber's home. She knew by now Wilber and Karen would have completed their physical reunion and would be doing evening affairs, most likely completing Dinner and relaxing. She was quite astute in her speculation.

The last person in the world Wilber would expect to ring his doorbell was Aida Abramova. Karen answered the door wondering who the beautiful woman was and asked, "May I help you?"

"I need to speak to your husband, Karen."

"You know who I am?"

"Yes, you are Wilber's lovely wife and I'm certainly jealous of you."

"What do you need to talk to Wilber about?"

"I have some evidence I want to give him, that he needs to give to his boss, John Burkette. He's expecting this, as it will put closure into one of the more difficult periods of his life."

"Alright come in."

Wilber was standing there in almost shock. He had just received a text message from John Burkette informing him the President caved into the Russian demand and none other than Aida Abramova would be going to Saturn with you.

Wilber played dumb and had on his poker face. He was not going to comment on that extraordinary change in Project Solaris crew to Saturn. Plus, his wife wasn't cleared to know they were going there.

"Hello Wilber."

"Aida what brings you here."

"I wanted to personally deliver this to you as I know John Burkette will know everything, we discussed about Pat is true." She handed Wilber the Ziploc bag.

"I'm not happy I have to do this, but thanks to your extraordinary abilities as a spy, we sometimes have to deal with people like Pat," Wilber said.

"Wilber, no man has ever done as much for me in my lifetime career as you have. You didn't plan on doing it, as much of it was purely coincidental, but you have made me a very important person in Russia now. This is my way of thanking you."

"It's kind of a strange way of thanking someone."

"Wilber, I know about your relationship with Pat. He back stabbed you often and when I was sleeping with him, he vented his vitriol for you and bragged at how many times he almost got you killed. He was surprised when you came home alive a couple times, but he knew he would have other opportunities to get you killed."

"We didn't get along, that's true."

Karen was standing there taking it all in. Her feminine intuition knew where there was smoke there was fire, and Aida was smoking in a metaphorical sense.

"Wilber, I'm not going to take up any more of your time, but I want John Burkette to know I'm sincere and delivered the proof we talked about. You are the only person I can trust to do this transaction. Nobody but you and me and Karen know this happened and after I'm gone you can explain to Karen why she should never discuss this because it would not only put me at risk, but it could also affect you and Karen."

"Karen will not divulge any of this to anyone. She's a smart lady."

"She must be utterly brilliant because she ended up as your wife. She may not know how lucky she is marrying such an extraordinary person."

Karens eyes were watering up a bit and she knew Aida was not far off the mark.

Aida soon left and Wilber decided it would be in Karen's best psychology to not know he would have further involvement with a very capable Russian Spy, and that the world had just got crazier because of the Saturn situation.

In the next morning, John Burkette called Wilber and said, "I'm going to pick you up and take you some place where we will be attending a meeting."

"Alright."

Soon after kissing and hugging Karen, Wilber was out the door and walked down the driveway where John Burkette's car was waiting and got in.

Before Wilber put on his seatbelt, he handed John Burkette the Ziplock bag and Said, "Here's Pat Barton's DNA mixed in with some of Aida's DNA."

That pretty much confirms it, I will have the lab boys confirm the DNA. We'll need to get a sample of Aida's DNA separately.

"I'll get that for you today. I know how to obtain it."

"How will you get it?"

"Don't ask, you might not think highly of me afterwards."

In due time the two arrived at a commercial office building where two more CIA people joined them, Snoopy and Brent. John Burkette then droves to Massachusetts avenue and was let into the Russian Embassy compound as there was a host there waiting to make sure they had no problems entering and to show them the parking spot reserved for the VIP's. He then escorted them into the Embassy and into a special room behind a cypher lock door. Inside were a group of Russians including Aida all dressed up nicely looking like Polina Gagarina's twin sister.

The meeting was held here for secrecy, the Russians were fearful to conduct it anywhere else because of their security protocols and competing interests.

The meeting lasted several hours and all the details of Aida's role in the mission were worked out and they knew Wilber O'Toole would be the mission commander.

When pressed for his intentions of his conduct towards Aida, she interjected her comment to quickly shut that conversation down and said first in Russian, then said

the same thing in English, "I've known Wilber for a while. He and I were not always enemies. I have complete confidence in him. Wilber and I will work well together, so don't be worried about the relationship he and I will have on Project Solaris Spacecraft."

The Russian ambassador asked, "What do you view as your role, Aida?"

From my viewpoint I'm there to help Wilber and support him and in our private discussions he and I know we need to work together on this because it's not an American problem or a Russian problem, it's an Earth problem" Aida said.

"We can't disclose Project Solaris to the rest of the world because it would cause a lot of political turmoil," The Russian ambassador said.

"We need to go get the job done and the mission accomplished so that our governments can figure out what to do next," Aida quickly responded.

Aida's attitude and her conversation quickly influenced all the Russians at the meeting they were embarked upon a mutual important mission, and it was very important they worked together well, just like they had accomplished during the international space station missions.

As they were all leaving the room after discussions died down, Aida said, "Wilber.

I want to talk to you privately and I'll give you a ride home as I would like to speak with Karen and let her know this is all professional."

"Sure."

John Burke raised his eyebrows but realized, this was all legitimate and probably a reasonable thing and that at some point in time Karen will have to know they were going to Saturn together and in the past, Wilber had boinked Aida.

Soon Aida and Wilber were driving from the Russian Embassy and heading towards Wilber's home when he brought up the DNA matter.

"Is there any way I can get some of your DNA to give our lab to prove that is your DNA mixed with Pat's DNA."

"The only way you are going to get my DNA is to put your fingers down in my panties and discover how wet I am and how much you turn me on."

"That works for me," Wilber said.

Aida turned into a fast-food restaurant and pulled up to an area where there were no cars parked. She then lifted her dress up and said, "Give me your hand which Wilber complied with. She then shoved his hand down to her vulva and it was very wet which Wilber felt and got as much on his finger as he could."

"That really feels good. I wish I could convince you to do more."

"I not only have to worry about your stiletto, but I'm also sure Karen has one too. I would rather not find out the hard way."

Wilber had a sheet of paper the Russians gave him that had all the meeting members phone numbers and email addresses so they could contact each other as they were now deemed the Russian contingent of the oversight team. He wiped all that wetness onto a portion of that piece of paper, then asked, "Would it be okay if I call my boss and have him meet us here and give him the DNA source."

"Sure, no problem but one of the days I'm going to seduce you into putting something besides your finger there."

"Thanks for the warning," Wilber said.

"If we both come back alive and achieve our mission, maybe I want do it one time for old time's sake," Aida said with an evil grin.

"We'll have to figure out a way to celebrate we are living because this will be a tough mission," Wilber said.

"I'm looking forward to it," Aida responded.

Wilber made the phone call and in ten minutes, a car pulled up.

"I'm going to have them give me a ride home. I'll see you tomorrow at the prototype."

"I'm looking forward to it. This means a lot to me and working with you on a joint project pleases me more than you realize."

"Even though I'm now married and must conduct my life differently, you will always be a wonderful memory for me. Let's always remain friends."

"We will."

Wilber got out of the car, walked over to the other car, and opened the rear door and got in. The car then backed out and drove off.

Wilber had a credit card holder shield so that a person could not remotely get to the chip on his credit card. Pulled the credit card out and Tore of the wet portion of the paper that had Aida's DNA on it and inserted it with some of the paper sticking out and handed it to John Burkette and said, "Here's Aida's DNA."

The following day Aida was brought to the prototype in a CIA car with a CIA driver. She was escorted into the prototype where they would start teaching her all Project Solaris Spacecraft intricate operations. This was a stunning development for the FSB.

At the end of the training session, the CIA driver took Aida back to her hotel where she was staying. After she left, John Burkette said, "Wilber we need to make a stop on the way home."

John Burkette had driven them to the prototype to make sure there were no issues integrating Aida into Project Solaris operations.

Wilber noticed they were soon heading West on Interstate-66. He suspected he knew where they were going.

After I dropped you off at home yesterday, I drove over to the facility that does our DNA fingerprinting. In case you don't know it, they have a machine there that can record and compare the DNA in fifteen minutes."

"That's neat, it usually takes a couple weeks."

We matched Aida's DNA to the prior sample that had Pat Barton's sperm in it. There were probably 50,000 sperm cells in the sample so there was lots of information. It proves Pat Barton slept with Aida and did not fill out the required foreign intelligence officer meeting forms that immediately made him a person of interest. I have reason now to believe Aida is not lying about any of this."

"Aida still has feelings for me. The fact she let me put my finger into her vagina to get that DNA sample shows those feelings still exist."

"Any chance of turning her into a double spy?"

"Only way that would happen is I would have to get divorced." "Maybe I can assign you an operation to seduce her and lie to her. We can have your wife briefed by her psychiatrist you are doing a special mission." "If you do that, she will end up like Xinxin."

***

Chapter Twenty-Four

Extraordinary Rendition

The car soon turned off the freeway and went up a two-lane paved country road with some nice landscaping.

They were soon at a private runway and hanger and the runway had lighting.

There was a private jet waiting. The pilots were on loan to the CIA by some unsavory Characters that were Cash in Advance contractors.

These were extraordinary rendition pilots who flew people the CIA tortured to 56 different countries. Egypt was one of their favorite destinations.

As soon as the car pulled up to the jet, several men came out of the hanger with Pat Barton in hand cuffs and leg restraints, wearing the suit he went to work that morning.

Pat Barton didn't look happy. They had not beat him or messed him up in any manner.

The CIA men in suits carried Pat Barton along under each arm. They stopped in front of John and Wilber.

"You will not get away with this. I have friends."

"Yes, including Russian Spies one of which turned you."

"Fuck you."

"Pat, I want you to look at Wilber, we have now confirmed you set him up to be killed three times. Do you want that to go to trial?"

"Fuck you, John."

"Pat, Aida gave us samples of your sperm she was going to use to blackmail you. When you bragged to her how you almost got Wilber killed three times in fratricidal activities, you crossed the line.

"It's too bad he wasn't killed, he pissed me off all the time.

"We could simply just kill you and bury you out in a forest somewhere, but we want you to experience what you almost arranged for Wilber in Beijing and Singapore.

We also know you gave Faye Wong information. Did you have sex with her too?"

"Fuck you, John."

"Pat, you are a disgrace. You are no better than John Walker, Aldridge Aimes, or Robert Hansen."

Pat made some physical movement as if he were trying to get a John Burkette, but with his hand cuffs and leg restraints being held by two bruisers it was a weak attempt.

"Put him aboard the plane and takeoff," John Burkette said.

Soon Pat was aboard the plane and additionally handcuffed to his seat. Eighteen hours later the Saudi Sheikh's plane pulled into a hanger. A white SUV was there. The hanger doors closed, and Pat was led out of the plane over to the SUV. Once they were inside the SUV, the hanger doors slid open and the SUV soon departed and joined two other white SUV's and they were soon driving across the desert. They soon came up to a man and his son with their Falcon.

Sheikh Omar walked over to the SUV that rolled down a window on the side of the vehicle of the car he needed to approach. There was Pat Barton. Sheikh Omar said, "Pat Barton, welcome to the Middle East. You will never leave here alive. See that boy over there? Wilber saved his life. John Burkette saved my wife Emily's life. They are my family. The young Turks will soon be teaching you the error of your ways."

Sheikh Omar walked back over to Zayd holding the falcon Olimpico and said, "That person I just talked to almost got Wilber killed a few times. The young Turks will soon teach him a lesson or two."

***

Chapter Twenty-Five

Departure

After all the training and construction training it was time to go. Russians and Americans gathered at Vandenberg Launch Complex 10.

Karen had just hugged Wilber one last time and was taken to the block house where she was standing right next to the DD/P Brent and Vladimir Osechkin.

Colonel Baker was there and knew Wilber would be on that spacecraft. Thus Colonel Baker personally became Mr. Quality Assurance. He left no stone unturned so when countdown hit T-0 he felt comfortable the seven people on the Project Solaris Spaceship was ready to launch fault free.

For Vandenberg this was an unusual sight. This was a super heavy payload and there were 8 booster rockets. Twenty water trucks were brought in to dump far more water simultaneously than they ever did before.

T-0 hit, and the Project Solaris Spacecraft was on its way. Specialized space suits, fusion reactors and all kinds of interesting devices flew that day.

The previous day at Launch Complex 5 and 6 other rockets were launched all going to Saturn. At the same time a TR-4 from Area-51 flew towards Saturn and would be a pathfinder through the asteroid belt for the two other large rockets carrying submarine parts.

After multiple days traveling Project Solaris Spacecraft came down on one of the very few rocky outgrowths of the planet. Since everyone was only seven percent heavier than they were on Earth, there were no major problems with weight.

Thanks to SpaceX and NASA, Project Solaris Spacecraft came down on a tripod landing gear that was designed to keep the spacecraft level. Because of the threat of high winds, the landing gear had individual electric powered drill bits that came down at a 120-degree angle providing a perfect anchor system. The highest winds expected on Saturn could not tip over the spacecraft after the anchors drilled down into the rock and provided that major stability.

This rocky outpost was selected for the perfect angle on the slope to assemble the submarine. It would launch into the liquid helium with no effort simply by lowering the submarine into the liquid helium via a powerful wench system. There would be more rockets coming. The command ship and habitat was designated Project Solaris-1.

The next ship which contained the track system the submarine would be built on was Project Solaris-2.

Subsequent Project Solaris ships numbered 3 through 35 arrived delivering modular sections, these self-made machinists and electricians bolted together. It truly was a fascinating adventure. The robotic arm of the Project Solaris ships that arrived on a tripod landing system lifted the section and placed in exact position and fastened to the rest of the submarine..

The ingenious bolt and torquing system pulled the sections together. Each modular section had what it needed. Whether hydraulic, electrical or some other resource. Everything was wireless which greatly reduced wiring. After a Solaris Spacecraft delivered a new section and bolted in place it took off and went back out into space and was herded back to earth for re-use if necessary.

Because of the unique construction techniques that relied heavily on robotics and artificial intelligence, from start to finish, the submarine was ready to launch in 30 days fully provisioned.

The initial plan included six people manning the submarine. A new plan came about. The rationale was not to risk half the people in case combat or something else happened.

Wilber, Snoopy, Aida, and Dominic deployed on Project Solaris submarine. Using their wrist communicators inside the submarine with all entrances closed and a green board lit up and fifteen-pound pressure test satisfactory the three remaining Solaris crew members operated the hoist that slowly let the submarine weighing almost 2700 tons to slip into the liquid helium on top of the skid that had been coated with graphite prior to adding each spacecraft module.

The submarine then went on sea trials nearby checking all the systems reporting back to the base camp a complete health check of the submarine. At the end of all the exhaustive tests, the submarine was certified for operations. The submarine slowly departed the area and using the Liquid Lense Helium calibrated surveillance system after it submerged and navigated its way towards the area of interest. Full ISR data was recorded and if trouble happened emergency transmissions would happen. Rocket powered slot buoys would be launched traveling at low altitudes away from the target area and broadcast the emergency message if required.

Constantly monitoring everything as they approached the Aliens utilizing the Liquid Lense surveillance system, no structures or indication of any civilization appeared until they approached the area where the blue weapons were fired. The submarine was placed in an ultra-quiet mode and crept forward.

Fifty miles from the place of interest the sensitive receivers of the Liquid Lenses system started picking up light. They slowed down even more and crept in.

Slowly but surely the distant light image became much clearer and soon the Liquid Lense system provided an incredible image of a submerged City inside a transparent dome. Coming up to approximately a mile to the edge of the transparent Hemisphere Dome City that contained and many advanced looking buildings and a few Alien creatures walking about their daily business created a sight to behold.

Snoopy and Dominic faces were glued to the Liquid Lense system and watching intently for Alien activity especially threats that might unexpectedly start coming after them.

Aida turned toward Wilber and grabbed him and pulled him close and kissed him more passionately than any person in her lifetime. Wilber would be her hero for life. He had done the impossible.

Wilber allowed Aida the moment. It was special since all they had been through together.

One big thing Wilber discovered about Pat Barton after the young Turks got done with him, there was going to be another attempt on Wilber's life that Pat Barton had negotiated with terrorists. Had Pat not been taken away by extraordinary rendition, Wilber might be dead by now. Aida had saved his life by her revelations about Pat Barton. It creates a strange sensation when you discover an enemy spy saved your life.

With Pat's confession the terrorists who came across the Mexican Border with several illegals were caught in a safe house and soon had an extraordinary rendition of their own, and later traded for hostages.

Pat Barton was never going to come back because he would file lawsuits and go after the CIA. The Young Turks barbecued Pat and put on some special sauces that would drive the vultures crazy with the aroma. Pat then ceased to exist, and all his belongings were buried in a deep hole in the desert that was soon lost in shifting sands. Pat disappeared forever.

***

Chapter Twenty-Six

Observation And Determination

After watching for a while, it became clear the Aliens had not detected the presence of the fusion nuclear-powered submarine. The submarine was black and dark and easily hid at a distance away from the well-lit underwater city with a glorious transparent dome. Thanks to the submarine's special exterior coating, the thermal image was minimal and easily buried in the background lighting of the large ocean of liquid helium.

Wilber then made a command decision; it was more important to go back to Earth with all the ISR data than to pursue alien communication and possible hostile reception. The submarine turned around and left the area.

Thanks to precise navigation the Project Solaris Submarine came back to the base camp. The three amigos that remained behind had applied graphite to the skids the submarine would be winched up on. The submarine partially drove up on the skid and at the point is stalled. The winch cable attached pulled the submarine the rest of the way up the skid.

They had one last act to do before leaving the planet, camouflage the submarine to make it available for future missions. It took them a day to accomplish that. With the reactors shut down and the submarine lifeless after uploading all the mission files. They could now leave. A tanker had refueled the spacecraft. With a lot of the weight removed because that equipment they delivered was on the submarine, and only a cargo of seven people there was plenty of fuel to get out in space on the opposite hemisphere of the submerged alien city where it got refueled again for its trip back to Earth.

As a special precaution, a TR-4 was there to help it navigate through the asteroid field. Major Barnes and Major Schmidt would do their upmost to get Wilber back to Earth alive.

Project Solaris Spacecraft finally made it back to Earth deployed parachutes coming down for landing. At 5,000 feet the rocket engines ignited to help slow the descent further and soon landed on three retractable landing gear on the designated concrete slab landing zone area at Launch Complex 10.

Project Solaris mission and submerged sojourn to Saturn's submerged city now ended.

Alien confrontation would have to wait for another time. With the Project Solaris Submarine left on Saturn with tamper monitors that would last for decades, Project Solaris now had a submarine they could come back and use. But first they would plan a way to meet and engage the Aliens. Would Wilber and Aida go out into space again together?

Paul D. Escudero

November 2023

Author's Note

Project Solaris - Solar System Investigations Novel is entirely fiction. There are no living people in the book or any space events that really exist. All characters are fictional. Any possible correlation with any real name is strictly coincidental.

If you read the Novel, you know the main character is the CIA agent Wilber O'Toole. The name was created out of the names of two of the most influential people in my lifetime.

First and foremost was Wilber Alvey, one of my math teachers in high school. Wilber was also a farmer and while he was living farmed several large farms north of the sleepy little town of Cheyenne Wells, Colorado, I assisted him for almost four years. I knew Wilber Alvey from 1969 up until he passed a while back, reaching over 90 years of age.

Wilber Alvey was the most influential person in my life at an early age when I needed adult leadership the most. Wilber Alvey was the only male adult other than the electrician Clark Osborne who had much to do with my early development. Clark Osborne is probably one of the major reasons why I got involved in nuclear submarines where I worked for many years. As an electrician Clark Osborne was in charge of the runway lighting system for a Military Air Base in Colorado during WW2.

Now you know why Wilber is the main character in this book as I am successful in life because of all the lessons in life he taught me.

Wilber's last name in this Novel is O'Toole.

When I was selected for a major role in a significant project, my interface was a gentleman named Raymond O'Toole.

Wilber Alvey went to his grave not knowing I had that involvement with Ray O'Toole's project, nor does my hometown. Now they might be curious after this book is published. My adventures with Ray O'Toole could be a book all to itself.

Project Solaris - Solar System Investigations also discusses a condition that when a federal agency gets inbred through nepotism and patronage, that results in members don't think outside the box and not discovering new realities until it's too late. Also, incompetent, and caustic supervisors cause incredibly unsuccessful results for organizations as depicted by this story.

Now for some dirty laundry. The people in government are not always protected from political and vindictive enemies. Thank God we have a few good people like depicted in the Novel that put lives ahead of their personal career paths.

Would you take a bullet for your country?

I've observed a lot of skull drudgery in government and just like in the book there are supervisors who believed agencies didn't have turf wars.

The turf wars existed such as between NUWC and SEABAT were legendary. There were other Turf wars at agency's that used to be places like SPAWAR, Keyport, and Newport. Turf wars come and go as people come and go. Question: Does the CIA and FBI get along now? Think 9/11. What did they fix?

This is for supervisors who love office warriors and didn't believe turf wars existed:

US acted to conceal evidence of intelligence failure before 9/11 | September 11 2001 | The Guardian

How did bars and nightclubs figure into all of this?

In the Sports Bar in Crystal City located near 23rd and Eads Street, important decisions were made as the book states. Foxhole which is closed and turned into a Gay bar with colored flags outside was a place where DEA agents hung out decades ago. I knew one of the DEA agents and attended a party at the 1702 club at Farragut Court in Washington DC for an undercover DEA agent I knew for many years, just before he went on his last mission. At that party I got to meet some of our nation's top DEA undercover agents. Incredible heroes, all of them.

There was also the Crystal City Tavern where you could get a T-Bone steak for $10 while watching the stripper's dance. You would be utterly shocked to know who went with me there (hint: one my former supervisors, who also was a Cowboy and one of the good ones).

The bar Faces (aka Feces) existed in the same building complex as the Naval Sea Systems Command before that organization moved over to the Naval Yard. Just like in the book Ivan was there sitting in Faces a couple bar stools down from Cash in Advance, or FBI agents monitoring him and his watcher sitting elsewhere in the bar.

If you read some of the Russian Defector books, you will discover there indeed was watchers and watcher-watchers sometimes. The

Soviets that ran the spy John Walker had watchers and sometimes watcher-watchers.

John Anthony Walker Jr. former Naval Radioman and Navy Chief Warrant Officer and communications specialist, passed away with the honor of General in the Soviet KGB.

John Walker (July 28, 1937 – August 28, 2014) was convicted of spying for the Soviet Union from 1967 to 1985 and sentenced to life in prison. How many people did he get killed in Vietnam? How did he change the outcome of the war? You might be surprised. Why he wasn't executed surprises me. He saved his own skin by doing a plea bargain to rat out his co-conspirators.

Project Solaris - Solar System Investigations Novel may not currently represent how CIA or NRO conduct their business in real life. However, a few of their managers might get some good ideas by reading this book.

There are some excellent non-Fiction books about the CIA I've read. The first two books on this list I highly recommend, especially if you want to read CIA's history.

Ron Kessler's book: Inside the CIA: Revealing the Secrets of... by Kessler, Ronald (amazon.com)

Thomas Evan's book: The Very Best Men: Four Who Dared: The Early Years of the CIA: Thomas, Evan: 9780684825380: Amazon.com: Books

Bill O'Neal's book: Secret CIA: 21 Insane CIA Operations That You've

Probably Never Heard of: O'Neill, Bill: 9781648450839: Amazon.com: Books

From the Soviet point of view: KGB: Andrew, Christopher: 9780060166052:

Amazon.com: Books

If you read all those books, then you will know information in my Novel isn't so farfetched.

What about space and the final frontier?

Amazon.com: US Air Force Secret Space Program: Shifting Extraterrestrial Alliances & Space Force (Audible Audio Edition):

Michael Salla, Jerry Lord, Exopolitics Consultants

***

In the story I use Vandenburg Launch Complex 10 for the early launches in the book that take place. Vandenburg Launch Complex 10 originally built by McDonnald Douglas in 1958 is no longer used for rocket launches and is now part of a museum. Vandenburg Launch Complex 10 was originally built to test intercontinental ballistic missiles.

In 1963 Vandenburg Launch Complex 10 transformed into a space launching facility. Prior to 1966 Space Launch Complex 10 West was known as Vandenberg AFB Pad 75-2-6.

Vandenburg Launch Complex 10 remains a rare pristine look at the electronics and equipment created in that era that helped the United States develop space capabilities.

The last launch from Vandenburg Launch Complex 10 tested a Thor booster in 1980. Vandenburg Launch Complex 10 was declared a National Historic Landmark in 1986.

Later in the story during the Project Solaris launches, they occurred at Launch Complex 6 which is currently operational.

Remember HAL 2000 on Space Odessey? In the early 1970's very few people would believe something like expansive artificial intelligence like we now have could happen. Artificial intelligence is now being developed in a dozen powerful countries investing vast sums into it. Google Japanese sex robots and you will get a huge surprise. That's AI at its finest.

In my Novel, Drones Robots Trains & Aliens now selling on Amazon Kindel eBook, the main character Ted has a personal humanoid robot Tensai. Is that going to happen? Yes, it's happening in China right now.

America needs to start paying attention, but when you have good ole boys like Pat Barton running the show, the Cash in Advance boys eventually find out about it a day later and a dollar short. Think I'm full of baloney? Scroll down to the year 2015 on this Wikipedia report, then you might just say WTF is happening? Why is the Fumble Before Indecision boys not all over this? Maybe they are too busy investigating Trump to do their charter: Counterintelligence Operations. I would say call MI5 and ask for help, but after the Cambridge Five, they may not be viable either.

List of security hacking incidents - Wikipedia

What do you think is important about that 2015 incident that happened under Obama's watch? Remember the Mission Impossible Movie where the high-speed train is going through the Chunnel and the spies are fighting over the NOK list? Think about it. It truly was an extraordinary breach. I rest my case.

Now for a reality check.

China has 2000 Einsteins as discussed in this book. In the last book I published, Clandestine Transporters, I point out a couple Chinese. One received the Nobel Prize for inventing fiber optics. The other is a female who figured out how to separate U238 from U235. Without her, America would not have been able to build the Atomic Bomb. I use part of her name in the Clandestine Transporter story as well as the man who invented fiber optics to give them honor, they richly deserve.

What about the 2000 Chinese Einsteins?

In the mid 1980's I was at a seminar in San Diego concerning modal analysis equipment used to design rockets and aircraft. There were six Mainland Chinese Research Scientists at the seminar. There was also an NSA agent probably observing them.

One of the six Chinese received her PhD around the age of 21. She could type 180 words per minute with no mistakes. Her fingers on the Keyboard were like Yuja Wang's fingers on the piano, in milliseconds or less at times. This young female Chinese at the time, helped design the Silkworm missile. What has she designed since? She's an expert in Modal Analysis and led us through all the simulations by the end of day two of the five-day seminar. The NSA dude I had lunch with was quite animated when I informed him about her capabilities in modal analysis including using advanced modal analysis software from companies like SDRC. Get that?

I study China all the time. I've published 3 Novels in the Chinese language. Now I'm going to explain China and their impact on technology.

In my past I wrote research white papers that went through ONR and full phase III development (meaning actual products were delivered). In the process of writing the white papers and coming up with goals and specifications I had to do significant research into signal processing.

I've studied signal processing techniques such as Stochastics Resonance (used to reduce granularity in satellite pictures and exposed Badge Man who killed JFK). Stochastics Resonance was pioneered at Saratov University in Russia under a U.S. Navy contract. Surprised? Where else can Stochastics Resonance be used? Medical equipment monitoring the heart as well as military systems.

I also studied Wavelet theory, Systolic Arrays, Chirp filters, and a lot of other signal processing processes. I was already well trained in FFT because I worked for Scientific Atlanta for a few years who built the fastest FFT processors at the time. I also studied La Place Transforms and Z transforms.

Oilmen use Wavelets to find oil deposits. Spies use wavelets to find bugs or for bug receivers. Wavelets are also used in espionage for signal recognition and acoustic fingerprinting. Understand the importance of Wavelets and signal processing now?

Now how do Wavelets and other signal processing pertain to what I'm going to tell you about those 2000 Chinese Einsteins?

10 of the top 20 Wavelet designers in the world are Chinese. If you go to a Wavelet seminar, you will likely meet Chinese Wavelet designers. Where did some of the past major Wavelet seminars occur? Hong Kong. [WORKSHOP ON WAVELETS AND THEIR APPLICATIONS (cuhk. edu.hk)]

To all you CIA office warriors, you need to wake up about China. They might be eating your lunch and you do not know it. Read and Weep:

[Artificial intelligence industry in China - Wikipedia]

In my last book I had some discussion about AI and discussed major developments in other countries such as Russia, China, Japan, Israel, Great Britain, France, etc. Let me tell you what I know for a fact. It's scary as shit. It really is. In that book Clandestine Transporters, it describes how Russia is credited with the first AI kill in human history.

In my book Soylent Caravan Chapter-11 exposes how AI is killing all the General's enemies. Think that's far-fetched? I firmly believe it will happen long before the office warriors figure it out.

What's something I think AI will do for mankind?

AI will be the entity that will expose government's awareness and involvement with Aliens visiting our plant, some of which allegedly are now at area 51.

I recently published a Novel about a Remote Viewer. This story is based on a real remote viewer I know. She was a technical advisor to the Novel. In one of my interview documents with her, I have well over 50,000 words. I did extensive research into her.

Because of my interests in Aliens and Space, I asked her if the government ever tried to use her to remote view Aliens. She said she tried but it didn't work because their brains are different, and their auras are different. But she said they figured the work around. She remote views those Earth people talking to the Aliens. Who are these Earth people? Russian Air Force Officers.

Paul D. Escudero

Personae Dramatis

Karlov group, elite Russian spies utilized for most important special operations. Vladimir Osechkin a senior member of the Federal Security Service of the Russian

Federation

Ian Monroe, who had the nickname Snoopy.

Jerry Nault, Wilber's Project Solaris controller.

Sandra waitress at restaurant who met Wilber in the past.

Rachel Sandra's personal friend.

CINCPACFLEET Intel, Halawa drive Kamehameha Hiwayroute 99.

Headquarters United States Pacific Fleet 5 story building.

Jennifer Thompson, a British fashion model (cover for her MI6 role).

Faye Wong, Female Chinese spy and lover.

Salma Rachid's music

Sheikh Abdulla, and Prince Bandar who were quickly introduced by Sheikh Omar.

Pierre Truffaut designed submarines for Jacques Cousteau.

Sheikh Omar from Dubai, UAE

Sheikh Omar's son Zayd

Sheikh Omar first two names as Władziu Valentino and middle name is Liberace." John Dunbar, one of Wilber's aliases.

Fullerton Bay Hotel Singapore   LA   BRASSERIE restaurant

LANTERN a Singapore rooftop bar set against the stunning panoramic backdrops of Marina Bay.

Idrak is Xinxin's cousin and head of security for Fullerton Bay Hotel, Singapore.

Paul Morgan, Norwegian Scientist who intercepted and pinpointed location of signals transmitted from Saturn.

Wilber O'Toole, CIA case officer for Project Solaris, the program to discover civilizations on Saturn transmitting signals and why.

Professor Proctor, Cornell University, and friend of Paul Morgan from Norway. Pat Barton, Senior member of CIA's Deputy Director of Solar System Investigations Wilber O'Toole's boss early in the story.

John Burkette, Deputy Director/Planning for CIA (Covert Opps) Also the director of Project Solaris.

Aida Abramova illustrious blonde Russian FSB Spy, one of Wilber O'Toole's lovers.

Dmitri Vasilyevich Bortnikov, Aida Abramova's boss.

Vasilyevich Bortnikov, Dmitri Vasilyevich Bortnikov's boss in the KGB (FSB).

Colonel Baker at Vandenberg AF BASE commander in charge of rocket launches. Xinxin Lin, Wilber's Singapore lover

Nov 2023.

454

9 781963 718492